Wolfhowl
Mountain

Dian Cronan

For D. K. W. –

thank you for everything;

For my ever-loving and supportive family and friends –
you made this dream possible;

And of course, for all you readers out there –
thanks for stopping by.

CONTENTS

Part One

Part Two

Jason McBride: The Third Owner

Part Three

PART ONE

Prologue
1851: How the Blight Came Upon Port Braseham

As he tried to remember how that quiet, wistful tune went, Eamonn Callaghan's mind wandered to sweet Alva. He had been so hard on her these last several months. He pictured her in his mind, standing limply, her petite body slouched around her swollen belly and her thin arms hanging at her sides. She stared at the floor, dark thoughts swirling in her eyes. So much had changed in such a short time. So much... Eamonn watched her heart break in her eyes each time he raised his voice toward her, each time he stomped angrily from the room. He didn't mean it, but didn't she know? Couldn't she see? It was all for her, for the baby.

But no, Alva did not understand. How could she? Eamonn had kept so many things from her that she could never understand the truth. But he had only wanted to protect her and the baby. Alva had become so delicate and he didn't want anything to jeopardize her health with the baby coming. He didn't want Alva to worry. And there was certainly no shortage of worries.

The strange storm that whipped the coast early last summer destroyed everything they had worked for. Eamonn couldn't pay his workers on the trawler or on their land because there had been no fish and no crops since the storm. He couldn't afford to repair the damaged and unfinished east wing of the house, and Alva had wanted so badly for it to be ready for the baby. Rather than explain to her they were losing money, rather than admit he was relying on his cousin Seamus for their necessities, Eamonn let her spend freely on the baby and the nursery. It made her happy, and he so desperately wanted her to be happy.

It was true Alva had asked what was wrong many times, but Eamonn was a proud man, so he lied. But the more he lied, the more curious Alva became or the more money she spent on the baby so every time he looked at his wife, Eamonn's head reeled with resentment. It was Alva who had wanted this land and this house, and who constantly asked when it would be finished. Alva who was so desperate to fill the house with their children. *Alva* who spent the money they didn't have. His resentment would build and build until he exploded at her, berated her. Nothing she did was enough to quell his growing bitterness.

Yet Alva did not complain. She went about her duties as wife and future mother much as she had before. But the circles beneath her eyes grew darker and the red blush of life drained from her cheeks. Her rich, dark brown hair faded and was slowly being taken over by gray. She looked weak and sick, sometimes too exhausted to even hang the laundry on the line.

Eamonn told himself she was exhausted from the housework and her pregnancy, from his outbursts. She was so exhausted in fact, that she started to have bouts of delirium, talking to herself or some invisible presence. He heard her sometimes in the nursery, or up in the library, talking as if to an old friend. "He does not know what he is saying," she would say. "He is a proud man and things have been hard for him since the storm. Things have been hard on everyone since the storm. Things will be better once the baby comes. Things will be better. When the baby comes." It was not until Alva accused Eamonn of hating the baby, of not wanting her or their child that he realized how cruel he'd become. She'd screamed at him, hot tears staining her cheeks as she threatened to throw herself into the Atlantic from the cliff behind the house.

Eamonn took her in his arms and whispered, "Hush, Alva. Of course I want you and the baby! Of course. I love you both. I love you." He rocked her back and forth, telling her he was sorry, that things would be better, *he* would be better. He promised her everything would be alright.

But the labor came, and then the baby, and... and nothing changed. The fish had all but disappeared from the coast and still no crops would grow on their land. Alva sunk into a deep depression and left the baby, constantly crying, alone in the nursery while she retreated to the library for hours at a time, and Eamonn didn't interfere. Although Alva refused to speak to Eamonn or spend even a moment in the same room with him, there was no shortage of whispered words when she was in the library. So Eamonn spent as much time as possible in town looking for work as a handyman, getting away from the oppressive sadness that now infected the house like a pestilence. However, if he was honest with himself, what really frightened Eamonn was sometimes it seemed as if Alva's voice wasn't the only one he heard slipping through the cracks in the walls. Sometimes he thought a voice whispered back…

Eamonn suddenly remembered the sorrowful notes he had been concentrating on and continued with his whistling. He pulled his coat tightly around his body, tucking in against the wind, toolbox swinging in his hand. He made a silent promise that he would be kind to Alva when he arrived home, that he would take her in his arms and kiss her as if it were their wedding day. He glimpsed for a moment that gleaming smile of Alva's on the face of Emily Lenore, his beautiful daughter, as he lifted her tiny body from her crib to hug her and tickle her and delight in her cooing noises like a good father should. For a moment, only a moment, he felt real joy, felt his family could be happy again. But then, in a burst of cold winter wind, it was gone.

The collecting dark clouds rumbled with rain overhead and Eamonn walked faster. Lightning illuminated the deep purple billows, and he was sure the sky would open up any moment.

Reaching the top of Wolfhowl Mountain, where their house perched precariously close to the cliff's edge, Eamonn saw the bane of his existence – Alva's dream house – looming on the horizon. Icy dread filled the pit in his stomach and he tried warding it off, thinking of Alva's smile and hoping if he were glad to see her, then she would be glad to see him, too.

At last, the gates came into view. He stepped through and chained them behind him, the clinking disappearing on the wind as the distant church bells chimed six o'clock. He made his way toward the shed out back. He made a mental note to check on the east wing as he walked by to make sure the open walls were protected from the coming rain. How strange, he thought, that they would be getting rain this late in the year instead of snow. He didn't think he'd ever seen Christmas Eve rain.

Eamonn was passing the east wing as a light drizzle began to fall. He looked up at the gaping hole in the second and third stories as another barb of lightning illuminated the darkness. That's when he saw her body swaying in the breeze like a ragdoll, hanging from the end of a rope.

___Chapter One___
The Delaneys

August 2007

I climb out of our beat up station wagon that has been the Delaney family home for the last five days. The crisp air of southern Maine is cooler than what I'm used to – although not by much – but anything is preferable to the broken air conditioning and recycled air of the Volvo.

My knees ache as I swing my feet to the gravel driveway, but god does it feel good to stand! I want to stretch, to bend over and touch my toes, or listen for the sound of the rolling surf I'm told is not far off, but from the moment Mother turned the car into the great looming shadow of our new house, all I can do is stare. Standing before me is the most beautiful, yet most terrifying house I've ever seen.

The strange Victorian hybrid eclipses the sun, sending the weed-strewn lawn into a chilly late afternoon darkness. It stands three stories tall, with octagonal turrets at each corner, capped off by sharply slanted roofs slicing open the clouds. Tall grass and weeds creep up the dilapidated wraparound porch. Ivy climbs to a second story veranda in thick green pipes and disappears around the side. The roof is missing a hoard of shingles, and several others seem ready to fly away on the next breeze. It's all angles, chipped paint, and rotten wood, sagging into the ground so that the front stoop frowns back at me. I feel as if this first meeting is meant to be seen in black and white, and I wait for the obligatory crack of thunder and burst of lightning.

But there's beauty in the old place too. The base of each turret forms a screened gazebo on either side of the porch, a sweetheart swing visible in each. The brittle railings have an intricate design carved into them, worn and softened by age. A few ramshackle stairs lead up to a set of wide double doors that look like they're the only sturdy things left on the house, complete with a fresh layer of bright red paint. _That's odd_, I think. _Why paint the doors and nothing else?_

"Rose, honey," Mother says, chasing away the dark skies and ominous thoughts. "You're gonna catch flies with that mouth." Her voice drips with the rich honey typical of the Texas drawl. She is pleased with my awe.

Immediately my anger and resentment toward Mother for this ridiculous move comes to a boil. How dare she move me twenty states away from all of my friends, I think, clenching my fists and gritting my teeth to keep an outburst at bay. How dare she force me to live in some podunk town in this tacky fortress of darkness? The bile rises in my gut and I take a few deep breaths, like my anger management counselor suggested. I close my eyes and picture myself far, far away. I'm in a meadow overgrown with flowers and golden wheat. I can almost smell honey beyond a rim of tall cedar trees. *Happy, happy, happy, I'm so happy,* I think as I take another deep breath. *Happy!*

It doesn't work. Standing in the cool silhouette of this decomposing eyesore makes me homesick for the hot, sticky summers of Texas, and I glare at the ground, silently gritting my teeth. The rough squeakiness they make in my ears as they grind against each other comforts me a little.

As I face my new house again, I see each door is decorated with a gigantic polished knocker in the shape of a cross, complete with an emaciated Jesus. I'm sure they meant something to the original owners, but in this day and age, it's kind of tacky and a little bit creepy. Being a (mostly) devout Irish Catholic herself, Mother's unlikely to have them replaced.

"Can you get your brother out of the car, please?" Mother asks over the roof of the car. "I'm going to speak to Mrs. Carroll about the paperwork." She turns away without waiting for a response.

I look at the car parked behind the station wagon just in time to see the realtor climbing out. She doesn't look like I expect. The annoyingly faint Maine accent that had been lilting over the phone at Mother the last few months had me hoping for a stout unpleasant redhead in an old beater. The real Nora Carroll steps lithely from a black sporty coupe. She's dressed in a charcoal grey suit with a knee-length skirt and conservative heels. She wears gold in her ears, something shiny on her wrist, and the biggest diamond ring I've ever seen outside of a museum. If we were standing in the sun, the glint off of that rock would've blinded me. In truth, Mrs. Carroll is quite beautiful. I'm disappointed.

Mrs. Carroll daintily shakes hands with Mother when I'm distracted by a smacking sound. I turn to see my five-year-old brother smush his freckled face into the glass of the back passenger window.

"Rosie, can I get out now?" Liam's cherubic voice is full of impatience. I stick my tongue out at him, but then release the beast. Five days in a car is tough on a five-year-old. Due to severe boredom, he's had several naps today already and is now a ball of energy.

"Wow!" Liam runs toward the house at full speed.

"Be careful!" I shout, chasing after him.

Up close, everything on the house is larger than normal, including the ornate stained glass windows on the first floor, colorfully depicting various religious scenes. They're skillfully done, but need cleaning and several panes are broken and boarded up.

The second floor is dotted with regular windows and rickety verandas, and the third with a few dormer windows. There's storm damage on the heavy roof as it begins a sharp incline half-way up the second floor, coming to a point at a widow's walk, barely visible from this angle. Most widow's walks are decoration these days, but with the strange design of this house, I wouldn't be surprised if this one is actually accessible. I make a mental note to check later. It might be a good place to hide out when I want to be left alone, which lately, is always.

I try picturing the house when it was fresh and new. I imagine the smell of fresh wood and paint. It must have been stunning. I bet the townspeople gazed at it jealously from the bottom of the great hill.

Then my heart stops.

Black soot covers the entire right side, starting on a second floor verandah and extending over nearly half the house. What I first took for moldy wood and old paint is actually fire damage. How did the fire start? Was it an accident? Did anyone die?

I lurch out and grab Liam's hand as he's about to put a pudgy foot on the bottom step. "Here, let me hold your hand. I'm not sure how steady these stairs are." I speak louder than necessary, hoping Mother hears me, but she's fully engaged with that realtor twit.

We ascend the porch together, the steps creaking noisily under our feet. I keep a tight grip on Liam's hand as he struggles to break free. "Let go, Rosie! Let go!"

"Where're you fixin' to go?"

11

"I wanna swing!"

"Okay, okay! Stop yankin'!" I let go of Liam's hand and follow him as he bobs along to the gazebo door. The screen is torn and hangs down from one of the top corners. The door itself has come off its hinges and is simply leaning against the doorway. I slide it to the side and poke my head in, grabbing Liam's arm to prevent him from going inside just yet.

The swing seems okay. It's newer than the rest of the house. I tug on one of the chains. The ceiling doesn't come crashing down and the chains seem sturdy. I picture another family enjoying this spot, an older married couple sipping iced teas as they swing slowly. Grandchildren playing in the front yard, trying to catch lightning bugs in mason jars... I'm both charmed and irritated.

The paint is peeling and the wood is splintered. The door opposite, barely hanging on its hinges, leads to a side porch. There's an old rag on the floor and a few cobwebs in the corners, but no spiders are home right now. An old wasp's nest, dried up and empty, lingers in a corner.

"Alright, squiggle worm." I pick Liam up by the armpits and set him on the swing, struggling a little bit. He's a little heavy for his age and my ballerina legs can hoist him fine, but my scrawny arms wobble. "Have at it."

I stand behind the swing, looking out at Mother and Mrs. Carroll while I push Liam. They walk toward the house in deep discussion, I assume. Mrs. Carroll has several papers in one hand and a pen in the other. They pause at the hood of the station wagon to go over the documents.

Mother's long and severely straight red hair is pulled back into a ponytail. It looks dull in the shade, but her pale Irish skin and green eyes are as bright as ever. I hate to admit it, but she looks better than she has in years simply because she divorced Dad. Since the split, I've watched her come alive again, gain control of her stubborn Irish temper, and smile more – real smiles, where your eyes smile too. She seems truly blissful. And that. Fills me. With rage.

The divorce had the opposite effect on Dad. He was devastated and steadily became more emotional and erratic, often on the verge of tears. It's a terrible thing to see a grown man cry and beg, especially if he's your father. His emotional instability made him completely inaccessible to me and Liam at a time when we needed him most. Liam's too young to understand, and sometimes he cries at night because he wants

Daddy to read him a story and no one else will suffice. I sometimes lay down with him until he falls asleep.

My feelings are… complicated. I love my father, and I miss him so much, but I can't be around him and his depression. It only makes my own worse. Alternately, I'm kinda happy to see Mother enjoying herself again, but fully appreciating that is difficult since I pretty much hate her right now. Mother's temper might be under control and her complexion is clear, but at the cost of our family. And now here I am, forced to pick up and move to some silly island because Mother's in a hurry to move on from her stale marriage, and all right before my senior year of high school – which, I admit, is my biggest complaint.

When my parents first separated, the courts said, at sixteen, I was old enough to choose to stay with Dad if I wanted. And I might've made that choice if Dad had gotten counseling, but he refused. And what about Liam? Liam isn't old enough to choose, and the courts awarded custody to crazy Mrs. Delaney. She might be happier, and she might've joined a program for alcoholics, but that doesn't make her a better mother. She's always worked long hours as a nurse, often on the night shift, but now she's home even less. Experiencing a mid-life crisis brought on by the divorce, she acts like a single college girl. She goes to bars at happy hour (recovering alcoholic who?) and comes home late (if at all). She flirts with younger men, and dresses like my classmates. Just thinking about it makes my stomach turn. And I'm not going to let Liam be subjected to Mother's ridiculous impulses without a buffer. It's only a matter of time before she starts bringing street trash home. But this new town, Port Braseham on Mount Desert Island, is small. The realtor told us it's a tight-knit community, founded on Irish pride and Catholic principles. I hope all the men in this stupid town are old, wrinkled sailors who smell like fish and believe in marriage before pleasure.

"Eww, look!" Liam's shout breaks through my angry haze. "What?"

Liam hops to the floor, the wood beams creaking loudly. I bring the swing to a stop and watch as he kneels into a corner. When he turns around, he's holding the longest, fattest slug I've ever seen.

I jump back. "Liam, that's disgusting! Get away from me!"

"Don't be such a baby, Rosie!" He says. "I'm gonna go show Mommy!"

I watch Liam totter off the porch, but don't follow him. He runs up to Mother, shoving the slug at her. Mrs. Carroll recoils, but Mother flashes him a placating smile and pats him on the head, then points toward the lawn. Liam shrugs and finds a patch of grass to sit on while he toys with the slug.

I turn away to avoid another burst of red-hot rage. I walk back toward the front doors, placing a hand on the porch railing. I feel the raised wood underneath my fingertips, but the design is no more discernible than it was from the driveway. Looking down at the spokes, I notice each is carved into twisting ivy. The leaves are especially delicate and many of them have broken off; some pieces lay in the gap between the deep grass and the muddy underbelly of the porch. I absently wonder if there might be a body buried down there.

The fresh blood red paint on the front doors makes them pop out from the gray background of the rotten wood siding. The doorknobs are old-fashioned crystal, and each has a large keyhole beneath that looks like it might take one of those old skeleton keys. I try turning them, but they're locked. I snort; as if anyone other than a few kids on a dare would bother breaking into this dump.

A small placard beside the doors catches my eye. Some letters are carved into it, but it's too dirty to read. I check to see if anyone's watching, but Mother and Mrs. Carroll are still leaning over the paperwork and Liam is watching his slug slurp around on his arm. I spit into my hand and rub it into the sign with my fingers. Slowly, some of the letters appear: W, H, M. If I want to see the rest, I need something more abrasive.

I remember the rag and retrieve it from the gazebo. Using the rag, I continue to work my spit into the filthy sign. It takes several minutes of vigorous rubbing, but when I'm finished, I'm able to make out the words.

"Wolfhowl Manor 1851," I read to myself and roll my eyes. "Creepy name for a creepy house. No surprise there."

Suddenly, a low gravelly voice erupts from the shadows of the porch. "Used tah beah sign at the bottom ah the hill theyuh."

Turning, I see the silhouette of a mammoth in front of the other gazebo. At first, my throat is so tight I can't even breathe. Then I scream.

Chapter Two
Over the Cliff

I launch away from the doors and stumble backward off the steps. I land hard on one of the large stones making up the path from the driveway.

"What on earth – Rose?" Mother stands behind me. She has several papers gathered up in one hand and the other placed firmly on her hip. Next to her, Mrs. Carroll's face is reserved in silent judgment.

"I uh, there's a, I saw –" I stammer pointing toward the porch. As if in answer, the mammoth shuffles out of the darkness, and I realize the mammoth is actually a Neanderthal of a man. His large hands are jammed onto the ends of arms that hang almost to his knees, and his jaw is set in a pronounced under bite like a crumpled old bulldog. He wears a green flannel shirt under worn overalls, and two large work boots covered in red paint flecks. He pulls a dirty handkerchief from a pocket and wipes some sweat from his forehead as he shuffles toward the stairs, the floorboards of the porch protesting loudly beneath him.

"Ah said," comes the low gravelly voice again, "theyuh *used* tah beah *sign* at the bottom ah the *hill.*" He speaks more slowly this time, but he's no easier to understand. I stare at his face, set with wrinkles deep enough to drop a quarter in. Two deep emerald eyes with pinholes for pupils twinkle beneath the folds of his unruly gray eyebrows. Either he's very old, or he's lived a very tough life. I'm guessing the latter and put him somewhere in his sixties.

"Yes, yes, the sign, Derry, *I know.*" Mrs. Carroll snaps, and then turns to Mother. "There used to be a sign at the bottom of the hill reading Wolfhowl Mountain, carved out of an old oak tree. In fact, it was carved by the original owner of the land. It had some pine trees on it, the full moon, and a few wolves. It was very... *unique* shall we say? Some vandals carried it off several years ago. It's a real shame," she adds insincerely.

"I see. Get off the ground, Rose," Mother snipes.

15

I get up, trying not to stare at this Derry monster. He stands deathly still, like a giant boulder, as if he's waiting for something. He scares the heck out of me.

Liam runs up behind us. "Look Mommy," he points. "A giant!"

"Shh, Liam!" Mother smacks his finger away.

"Mrs. Delaney," Mrs. Carroll says, "This is Derry O'Dwyre. He and his son are the caretakers of Wolfhowl Mountain." Her carefully controlled accent is much less pronounced than Derry's, whose accent sound like some overdone impression from *Saturday Night Live*.

"The O'Dwyres tend the grounds," Mrs. Carroll continues. "They'll be available for anything you need, including repairs. They've made quite a few already in preparation for your arrival."

I'm unable to stifle a snort and Derry's eyes flick to me. His gaze is intense and I can feel him sizing me up.

"As stipulated in the sale of Wolfhowl Mountain and the agreement with the Port Braseham Historical Society, the O'Dwyres' services are the equivalent of rent as long as they live in the small cottage on the side of the hill," Mrs. Carroll finishes, gesturing to the right side of the house, where the hill drops sharply. I can just glimpse the roof of the cottage.

"Yes, of course," Mother says. Her smile falters when she meets Derry's gaze. "It's a pleasure to meet you, Mr. O'Dwyre."

Derry gives an apelike grunt, as though he's not happy someone is moving in. Probably makes more work for the lazy elephant. He tips his dirty ball cap to us, gives me one last lingering glare, and turns to leave.

"Derry," Mrs. Carroll calls before he gets far, "we were actually getting ready to take a quick tour of the interior. Would you like to join us in case Mrs. Delaney has any maintenance requests?" Her voice is lighter all of a sudden, hopeful. Why would this delicate flower spend any more time with this big ox than she has to?

Derry pauses in his retreat. He keeps his back turned until she finishes her question, and then shuffles into the shadows of the porch.

"Well!" Mother's hand flies to her chest.

"Uh," Mrs. Carroll's voice falters, "don't take it personally, Mrs. Delaney. Derry just has one of those gruff personalities. I assure you, he'll be most helpful to have around once you get settled, which reminds me, your belongings arrived the other day as anticipated. The O'Dwyres placed the items in their proper rooms based on your labels."

"Thank you." Mother follows Mrs. Carroll to the front door, Liam and I close behind.

To my sheer glee, Mrs. Carroll pulls out a set of skeleton keys.

"Now, there are four keys to the house," she says. "They're quite old, but sturdy, made of iron. The previous owners appreciated the antique design of them, but you can have them replaced with something modern if you'd like. There are two keys each for the front, back and side doors; one key for the attic, and one for the basement." She holds up each key as she indicates its purpose, but they all look the same to me.

"Awesome!" Liam says, hopping up and down. "Can I open the doors? Can I do it?"

"Sure, sweetie," Mother reaches for the keys, but Mrs. Carroll jerks them out of her reach and says, "I want to stress to you, Mrs. Delaney, this must be a quick tour. I have a pressing appointment in Bar Harbor." Her voice is stern, like a parent issuing a new household rule. "A quick tour, do you understand?"

Mother and I exchange a quick glance.

"Sure, that's fine," Mother replies. "We want to get settled in for the evening anyway. We're exhausted from the trip."

"I'm sure." Mrs. Carroll relinquishes the keys to Mother, who sticks the key for the front door into the keyhole and lets Liam turn it. There's a loud and heavy click as the lock releases. Liam turns the crystal knob impatiently and throws himself through the door. Mother and I follow, but Mrs. Carroll hesitates.

Once my eyes adjust to the darkness within, I'm awestruck all over again.

The double doors open onto an oval-shaped foyer exposing the second floor. The sides are framed by large staircases straight out of *Gone with the Wind*, each lined with faded, dusty red carpet. Beneath each staircase, an archway leads into a room beyond. The colored light from the stained glass windows glows on the weathered floorboards. Straight ahead is a short hallway with a closed door at the other end and another small door to the left. Centered above the front doors, and three times the size of the other stained glass windows, is another stained glass portrait, this one of the Virgin Mary.

Mrs. Carroll sneezes daintily. "Oh, bless me! Um, it's a little musty, but nothing a good spring cleaning won't fix." She laughs nervously. "Now, where is that light switch?" She lifts a finger with a French manicured nail along the wall until she finds the switch.

The foyer illuminates in a soft yellowy light. Above is a large crystal chandelier. The crystals catch light from Mary's window and throw rainbows around the hall. My eyes follow the colorful splashes down the walls. The pine green wallpaper is peeling and patchy. Spring cleaning… suuuure.

Liam starts running toward a staircase, but Mrs. Carroll lurches out and grabs him by a shoulder.

"Just a minute, young man!" She grips him tightly with her manicured claws. "Do not go roaming around this house alone, do you hear me?" When all he does is stare back with wide, frightened eyes, she shakes him. "Do you hear me?"

I jump forward and smack Mrs. Carroll's hand away from Liam. I consider cussing her out, but refrain, afraid the shock will be too much for such a high-class woman. Besides, her look of shock tells me being smacked by a Texas redneck is clearly insulting enough.

Liam starts crying, a little simper at first, but before long it's a full on tantrum. Mother reaches for him, but he ducks away from her and buries his head in my side. I hold a hand protectively on his head and glare at Mother. *"Do something,"* I mouth to her.

Mother looks at the realtor, but doesn't know what to do or say.

Mrs. Carroll recovers quickly. She shakes her head as if trying to rid it of a stray thought and looks at Liam apologetically. "I'm sorry. I did not mean to scare you. It's just – " She forces a smile. "It's just this is an old house and there are a lot of places one might get hurt. Stick close to your mother until you've familiarized yourself with the house, alright?" When the silence persists, she gestures toward the stairs. "Shall we?"

Mrs. Carroll clasps her hands together and throws herself back into realtor mode. "This is the main foyer," she says, pronouncing it pretentiously as *foi-ay*. "As you can see, it has two grand staircases leading up to the open hallway on the second floor. There are four rooms off of the foyer." Mrs. Carroll points to each door, beginning with the one on the right. "The dining hall, a hall leading to the kitchen, the drawing room, and the living room. Now, as I told you over the phone, this house is very old and the original owners were quite eclectic in their tastes. It might seem a little odd to have a drawing room, for insistence, but you might find the extra space useful for cocktail parties and the like."

I suppress an eye roll. Does anyone actually throw cocktail parties outside of Hollywood?

"Now if you'll follow me, Mrs. Delaney, I'll take you through the upper floors." Mrs. Carroll walks as quickly as she talks.

"Oh," Mother says disappointedly, "I was hoping you could take me through each room, explain the history a little?"

"As I said, Mrs. Delaney, I have another appointment and I really am in quite a hurry." I believe her; she doesn't even pause to turn around and continues up the stairs. "All the information on the history of the house is included in those documents I gave you. If you have any other inquires, the head of the Port Braseham Historical Society, Mr. Quinn, can surely help you. Now come, come." She snaps her fingers.

Mother shrugs at me and starts following Mrs. Carroll up the stairs. "Are you coming, honey?"

I shake my head. "We're just gonna poke around down here."

"Well, kiddo," I say when we're alone, shaking his shoulders slightly. "Whaddya say? Wanna take a peek around? Maybe we'll see some *ghosts.*"

Liam looks up at me with wide eyes, his mouth agape. "Ghosts?"

I shrug. "You heard that evil woman. It's an old house. Who knows? Maybe it's even built on top of a graveyard!"

"Cool!"

"Now, I bet," I say, trying to distract Liam from his sour mood, "if we snoop around, we might find some cool things from the previous owners."

"Like dead bodies?" Liam asks and I laugh.

"I was thinking photo albums and trinkets, but you never know…"

"Let's look in here first!" Liam flings himself through the archway into the dining room.

It's shaped strangely; a rectangle with an oval cut in one corner from the foyer's curved wall, and half an octagon in the opposite corner from the gazebo. A small door allows access to the gazebo. There are two stained glass windows at the front, and a set of French double doors open onto the wraparound porch.

Liam crawls around underneath a large dining table. It's long and skinny with one wing-backed chair at each end, the cushions lined with the same blood red fabric as the stairs. The wood is stained so dark it's almost black. The simple dining set looks out of place with the rest of the room. There's an ornate fireplace and crown molding around the high ceiling and chair railing. I wonder if these detailed touches were carved by the same skilled hands that carved the ivy into the porch railing.

I walk to the double doors. Peeling the sheer, moth-eaten curtains aside, I see the hill drops severely on this side and I can just make out the roof of the O'Dwyres' cottage. The porch itself is blackened, a large section missing entirely, as if it melted away. I assume it has something to do with the fire and then, remembering Derry's intimidating form, reach down and make sure the doors are locked.

"Don't go out these doors, Liam, okay?" I say. "It's not safe on this side of the porch." I turn around, but Liam has disappeared. I check under the table, in the fireplace, and back in the foyer. "Liam?"

"I'm in here!"

I notice a small skinny door in the back corner of the room that I at first took for a closet. Pushing through, I find a massive kitchen. To the left of the door is a fireplace identical to the one in the dining room. Peering into it, I realize it's the same fireplace, accessible to both rooms. Cool.

There are two windows on the right, similar in size and shape to those on the front of the house, but with normal panes. Popping out of the back corner is the pantry, in the same shape as the gazebos on the front of the house. So there's a turret back here too. I find Liam in the pantry – no surprise – poking around some items on the shelves.

"What'd you find?"

"Nothin' really." He's nosing around several old and dusty cans of food at eye level. "What's this say?" He asks, thrusting one of the cans at me.

I wipe the dust away, revealing a familiar green and yellow label. "It's green beans," I say, and then laugh, "from nineteen eighty-one!"

"Gross," Liam says and continues poking around. We find several more old cans of vegetables, a loaf of bread that's turned into a moldy green rock, and a bag of old sugar full of ants.

"You know what I wanna know, Rosie?" Liam asks as I pull him away from the dust and bugs.

"What?"

"Why'd they leave without food?"

"They were in a hurry I guess."

"That's crazy!" My portly brother can't wrap his head around such an idea. He walks off, looking into every cabinet he can reach.

A door in the opposite corner from the pantry leads into the drawing room. Next to it is a doorway to another staircase. I wonder if this is one of those houses that used to have servants, and if this was the access to their quarters.

I turn to the dingy glass of a small window above the kitchen sink and drink in the view. Mrs. Carroll is right about one thing: the view is astounding. The grass lies tall and un-mown, bending this way and that as the breeze speeds up from the cliff where the land suddenly drops away. Old pines line the edge of the property up to the dropoff and part perfectly so the sun is visible along the edge of the water, just beginning to dip below the horizon, sending up a rainbow of colors along the skyline. I feel my lips curling into a smile, and for the first time in a long time, I don't fight it. For a minute, it feels like my happy place has come to life, only it's more perfect than I dreamed. I feel the urge to go outside, kick off my shoes, and twist my fingers in the grass.

Above, the heavy floorboards creak as Mother and Mrs. Carroll tour the second floor. Looking up, plumes of dust and dirt slip through a crack in the ceiling and hit me squarely in the eye.

"Ack!" I clutch my eye and bump into the counter, blindly searching for the faucet. My fingers find it and I throw my head under the water, prying open the afflicted eye to flush it out. "Liam! See if you can find me a towel or something!" I start coughing as the coppery water hits my nose and slides down my throat. "Arg! Liam!" He must've wandered upstairs in search of Mother.

I pull myself out of the sink and rub my stinging eye vigorously, bringing pinpoints of light to my eyelids. I feel along the counter until my hand slides across something soft and dry. Without caring what it is, I grab it and dry off my face. I cautiously open my eye, blinking several times. When it doesn't immediately start burning, I sigh with sweet relief and look down at the towel in my hands. It's surprisingly clean, pale pink, and embroidered with the initials E. L.

"Hmm." I shrug and use the towel to soak up excess water from my hair. I saunter to the back door to admire the view again. Sighing, I admit eerie Wolfhowl Mountain and sleepy Port Braseham might not be so bad – not that I'll ever admit it to Mother.

I imagine how nice it'll be waking up and starting each day with such a startling view when a small figure appears between the sun and the house. Pulling the old door open, I peer through the screen as a soft breeze blows Liam's giggles toward me.

I toss the old towel onto the counter and step onto the back porch, descending a few stairs and shielding my eyes from the sun with a hand. "Liam, you shouldn't be out there by yourself," I warn. As if sensing my next warning, Liam totters toward the edge of the cliff.

"Don't get too close to the edge! You'll fall," I continue down the steps, my pulse quickening. I take a few cautious steps into the yard, as if the cliff will creep up on me while the grass tangles around my legs like living vines.

Liam turns back and waves a pudgy little hand, smiling brightly and laughing his infectious laugh. Despite my irritation, I smile and wave back.

Then Liam breaks into a reckless run, heading directly for the dropoff, his red hair glowing like fire in the sun's sinking light.

"Liam!" I take off after him. "Liam, stop!" Panic thrusts up inside me.

I chase Liam, gaining on him as the edge of the cliff looms closer. The sharp blades of grass and weeds slash my legs as I pump my arms as fast as I can to close the gap between us. I'm nearly on top of him, just one more inch…

As Liam's little feet leave the earth I make a crazy lunge, grabbing at the collar of his shirt. But just as I reach him, he vanishes, sinking over the edge of the cliff and then I, too, sail over the edge after him with the momentum of a steam engine.

Time stands still. There's no trace of Liam plunging toward the sea below as I stare down at the jagged rocks, at the black waves violently hurtling themselves against them. The water churns and sparkles in the sunset and the salty air burns my lungs. For a moment, all is silent. But then I hear a scream, as if from far away. It grows louder and louder until I finally recognize my own terrified voice as I rocket toward my death.

Chapter Three
Don't Believe Everything You See

Warmth grips my wrist so tightly something cracks. A hand, strong and rough, grabs me before I completely disappear over the brink. I swing out over the churning waves far, far below and then, like a pendulum, back toward the cliff, slamming into its soft earthy side. I barely have time to contemplate my near death experience before I'm being hauled toward safety. I grab onto every root or blade of grass within my reach with my free hand as my sneakers scramble along the side of the dropoff. My torso hits horizontal land and I furiously kick and claw at the grass, scampering until my feet find the ground, and then crawl as far from the edge as my body will allow before I collapse, trembling and exhausted.

My mind races as I catch my breath. Someone has just saved my life, and that someone is now only a few feet away. I roll onto my side to take in my savior.

Familiar bottle green eyes alive with adrenaline peer out from behind a freckled face and shaggy, reddish brown hair. Even lying in the grass, he cuts a tall figure; a figure made of hard manual labor, lean with worked muscles. I remember the sensation of his rough hand on my wrist and look at his hands, running through his hair. They're cracked and dry, much older than the rest of him; he couldn't be more than twenty or so. His green eyes find mine and his parched lips part. "What the *hell* d'you think you were doin'?"

His words trigger my memory and I'm on my feet again, heading for the cliff. "My brother! Liam! *Liam!*" I scream before I'm tackled.

The stranger's heavy body falls on top of mine. I kick and struggle as I try to get away. "Get off of me!" I scream, and with a deep breath, take in the stale taste of cigarettes and sweat on my tongue. "Liam!"

"Hey!" He straddles me, pinning my arms to my body with his knees. "Hey! Crazy girl!" When I don't stop struggling, he smacks me across the face; not violently, but hard enough to get my attention. He places two strong hands on my shoulders, pinning me to the ground. I glare into his piercing eyes as they hover above me, still feeling the tingle of his slap on my cheek. "Are you out of your evah lovin' mind?"

"Get off of me!" Tears build behind my eyes. *Liam…* "My brother just fell off of the cliff!"

"No he didn't!" He refuses to budge. "The only crazy idiot out heeah jumpin' off cliffs is you!"

"No, my brother! I –" Before I can finish my sentence, I hear the clamoring of feet on the porch and turn toward the house. There, scuttling down the stairs, are Mother, Mrs. Carroll, and *Liam*.

"Liam?"

My rescuer finally lifts his hard body off of mine and offers a helping hand, but I ignore it, getting to my feet, my knees still shaky and weak.

"What's going on out here?" Mother demands as the group approaches. "Who the hell is this?"

Mrs. Carroll places herself between Mother and the stranger, who now fruitlessly pats at dirt and grass stains on his clothes. "Mrs. Delaney, this is Derry O'Dwyre's son, Beckan." She lowers her critical gaze to me and then flicks her eyes to Beckan's rumpled clothing. "And I'm sure he has a very good explanation for this *display.*"

"Oh, erm," I'm suddenly self-conscious. "I uh, I thought I –" I break off when I realize the complete absurdity of what I'm about to say.

"She got tah close tah the edge," Beckan says quickly. I notice that, although his accent is stronger than Mrs. Carroll's, he's much easier to understand than his father. His mouth twitches as if to say something more, but he makes no more attempts to explain.

"I slipped," I add. "Beckan," I hesitate, not sure I'm pronouncing his name correctly, "helped me out."

Beckan and I exchange furtive glances, both disguising our awkward smiles and hoping this is explanation enough. When the awkward silence continues, Beckan sticks out a large hand to shake with Mother.

"Right, well it's nice tah meet you, Miss Delaney." He smiles warmly and she blushes at his formality.

"Oh, ha!" She giggles and tucks an errant strand of hair behind her ear. "It's actually Mrs. Delaney, but please, call me

Moira." I roll my eyes. "And this is my son Liam." She puts her hand on Liam's shoulder as he absolutely beams at Beckan.

Beckan exaggeratedly shakes Liam's hand. "Strong grip you got, young man."

"And you've obviously met Rose," Mother eyes me. "Thank goodness you were here to help her." She's smiling, but I recognize the tone of embarrassment and irritation. Not even an hour in town and poor little Rose needs rescuing from a cliff. "She can be such a klutz sometimes."

"Oh, it's nothin'," Beckan insists, all Aw shucks, Ma'am, and blushes.

"Well," Mrs. Carroll forces a smile. "Mrs. Delaney, why don't we go back around front and make sure you're good and settled. I'll need to be on my way to my appointment right away." I watch the realtor struggle not to look down her nose so obviously at us before she turns away. She walks expertly in her heels, even in the soft grass, one foot placed quickly in front of the other, as if she can't get away fast enough.

Mother, with a warning glance at me and a smile for Beckan, follows Mrs. Carroll and disappears around the corner of the house, Liam bounding after her. Silence persists between us as the sun continues to set, throwing the yard into a bright orange glow and setting the horizon on fire.

"So, Rose," Beckan says, my name rolling beautifully off his tongue, "you want tah tell me why you're throwin' yourself off a cliff two seconds aftah gettin' intah town?"

"I was *not* throwing myself off a cliff!" I stamp my foot. "I thought I –" I stop again, remembering what I saw – what I *thought* I saw. I saw Liam, saw him so clearly, his little figure darting toward the edge of the cliff. Thinking about it, my eyes are forced back to the dropoff.

"Thought you saw somethin' you didn't see," Beckan offers ominously, his soft voice suddenly very hard to hear.

"I –" I hesitate, but something in his voice makes me continue. "Yes. I was sure, so sure, I saw my brother runnin' off that cliff." I point like an idiot, as if Beckan wouldn't know which cliff I'm talking about.

Beckan nods. "Ayuh… The sun has a way of playin' tricks on you 'round heeah."

Beckan's tone sends shivers down my spine and as the wind picks up, I hug myself to chase away the chills. "What do you mean?"

"I just mean… don't believe everythin' you see 'round heeah." His tone and eyes are so serious, that I can't keep the warmth inside anymore. "Anyway, stay safe, Rose Delaney." Beckan turns and walks toward the side of the house. I watch him until he disappears.

*   *   *

The small one-level cottage built into the back of the hill is already cloaked in darkness. The outside décor mimics the main house, but on a smaller scale, and is just as poorly kept together. Beckan looks at the peeling paint and battered shingles and sighs; just two of the many things he and his father had been meaning to fix for a long time. The weathered front door slowly creaks open and an energetic bloodhound bounds out of the darkness.

Beckan braces himself, accepting Lady's paws on his chest as she jumps on him. He rubs her big floppy ears and notes the white fur creeping in around her eyes and snout. As Lady drops down and runs circles around him, wagging her tail, another figure emerges from the shadows. Derry is every bit as tall and freckled as Beckan, but he's twice his size in old muscles that have started going to seed. Beckan meets his father's beady stare and continues toward the house. He passes Derry on the porch without a word.

"She's gettin' stahted ah little early this time 'round, eh?" Derry says in his typical gruff voice.

Beckan doesn't respond but follows Derry's gaze up the hill to the attic window. He flinches as the shadow, slight and fast, flits across the dark panes.

"That girl, she's cunnin'," his father says, "but she's gonna beah trouble. Mahk my words."

Beckan sighs. "Ayuh." The uneasy feeling grows in the pit of his stomach as he goes inside, where a hot shower and a cup of tea will cleanse him of the spooky feeling that's followed him home.

Chapter Four
The Fire

"Boy, that woman was jumpy wasn't she?" Mother closes the door behind her as she breezes back into the house. Liam and I sit on one of the bottom steps, chins in our hands and elbows on our knees, disappointed and bored. "And in a hurry too!"

"Yeah, for her 'appointment'." I hold up air quotes, rolling my eyes.

"What do you mean?" Mother leans against the door with a sigh. For the first time all day, she looks tired. The jade of her eyes is dull and several strands of hair are matted to her forehead with sweat. She wipes them away with a light smile.

"A pretty woman like that doesn't dip out on the biggest sale of her career for just **anything**," I say. "I'm guessing she's got a sugar daddy at the nearest motel."

"Rose! That's an awful thing to say!"

"Sugar daddy?" Liam asks. "Like the candy?"

I ignore him. "Why else would she be in such a hurry?"

"Maybe she's scared," Liam frowns and fiddles with a shoelace.

"Scared? Don't be silly." Mother pushes away from the door and makes a space for herself between us. She places an arm around each of us and I manage not to recoil.

"There is nothing to be scared of here," she says, giving us a squeeze.

"Mom," I say seriously, "this place is a fire-eaten museum and it has more shadows than a graveyard. It's ancient! It'll probably collapse any minute." One can hope.

"Look kiddos," Mother sighs heavily and her shoulders sag; she's weary of my never-ending negativity, "I know this move, among other things, has been tough on you, but this is a fresh start for us. Let's not take it for granted." She looks pointedly at me. "And, yes, this place is a *tad* gloomy, I'll admit, but all it needs some love. A little paint, a little wallpaper..." She gestures to the large foyer around us and her voice falters. "It'll be good as new."

Mother hugs the dubious Liam tighter. "The most important thing to remember is it's just a house. Yes, it's old, and yes, it's been a long time since anyone's lived here, but there're no ghosts. There're no goblins. There're no monsters. It's just *a house*. Okay, kiddo?"

After a pause, Liam says, "I'm hungry." Mother and I laugh. If Liam's hungry, then all is right with the world.

"Alright. Let's finish unloading the car," Mother says. "Then we'll figure out something for supper. Deal?"

"Deal!" Liam runs at the front doors and Mother follows. "Rose?"

"I'll be there in a minute," I say. "It's kinda chilly in here. I need a sweatshirt."

"Mrs. Carroll said our packages arrived a few days ago and the O'Dwyre's divvied them up for us," Mother says without turning around. "Your things are in the room at the top of the stairs."

I'm already halfway up the right-side staircase when I remember there are two staircases. I turn around to ask which staircase she means, but Mother's already disappeared through the doors.

The second floor of Wolfhowl Manor is perhaps more overwhelming than the first, if only because there are so many rooms up here. Six doors lead off of the open hall. It's darker than the first floor, the paneled walls absorbing most of the light. The only window looking in on this part of the house is the great stained glass of Mary, but no light shines through it now. The chandelier hanging just below the second floor level emits a dim, ineffectual light. I hate to admit it, but after what happened on the cliff, I'm a little creeped out.

I go for the room at the top of this staircase first. Fifty-fifty shot, right? I nudge the door open with a loud echoing *crrreeaaakkk,* drowning out Mother's cry as she reenters.

"No, Rose! Not that one!"

But it's too late.

I know instantly the fire started in this room. A huge blackened scorch marks the center of the floorboards like a bomb blast. The fire-eaten wood beams hang crookedly from the ceiling, ready to disintegrate at the slightest touch. A hole yawns in the ceiling beyond the damaged beams, boarded up with few pieces of plywood. A similar shoddy repair has been made to an outer wall. The framing of the bay window opposite the door is equally black and soot covered, and the broken panes are also boarded up. The same octagonal cut from the dining room below is in the front corner. There's a small door in one of the walls of the turret, but I can't even begin to guess what's behind it as a wave of nausea overtakes me. I sway on my feet and throw a hand against the wall for support. I'm scorching hot and the taste of bile creeps into my mouth.

Mother rushes in behind me, yanks me from the room, and slams the door.

In the hallway, I wrench my arm from Mother's grasp and lean against the banister, fighting the urge to faint. I wipe sweat from my forehead with a clammy hand.

Liam runs up the stairs. "What's wrong? Mommy? Rosie?" Mother's back is against the door to the fire room. "Hey, what's in there?"

Neither of us replies.

I feel the world dimming and I focus my thoughts in an attempt to stay conscious. Really, I can't be that shocked, can I? I knew there'd been a fire, but I assumed the damaged parts had been restored, at least on the inside. What the hell else were Derry and Beckan for it not for that? But it isn't the sight of the room that really bothers me. It's the way the room makes me *feel*. It's a stifling, desperate, miserable feeling. In the few seconds I stood in the doorway, that horrible feeling flooded my senses. I can still feel the heat of the wall on my hand, burning like a hot stove, and I check to be sure it isn't actually burned.

Finally, I find my voice. "Mother... that room –"

"Rose, I'm so sorry." She interrupts.

"What happened in this house?" I ask, finally beginning to feel normal again.

Mother sighs and shrugs. "There was a fire several years ago. Mrs. Carroll didn't give me the details and I didn't ask. She mentioned repairs had been made and I guess I just assumed all of the damage had been repaired."

"You just *assumed?*" I ignore the voice in my head reminding me I'd made the same mistake.

"I'm sorry, Rose," Mother says, her voice stern, "but what do you want me to tell you? We needed a place to live and this place was affordable."

"Affordable," Liam says. "What's that mean?"

"It means cheap," I hiss.

"Yes, Rose, it was cheap," Mother says. "I'm sorry this house isn't to your liking, but you're just going to have to buck up and deal with it. This is our home now. It may not be perfect, but it's ours. Luckily, we have two handymen hanging around, whom I'm sure can help us restore the damage. It'll be like new before you know it. Now, if you still need a sweatshirt, your clothes are in the room on the other side. Go get one and then help Liam and me get his room ready, so we can get some food and get to bed." She picks up the box she dropped at the top of the steps and disappears into a doorway without another word.

Liam shrugs and follows her into his new bedroom, oblivious to the tension in the air. I'm so angry I'm practically growling as I stalk to my room and stomp through the door. As I flip a light switch, my anger dissipates almost immediately. To my chagrin, my bedroom is actually pretty amazing.

Dammit.

Two bay windows lined with cushions of light green and pink greet my eyes on the opposite side of the room. The sheer pink drapes gathered on each side look nice with the faded mint green of the walls. The cool colors soothe my emotions. The cutout from the turret with the funny little door in it is in the front corner. The second best feature of the room is the set of French doors leading out to my very own balcony. I peer through the translucent curtains onto the dark front lawn, the lights of Port Braseham tinkling back at me from the bottom of the hill. I feel a little like Rapunzel awaiting her prince.

The best part of this move by far is the large canopy bed in the middle of the room. Mother said she'd bought me a new bed since most of our furniture had been left behind to reduce moving costs. I've always dreamed of having one for the same reason I've continued with ballet all these years – it makes me feel like a princess.

Running, I leap onto the bed and almost launch myself off of the other side. Up close I can see a moth-eaten hole in the canopy and feel the mattress springs in my back; it's used, but so what! I sigh to myself and stop fighting the grin that's been struggling to contort my face all afternoon.

Reluctantly, I get up, remembering I'd come for a sweatshirt. If I don't resurface soon, Mother will be even more annoyed with me. I do a quick scan for my belongings, but don't see any. There's a door opposite the turret. When I open it to reveal a large walk-in closet, I discover, as with the rest of the room, I'm in love.

*   *   *

I help Liam with his room while Mother unpacks the kitchen things we'd need right away. As Liam starts to complain of death by starvation, Beckan shows up with some milk, sandwiches, and a big bag of Cape Cod kettle cooked potato chips for our dinner. Mother fawns over his thoughtfulness and invites him to stay with a light touch on his arm, but he declines with a simple smile and a "No thank you." I watch him from the top of the stairs. He doesn't put one foot inside the foyer, but leans over the threshold to hand Mother his food delivery.

After dinner, Mother disappears to "investigate this quaint little town," which means she's checking out the local bar scene. Liam and I are left to our own devices in our dark new house. We spend the time together, getting the rest of his room unpacked before I announce it's time for bed. We've just finished bedtime stories and I'm pulling his covers up to his chin when Liam says, looking very serious, "Rosie? Do you miss Daddy?"

"Umm." My voice catches in my throat, Dad's face floating before my eyes. "Yeah... yeah, squiggle worm, I do."

"Do you think he misses us?"

"Of course!" I hug Liam tightly. "Of course he does!" Pulling back, I look straight into his baleful eyes. "Every minute you're thinking of him, he's thinking of you. I promise. Okay?"

"Yeah." He frowns. "Rosie?"

"Liam?"

"I'm thirsty."

I laugh. "Of course you are." This is Liam's routine, a last ditch effort to avoid bedtime for a few minutes more. I'm about to let him out of bed when I see a full glass of water sitting on his bedside table.

"Hold it, trickster! What's this right here?" I hand him the glass.

"That's not mine," he says, selling his confusion with furrowed eyebrows.

"Yeah, sure." I shake my head. "You almost got me. Alright, back to bed you go." I let Liam take a few sips of water and then set the glass on his nightstand. I leave his room in the warm yellowy glow of his nightlight, and his comforting silhouette under the quilt stays on my eyes an extra few seconds. I feel my way down the hall to my room in near pitch blackness and I feel the yawning expanse of the foyer on my left rather than see it.

At night, my new room has a different feel. A small lamp on my nightstand spreads its cheery warmth in a tiny circle of light before being swallowed up by the heavy darkness of the rest of my room. It's chilly and still. The floorboards groan with each step and echo throughout the empty rooms of the rest of the house.

I stifle a shiver and slip under the covers of my new bed in an old t-shirt and warm socks. Sitting close to the light, I grab my worn copy of Pride & Prejudice. I've read it a dozen times at least. The story is familiar and comforting. Handsome and arrogant Mr. Darcy and flippant, reckless Lydia will let me forget my troubles for a while. I sink into my pillows and begin reading.

It is a truth universally acknowledged, that a single man in possession of a good fortune, must be in want of a wife...

*   *   *

I'm sitting straight up in bed, clutching my book, still open in my hands, against my chest. I must've fallen asleep reading.

But why am I awake? Why is my heart trying so hard to break my ribs? Did I hear something? Yes... I *heard* something.

I listen intently to the unsettling silence. Then, from somewhere very near the house, I hear the wild lament of a wolf, howling at the moon. His cry is answered by another mournful howl, even closer to the house, and then a third.

They're right under my window.

The final howl resounds throughout the house, a hollow, lonely sound.

Only when the wolves are finished howling do I lean back on my pillows, shivering from the very chill in my bones.

Chapter Five
The Flatlander

The start of the school year is still a few weeks away. I'm bored the second I crawl out of bed, escaping a fitful night of sleep. It was hard to fall asleep after the chilling howls of the wolves echoing through the halls of this mausoleum. Then I couldn't sleep because I was waiting for Mother to come home, smelling of booze and cigarettes – as usual – which happened around 2 a.m. When I finally did sleep again, I had strange dreams. Dreams about my old friends melting away. Dreams about Dad, about a strange, dark presence hovering over me, watching me sleep.

It's early, but I know there's no going back to bed, so I take a shower and wash off the accumulated film of a sweaty car trip and a night of heavy lifting. I'm impressed by the bathroom, which is down the hall between Liam's room and the fire room. Everything is pristine, white, new. The rising sun filters in through a large bay window with sheer curtains. It's so bright and cheery in here that I almost forget about the blackened scar of a room behind the mirror. Almost.

Looking through the window, I can see clear down the steep hill to the O'Dwyre's cabin. A thin spire of smoke wafts from the chimney and there's movement on the shaded porch. Thinking about Derry and his intense stare makes me shiver, but thinking about Beckan's handsome green eyes warm me again. I pull the shade down and turn on the water. It's lukewarm and low on water pressure, but it feels so good to rinse away the grime and creepy feelings.

I dress quickly with barely a glance at my pale skin in the mirror. I've got my long, nearly black hair in a bun and a bike under my feet while Liam still sleeps and Mother snores away her hangover.

I venture into Port Braseham proper to see what it's all about. Maybe, if I'm lucky, I'll find a hidden KFC or an old-fashioned Wendy's in some hole-in-the-wall shopping center. My stomach complains loudly at the thought of an ice cold Frosty.

I realize why Wolfhowl Mountain is called a mountain instead of a hill. It hadn't looked so vertical from the safety of the station wagon yesterday, but my bike reaches such a high speed near the bottom that I'm afraid my wheels will roll right off. But the wheels remain attached and I have the perfect momentum to coast through the curvy, tree-lined main drag into town.

After a mile of monstrous pine trees and the smell of cedar and juniper, downtown Port Braseham explodes before me. The streets are lined with tall Victorians painted in bright teals, yellows, and lavenders. White trims fly around the turrets and French windows. Green grass surrounds stone walks and short picket fences. Most of the Victorians downtown have been converted into businesses with names like Murphy's Estate Law, Doyle's Taxidermy, Port Braseham Bait & Tackle, Downeast Cah Shop.

I scoot around town for a few hours, gawking at how different Port Braseham is from Texas. Aside from the massive trees, everything else is so quaint and tiny. Trees are everywhere, but cars and people aren't. Trees dot yards and side streets, separating neighbors from each other. Houses are more than ten feet apart on large tracts of land. I haven't seen a single apartment building, movie theater, or Starbucks. I guess tiny towns like this hold some kind of *Andy Griffith* charm, but I'm still not sure if a place like this is going to work out for me. What the heck do people do for fun around here?

At eleven a.m., I'm drawn toward the peal of a bell ringing from a steeple high enough to see the tip above the treeline. Following the sound, I finally encounter some locals. As I sail by them, observing, I notice they're also observing. And while I'm looking at them with mild curiosity, they stare at me with piercing, scrutinizing eyes. Are they hostile? Am I trespassing? Can it be this town is so small that they know I'm an outsider at first glance?

Everyone is heading for the building with the bell. Women and girls wear conservative dresses and skirts, and I'm suddenly self-conscious in my tank top and tight capri pants. The men and boys wear suits and shiny shoes. A small girl fiddles with her hairbow. A mother bends down to help her son with his tie. This is obviously their Sunday Best, and as I come to a break in the trees, I see the source of the bell: church. Of course. They're staring at the heathen's cleavage as she heads away from the church instead of toward it.

I stop and stare right back at the townspeople as they disappear inside the church. I wait until the last righteous coattail is inside before pedaling off to find a comfortable place to sit, think, and pout.

I find a small beach access at the bottom of a stony cliff. I sit on a boulder and let my bare feet dangle in the cold, wet sand. The beaches here are so different than those on the Gulf. The sand is full of tiny pebbles of various size and color. It's more pebble than sand really, and it reminds me of a scene Seurat might have painted, dotted with grays, blues, and muted reds. Large rocks pop out of the ground everywhere, surrounding this perfect little clearing resting between them.

The whitecapped waves roll in. There's no one else on the beach, no swimmers in the choppy water. There are a few fishing boats in the distance, coming inland for lunch. It's quiet here in this spot, and I enjoy it as long as I can before I'm so desperate with hunger that I have to eat something or die.

I shake the sand off my feet and slip them back into my sneakers. I haven't seen a single fast food restaurant I recognize since getting off the ferry. There isn't even a ubiquitous McDonald's, but there's an old-fashioned diner car across from the beach access called The Wharf Rat. I throw a glance on either side of it, but I'm met with more ghosts of buildings, former sentinels watching over the empty boardwalk. Hunger draws my heavy feet across the street. I take a deep breath and slink through the door in my best attempt to be invisible, keeping my eyes on the ground and shrinking into my shoulders, trying to look small.

The small diner is crowded, the atmosphere close and humid. There's one open stool around a dingy white bar. I squeeze between two fishermen who smell like they just walked off the boat before anyone else can take it. While I put away my invisibility cloak and wait for the waitress, I take a chance and walk my eyes around the room.

Most of the customers are fisherman or early birds here for the dinner special (grilled mystery fish and biscuits with ambiguous looking gravy). The restaurant has the usual hum of several conversations going on at once and the tinkling of dishes and silverware. Music pours from a jukebox near the door, but I can't make out the tune. I eavesdrop on some of the nearby voices, but they all sound like ol' Derry. I can't understand any of their slack jawed warbling and I feel like I'm all alone in a foreign country. I miss the honeyed southern drawl of my friends.

There's an old woman with wrinkles deeper than Derry's in one of the booths at the end of the dining car. Her white hair is pulled into a tight bun, but several strands have come loose, giving her a wild look. Her two milky blue eyes stare blankly, like she has a bad case of cataracts. Then the old woman's eyes shift, and it's like she's looking right at me. Her stare is vacant but intense. It makes me uncomfortable and I shrink back on my stool so the fisherman next to me blocks the old woman and her strange eyes.

"What can I do ya fah?" The waitress comes up on me suddenly and I'm startled.

"Oh, um…" I look around and realize I don't even have a menu. "Can I see a menu?"

The waitress, a heavyset redhead with long, manicured red nails and a nametag reading 'Flo', stares at me. "A menyah?"

"Yeah, you know," I struggle to come up with another word, but can only repeat, "a menu?" with more emphasis.

"Theyuh ain't no menyah heeah deah," Flo says. "Fish. Burgah. Chicken sahlad."

"What's in the chicken salad?"

Flo rolls her eyes.

"Never mind. I'll just have a basket of fries please. And a bottled water. To go."

Flo huffs a strand of crimson from her eyes with a hand on her hip.

"A *glass* of water?"

Flo stomps off to shout at the kitchen staff and I put my head in my hands. I hate this place.

"Flatlandah, eh?" The fisherman to my right asks.

"Huh?"

"He means yah ain't from heeah ah yah?" says the fisherman to my left.

"Oh. No."

Silence between the three of us endures. I look left, and then right. Both hairy geezers stare at me in an expectant, friendly manner.

"Texas," I say.

"Ayuh, ayuh." Both men nod knowingly. "Vacation?" One of them says.

I shake my head and stare into my lap. "No. Just moved here. Yesterday." It's a struggle not to add "Unfortunately."

The silence between us continues. When I look up again, the old fishermen are pointedly looking away from me, sipping away at their coffees.

"You know, the mountain?" I say as Flo brings my fries and a Styrofoam cup of lukewarm water.

"The Mountain?" Flo says loudly enough for most of the customers to hear, and I can tell by her tone there's something wrong in those words, something unwelcome. Those in the immediate vicinity turn and stare. Others simply turn an ear.

"Yeah," I say uncertainly. "Wolfhowl?"

The only perceptible noise for several long seconds is the clinking of glass and silver. It's a silence heavy with meaning I don't quite understand and it takes a loud "Order up!" from the cook to bring everyone back to Earth. Flo disappears to grab the order and the patrons return to their late lunches and early dinners.

"Yah ain't welcome heeah." It's my new friend on the left.

"What?"

"Yah heard him." The fisherman on my right says. "Git."

Git? Seriously? Who says that to a person? I look around the diner and see that, although the other patrons have gone back to their meals, their voices are lower and they keep sneaking glances at me. But why? What did I do? I feel the heat rising on my cheeks and it's too much. The weight of their judgment makes it hard to breathe. Shoving myself off of the stool, I scoot for the door, feeling their stares burning a hole in my back as I do.

As I slink away from the dining car, I look over my shoulder. There, in the back window, are the old woman's clouded eyes. And they're looking right at me.

Chapter Six
It's the House

I haven't shaken off what happened at the diner by the time I reach the base of Wolfhowl Mountain. Dragging my bike along beside me, I go over the conversation for the hundredth time. Did I say something wrong? Did I offend them somehow? You aren't *welcome* here... Why the hell not?

I stop at the incline of the long drive and sigh. It was easy breezing down it. Going up is another matter. My body is tired from heat and hunger. I'd skipped breakfast and I left my fries at the diner in my hasty escape. I'm not sure I have the energy to climb all the way up the hill just to deal with Mother's wrath because I disappeared without leaving a note. Hopefully she woke up in time to do something about breakfast for Liam. I feel a fresh pang of guilt for not considering that before I left.

The loud roar of a diesel engine emerges behind me. Beckan stops his rusting blue pickup beside me, the brakes protesting loudly. Looking through the open passenger side window, he asks, "Need a lift?"

I almost say no. I'm not in the mood to talk, much less to this strange ape who tackled me yesterday. But I also don't want to walk all the way up that damn hill, and there's something alluring about Beckan's crooked smile. "Sure. Thanks."

He jerks his head toward the bed of the truck. "Toss your bike in the back."

I bring my bike around to the bed of the truck, but it's higher than I realized. The bumper is three feet off the ground and my bike is heavy and awkward. Beckan watches me struggle for a minute or two in the rearview mirror before getting out to help me with a chuckle. Taking the bike from me, he hoists it into the truck bed with one arm.

"Explorin'?" He asks once we're both in the cab.

"Yeah."

"I guess it's pretty different up heeah."

"That's an understatement."

It's awkwardly silent and I stare straight ahead, watching the tall pines jog by. I feel his green eyes on me and find myself wanting to look at him, but I'm stubborn and let the thundering rumble of the engine drown out my thoughts.

Beckan parks with a lurch on a small patch of gravel at the top of the slope toward the cabin. He takes off his seatbelt, but doesn't get out. Instead, he turns toward me. Instinctively, I press my body into the passenger door.

"Want tah talk 'bout it?"

"About what?" I snap.

"Whatevah it is you're so fired up about," he says, waving a hand in my direction.

I glare. He's smirking, which only irritates me more. "I am not *fired up.*"

"Yeah, okay." He crosses his arms, hunches his shoulders, and aims his bushy eyebrows down over his eyes.

He's mocking me. I uncross my arms and try to loosen my muscles. "I am not fired up," I say, this time staring straight into his bottle green eyes, hoping that'll be more convincing. Because I am good and fired up. I'm pissed at Mother, hate this whole stupid town, and I certainly do not want to talk to one of its very own country bumpkins about it.

"I'm a good list'nah." Smiling, he puts a cigarette between his lips and lights it with a fancy butane lighter with his initials carved into it. It's a little frilly for someone as rough around the edges as Beckan, and I figure it must be a gift from his biker chick girlfriend.

"It's none of your business." I cross my arms again.

He shrugs and exhales some smoke into the cabin, making no attempt to blow it away from me. Rude.

I stifle a cough. "Those things are bad for you, you know."

He shrugs again, but remains silent, waiting me out.

I roll my eyes. "Whatever." I throw open my door and stomp around the back to retrieve my bike. I'm determined to get it down without Beckan's help, but he hops out and helps me anyway.

"I can get it," I say with a little snake venom.

"Wouldn't want you tah strain those pretty little balleriner legs." Chomping his cigarette with his teeth, he lifts my bike out and sets it on the ground next to me, waiting for me to take the handlebars.

I squint at him. "How'd you know I'm a dancer?"

"You're not just a dancah," he says. "You're a balleriner. There's a difference." The way he mispronounces ballerina is kinda cute, but it's disconcerting that he seems to know so much about me.

Mother enrolled me in dance when I was too young to even remember. As I grew older, I began to appreciate ballet more, and have exclusively studied it in my spare time since I was ten. But I haven't said a word about it since we arrived, least of all to Beckan. How'd he know? Did he and his father rifle through our belongings when they were "placing" them in our rooms?

"Yeah, whatever." I say, irritated. "How'd you know?"

"I dunno. It's the way you carry yourself, the way you walk," he says. "My muthah used tah walk with the same grace. That's what Pop called it."

I blush and look at my feet. He's been watching me walk? "Your mother's a dancer?" I assumed some broad, as equally ape-like as Derry, resides in the little cabin on the side of the hill. After all, how could a woman with the delicateness and refinement of a ballerina marry a brute like Derry, or raise a rough-n-tumble guy like Beckan? He's all muscle and dirt and grease. Someone raised by a ballerina should be softer, more intelligent.

"She was," he says solemnly. "She's been gone a long time."

I know by his tone that Beckan doesn't mean his mother ran off with some trucker passing through town. I understand his mother is in a place people don't come back from. "I'm sorry," I say quietly.

Beckan shrugs again and scratches the back of his neck. His cigarette has burned down to the filter and he uses the fading ember to light another. I feel badly about how I've treated him. Less than twenty-four hours ago he saved my life. Don't I owe him something? My mouth opens, closes, opens again. Beckan senses my hesitation.

"Spit it out girl," he says as he rolls the cherry out of his dead cigarette and pockets the butt.

My eyes on the ground, I speak to him as if I'm in confession. "I went to that diner by the beach. The Wharf Rat. These two fishermen started askin' me questions about where I'm from. They thought I was a tourist or somethin'. When they found out I just moved here, they... they said I wasn't welcome." I roll my eyes, ready for Beckan to be shocked, to tell me that's ridiculous. But he doesn't.

Beckan sighs and his shoulders sag. His serious eyes settle on me.

I squint at him again."You know why, don't you?" I yank the handlebars of my bike away from him. "You know why those Wharf Rats said that." Beckan starts to look away and I shout at him. "Well? Tell me!"

"All right, calm down," Beckan holds up his hands. "Geez." When I'm calm, he shrugs again and spreads his arms wide, like he's going to tell me something unbelievable.

"It's the house." He says it so simply, as if those words should be enough, as if I know exactly what he means.

But of course, I don't. "The house? What does that even mean?"

"They think it's cursed."

"Who?" I demand.

"Everyone. The whole town. And if you live in the house, then you're cursed too."

*   *   *

Cursed. How ridiculous! It's so ludicrous I'd actually laughed. Even now, remembering how serious Beckan was, I'm shaking my head and laughing to myself. This is just *perfect*. As if I'm not enough of a pariah in this town because I'm from Texas, now I'm the girl who'll bring a curse down on the entire town. *Freaking awesome.*

When I got home, I discovered Mother had not only fed Liam, she'd even been to the market and stocked the pantry and refrigerator. I wasn't in trouble for going missing because she didn't even notice I'd left. Mother assumed I was sleeping in and then forgot about me altogether. I don't know if I'm relieved or insulted.

Mother fixes sandwiches for the three of us and we eat at the same kitchen table we used in Texas. The same table where Dad ate with us, in the empty chair across from Mother. The same table where we'd talked about our day, told stories, laughed... Now the table feels huge and empty, and my turkey sandwich is hard to swallow. I turn to the window and check out of the conversation.

When Mother starts cleaning up, I tune back in. She's babbling about going to the hospital in nearby Bar Harbor to talk to the head nurse about her first day. She landed a job as an intensive care nurse at the hospital via a phone interview a week ago. In typical Moira Delaney style, she didn't iron out the details. I'm hoping for a lot of night shifts. It'll keep her out of trouble – and of the bars. Mother's taking Liam with her and asks if I want to tag along and explore some of the sights Mt. Desert Island has to offer afterward, but I decline. I've had enough of the outside world for one day. I'm not going to press my luck.

By three, Liam and Mother are gone and I'm staring at countless bags of clothes in my new closet. When I'd been hastily cramming my clothes into these same bags a few weeks ago, Mother bitched at me for being such a clotheshorse and went on and on about the shipping costs and how this move was already costing her enough. I cussed her out and screamed that this move was costing Liam and me a hell of a lot more than she could even begin to comprehend. It was an explosive argument, but I don't feel the least bit bad about what I said. I meant every word then, and it rings especially true now that we're the new outcasts in town.

I'd intended on tackling the arduous task of unpacking my room, but just as I'm getting into the mindset, I catch sight of that funny little box in the turret. I find myself wondering… Could it be a door? It's the perfect little mystery to prolong my procrastination.

My bedroom is on the front of the house and one of the tall turrets runs through the corner of my room, creating that odd little cutout I saw in the kitchen and dining room. In the middle section of the cutout sits this little door, like something out of *Alice in Wonderland*. There's no knob, but the more I look at it, the more positive I am it is a door. I rap on it with a knuckle and the hollow *thud* of a hidden chamber beyond answers.

I kneel by the door and run my hands around the edges, feeling a draft. Wedging my manicured nails into the tiny gap between door and wall, I pull, but nothing happens.

I push.

Wiggle.

Pound.

Pry.

The only result is a broken nail. I cuss and kick the door with all my might.

I hear something, I'm sure. A noise, quiet and muffled, and it's coming from behind that door.

I can feel my heart in my chest and go at the door with renewed energy. I manage to get a whole fingertip between the door and the wall, and with one final yank, pry the door off. I fall backward, cradling the door in my hands. Throwing it to the side, I sit up on my elbows. The opening is pitch black and I peer into the darkness, prepared to greet whatever's in there.

And when I do, I scream.

Chapter Seven
The Search

I'm glad no one witnesses my idiotic behavior. As soon I have the door removed, a huge black crow comes cawing out of the darkness. Its flapping wings flutter over me and I scream like a child for the second time in twenty-four hours.

"I hate this God forsaken place!" I scream and stomp my feet. I cuss for a good thirty seconds while the dark beast circles the room.

The crow flits into walls, the ceiling, the furniture, desperately trying to find a route of escape. The dumb bird darts into everything except the open bedroom door. I get up and slam my closet door shut before it can get trapped inside and crap all over my clothes. I swing a pillow around, trying to coach the crow into the hall.

The bird senses sunlight from the bay window and changes direction, flying into the window at top speed. The solid thwack makes me flinch. The crow falls to the bench, its neck broken. Panting as I swipe a few loose strands of hair from my face, I prod at it with a toe. It doesn't move. I stare at it, waiting for any more damned surprises.

When nothing happens, I consider how to proceed. The thought of a dead bird laying there to rot is unpleasant, but not as unpleasant as the idea of touching it, and finding some way to dispose of it. I turn my back on the bird and decide to worry about it later. Maybe Liam will do it for me when he gets home. Or maybe I can call... No. Beckan already thinks I'm prissy enough.

I cautiously return to the dark cavity in the turret. I take off one of my sneakers and toss it into the abyss, hoping to stir any remaining crows or bats or...whatever. When nothing happens I poke my head inside.

The space is the same shape and size as the gazebo below. It's damp, and as my eyes adjust, I see scrawling on the wall. I grab the light from my nightstand and plug it in closer to the turret so I can shine the light inside. The scrawling is actually a child's crayon drawings: a little red dog, a big gray airplane, and a stick-figure girl with a pink dress and brown wavy hair. They're signed with the initials E. L., which sound familiar, but I'm not sure why.

Playing the light around the walls, I gasp. Three of the walls are covered by more colorful drawings. There's a church with a crooked cross at the top, several houses with children playing outside on green squares of grass. There's a blue bay with small sailboats, and a red hot sun overhead. Buildings sit along the water, all white blocks with small black doors. Reading some of the signs, including one reading Wharf Rat, I realize it's a drawing of Port Braseham. I see the main road now, with its pastel Victorians as the road winds past the church.

Hmm... I back out of the turret and go to my balcony. Pulling the curtains aside, I realize the drawing is a map of Port Braseham as seen *from this very spot!* I look back at the little door. What a strange secret little room.

The turret offers nothing more. A few cobwebs and some bird crap. That's it. No secret passageway. No more crows, or even a bird's nest. There isn't even a hole where the crow could've gotten inside. How'd it get in there in the first place?

I sit back on my heels. Why am I so disappointed? What did I expect to find? It's just a house. A regular old house, albeit with a strange floor plan. This isn't the Adams Family mansion. It's not Rose Red. It's *just a house.*

Beckan had said it's cursed. But I'm a logical person and my rational mind recognizes there's no truth to this preposterous idea. It's just myth. Conjecture. A spooky story for townspeople to tell to children hugging hot chocolates around campfires. But... the idea originated somewhere, right? At some point in time, something happened here to start that rumor.

Now that *is* an interesting question: What *happened* here?

I officially abandon any pretense of productivity and succumb to my morbid curiosity. If I'm going to be rejected by society for living in this eyesore, I want to know why. The house itself might have something to offer up, full as it is of the previous owners' junk. In the last twenty-four hours, I've been in the kitchen, the dining room, Liam's room, and the upstairs bathroom. (Let's ignore the fire room for the moment.) The question now is, where do I start?

I decide on the basement. After all, all things creepy start with the Indian burial ground in the basement, right? Wolfhowl Manor has a basement, but it's so stupidly large, and has so many damn doors, I'm not sure where to look for it. I start in the only place that makes sense – the foyer, the nucleus of the house, from which all things spread out.

I remember the only doors in the dining room go to the kitchen and the porch, so I begin in the room opposite, the living room, which is a mirror image of the dining room. Two stained glass windows on the front, the gazebo cut out in the far corner, and a set of glass double doors leading to the porch. This side, happily, is not damaged by fire or sagging with mildew. Looking out onto the side yard, I see the blades of grass glowing in the afternoon sunlight. It's dotted here and there with rose bushes and patches of what used to be a vegetable garden. Beyond that is a thick sloping forest of skyscraper pines, red spruces, and beeches. A few wispy clouds float above. I can't stifle the contended sigh this sight releases. I again admit to myself the beauty of our new little perch. At least on the *outside.*

I frown at the dark red wallpaper suffocating the walls. At one time it'd probably been the same velvet red as the carpeting on the stairs, but it's dingy with dust and age and reminds me of congealed blood. Mother decided this would be the TV room. The flat screen hangs on the wall between the two stained glass Saint Whomevers and our ratty old couch sits against the opposite wall. I sit, sinking into the flattened cushions, wondering why this piece of crap wasn't left behind with everything else. There isn't much left to this room. A few boxes of old family photos and a coffee table complete the tour. Blah.

I move to the drawing room. A previous owner must've redecorated because it's the only room I've seen so far that has a little class. The once glossy golden floorboards are scuffed and darkened by age, but the walls are covered in frilly wallpaper with white lacey patterns on a baby blue background. The large fireplace is more ornate than the one in the dining room. A leafy pattern is carved into it, like the porch railings out front. It's too pristine to have been made by the same skilled hands as the ivy banisters, but maybe Ol' Derry polished it before we arrived.

I walk the length of the fireplace, dragging a fingertip along the mantle, creating a clean line in the dust. I knock an unexpected obstacle to the floor. Picking up the small gold frame, I see my parents' wedding portrait.

Mother wears the hairspray helmet common in the early nineties and a simple white gown with a hideous veil, an angry tulle monster trying to eat her face. The only bright side is it softens the bright blue eye shadow painted up to her eyebrows and her hot pink blushed cheeks pulled back to her ears. Dad is more classically handsome in a tuxedo, very James Bond. He looks so happy. The cheap flash on the Polaroid camera reflects off of his perfect teeth and a smile tugs at my lips. I can't remember the last time he smiled like that. Liam looks just like him when he laughs.

I fight the burning in my eyes. There won't be tears today, not over him. In a burst of anger, I fling the frame across the room and it cracks into the floor behind a stack of boxes of more yet-to-be-unpacked Delaney family junk. Squaring my shoulders, I turn my back on two bay windows and stomp by the smaller window looking out on the cliff, which I ignore. I pass through another door and find myself in the kitchen between the old servants' stairway and the hall leading to the foyer.

The hall has two doors leading off of it. The first is a tiny half-bath that has to be original construction. There's a small washbasin low to the ground and an old toilet with a tank and a pull chain hanging near the ceiling. A skinny pipe trails down the wall to a toilet bowl, which is so short I'm sure my knees will touch my chin if I sit on it, which I won't, because it obviously hasn't been cleaned in ages.

The second door puts me exactly where I want to be – standing on the precipice of a rickety set of stairs descending into inky blackness. I recoil from the musty scent and damp air floating up from the dark. A draft pulls a strand of hair loose from my ponytail with a sensation so much like delicate fingertips that I shiver.

Maybe this isn't such a good idea. Putting my room together is certainly more productive… Oh hell, this is ridiculous!

I slowly work my way down the stairs and into the dark pit, each step groaning more loudly than the last as dust and silt sift to the floor. In my head I repeat a ceaseless mantra: *It's just a house. It's just a house. It's just a house.* I use the railing to guide my way to the bottom until a splinter lodges itself under one of my nails. Dammit! I suck on my finger. I reach the floor and grab blindly for a light switch.

A dim light emits from one tiny bulb in the center of the vast space. It does almost nothing to beat away the darkness, nor does it calm my rising fear. Although fear isn't exactly the right word; I simply feel ill at ease. There's something not quite right about this basement. Something not quite right in how the walls lean away from the light. I reconsider going back to my room, but remember Beckan and his silly curse. I feel an urge to show him I'm not afraid like he is, that I'm stronger than he thinks. There is no curse. It's just a scary story, local lore. There are no such things as curses. *It'sjustahouse.It'sjustahouse.It'sjustahouse.*

This basement is no different than any other. Exposed floorboards above and a concrete slab floor below. Tiny windows at intervals around the ceiling. A few rooms have been hastily created behind the stairs at some point. In the farthest corner, I see the laundry closet with the new washer and dryer Mother ordered. They're of the large expensive variety with a giant portal in the front of each machine so I can watch my underwear flop around for hours of mindless entertainment. Mother picked the cherry red versions to match her nails and lipstick.

The door next to the laundry room is an incomplete bathroom. In keeping with the general atmosphere of the basement, this room absorbs the light. I barely make out the tiling on the walls and floor, completed in an old-fashioned black and white pattern. Pipes protrude from the floor and walls for a missing sink, tub, and toilet. Eye level with me is a large mirror with a spider web of cracks running throughout. A kaleidoscope of me's wink back.

A small weathered door is hidden behind the stairs. It takes several bouts of jiggling and cursing to wedge the swollen door out of the jamb. When I peer inside, I wish I'd turned around at the top of the stairs.

The floor is pure mud. The concrete has been jack hammered away. What remains is littered with decaying toys. An old red tricycle, an elegant dollhouse like something out of *Little House on the Prairie,* alphabet blocks, yo-yos, fire trucks, several creepy dolls missing various limbs. Every toy is caked with mud dust. In a corner I see a patch of mud uncluttered with toys. The dirt floor is especially churned here. *This* is Wolfhowl Manor's Indian burial ground. It's more than a collection of junk from previous owners. Standing here staring at these things, I'm overwhelmed with nostalgia that almost brings me to tears. Someone hoarded these things down here not because they were in the way, but because they mean something; I'm sure of it. These aren't trinkets. These are *keepsakes.*

I have to investigate; the urge to know is strong. I move to enter the room and *BANG!* The door slams shut, nearly smacking me in the nose. I stumble backward. My heart hammers in my chest. I stare at the door. I repeat my mantra: *It'sjustahouse.It'sjustahouse.It'sjustahouse.*

An old house, lots of drafts... That logic could rationalize the door slamming shut on its own. But it doesn't explain the hand on my shoulder, the pinch of fingernails digging into my skin.

I'm too terrified to scream. I run. I stumble up the stairs, down the hall, and scramble for the front doors. The firm and alien hand pushes against my back, propelling me out of the house.

I tumble down the porch steps into the grass. I turn around in time to see the blood red doors slam shut with enough force to crack a pane of stained glass. The porch frowns at me disapprovingly. The crooked doorframe glares at me.

I can scarcely come to any other conclusion. The house is angry with me.

Robyert and Barbara Olenev
The First Owners: 1900-1903

Robyert Olenev accompanied his aging parents to America in 1898. His parents desperately wanted to escape the poverty and persecution of Russian Czarist imperialism, but Robyert, who gladly parted with the Russian spelling of his name for the more Americanized Robert, was full of love for the free America. In Russia, his family had been poor and struggling, but in America, their fortune would change, just as the fortune of millions of immigrants had changed for the better. Or so he thought.

The Olenevs settled in a New York City slum, sharing a tiny apartment with an uncle's large family, who'd arrived a few years earlier. His uncle worked in a meat packing plant while his aunt stayed home with their five children and worked as a seamstress. Robert worked at the plant with his uncle, but his parents were in their late sixties and too frail for manual labor, and his father couldn't stomach the gore that came with slaughtering animals. So his mother, Viktoriya, began taking in seamstress work while helping his aunt with the children. His father, Grigory, started a pushcart business on the streets of the city, selling traditional Russian food like Okroshka or Varenyky. The menu depended on what he could afford at the markets each morning. Sometimes it was a nameless, rancid smelling mush, but it was cheap food and anyone hungry enough and poor enough would buy it. Usually the ingredients were stale and slimy, but if you made it just right, and used enough spices, no one would really know.

It didn't take long for Robert's parents to fall out of love with their move to New York. They were still poor, and many times the prejudice against them made the persecution in Russia seem less troublesome. Robert, younger and more able bodied, managed to stay positive despite the difficulties. "Our luck will change," he'd tell his parents. "We will be patient. Time and hard work, they will earn us our reward. You will see."

It wasn't until his parents' deaths that Robert finally lost his optimism. After the new year of 1900, Viktoriya succumbed to influenza. By March his father, suffering from a broken heart, followed her. His parents had been together since they were bright-faced fifteen year olds and the world still seemed their oyster. Now they would be together for eternity. At thirty-one, Robert was an orphan in a foreign place. For the first time in his life, he felt alone and hopeless.

It was Barbara Irvine who reinvigorated Robert and brought him back to life. She was a young seventeen with a sweet face and naiveté of spirit that defined affluent children. More importantly, she was kind and loved helping others. She dreamed of becoming a nurse or teacher, but from the time she met Robert, all she dreamed of was a house filled with their children.

Barbara and Robert met on the streets of New York. She was touring the city with some of her pretty cousins when Robert, lost in his world of despair, bumped into her and sent her reeling into the streets on her pretty little behind. Her light pink dress was soiled by a pile of horse manure and Robert was mortified. He apologized profusely in his broken English. Luckily for him, Barbara found his aloof nature and awkward apology charming. They began courting, quietly at first, for fear her family would not approve. When he proposed only two months later, their fears were confirmed. Barbara's father absolutely forbade her to marry the Russian immigrant who was only after her inheritance. So, sick with Romeo and Juliet syndrome, Barbara defied her parents and the couple eloped.

Craving a fresh start, the happy couple went north. Robert, with many fond memories of helping cousins on a family farm in Russia, had dreamed of having his own plot of land to fiddle with. He was sure planting crops and buying livestock would lead to the financial security they needed to raise a family. Barbara, full of young love for her husband, followed him to Maine, where they settled in a large home on a decent plot of land known as Wolfhowl Mountain. Barbara discovered the property listing in the back of a little known newspaper. The print was small and tiny, as if it was trying to stay a quaint little secret, and she found the ominous name to be one of its many charms. Robert found her enthusiasm for the property rather cute. It was relatively cheap and they could just afford it between Robert's miniscule inheritance and savings, and the little money Barbara had in her own name. They purchased it sight unseen in May of 1900.

For a time the Olenevs lived in the wedded bliss of the honeymoon period. They planted crops and bought cows and goats. They lived their lives for each other, completely unaware of the strange stares from the townspeople. They were oblivious that many ignored them, that they hadn't made any friends, and that it was very obvious there was something dreadfully wrong with their idyllic home. The couple stayed blissfully ignorant until Barbara and Robert conceived a son in November 1902.

It wasn't until the pregnancy that the couple began to notice the strangeness of their perch atop the world. First, it was the land. Corn stalks grew without ears of sweet corn. Apple trees grew without a bounty of fruit. Then it was the animals. Milk from their cows came out sour and curdled. Meat they took from their bones was bruised and inedible. Goats stopped eating and began to starve, dying off one by one. Then it was the stares. Women stared at Barbara. Sometimes it appeared they stared at her with a sad sympathy, and sometimes the glares in their empty eyes were full of hate and envy.

Slowly, as Barbara's belly swelled, she began noticing the lack of young and happy children in Port Braseham. The church playground was silent and empty. No stores nearby sold baby clothes and no seamstresses in town made them or quilted cute little blue or pink blankets. The youngest children at the small school were nearly twelve.

One cool morning after church, strolling hand in hand, Robert and Barbara walked through the graveyard and made a chilling discovery.

In a far back corner of the graveyard, covered in brown pine needles and lifeless rose bushes, were several granite gravestones that were not yellowed or rounded with age. Fresh flowers dotted several of them in recent memoriam.

Barbara bent over one of the gravestones nearest the path and read the epitaph. *Here lies our angel Kaitlyn. Born April 2, 1852. Died April 3, 1852.* Robert kneeled beside her. Together they read first one, then another, and another.

Sean, our angel. Born March 1, 1858. Died March 3, 1858.

For Erin, our dearest child, called Home too early. February 14, 1852-February 18, 1852.

Here lies our sweet Clare, whom we were lucky to know, if only for the briefest moment. December 24, 1855-December 26, 1855.

To our dear Aidan, we will always love you. December 25, 1854-December 25, 1854.

Corey, who bore our sad curse, we will always love you. Born January 1, 1859. Died January 6, 1859.

In all, Barbara and Robert discovered thirty-three infants buried there. Many of their mothers were also laid to rest close by. Robert knew his wife was a superstitious woman, and did his best to calm her thoughts, but he also knew he'd be unsuccessful. Barbara was convinced their child would suffer the same cursed fate as all of those infants in the graveyard. She was even more dismayed when no one in town would discuss the dead children. Through her own determined digging, Barbara discovered there hadn't been a healthy child born in Port Braseham since 1851. What had killed all of these children? Why were so many of their mothers also dead? Was God punishing the poor families of this town? If so, why?

Though the last trimester of her pregnancy was fraught with worry, Barbara and Robert's son, Shane, beat the odds. He was born atop Wolfhowl Mountain, happy and healthy the summer of 1903. Word spread through the town and though the townspeople were flabbergasted, they were also elated. Was the curse broken? Had this young, happy couple finally brought salvation to Port Braseham?

Sadly, their joy was short-lived. Less than two weeks after Shane's birth Barbara was dead. In a bout of depression, she hung herself in the one of the upper bedrooms. Robert was devastated. For a few months, he struggled with the farm, trying to make money and take care of his young son without his beloved.

At first, Robert and Shane were seen in town often, at church or the market. Townspeople offered their condolences and their services. They volunteered to help him with his bright and healthy child, all too happy a baby had finally survived. But as the months went on, Robert came into town less and less. The townspeople were so concerned about Shane, so envious, they worried for his safety. When a few weeks went by without seeing either of them, a few representatives from church finally went up to Wolfhowl Mountain to make sure they were okay.

They found Robert locked in his bedroom, dead from starvation. Shane lay in his crib in the nursery, happy and fed and well taken care of despite the fact that his father had been dead for several days. Robert was buried next to poor Barbara, and Shane was adopted by the pastor and his wife. Several weeks after Shane was stolen away from Wolfhowl Mountain, on Christmas Eve 1903 the child died... and the curse lived.

Chapter Eight
New Girl

I didn't tell a soul what happened in the basement, nor will I. I've searched for a rational explanation, and I've decided the slamming doors were due to a drafty half-repaired house with openings and cracks all over the place. And the hand... well, the hand I must've conjured up on my own. After all, I'd gone looking for something ghostly hadn't I? I'm a (relatively) good, modern Catholic girl, and I don't believe in spooks haunting up my house, unlike Grammy Delaney, who would've gone crying to the local priest for an exorcism.

There is, however, one thing I can't explain away – my fear. I know it's a silly, irrational reaction to the dead crow and the creepy basement, but that doesn't send the goose bumps away.

I sit in one of the porch swings and sway idly for an hour before Beckan walks up the hill with his toolbox, intent on taking care of a few things from Mother's honey-do list. How disappointed she'll be to know she missed him.

When Beckan notices me approaching from the side porch, he smiles. "Long time no see," he says. "How's it goin'?"

"Well..." Obviously, I can't tell him the truth. "Mother and Liam are out runnin' errands, so I thought I'd just hang back and enjoy the weather, take advantage of a little alone time." I force a confident smile and shove my hands into my pockets.

"Ayuh. I know the feelin'." For a few seconds we look at each other, me trying to convince him everything's fine, and Beckan tilting his head as if he doesn't quite believe me.

"Anyway," I say to end the awkward silence, "maybe you can help me. Since you're already here and all."

"Yeah? How's that?"

"Well, I had the balcony doors in my room open earlier, to let the fresh air in, you know? And a damn crow flew right in." Beckan raises his eyebrows. Can he tell I'm lying? "I tried to steer it back out, but it flew into a window and broke its neck. Would you mind gettin' rid of it for me?"

Beckan stiffens. "Um…"

He's reluctant, so I try convincing him with my best southern belle routine. I pout subtly, a finger twirling a loose lock of hair. "Pretty please?" I ask in a sickly sweet Southern drawl.

Beckan rubs his neck and looks toward the doors anxiously. I'm about to ask what he's so worried about, but he finally agrees. "Ladies first."

"My hero!" I smile, leading the way.

There's just one problem when we reach my room. The crow's gone. It's disappeared.

"You sure?" Beckan asks when I turn away from the bay window.

"Yes, I'm sure! D'you think I made it up?"

"Maybe it was just stunned," he says, but I can tell he doesn't believe me.

"No way," I insist. "If you'd seen how hard it hit the window… It was *dead.*"

Beckan shrugs. "Well, if there's nothin' else, I'll be in the kitchen working on those squeaky cabinets for your muthah." He shuffles off, but not before throwing me one of those *that-crazy-girl* looks over his shoulder. I'm starting to feel a little crazy myself.

*   *   *

I spend the rest of the afternoon unpacking and cleaning my room, trying to keep my mind off of the hand on my back and the crow that wasn't there. Even though Beckan's in the kitchen and all sounds of his presence are silenced by the walls of Wolfhowl Manor, knowing I'm not alone makes me feel better.

Mother and Liam return with takeout pizza for dinner. Beckan is just finishing changing out the hinges on the old cabinets and spraying WD-40 on the new ones to keep them limber when Mother breezes into the kitchen to fawn over his handiwork. She tells him his muscles must be tired, while gently massaging them, and insists he stay for dinner. I've lost my appetite.

Beckan insists he can't– a little hastily, if you ask me – slipping his arm out of Mother's grasp, and leaves.

We again arrange ourselves around the kitchen table. I pretend to listen as Mother drones on and on about the hospital and their afternoon gallivanting around Bar Harbor. When she finally asks me how I spent my afternoon, I say, "Oh, I unpacked a little," and leave it at that.

*　　　　　　*　　　　　　*

Fortunately for my sanity, the next two weeks fly by without any more ghostly occurrences. I stay busy, helping Liam and Mother unpack and put the house into some kind of order, while Beckan and Derry putz around the grounds, following up on Mother's growing list of wishes and repairs.

Derry spends all his time working outside the house, I've noticed. He mows the lawn and turns the garden over because Mother insists on a place to plant things, even though she hasn't spent a second in gardening gloves for ten years running. He also does a lot of staring at the fire-eaten portion of the porch, and the burned shingles and siding, but he doesn't seem to have a plan.

On the inside, Mother keeps Beckan busy. After he fixed the cabinets, she decides she wants them refinished with a touch of honey. Then she has him hang pictures, trinkets, and curtains. She has him fix squeaky door hinges and give the bathrooms a good scrubbing, despite my reminder that the O'Dwyres aren't our personal butlers. But Beckan is polite, insisting it's no problem. Mother supervises him at every turn, of course, bringing him sandwiches and lemonade like a good hostess. It makes my stomach turn over.

Mother's to do list keeps me busy too. When I'm not unpacking my own things, I'm unpacking Liam's or Mother's, or sweeping or cleaning or washing dingy wallpaper. I retreat to my bedroom whenever possible to avoid watching Mother's shameless flirting and get away from her newfound even keel attitude; both are equally sickening.

Liam keeps himself busy too, and he's adjusting and enjoying himself here. The last year has been so hard on him, but lately he's all sunshine and rainbows. He loves his large new room with an attached playroom for all of his toys, and since I spoil him, he has a lot. The front yard is big enough for him to tool around on his bike and play fetch with Lady.

Although Liam is a little afraid of Derry, he takes an immediate liking to Beckan. He follows him around like Scrappy

Doo, constantly talking, asking questions, and boasting about his own impressive five-year-old abilities. Liam goes to the cottage to play with Lady and see what Beckan's doing whenever he can. Beckan lets Liam tag along on his errands into town. Beckan takes my brother's unabated admiration in stride, tolerating Liam's constant presence with a smile, and even with a little enjoyment. Sometimes he's here so late that it's Beckan who takes Liam up to his room and regales him with exciting bedtime stories that beat mine by a mile.

I catch the two of them on the back porch one night after dinner, sitting side by side, watching the sunset. They cut a beautiful silhouette and I watch them for a long time. Maybe there's more to Beckan than the tough guy exterior. But then his shadow morphs, changes into Dad's distinctive broad shouldered slouch, and I look away.

Liam has come alive since moving to Port Braseham. Seeing the perma-smile on his face every day lifts a weight off my shoulders. Seeing my brother enjoying himself again is nearly worth being uprooted. And the happier Liam is, the more I begin to ignore the uncomfortable prickliness at the back of my neck whenever I'm in the house. If Liam is happy, that's all that matters. He has a chance to recover from our parents' divorce, to move on, and I'm going to help him do that any way I can.

*   *   *

By the Sunday before school starts, the house actually feels more like home, and seeing our belongings spread around comforts me. As a reward for all our hard work, Mother wants to go out as a family. The cool morning gives way to a warm afternoon, and we decide to go on a picnic. There's a park next to the church with picnic tables, a playground, and a cracked basketball court with weeds protruding all over. Mother insists the O'Dwyres join us, despite my repeated objections. Derry lets out his ape-grunt and retreats into the cabin, but Beckan gives in to Mother's persistence and joins us.

We enjoy a spread of sandwiches Mother and I made together, store bought potato salad and macaroni salad, kettle cooked potato chips, and my grandmother's secret ambrosia salad recipe. Once we've eaten our fill, we break apart across the playground. Liam is at the top of a wooden castle, pretending to save a damsel in distress. Lady plays the dragon, barking wildly from below. Mother strolls along the edge of the park where a line of wildflowers flourishes, picking a few and putting a daisy in her hair with a wave back at Beckan and me, still sitting at the table. I grit my teeth and start cleaning up, throwing away our trash and putting leftovers in the basket.

I take several sidelong glances at Beckan as he politely helps. I'm still trying to wrap my head around this guy. I'd initially pegged him as an uneducated ape. On the surface, everything about him is rough and uneven. His hair is shaggy and un-gelled, the opposite of the boys I dated back in Texas. He has a permanent five o'clock shadow and his eyes are deep-set like his father's. I can see a younger version of bulldog Derry, but just barely. He must look an awful lot like his mother and I wonder what she was like. How did a delicate ballerina fall in love with a blue-collar type like Derry?

"Somethin' on my face?" Beckan asks, smirking.

"Huh?" I'm embarrassed he catches me staring. "No, sorry. I was just thinkin'."

"'Bout?"

I shrug and change the subject. "So you and your dad," I say, "what do you do around here besides work on the mountain? I mean, we don't pay you, so how do you make a living?"

"Pop and I are good with our hands," he says as we sit back down at the picnic table, across from each other. "We do a lot of thins… make custom furniture, fix thins that need fixin'. If it's a good yeeah for fishin', then we make money doin' that. Cahn't count on that though."

"Seems kinda boring around here."

He nods. "I suppose it seems that way tah someone from a big city."

"Don't you ever want to get away?" I ask. "Get out and see the world?"

He shrugs, but doesn't reply. Like maybe he does want to see the world, but he can't.

"College?" I ask.

"Nah." He looks down at his hands and picks at his cuticles. "I didn't even get a diploma. School was nevah really my thin'. You?"

"I haven't gotten around to it yet."

He raises his eyebrows. "Aren't you gonna beeah senior?" I nod. "Isn't that somethin' you should be workin' on?"

"I guess," I say. "But things were sorta turned upside-down for us just when I was startin' to think about it. Between my parents' fightin', lookin' out for Liam, and the move... It took a backseat to everythin' else."

"What 'bout now?"

I shrug, imagining myself dancing on a large stage at the University of Arizona, or Oklahoma. In my wildest dreams, Juilliard. Then I'll move to New York City and find a loft and a job with one of the top theaters... But that's just a dream. "It's a nice day," I say. "You don't see many afternoons like this in Texas. Too sticky."

"Well, we won't see but a few more like this, even 'round heeah," he says. "We'll hit the rainy season in the next few weeks. You won't see the sun again 'til May."

As if waiting for Beckan's permission, the sun dips below the tree line. Mother comes back over, Liam trailing behind her.

"You know," Mother says, "it's odd."

"What is?" I ask.

"Well, it's a nice Sunday afternoon, the last one before school starts," she says. "You'd think there'd be more people here. There should be more kids enjoying their last day of freedom. I was kinda hoping to meet a few of Liam's classmates or their parents. Maybe ask them what the school is like."

There are a few seconds of silence as we all look at each other, the only sound the rising chorus of crickets and cicadas.

"Well," Beckan says to Liam, "we bettah get you back home. We don't want you ovahsleepin' and missin' the first day of school! C'mon – race you tah the cah."

Beckan and Liam take off running. Liam pumps his arms at full speed and Beckan trails right behind him, letting him win. I sigh, feeling relaxed. Why can't every day feel like this?

*   *   *

September

I look at the old-fashioned red brick building uncertainly. It looks like it came in sections and was cemented together by a local church group over a hot summer weekend. It's boxy like a factory, all purpose and no fashion.

I feel claustrophobic. My old high school had more than four thousand students enrolled in grades nine to twelve. Port Braseham's schoolhouse holds less than a third of that – in all twelve grades. In a town where everyone knows everyone, the students are sure to know everything about everyone, a thought that makes me break out in a sweat. Gossip's a mean machine when you're just a number. How much worse is it when you have a name and a face, especially when you're the new outsider living in a cursed house?

I felt like a character out of a sitcom getting ready for school this morning. Mother and I got up and ready about the same time. I took the task of getting Liam together while Mother made breakfast for the three of us. We sat and ate together at a leisurely pace. As far back as I can remember, this has never happened in our family. Back in Texas, mornings in the Delaney household were hectic. Mother was always working and never around when it was time to get ready for school. I was out of the house by six thirty. Dad just managed to get Liam ready and dropped off at day care on his way to work.

In Port Braseham, since all students go to the same school, all classes start at the same time. Mother got a normal nine to five shift at the hospital to allow her a little more time to get settled into the house. The hospital is far enough away that it's going to be a stretch getting us to school on time, which is why, at this moment, I'm in Beckan's loudly idling truck sitting at the curb by The Catholic School of Port Braseham. We let Liam out by the kindergarten doors along the other side of the building. Now that it's my turn, I'm hesitating.

"Are you gettin' out or not?" Beckan asks.

I look at the building again and then back to Beckan. "I guess." I make no move to get out.

Beckan sighs and reaches over me for the old-fashioned chrome door handle, tugging stubbornly on it until it releases. I melt into the seat to avoid direct contact with him. I feel his body heat as he leans over me. He shoves the door of the old Ford open, making an ear splitting *crrreeeeaaaak,* and several students catching up on the manicured lawn turn to stare.

"Off you go, girl." Beckan smiles at me and nods at the open door.

I glare. "Thanks for the ride. I'll walk home." I slide out of the high seat, keeping my hands on the back of my short pleated skirt to prevent a free show. It's impossible not to slam the door of his pickup, but I try anyway. The churn of the diesel engine driving away earns more stares. I let my hair fall in front of my face and hug my bookbag tightly to my side. Where's a wall to melt into when you need one?

I look everywhere except into the eyes of the other students. The campus grounds are nice. Each healthy green spread of grass is dotted with dogwood trees and flower bushes all the way around the building. There aren't any busses, but several parents are dropping kids off in a designated drop off zone.

I'm ambling along in the direction of the main doors as if I'm heading to the electric chair when suddenly, something small and cold grabs my wrist.

"OMG! Did you just get out of Beckan O'Dwyre's truck?" The small thing is a frail looking girl about my age with short black hair. The cold thing is her tiny hand on my arm.

"Um…"

"You're going to get the rumor mill going before school even starts. Well, who am I kidding? The rumor mill started the second that eyesore was sold!"

The small girl turns out to be one Letta Bauer, another Port Braseham transplant. She moved from Maryland with her parents a few years ago and I'm glad to finally meet someone who'll talk to me and I can understand. I shake Letta's eager hand and introduce myself.

"Oh honey, I know who you are!" Letta laughs. "We all do."

"Great." Back in Texas I was popular, but in a good way. I'm pretty. I was on the cheerleading team, and I'm a talented dancer. I had my pick of dates on Friday nights. I was invited to all the parties, threw a few of my own, and incited a little more girl drama than was necessary. Sure, there were people who disliked me, but I was important and they weren't, so I didn't really care. But in Port Braseham, I can tell things are going to be very different.

Letta leads me toward the building. I notice I'm at least a head taller than her. Letta talks the whole way, barely stopping to breathe unless she's asking me a question, and even then, the pause is short. Apparently, everyone knows my name, that I have a younger brother, my mother is a divorced nurse and designated "hot M.I.L.F.", and we're the newest owners to take possession of the blight on the hill.

"And they know you're from Texas, so don't expect them to be too friendly on that account," Letta says. "Southerners aren't too highly regarded up here, trust me."

"Tell me about it," I say. "I was kicked out of a restaurant for Pete's sake!"

"Pfft. That's nothing," Letta says. "At least you're Catholic. That's about the only thing that'll save you around here."

I roll my eyes. "Is anyone in this town not Catholic?"

"Me." Letta smiles. "I'm Jewish, which doesn't exactly make me popular either, but I've managed to survive and you will too. Trust me, not everyone in this town is as judgmental as some of the old fogies around here. You'll get used to it."

I sigh with resignation – or anxiety, I'm not sure which – as we enter the building. The inside of the school looks like what I expect of a high school. There are halls of brightly colored lockers, wooden windowed doors, and students bustling around and catching up. I feel a pang in my stomach. I wonder how my friends back in Texas are doing. They have a couple more hours of sleep, but then they'll go to school and catch up and flirt with the boys... and I'm here. In the smallest town on the planet. Branded with the scarlet letter of haunted houses. God I miss Texas.

I ignore the heads turning in my direction, and continue talking to Letta. "Well what's the big deal about arriving with Beckan? How's that any worse?"

Letta explains, "Well there's the obvious reason – he and his father take care of your house. The O'Dwyres have handled the property for generations since no one else around here will touch it because of the curse." She rolls her eyes.

"Is there a less obvious reason?"

"Well... a few years ago Mr. O'Dwyre had a disagreement of sorts with Seamus Quinn, the head of the town council and President of the Port Braseham Historical Society. I'm not sure what it was about because it was before I moved here, but rumor has it that it was pretty nasty. Mr. Quinn's son, Ronan, is the most popular kid here. It seems you're either on Ronan's side or Beckan's – and Beckan's is the wrong side to be on."

"Why should it even matter?" I ask. "Beckan isn't even a student here. He's what? Twenty-two? Twenty-three?"

"I think he turned twenty a few weeks ago."

"Really?" Does that matter to me? I'm not sure. But I'm curious to know how Letta knows Beckan's birthday.

"Anyway, he dropped out his freshman year, but it doesn't matter. This is a small town and you run into everyone everywhere. Beckan and Ronan had it out near the end of the school year last year down on the docks. It was a huge fight. Beckan nearly knocked Ronan unconscious and they had to fish him out of the water. But man, was it awesome! Ronan deserved a good kick in the teeth. And Beckan looks pretty hot all sweaty and breathing heavily in a ripped shirt." Letta's eyes go glassy.

A shrill bell rings, a real honest to goodness bell, not an electronic counterfeit.

"There's the warning bell. I better show you where you're going." Letta grabs my arm and pulls me to a poster on the wall with a list of letters and room numbers. "There's your homeroom with Mrs. Brennan, the crazy old bat. Her room is right around the corner."

"Thanks."

"Anytime. Hey, maybe we can sit together at lunch. If you make it that far." Letta smiles.

"I'm already cursed," I say. "How much worse can it get?"

"You'll see." Letta winks and disappears into the throng of students hustling by.

Right as I turn toward Mrs. Brennan's room, a group of large boys run by me, pushing everyone in their way and leaving destruction in their wake. I'm knocked into a wall and fall on my butt. Several students watch it happen and stare at me with uninterested, crossed arms. When my supplies spill out of my backpack, several sets of feet stomp all over them, and no one stops to help me.

I. Hate. This. Town.

I grit my teeth, gather my belongings, and go off to begin what will be my worst day in Port Braseham yet.

Chapter Nine
Humble Pie

Mrs. Brennan must be the oldest active teacher in the United States. Her salt and pepper hair lays in a long braid down her back. Despite the late summer heat and lack of air conditioning, she's dressed like a nun. Her dress starts at her chin and goes all the way to her skinny wrists and ankles with tiny buttons all the way up the front. I try guessing her age from the angle of scoliosis in her back and wonder how she got all those buttons done up with her long brittle nails. Maybe she didn't. Maybe she sleeps in it. Maybe her husband used to help her with the buttons, but he died and she's been stuck in it ever since, and she just spot cleans it as necessary. I look forward to tomorrow with mild curiosity.

One other student, a brooding blonde boy, sits in a desk by the windows, deliberately ignoring the rest of the room. You and me both, brother.

I choose a desk at the back, an old contraption with the desk and seat welded together. I can't keep my feet under the desk and my bag out of the aisle at the same time so I set my shoulder bag next to my feet and do my best to keep it out of the way.

More students file in and take seats. The goody two-shoes collect in the first row while the rest fill in from the back. Though there's no school uniform in the clichéd blue, red, and green plaid skirts and jackets, I notice everyone is dressed conservatively. Boys wear collared shirts with little embroidered alligators or tiny men on tiny horses. There are no bare shoulders in sleeveless shirts for the girls, and all of their skirts fall to just above the knees. I pull at the hem of my short skirt self-consciously, wishing it were longer for the first time in my life. I know with my body type, my skirt is a shade shorter than my fingertips, which is possible to get away with at a city school back in Texas. Here, my outfit makes me stand out and, although that's something I usually enjoy, I have a feeling it's going to get me noticed in the wrong way.

The other students smile and chatter at each other, still catching up on the first day jitters. Some of them glance back at me politely, but without smiling. Others stare without embarrassment. I might be the new kid in town, but Letta's right – they know exactly who I am. I've never wanted to blend in so badly in my life.

Last to enter is the obligatory model, tall and gorgeous. Everyone greets her by name ("Hey Mary!") and tries to get her to notice them. A wave, a smile, a loud "Hey! Over here!" and a motioning hand. Her smile gleams with perfectly whitened and proportioned teeth, a dentist's dream. Long legs strut gracefully beneath a pair of khaki capris and a form fitting pink polo shirt hugs her shapely torso. Girls glare at her with veiled jealousy and boys tell her how great she looks. This girl is exactly who I used to be, pretty and popular, stylish and important. An uncomfortable – and unusual – pang of jealousy turns my stomach.

The only seat left is next to me, by a bunch of insipid chatty girls going on and on about how fat So and So got during the summer hiatus. I judge them critically, even though I know I'd be doing the same thing with my friends back home – *friends* I've heard nothing from.

Mary stalks to the last desk like she's strutting down a catwalk, flinging her shiny brown mane and pouting for a couple of the staring boys. She kicks my bag out of the way with her black flats and sits, turning her back to me and talking to her friends.

"Excuse you," I say loudly as I right my bag.

Mary throws an insincere "Oh, sorry" over her shoulder without paying the slightest attention to me.

"Bitch." I whisper, feeling only a little guilty for cussing in God's schoolhouse.

The bell rings and a flood of beginning of the year announcements crackle over the PA system. The din of gossip continues straight through and I only catch a few words that don't make much sense: "robotics...ing tryouts...first home game...come back!"

Mrs. Brennan, perched by her desk, hands out our schedules in alphabetical order, forcing everyone to go up front to get them. She probably can't see beyond the front row despite those

Coke bottle glasses. I bet if I held those puppies up to the sun, I could burn an entire anthill into oblivion.

I dread my name being called and having to walk up front to be eyeballed by everyone. Fortunately, or unfortunately, my dread is short lived. Being close to the beginning of the D's makes Rose Delaney the fourth name Mrs. Brennan calls out. I keep my eyes on the ground and a hand on my hem, as I get up and approach Mrs. Brennan.

"Oh, you must be new deeah," says Mrs. Brennan without relinquishing my schedule from her gnarled hands, despite my firm tugging on a corner of the folded paper. "How exciting! Why, we haven't had a new student since little Letta Bauer a couplah years back. Let me get a good look at you."

Mrs. Brennan lets go of my schedule and holds my shoulders at arm's length with her knotted claws, drinking me in. "My, well aren't you pretty!" Mrs. Brennan adds in what she probably thinks is a whisper, "But you might need tah pull your skirt down a bit deeah. It makes you look a mite desperate."

A murmur of laughter spreads through the room as my cheeks heat up.

"Where are you from, Rose?" Mrs. Brennan asks.

Before I can reply, someone in the back calls out in a faux southern accent, "Why she hails from good ol' Texas ma'am! She's the new spook sittah!"

"Oh deeah," Mrs. Brennan holds a dismayed hand to her lips.

I grit my teeth and retreat to my desk. I glare at everyone. If these idiots actually believe in this stupid curse, maybe an evil glare might make them fear me the way the kids in the movie should have feared Carrie.

I take my seat. Mary mutters under her breath, "More like spooky slut."

I throw my glare at Mary and can tell I've caught her off guard. She clearly thought the smear would only be heard by her friends, but it only takes her a second to recover, and she shoots me a snarky smile and raises a perfectly plucked eyebrow, as if to say, *You heard me, Spooky Slut. What're you gonna do about it?*

I clench my fists, close my eyes, and allow the hum of the room to disappear into the distance. I'm in my happy place. *Happy, happy, happy!* I do everything in my power to control my volatile temper, but I have a feeling, before the year is out, Mary's perfect smile will have an unpleasant conversation with my fists.

*   *   *

I manage to make it through the first two periods with relative ease. Most students toss guarded glances in my direction, but that's all. I'm grateful no one makes me stand in the front of the room to introduce myself, because as my new English teacher Mrs. Clancey put it, "We know who you are already!" It's both relieving and unnerving.

From English, I go to Chemistry, where no one chooses to be my lab partner for the first semester. In a class of nineteen, this makes me the odd one out, destined to be lab partners with the nerdy, but seemingly capable Mr. McLoughlin. Looking him over, I decide he's in his mid-thirties and without the black framed glasses, even a little cute.

After Chemistry, I follow the throng into the cafeteria. It looks much as a school cafeteria should, but it's tiny compared to what I'm used to, and most of the tables are already full. I allow the crowd to carry me through the lunch line for cold instant potatoes, today's mystery meat, and a stale brownie. By the time I exit with my tray, half of my lunch period is over and all of the tables are taken. With a sigh, I wander around looking for any spot I can squeeze into. From a far corner, I spot a small, pale hand waving at me. Relieved, I scuttle across the cafeteria and plop down next to Letta.

"Thank you!" I say. "I was starting to feel like a plague victim. Everyone's leaning away from me like I'm contagious."

Letta laughs. "I'm glad to see you've made it to the halfway point. Allow me to introduce a few more allies." She points at the three faces smiling from across the table. "This is Shane, Patty, and Eileen. They accept me for my Jewish inheritance and they'll accept you for your curse."

"Nice to meet you," I say, surprised to realize I actually mean it.

"So how goes it?" Letta asks, piling the potatoes into her mouth.

"Okay I guess. It's a heck of a lot different than Texas. Everyone thinks I'm the slutty spook sitter. And some bitch seems to hate me for no reason."

The four faces around me exchange glances and say in unison, "Mary Donovan."

"Yeah," I say. "How'd you know?"

"She's the Queen Bitch," Eileen says. She's pretty in a classic way, like Janet Leigh or Doris Day, with her blonde bob and dark eyebrows.

"She's also Ronan's girlfriend," Shane adds. "She's the unofficial prom queen. His popularity and his dad's position make him pretty much in charge 'round heeah. She fulfills her first lady duties pretty well." Shane is the stereotypical Irish kid. He's a tall, scrawny redhead blanketed in freckles. He probably goes around cursing his affliction, but I've always thought freckles were cute.

"Speakin' of Ronan..." Patty says, throwing her deep brown eyes over my head. "He's coming ovah heeah!"

"Tah speak with the commoners?" Shane says in mock bewilderment. "Is the student council campaignin' stahtin' up already?"

"Well he sure ain't comin' tah talk tah us," Eileen says, turning to me.

I turn to look at the Adonis that is Ronan Quinn. The only thing Irish about him is his name. He's tall and brawny like Beckan, but in a polished way that says his muscles are sculpted by a strict gym regimen. His skin is smooth and clear. He wears a light green polo over a pair of white cargo shorts and Sperry's. He's exactly my type. He tosses his head to the side to get a few stray chestnut pieces of his shaggy 'do out of the way, and throws a glossy smile at me. My pulse quickens.

"Hi, Rose," he says as he approaches, reaching out a hand for mine.

"Hi, Ronan," I say, taking his soft hand. He shakes mine gently, as if afraid he'll break my delicate fingers. If this is the king of the idiots, then I'm going to win him over. Maybe then the commoners will stop looking at me like I'm the devil.

"I see you've been talkin' about me already." His smile widens. "I'm glad." His accent reminds me of Mrs.Carroll's, carefully controlled.

I smile, but inwardly I roll my eyes. A master of fake charm myself, it's easy to spot it in others. The question is, why's he bothering to charm the girl everyone's determined to hate?

"Well," he says, "I'm sorta the unofficial welcomin' committee. Why don't you grab your lunch and join us?" He motions to a table filled with an equally preppy and fake group, including Mary Donovan. The others chatter excitedly, but if Mary's eyes could kill, I'd be very, very dead.

I have zero desire to sit next to Mary, and I'm pretty comfortable chatting with Letta and her friends, so I'm not especially inclined to accept Ronan's offer. Not yet anyway. Just because I'm new doesn't mean I'm easy. "I appreciate the offer," I say, "but I'm just fine here. Maybe another time." I smile lightly and turn around, but apparently, Ronan isn't used to hearing no.

"Come on, Rose," he says. "You wanna make sure you get in with the right group don't you?"

I bite my tongue and hold my sweet smile for as long as I can, but I already know this will end badly. I know Letta and her friends aren't exactly the cool kids, but they're the only people who've been nice to me, and I don't think it's fair of Ronan to insult them like that.

"What do you mean?" I ask as my previous desire to win Ronan over morphs very quickly into a stubborn desire to spite him.

"Well," Ronan seems confused, "I mean you wanna make the right friends around here. You don't wanna get in with this gawmy group. You've already got a unique challenge in front of you."

"Oh? I feel the urge to call forth my happy place, but force it to the back of my mind. "Please, enlighten me."

"Well, Rose, come on." He spreads his hands. "I know about what happened at The Wharf Rat, and I know you know about the unfortunate history of your house. You've already been seen around with Beckan O'Dwyre. Why don't you make the right choice this time, and come hang out over here? We're real fun, I promise." He smiles at me one last time.

I take a deep breath, but anger sweeps over me and there's nothing I can do to stop it now.

"Listen, Ronan," my sweet tone disappears, "I might be from the south, but I ain't stupid. You're bein' about as real as Kim Kardashian. I don't know what your game is, and I don't particularly care. I wanna sit here and enjoy my lunch with these lovely people, and I don't much appreciate being told who my friends should be or what my situation is. Now, you run along and go play with your little friends. Mkay?" I swivel back around to meet the four pairs of large eyes staring at me. I pray Ronan will do what's best for him and save himself further embarrassment. But he doesn't.

"Look what kind of bitch we have over here!" Ronan shouts to his friends. "The spook sitter is too good for us!"

"Alright," I say to myself. "Alright then." I stand, holding my untouched lunch tray. I take another deep breath and when Ronan turns back around, I smash my tray into his expensive shirt and rub it around a few times. In the shock and silence that falls over the cafeteria, the Styrofoam tray slowly slides down his shirt before falling and landing on his Sperry's. Ronan stares at his shirt and then at me, eyes and mouth wide in disbelief. I dip my hand in the cold potatoes and gravy and smear it across his reddened cheek. I flick the excess on his pants and then lick my fingers to clear the rest.

"Mmm," I say. "Humble pie just like Grammy used to make. You should have some."

From behind me, Patty breaks the long silence.
"Oh...my...gawd!"

Chapter Ten
The Second Fire and the Mystery Sandwich

I spend the rest of my day ignoring sneers and insults. Although plastering Ronan with my lunch is satisfying, it also cements my isolation. In Latin, a boy actually scoots his desk away from mine. I wish I could. Mostly I just hope for a friendly face, like Letta or one of her friends, but I don't see them again until the end of the day. Letta, Shane, Patty, and Eileen walk home with me, still full of praise.

"I can't believe you did that," Patty says. "I mean, Ronan's had that comin' a long time, but for someone tah actually *do* it..."

"I can't believe it took someone until senior yeeah!" Eileen laughs.

"We worship the ground you walk on." Shane bows and begins chanting, "We're not worthy! We're not worthy!"

"Thanks," I laugh. "I think."

The weather is warm, but a breeze rustles the trees. I look up at the blue sky dotted with cotton ball clouds and sigh. I'm more relaxed now than at any other point since moving to Port Braseham – well, actually, more relaxed than the last two years, perhaps because I'd finally released some of my pent up anger. Maybe tomorrow I'll take my bike to school. If tomorrow is as crappy a day as this one, I'll be able to burn off some excess anger on the ride home without hurting anybody. If I get suspended again, Mother'll kill me.

Letta and her friends drop off one by one as they make their way home. By the time I reach the bottom of the hill, only Letta remains. We stand at the corner of Letta's street and my driveway as the silence passes between us. Letta stares up the mountain at the tips of the turrets, just visible on the horizon, and I follow her gaze.

"What do you think?"

Letta looks back at me owlishly. "I don't know much about it." She shrugs. "All I know is most of the town is afraid of it."

"That makes two of us," I say. "Even Beckan thinks it's haunted, and he practically lives in it."

"It's about more than ghosts," Letta says. "People are afraid of it without going anywhere near it. It's the curse surrounding it that everyone's afraid of."

"Yeah, but what *is* the curse? I mean, what's scaring an *entire town?*"

Letta shrugs again. "I don't know. People don't talk about it, like there's an unspoken rule or something. Those who do are kids who aren't really sure because their parents won't talk about it either. Sometimes I get the impression no one actually knows the truth behind it. It's just about tradition."

"Why don't they tear it down?" I ask. "It's ugly as sin anyway."

"I dunno that either," Letta says and then winks. "But I bet Hot Beckan O'Dwyre would."

I laugh. "He's *not* hot!" Maybe a little cute, but hot is an exaggeration.

"Yeah sure," Letta says, starting down her street. "Try telling my dreams that... See you tomorrow." She turns her head in a short, dark wave of hair, and meanders down the long drive into the shade of the trees.

I walk up the hill slowly, in no hurry to return to Wolfhowl Manor. As much as I want to believe the house is *just* a house, I still don't feel right inside it. Is it just the townspeople's blind belief in the curse that scares me? Does it just give my mind something to focus on because I want so badly to be back in Texas? Am I just looking for a reason to hate a perfectly good house?

Or is the tingling at the at the back of my neck a sign? Is the sensation of being watched real? Does my depressive nature press down on me inside of the house because I'm unhappy to be in Maine, or because the house wants us gone? And then there's that first day on the cliff. And the ghostly hand in the basement.

This is ridiculous. All I have to do to know the curse isn't real is look at Liam and see how happy he's been since coming here. If the house really is cursed, wouldn't Liam notice too? Wouldn't Mother? We've all been in and around the house, poking around in all the nooks and crannies. If something's really off about this place, wouldn't they feel the same uneasiness I do? As far as I can tell, neither Liam nor Mother has noticed anything out of the ordinary. Maybe I really am just fixating on all the negativity I feel about my life right now. It's not like that would be surprising.

I detour by the O'Dwyre cabin. Liam, whose kindergarten class releases at one-thirty, a full hour and a half before my classes, is sitting on the front porch with Lady, scratching her ears while Beckan whittles a stick down to nothing in the rocking chair. If we keep this arrangement up, we're going to have to find a way to thank Beckan for all his help with Liam.

"Hi, kiddo!" I say, forcing a smile. "How was your first day?"

"Hi, Rosie!" Liam runs over and hugs my waist. "I had a great day! How was yours?"

"It was good," I lie, and Beckan smirks. "What are you smilin' at?"

"You aren't going tah tell him the truth?" Beckan is stifling laughter.

"I don't know what you're talking about," I say evasively, avoiding his gaze.

"So you didn't dump your lunch in Ronan Quinn's lap?"

Liam gapes up at me. "You started a food fight?"

"No, of course not," I say. "It was an accident. I tripped. How would *you* know anyway?"

"It doesn't take long for word tah spread 'round heeah."

"I know, but seriously, *three* hours?"

Beckan shrugs. "Welcome tah small town life."

"Roo-sssie!" Liam tugs on my skirt so hard I have to grab it before Beckan sees my underwear. "I'm hungry!"

Beckan holds up his hands innocently. "I swear, I gave him a snack not an hour ago!"

I sigh. "A bottomless pit, you are. Alright, let's go."

"I'll walk you up. I want tah check on a few thins anyway." Beckan follows us as Lady runs circles in our wake. Once the house is fully visible, about seventy-five feet from the side porch, Lady whimpers and sits. She looks back toward the cabin and then at Beckan a few times.

"Come on, Lady," I coax gently. "You're allowed inside." Lady looks at me with piqued ears, but doesn't move. She sinks to her belly and flops her tail. We're a pet household, always have been. We had a dog when I was younger, but he died a couple of years ago. I'd tried convincing my parents to get another pet for the family, but then they split and the whole idea was lost in the chaos.

"What's wrong with her?" I ask.

"Aww, Lady's just a scardey cat," Beckan replies.

I punch Beckan hard in the arm before Liam turns around and asks, "Scared of what?"

Beckan looks at me. "Oh erm...nothin'. She just doesn't like bein' too far from Ol' Derry is all." He whistles at Lady, and granted permission, she pops up and trots back down to the cabin to wait on the porch.

Beckan says he wants to check out the fire damage on the side porch so he can let Derry know what supplies are needed for repairs. Now that someone lives here, especially a child, the O'Dwyres don't want any preventable accidents occurring on their watch. I send Liam inside to wash his hands and tell him I'll be in to take his snack order momentarily. I follow Beckan and watch him inspect the fire-eaten wood from the lawn.

Beckan stares at the porch for a solid minute, taking in every charred beam, every compromised step. He pushes on a few places with a foot to see how weak it is, each time collapsing the blackened wood under the slightest pressure. He takes off his ball cap to scratch at the wad of bronze hat-head underneath. He replaces his hat and takes out a tape measure, writing measurements down as he takes them.

"So when was the fire?" I ask, trying to sound disinterested, like I'm only curious rather than finding an excuse to stare at him a little longer. I *suppose* I can see what Letta was talking about as he pinches his pencil between his teeth and takes another measurement along the bottom stair. He's kinda hot, if you like the tough, blue-collar type.

He writes down a final measurement and slides the pencil behind his ear. "Which one?"

I'm startled by his reply. "Which *one?*"

"Yeah," he says, putting his writing pad and tape measure into a back pocket. "The house has been on fire a couplah times."

"Really? Why?"

He shrugs, coming closer to me, and I fight the urge to back away from him like he's a leper. "Not sure about the first time. It was way back, early nineteen hundreds. The second fire was in the sixties."

"Accidents?" I ask hopefully.

He shakes his head. "The fire in the sixties was set." He looks into my eyes as he explains, and I think his are a beautiful shade of green. "This crazy lady, Enit O'Sullivan, set it. That's what this damage is from." He waves a hand at the porch. "It woulda taken the whole house down if the sky hadn't opened up at the right moment."

"Why'd she set her own house on fire?"

"Oh, she didn't live heeah." He shakes his head and chuckles.

"What? Then why'd she set it on fire?"

He shrugs again. "She's loony? No one really knows, but I s'pose you could ask her. She still lives in town."

I snort. "Is she a hero?"

Beckan smiles and I notice how white his teeth are against his tan skin, and how his eyes crease at the corners like Derry's. He has a swath of soot on the side of his five o'clock shadow, and without thinking I reach up and swipe it away just like I'd do to Liam. It's only as I'm rubbing my thumb down his cheek that I realize how awkward it is.

I pull my hand back. "Sorry. Habit."

"S'okay," he says, still smiling. "I don't know if Enit's considered a hero, but I don't think she was jailed. She doesn't deny it either."

"Did she say why she did it?"

"Nope."

"Oh come on," I say, stepping so close to him I can feel his warm breath on my face. I poke him in the chest. "You're holdin' out."

He spreads his arms wide and says innocently, "The house is evil." He winks at me and turns to leave. He pulls out a rag and wipes at his face and neck as he heads down the hill. "Bettah get inside tah Liam," he calls over his shoulder. "Don't want tah leave him alone too long."

I watch Beckan until he's out of sight, mulling over what he said. I find Liam at the kitchen table gulping down a peanut butter and jelly sandwich with more jelly on his face than in his mouth.

"Liam!" I shout, arms akimbo. "You're gonna spoil your supper!"

Liam pauses mid-chew. "Then why'd you make me a sandwich?"

"Liam, don't fib to me! I didn't make you any sandwich."

"It was on the table when I came outta the bathroom," he says. "I swear! I thought it was my snack."

"Liam, I've been outside with Beckan. I didn't make you anything!"

Liam puts his sandwich down very slowly. He stares at it a few seconds before turning his glassy eyes to me. "Then where'd it come from?"

Chapter Eleven
The File

The sandwich episode doesn't end well. Though Liam swears up and down he didn't make the sandwich, I don't believe him. It's obviously freshly made, and unless the sandwich fairy made a trip to Wolfhowl Manor, nothing else makes sense. Cursed this house might be, but it is not making sandwiches out of thin air. But Liam's so upset that I don't punish him. I scold him often enough about his voracious appetite, I'm worried I'll make him anorexic. Instead, I make him promise to get approval for any snack before he eats it, whether it appears out of thin air or not.

We sit down for dinner together. Between the divorce, the move, and our hectic lifestyle, it hasn't happened much lately, and if it does, it's usually a silent affair. The only sound between us is Liam's loud smacking and Mother's irritated voice reminding him to chew with his mouth closed.

Tonight is different. I help Mother in the kitchen while Liam plays in the drawing room. Mother and I talk about our days as we boil pasta and bake garlic bread. I'm used to keeping most things from Mother out of spite or rebellion, but this time my motives are different. This time I keep the episode at lunch to myself, not because I don't want to get in trouble and get lectured about my temper, but because Mother's in a good mood and I don't want to ruin it. I ask about her first day at the hospital. Her day went well. She met a lot of nice people, and feels she's really going to belong at Mount Desert Island Hospital. At her job back in Texas, things between Mother and the head nurse had always been tense, but the head nurse at the new job sounds pleasant and easy going.

"I'm actually looking forward to tomorrow," Mother says as she tosses a salad together.

"I'm really glad to hear that, Mom." Mother knows it isn't easy for me to say anything nice, especially to her, so she merely smiles back and winks.

"Supper's ready!"

I summon Liam and help Mother carry the pasta, a saucepan full of homemade meatballs, and the salad to the dinner table.

Liam talks animatedly about his first day of kindergarten. "Miss Colleen is a lot nicer than the scary monster! And she's pretty too!"

The scary monster is Mrs. Abernathy, one of the women at Liam's daycare back in Texas. Most of the employees were nice, but Mrs. Abernathy was a real hag. Our parents even had to go in and talk with the owner of the daycare. Liam's interactions with her were limited from that point on.

"What about your classmates," Mother asks. "What are they like?"

"Okay I guess," Liam says, slurping a spaghetti noodle into his mouth. "Flynn let me play with his fire truck and Carin shared her brownie with me. And Kelly's mom brought in chocolate chip cookies at snack time! They're just like the ones Daddy used to make."

I feel a pang in my stomach. Dad wasn't a great cook, but the one thing he never messed up was a good batch of chocolate chip cookies. The batter was sweet, the chocolate chunks were huge, and he used the perfect amount of walnuts.

"Carin, Kelly, and Flynn. Well," says Mother, "Do you know everyone's name already?"

"Duh," Liam says, "there's only four of them."

"Four?" I nearly spit out my soda. "Do you mean there are only four students in your group?"

"No, there are only four in the *whole school.* Miss Colleen says we're special."

"Four!" I repeat. The largest class I was in today had only nineteen students, so I expected Liam's class would be equally small, but four... Only *four* kindergarteners in the whole town?

"Rose," Mother says sternly, "close your mouth before you start catchin' flies. We knew when we moved here that things would be... small."

"Yeah, but Mother," I say, *"Four?* That's crazy!"

Mother's face tells me to drop it. Clearly, she doesn't think it's an important discovery and I let it go. We talk about the nice weather, about taking another trip to the park before the weather turns, and about the O'Dwyres and all the work that still needs to be done in and around the house. Mother winks at me at the mention of Beckan's name. I almost throw up.

*　　　　　*　　　　　*

After dinner, Liam takes his bath and Mother assists. I'm left alone with my swirling thoughts and curiosity. Unsure where else to look, and unwilling to walk through the house alone, I swipe the file Mrs. Carroll gave Mother the day we moved in, which is inconveniently hidden at the back of Mother's closet under a pile of shoeboxes.

Lounging under the canopy of my bed, I leaf through the pages of the file, certain I'll find something to satisfy my curiosity, if only because Mother was so determined to keep it from me. What I find doesn't disappoint, but it raises more questions than it provides answers. I make a list of findings in a notebook:

Three police reports:

- One police report details the discovery of Robert Olenev's body on Thanksgiving Day, 1903. Robert Olenev, 34, died of starvation. His wife had died several months before, during childbirth. The child was found unharmed in another part of the house. It was believed at the time that Robert died of a broken heart.

- One police report about the fire in 1934. The cause of the fire was unknown and the report is remarkably lacking in details. It simply states there had been a fire in an upper bedroom and the owners, Hagan Boyle, 29, and his wife Alison, 27, had died of smoke inhalation.

- One police report about the fire in 1964. Enit O'Sullivan, 48, was dragged from the flames by a fireman. The officer's account said the police department had been notified of the fire by the caretaker's son, Derry O'Dwyre, then a sprightly 16. Enit was found in an upper bedroom and demanded the firefighter put her down because she intended to die in the fire. She'd admitted to starting the inferno with the intent of destroying both the house and herself. The police questioned Enit as she was being loaded into the ambulance, but rather than transcribe her actual words, the reporting officer stated she spoke in "spastic crazy talk about the devil and a cockamamie curse."

The original deed to the property dated December 17, 1849, listing Eamonn and Alva Callaghan as the owners.

Several news articles from various incarnations of *The Port Braseham Courier*. These articles detail events surrounding the house and a few that appear unrelated. Several obituaries are included, many of them children. I'm surprised how far back they go. The earliest is dated in 1852. The causes of death are mostly undetermined. A few listed an illness I've never heard of called wasting disease. I notice many of the women who'd given birth to these children had also died, some during birth and others from infection several days after a difficult delivery. The town appears to have a tragic history of infertility and child deaths, but I don't understand what these have to do with my house. None of these women or children lived here.

Several articles about strange weather events. Freak thunderstorms on Christmas Eve followed by months of failed fishing trips. Wind storms that carried crops away or droughts for months on end so nothing grew. When the crops died so did the grass, which lead to the death of cattle and other livestock.

I flip back through the pages of the file and my notes, more confused than before. Who put this file together? It's filled with information a realtor would have no interest in giving to a client. The death toll of owners alone is enough to scare off prospective buyers. Looking at the front of the file, in a script nothing like the realtor's neat and curly cursive, someone had shakily scrawled "Wolfhowl Mountain." So someone prepared this and gave it to the realtor. Mrs. Caroll probably never even looked in it. Maybe it came from one of the previous owners – if any of them were even still living.

I shove the brittle, aged pages back into the file, one lone article falls out. The headline is "Woman's mysterious death on Wolfhowl Mountain," a brief article written in December 1996. All it includes is the date and time, Christmas Day around six in the morning, and a short description on a cut-out no larger than a post-it. A woman was found dead inside Wolfhowl, but details were not immediately available. The woman appeared to be in her mid to late forties and in good health. At the time, the woman's identity was unknown, but she was believed to be a local wife and mother who had been reported missing the night before.

Information overload.

I leave the file and my notes on my bed and walk to the balcony doors. I peer out over the town, twinkling under the full moon. Although the evening is cool and I wear only a long t-shirt, I step out onto the balcony and look around. It's clear enough to see all the way to the other side of town. Some windows are still lit, but most are dark. It's a peaceful night and I hear the waves crashing below the cliff behind the house. A light wind prickles the pine needles and plays with my hair. Why can't the townspeople be as nice and fair as the weather?

I catch movement at the edge of the trees near my balcony. I can hardly make out the dark shape, but I know it's a wolf. Sensing my presence, it moves closer and turns a black head toward me. Suddenly, I hear its loud howl as it bays, not at the moon, but at me. My skin pimples and I shudder. I hug myself and back away from the railing. The howl sounds eerily like a warning.

Unnerved, I retreat into my room, shutting the doors and locking them. Somehow, the tiny little button on the knob doesn't seem strong enough to keep what's on the outside *out*. I make a mental note to ask Derry or Beckan to install a deadbolt. Unlikely as it is a wolf could scale the side of the house and find its way inside, I'm more concerned about what an angry town mob might do. The house is so old it barely keeps out a light wind, much less a crowd of angry people with burning pitchforks, screaming for the destruction of the house from hell.

As I lock out the noises of the night under the full moon, I'm uncomfortable in the sudden silence. Why?

Because it isn't silent.

Turning an ear toward my closed bedroom door, I listen intently. I barely hear the whisper of a conversation. Opening my door with a slow *crrreeeaaaak*, I tiptoe down the hall.

I creep by the dark pit of the foyer below. My right side tingles with fear as if I'm creeping along the edge of a cliff. Standing outside Mother's closed bedroom door, I hear the comfortable snore of a deep sleep. Then I see a tiny rectangle of light coming from underneath Liam's closed door. I tiptoe further, until I'm right outside his door. "Liam?" When he doesn't reply, I slowly turn the knob and ease the door open.

The bedside lamp highlights Liam's empty bed. Panic immediately wells up inside me, but then Liam's voice floats in from the cracked door to the adjoining playroom, but who is he talking to? Mother's asleep and I'm right here, so…? Could Beckan be in there telling Liam a bedtime story? At midnight? Not likely. There must be a stranger in the house! What other explanation can there be? What do they want with my brother? I'm not going to let them out of here without some bruises or a broken nose.

I search Liam's room for a weapon, while my heart does its best to leap out of my chest. All I find is a plastic Wiffle Ball bat resting behind the door. I pick it up and, as quietly as I can, stalk across the room to the playroom door.

"My sister's okay," I hear Liam saying in his sleepy voice. "She takes good care of me... when she isn't busy being mad at stuff."

I can't hear the other end of the conversation, only silence, but Liam replies as if *to someone.*

"She gets mad a lot, but she doesn't mean it when she yells. She tells really good bedtime stories. Beckan's are better. *But don't tell her I said that."*

I peer around the corner of the doorjamb into the dimly lit room. Unable to escape my rib cage, my heart is now in my throat, and hammers in my ears. I raise the bat high above my head, prepared to beat this stranger into submission. I should've grabbed the phone in the hall and dialed nine-one-one before I came in here like an idiot, carrying a *plastic* bat.

Easing the door open a little wider, Liam is revealed, sitting on a rug in the center of the room. His back is to me and he leans over, his pudgy little hands fiddling with a few of his beloved G.I. Joes. I'm shocked to discover he's alone.

He shrugs his shoulders. "I dunno. I guess."

"Liam?"

He shoots up like he's just been pinched, whirling around with a hand over his heart. His little blue eyes are frightened. "Rosie! You scared me!"

"Me?" I say, entering the room. *"You* scared *me!* Who're you talking to? Why the hell aren't you in bed?" My eyes search the dark corners beyond a couple of toy chests and shelves of board games.

"I wasn't talking to anybody. I was just playing." Liam scoots his pajama feet along the floor as he crosses the room, grabs my hand, and tries leading me back to his bedroom, but I resist. I continue analyzing the room, squinting into every corner and under every piece of furniture, wondering why Liam's in such a hurry to leave.

"I heard you," I say. "You were talking to someone." I shiver suddenly, and goose bumps break out on my skin. "Why's it so cold in here?"

"I was only playing, Rosie, I promise."

I narrow my eyes, waiting for him to crack. He doesn't. Now I'm feeling a little guilty. Maybe he's being honest and he *was* talking to himself. Maybe he was talking about me to his G.I. Joes because he isn't getting better like I thought. Does he need someone to talk to so badly that he's created an imaginary friend? Am I really that inaccessible to my own brother? I've tried to be better about listening to him and comforting him and being less selfish, but maybe that's not enough. Maybe he needs to go back to counseling.

I let Liam to pull me into his room where we're greeted by Mother, sleepy-eyed and disheveled.

"Mother, what are you doing?" I ask.

"Me? What are *you* doing?" She says, stifling a yawn. "It's after midnight."

"I heard Liam in here talking to someone." I blurt the words out before thinking, like a tattle-tale desperate to save her own skin.

"I wasn't talking to anyone!" Liam huffs and stalks to his bed.

"Mother," I say seriously, "I heard him. He was having a conversation. I think —"

"I'm really not interested," Mother interrupts. "It's late, you have school in the morning, and I have to work. Get back to bed, both of you." Liam is already under his covers.

"But Mother —"

She cuts me off. "I don't care, Rose. It's late and I'm tired. Stop bickerin' with each other and get back to bed." She turns on her heels and leaves.

"I'm sorry, Rosie," Liam says. "I didn't mean to get you in trouble."

I sigh. "It's not your fault squiggle worm. I'm a little cranky, that's all. But no more playing in the middle of the night. You need your beauty sleep." I pinch his cheek, pull the covers up to his chin and turn out the light. "Goodnight, squiggle worm. I love you."

"I love you too."

I slink back to my room feeling guilty. As I sink into my mattress, the wolf howls again. I can't be sure, but this time he sounds like he's directly below my balcony.

Chapter Twelve
History Class

The next morning, I leave early to try and catch one of the O'Dwyres to ask about a deadbolt for the balcony doors and all the doors opening onto the lower porch. Just to be safe. Maybe if I have the guts I'll ask them about the dead mystery woman. It didn't happen that long ago, so Derry and Beckan must've known her.

I climb onto my bike and I'm ready to kick off before I remember Liam's with me. He's playfully skipping along behind me, *Spiderman* backpack on and *SpongeBob* lunch pail in hand. He isn't as graceful as I am on a bike – or on his feet – and I certainly don't want him going down that steep incline. Hand in hand and walking on solid ground, I lead Liam down to the cottage.

Beckan and his truck are nowhere to be seen, but Derry sits on the porch, smoking his pipe with a snoring Lady at his feet. Other than a few glances of his back as he shuffles away from the house, I've barely seen him since that first day. He's made one or two small repairs to the gazebos and first floor windows, but still hasn't made any moves on repairing the fire-eaten porch. The old grump is always unavailable, either tending to some small repair on the cottage or else in town on an errand while Beckan does the heavy lifting.

"Hi, Mr. O'Dwyre," I say, forcing a smile.

"Ah ain't nah taxi service," Derry grunts in our general direction, but his eyes remain staring off into the distance behind me, fixed on the house. It gives me the creeps how he doesn't even look at me when he talks.

"Huh? Oh, no," I say, deciphering his ape-like grunts. "We're gonna walk. I was just wondering if it would be possible to get deadbolt locks installed on the balcony and porch doors. It would help keep things safer for...Liam."

Liam perks up next to me when he hears his name, much like Lady would've. Derry's eyes stay focused on the same spot

above my shoulder for so long I start to wonder if he heard me.
"Mr. O'Dwyre?"

"Ah don't do inside repaihs," Derry says slowly, moving his piercing stare to me. He gazes at me for a long time, as if inspecting me, like he's looking for something, for some sign of...what? I'm unnerved by it, just as I was that first day.

"Well it's just a little thing —"

"Ah. Don't. Do. In-side. Re-pai-ahs," he repeats more forcefully. His eyes leave me and I understand I'm being dismissed. He leans back into the rocking chair, patting Lady's raised head gently and continues smoking his pipe.

"Mr. O'Dwyre is really grumpy," Liam says as we walk down the hill. "He's kind of like you." I frown with fresh guilt.

At the bottom of the hill, we meet Letta waiting for us. Her dark hair is pulled back into a tight French braid and she wears a blue t-shirt over khaki shorts and a pair of flip-flops. Letta's pretty in a quiet way. I bet she doesn't even own a tube of concealer for her perfect porcelain skin. Letta smiles and waves, and I'm relieved there's at least one person in this town who likes me.

"Oh good! I was afraid I'd missed you. You must be Liam." She smiles and shakes his hand. "I'm Letta. I'm pleased to meet you."

Liam furrows his eyebrows. "I'm pleased to meet you too?" He speaks self-consciously, not sure if he's understood Letta, and I laugh.

Letta bumps me with her shoulder as we begin our walk. "No ride from You Know Who today?"

I roll my eyes as Liam skips ahead of us. "Oh har har. I'm not sure where he is this morning. I talked to Ol' Derry for a minute though, and he assured me he's not a taxi service. Stay out of the road, Liam!"

"You wahlk. Me nah taxi." Letta imitates Derry's gravelly voice and deep accent perfectly. She laughs. "He's such a caveman."

"You know him?"

"No, not really. I mean, I've seen him in town, but I've never spoken to him. People around here talk about him though. Either he's the king of town or the scum of the Earth. It depends on whose side of the feud you're on. Oh hey," Letta interrupts herself and pulls out a bright red cell phone, which I find strangely flashy for her Plain Jane style. "I was going to text you last night to see how you were doing, but I forgot to ask for your number yesterday."

"Oh..." My cheeks flush with embarrassment. "I don't have a cell phone."

"Oh. Okay." She shrugs and puts her phone away like it's no big deal. I'm glad she doesn't ask me why.

"What she means," Liam shouts over his shoulder, "is she *used* to have a cell phone."

Dammit Liam.

"Used to?" Letta says.

"Who used tah have a cell phone?" Shane, Eileen, and Patty, who'd been chatting at a corner, fall into step with us.

"Rose apparently," Letta says. "I'm sure there's a story there." She looks at me expectantly, one thick eyebrow slightly raised.

I sigh. "Mother took it away when we were still in Texas."

"Why?" Patty asks, absently twisting a strand of her red hair around a long finger.

"Oh," I shrug nonchalantly, trying to play it down, "she decided I didn't need a phone when I decided I didn't need to respect her rules anymore." I hope this is explanation enough. I don't want to admit to them that I'd been suspended from school, which resulted in Mother grounding me for eternity and the loss of my phone, for getting into an argument with another cheerleader over a guy. I knocked the girl to the ground and stomped on her head during a basketball game. It seemed like a good idea at the time – the girl deserved it. You don't mess with Rose Delaney's man, but it's starting to feel like it was more trouble than it was worth.

"Well that's not a big deal," Shane says. "Find where she's hidin' it and take it back."

"Yeah, that might work," I allow, "if she hadn't driven over it with the station wagon a few times."

"Wow," Eileen says. "Your mom was wicked pissed."

"Yeah, she does dumb stuff when she's mad." Just like me. I'd kill for that phone right about now, and although I still don't exactly regret stomping on that bitch's head, I do regret the consequences. If I still had a phone, I could reach out to my old friends and maybe feel a little less isolated.

"You look nice today, Rose," Patty puts in, sensing a change of subject is in order and I'm grateful. I thank her. Truth be told, I'd put much more thought into my second day outfit than my first. I'm wearing a loose fitting t-shirt over a pair of skinny jeans and white sandals. Although one of the shoulders of my shirt tends to slide down a bit, I'm hoping today's outfit will prevent me from having to respond to "spook slut" for the second day in a row. I'm pleased Patty notices my effort.

"No interest in Mrs. Brennan tellin' you how desperate you are again?" Shane laughs.

"Definitely not!"

"So what's on the agenda for today?" asks Letta. "Flying under the radar or boldly accepting the spotlight with an incident as dramatic as to rival yesterday's lunch?"

I shrug as we approach the schoolyard. "I was hoping to fly under the radar, but trouble seems to find me regardless."

We migrate to a grassy patch, where I stop and kneel in front of Liam. I tighten his backpack straps and ruffle his curly hair before he ducks away.

"Listen, kiddo, have a good day, okay?" When he tries to trot off without a response, I grab his arm gently. "Hey, I'm serious. Have fun today... and you tell me if anythin' is bothering you alright?"

"Yeah, okay," he says, blue eyes staring at his shoes. I release him and he runs off without looking back.

"How's your brother adjustin' tah the move?" Eileen asks as we head inside.

"Well, I thought he was adjusting fine, but..."

"But?" Shane says.

"I dunno. He seemed really happy once we got here," I say. "He had some trouble before we left Texas. The divorce, you know? Then yesterday I caught him in a, lie yet he refuses to come clean, and last night I caught him talking to himself in the middle of the night."

"Talking to himself?" Letta says. "About what?"

"I'm not sure. I only heard part of it. But he's never talked to himself before. I'm afraid he's regressing, that he needs someone else to talk to."

"Are you sure he isn't talkin' tah a ghost?" Eileen says.

"Seriously?" I laugh.

"Hey, I'm not 'fraid of the house," Eileen says, "but that doesn't mean I'm not a believer."

*   *   *

I spend the first half of my day doing my very best to melt into walls and avoid notice. Unfortunately, I do not avoid the notice of that old bat Mrs. Brennan (wearing an exact replica of the dress from yesterday in a different pattern). When my shirt slips off my shoulder and my black bra strap is visible for a split second, Mrs. Brennan feels the need to let everyone know good Catholic girls don't wear black underwear. This, of course, is followed by Mary Donovan repeating her spooky slut declaration from yesterday, boldly and loudly this time. Foiled dammit.

During the garbled morning announcements, I hear what I think is an announcement about cheerleading tryouts coming up in the next few weeks. My heart flutters. I'd had a lot of fun as a cheerleader back in Texas, despite the incident. I wonder if joining the cheerleading team here will help me acclimate...or cause more drama than I need right now. It would certainly eat up some of my boredom. If Mother even allowed it, and that's a pretty big if.

At lunch, I follow my new friends to a small courtyard where students are allowed to eat outside. The weather is a bit cooler than yesterday and a nice breeze keeps us comfortable in our spot under a birch tree. I successfully avoid a repeat of yesterday's excitement, though I catch Ronan's head peaking out a window, his eyes scouring the courtyard. I turn my head away to hide my face with my hair. *Is he looking for me?*

My day remains boringly sedate until I get to history class, arriving with a small collection of faces I'm starting to recognize, including the brooding blonde boy from homeroom. Mr. Lindsay, a small man with a kind face, ignores the strangeness of my presence that my other teachers always call attention to. He treats me like I'm anyone else and not That Girl from That House.

"Good afternoon class!" Mr. Lindsay greets us warmly, and without the telltale accent of one born and raised in Maine. I wonder where he's from and how he ended up at this tiny dot on the map. "How are we this second day of school?"

There's a dull attempt at a response from a few students, but most just stare at him, waiting. *Yeah, yeah, Teach. Whatever.*

"Well don't all start talking at once about your great love of history!" Mr. Lindsay chuckles to himself. "Now, I know we don't all love history as much as I do, but this should be your favorite year. This is the year you get to learn all about the great state of Maine!"

There's some grumbling and someone behind me mutters, "Again?"

Though I'm used to being on the honor roll, I don't love all subjects. My second favorite subject is English because I love reading, but hate the constant writing and analysis. My favorite subject by far is history. I love learning new things, be it about the history of the United States or basket weaving. It's all interesting to me, thanks to Dad, the great historian, who managed to make any history lesson exciting. He'd studied history in college, and although his job as an accountant had nothing to do with it, he put it to good use with his kids. Some of my favorite memories are of spending evenings with Dad while he regaled us with great narratives of the Mexican-American War or dangerous missions into the Congo by explorers never to be heard from again.

"By the end of the year," Mr. Lindsay continues, undeterred by his students' disinterest, "you'll be well versed in how the two thousand islands off our coast were formed, the battles of the war-torn Mimacs of New Brunswick, what the Vikings have to do with our colonization, our role in the French and Indian War, *and* the strange weather pocket that is Port Braseham and what it has to do with the failure of our fishing industry."

Weather pocket? My brain reaches up and plucks the words from the air. Some of the articles from last night were about the severe weather Port Braseham has experienced since its establishment. I raise my hand, but Mr. Lindsay is already turned away, scrawling our first assignment in his chicken scratch handwriting onto an old green chalkboard. He has a small balding spot on the back of his head and chalk on his shirt collar.

"Excuse me, Mr. Lindsay?"

He turns around with a warm smile, excited about the first question of the day. "Yes, Rose?"

I guess I shouldn't be surprised he knows my name. "What did you say about strange weather?"

"Ah, I was talking about the strange weather pocket that seems to surround us here in Port Braseham."

"Could you elaborate?"

The effect is immediate. It's as if all of the air has been sucked out of the room. Desks creak as my classmates lean forward.

Mr. Lindsay smiles. "Of course! Keep in mind I'm not a meteorologist, but there's a significant history to our weather pattern here." Mr. Lindsay's eyes come alive, just like Dad's used to. "Here's something you should keep in mind before I get too far: The state of Maine has fewer thunderstorms than any state east of the Rockies. On average, Maine has about twenty thunderstorms a year across the state – unless you include Port Braseham."

Mr. Lindsay lets the pause pass slowly with a raised eyebrow. "Port Braseham has nearly *thirty* thunderstorms a year, all of them devastating to the land. Each storm leaves the coast devoid of fish, many of them skimmed dead from the surface the day after. Crops are drowned, uprooted, or otherwise destroyed. Just as the sea seems to recover, another storm befalls us. That's exactly the kind of weather that crippled our fishing industry in the 1800s, an industry this town was founded on.

"Other strange weather events include strong windstorms that literally carry the crops away, making it difficult for farmers to survive around here. The soil's usually barren anyway, but just as we seem to get a few ears of corn or a few fields of wheat, a storm rips most of it away. This, in turn, causes livestock to die of starvation. Now, it isn't like this every year. We may have several years of calm between these devastating events. It is a cycle, but it's not a *reliable* cycle. By that, I mean it doesn't have a predictable pattern. We don't know when the cycle will occur, just that it will. It's a hot topic in the world of meteorology."

"What about Christmas Eve?" It's the blonde boy who's spoken, his voice as sullen as his expression. I wonder what he's so depressed about.

"I'm glad you asked! I almost forgot the most perplexing weather event of all," Mr. Lindsay says, "the Christmas Eve Thunderstorm. Every year without fail, we have a severe thunderstorm on Christmas Eve. It comes without warning, it's strong enough to knock out the power, and it lasts sunset to sunrise. Considering how rare thunderstorms are in the winter, how especially rare they are in Maine, and the fact that we have one every year on the same day is both exciting and perplexing."

"How many years has that been happening?" I ask.

"Well, as near as we can tell," Mr. Lindsay says, looking away from me, "it's happened every year since 1851. It all started on the Christmas Eve when the builders of Wolfhowl Manor...died."

*　　　　　　*　　　　　　*

After history, I keep my mouth shut for the rest of the day. I'm tired of being stared at, and it's pretty hard to get away from people in a small school.

My determination to consider the house as just a house is wavering under the sheer faith the people of Port Braseham have in the supposed curse. So convinced are they that Wolfhowl Mountain is cursed, they actually believe it controls a continental weather system. They haven't made me a believer – yet – but I'm certainly curious. Maybe I can find some evidence to disprove all of this silly superstition and cure the town of their blind belief in something so sinister and ridiculous. And even though I think that's about as likely as me sprouting feathers, I'm going to do more research for my own piece of mind. I want to find out what's really behind the story of Wolfhowl Manor.

I walk home with Letta and Shane. Eileen and Patty disappeared into the shop classroom with a gaggle of the geekier looking kids.

"Robotics." Shane says. "Brains ovah beauty... Not to say they aren't pretty – I didn't mean... ah never mind." His cheeks are beet red.

Letta laughs and pats Shane on his scrawny shoulder. "So Rose, how was day two?"

"Eh."

"Eh?" Shane says, as if I'm speaking a foreign language, and his red eyebrows furrow over a blanket of freckles. "What is eh?"

"Less bad than good?" Letta guesses. "Evenly good and bad? Bad, but not as bad as yesterday?"

"I dunno. It was alright I guess," I say, trying to figure out a graceful way to bring up – of all things – the weather. I wonder if it's as taboo as Wolfhowl Manor. "History was interesting though... I got a lesson on Port Braseham's weather."

"And the storm of the year no doubt." Letta rolls her eyes.

"So it's true?"

"A thunderstorm every yeeah on Christmas Eve?" Shane says. "Sixty-five degree weathah? Not a snowflake in sight? Tornado-force winds? All night power outage? Every yeeah? Yup. All true."

"Bizarre."

"So why the funk?" Letta asks. "Does weird weather make you a believer?"

"Not by a long shot," I say, "but it *does* make me more curious. I'd like to play detective and find out what this town's so afraid of, especially since it seems like no one's scared for a real and tangible reason."

"Not that they'll say anyway," Letta says.

"What's the worst I can do?" I say. "Cure their fear?"

"No," Shane says, shaking his head. "The worst you can do is confirm it."

*   *   *

I part with Letta at the bottom of the hill as I had the day before, but this time with her phone number. Letta insisted she'd make a great Watson to my Sherlock if I want help, but I don't expect to do much research tonight. I have calculus homework due tomorrow and since I'm terrible at math, I plan to work on it most of the evening.

I pick Liam up at the O'Dwyre's. When I arrive, he's playing in the yard with Lady and Beckan's out on another errand. Derry's exactly where I left him this morning, sitting in his rocking chair, smoking his pipe and humming to himself, eyes closed. I'm sure he hears my approach, but he doesn't acknowledge me. Liam grabs his bookbag from the porch and we head up the hill.

"Mr. O'Dwyre isn't as much fun as Beckan," Liam whines.

"Oh yeah? Why not?"

"He's too quiet. He didn't say anythin' the whole time!" Liam, constantly babbling about the most inane topics, finds silence intolerable. "When I tried to tell him about SpongeBob – which he's never heard of! – he said we were playing the Quiet Game."

"Sorry, kiddo." I unlock the door with the skeleton key, which still fills me with silent glee, and lead Liam into the kitchen because I'm sure he's starving. Together we have a snack and then I follow Liam to his playroom. He putters around with his toys while I attempt my homework.

It takes an hour for Liam to get bored and for me to lose all patience with calculus. Liam goes downstairs to watch television and I retrieve the realtor's file from beneath my mattress. I doubt Mother knows it's missing yet. Before long, I'm sprawled out on my bed with the contents of the file spilled around me. I look back through the articles and weather reports, but find no new insights, just the same questions I had last night. I find myself wondering why that bothers me so much.

Chapter Thirteen
The House of Forgotten Sorrow

I spend the rest of September trying to bury my curiosity. Between helping Liam with his homework, my own schoolwork and chores, and getting to know my new friends, I don't have much time to think about a bunch silly superstition anyway. It's only as I'm laying my head down to sleep that I remember this house is still a mystery to me, a puzzle waiting to be solved – *Put me together, Rose.* I fall asleep each night listening to the howls of the wolves in the woods and remembering the sensation of being watched, stalked, shadowed every time I'm alone in a room. I wake each morning with a vague sense of uneasiness and the feeling I haven't really slept at all.

Liam and Mother, on the other hand, are flourishing in Port Braseham. The history of the house is of no interest to Liam, and even if Mother had the time to think about it she wouldn't, because "history was your father's thing." She's more interested in romance novels, Beckan's rear end, and *The Real Housewives of Wherever* – not that she has time for those things either. She's constantly at work, picking up extra shifts whenever she can to try to cover the cost of our move. Sometimes breakfast is the only time we see her, which is just fine with me.

Although my new friends are very different from the friends I'd left behind in Texas – or rather, *they* left *me* behind – I like Letta's group a lot. They don't go to wild parties four or five nights a week, or do anything terribly dramatic or exciting, but when they ask how I'm doing, they *mean* it. I never realized how selfish my old friends were – and how selfish I'd been – until I knew what it's like to have people who genuinely care about my wellbeing. If this were a Hallmark movie, this is when my character would realize there's more to the world and start growing and maturing. The evil bitch becomes the heroine, resolution, The End.

Shane's always great for a good belly laugh. He's silly and makes me think of what Liam might be like as a teenager. Letta's funny too, but in a more sarcastic, burning way. Her quips are like small jabs in the ribs from your favorite uncle. Patty's quieter, but she smiles a lot and likes asking me about growing up in Texas and what it's like to go to such a big school, which I won't lie, makes me feel important in a way I miss. She also has a flair for fashion and I eye her outfits with envy because she makes it seem so effortless. Eileen's different than the others, a little more like me, or like the old Rose – Texas Rose. She can be mean and fake, or nice and genuine. She fits in with our group, but fits in equally as well with Mary and her minions. It all depends on what kind of mood she's in, what kind of day it is. Altogether, my new friends make me feel like a flower being fertilized and cultivated. These are the people who will help me survive the seventh circle of hell, otherwise known as Port Braseham.

But there are still two people lurking in my periphery – Ronan Quinn and Beckan O'Dwyre. I see Beckan on an almost daily basis. If he doesn't drive Liam and me to school or have a project in the house to work on, he'll find a reason to stop by and check on us. He usually says he's coming by to check on Liam and satisfy his long lost wish for a little "bruthah." And although he *does* spend a lot of time with Liam, he also spends a lot of time with me, and we get to know each other a little more each day.

I haven't actually spoken to Ronan since that first day, but I always feel his eyes on me. Just as surely as his arm is wrapped around Mary's waist, or his fingers intertwined with Mary's, his eyes are on me. It's like he's analyzing me every chance he gets, looking me up and down like a piece of meat. It isn't only that he finds me attractive – and I know he does – it's that he looks at me the way a dog looks at you when you whistle, head slightly tilted to the side and eyebrows furrowed. What exactly is he looking for when he looks at me like that? And from the way Mary glares at me, I know she's wondering the same thing.

*　　　　　*　　　　　*

October

On the first day of October I finally find myself with the time and curiosity to look into Wolfhowl Manor's history. I'm ignoring the calculus homework peeking out of my binder, waiting to infect my brain with frustration. I grab my laptop. It's the one electronic device Mother let me keep after the cheerleading incident on the condition it's for school use only. Before I open Google, I check my email. Plenty of spam, but not a peep from any of my friends back in Texas. I don't even know why I'm still checking. I quickly tap out a message to my (former) best friend Jennifer. Maybe my old friends need me to start the line of communication since they're really texters anyway. I throw in some details about the house and our new "servants", trying to invite both jealousy and curiosity, baiting Jennifer to respond.

Then I spend an hour using different key words to see if I can find any information about Port Braseham or Wolfhowl Mountain. I don't find much of interest. In a couple of cases, I bring up an article from the realtor's file, but mostly I find advertisements for local businesses. Apparently, there's a well-known furniture restoration business in town, Captain's Peg Leg, and I actually find a review for The Wharf Rat; I'm very glad I didn't eat those fries.

It isn't until I combine the search terms "Port Braseham", "local history", and "cursed" that I come across an enlightening article written for a travel magazine specializing in New England destinations called "The House of Forgotten Sorrow," which I read with great interest.

> *If you allow yourself to get far enough off the map in eastern Maine, you might find yourself taking a cool dip in the Atlantic. But, swim far enough out and you'll arrive in the small hamlet of Port Braseham. It looks a little bit like the town time forgot and a little bit like a town still recovering from The Great Depression. It's a town ripe with old-fashioned values, simple living, and a heavy dose of Irish Catholicism.*
>
> *The beautifully quaint coastline is covered in pebbled beach with sea foam waves lapping at the edges. Several fishing boats skirt across the horizon, but you won't find many sightseers here to enjoy the postcard view, nor will you find them along the rotting and deserted boardwalk. Indeed, all you* can *find there besides aged fishermen smoking their fragrant pipes is a small diner known as The Wharf Rat with a very simple* menyah *– fish, burger, or chicken salad – and an indifferent proprietor by the name of Flo. A word of warning: all three dishes taste exactly the same, sit like a brick in your belly in the same way, and for the same uncomfortable amount of time.*

The busier — I use that term loosely — downtown area of Port Braseham is quite lovely. Several mom n' pop businesses line the main drag of town, resting inside converted Victorian homes the colors of an exploding kaleidoscope a la Monet. Picket fences, winding brick walks, and monstrous pine trees make this a great destination for anyone in search of rest and relaxation, especially if you enjoy having nearly nothing to do but meander and stare at birds.

But there's another side to this seemingly peaceful town, a darker side the townspeople don't want you to know. And it all centers around what I like to call The House of Forgotten Sorrow, a great monstrosity of a house built on the tallest hill in town.

Eamonn and Alva Callaghan were a pair of young first generation Irish immigrants in search of a better life in America. Maine was a logical place for them to settle, not only because it had the fertile farmland they were looking for, but because the wide rolling green hills reminded Alva of the Irish moors where she was raised. In fact, it was the seventeen-year-old Alva who convinced her thirty-two-year-old husband to settle on the piece of land, which would come to be known by the sinister moniker of Wolfhowl Mountain, in 1849.

It was a grand dream for a humble fisherman and preacher and his devout piano teacher wife. They struggled at first, but Eamonn's fishing and farming business grew and before long, the couple had saved enough money to build a house in Alva's perfect vision. It was Victorian by design, but Alva's specific modifications turned it into a strange and ugly beast scowling down upon the town. A widow's walk was pinned to the roof so Alva could keep an eye on Eamonn's fishing boat and pray to St. Elmo for his safe return.

Slowly Eamonn toiled over the construction of the house, adding room after room and floor after floor to achieve Alva's dream. And the bigger the house became, the more determined Alva was to fill it with their children. Eventually her wish came true and she became pregnant. While she was thrilled, Eamonn was secretly panicking. The summer of 1850 was a violent one for weather. Storm after storm whipped the coast of Maine and Port Braseham had been struggling with their crop and fishing industries ever since. Land seemed nearly barren and the sea swallowed up all of the fish. Eamonn's business began to struggle, but he did not tell Alva. Of course she knew things had been hard, but Eamonn always told her they would be all right, and she believed him.

Their child, Emily Lenore, came sometime in late November 1851. The couple should have been beside themselves with joy, but this does not appear to be the case.

The Christmas Eve several weeks after Emily Lenore was born was a tough one marked by the strongest thunderstorm of the year and unseasonably warm weather. On Christmas Day, when the couple did not show up to church, a few of the townspeople went to check on them. Both Eamonn and Alva were found hanging from the rafters in an unfinished portion of the house. It was ruled a double suicide, but no note was found.

And what of Emily Lenore? Good question. After some of my own research, all I could find of the girl was a birth certificate. After birth, she disappears from civilization like a Mayan baby, as if someone went to great lengths to erase her entire existence from the planet. Was she raised by friends in town? There are no gravestones bearing her name behind the only church in Port Braseham. Was she sent to live with relatives in Ireland? There is no record of her leaving the country. Was she adopted under a new name? No paperwork exists to support this theory. No one really knows the true fate of Emily Lenore. Yet this is why the people of the town seem to think the house is cursed; Alva's ghost wants her stolen child returned.

I'm not much of a believer in ghosts, but there is some pretty convincing evidence to this dark little tale. For example, the death toll of the house: nearly every owner since the Callaghan's has died. The first couple died after the birth of their son; she during childbirth and he presumably from a broken heart if local legend is to be believe. And the child didn't live much longer than his parents, dying mysteriously a few weeks later. The next childless owners died in a mysterious fire. A carpenter bought the house in the sixties to fix it up and resell, but he was shredded by his own saw after falling through the rotting floor. The last owners fled in the early eighties, leaving the house in foreclosure.

Then there's that weird weather. Going back as far as records allow, Port Braseham has had a thunderstorm on Christmas Eve every year since 1850. Each storm leads to a period of barren land and empty fishnets for anywhere from several weeks to several months. At first, the townspeople seemed to think they had landed themselves in an odd little weather pocket and didn't give the storms too much consideration. But after several years, the Irish Catholic town members sought a different answer, an explanation from God. It was Eamonn's own eccentric successor as preacher who began steering the town toward the supernatural, based on a sermon I unearthed from 1859. He believed the town was being punished for the sins represented by Eamonn and Alva's suicides.

And then there's the part literally no one in town will discuss with an outsider like me – infertility and infant deaths. Since the deaths of the Callaghans and the disappearance of the child Emily Lenore, there has been a significantly high rate of infertility and infant death in Port Braseham. Through public records, I was able to confirm Port Braseham has the highest rate of miscarriages in the state – and it's one of the smallest towns! The ancient overgrown graveyard of Saint Perpetua, Our Lady Martyr has several headstones per year for children less than a year old. Taking my own little tour, until I was kicked out by the locals, I noticed when these gravestones started popping up – in early 1852. Could it be a coincidence?

Several times the town council has voted to tear down Wolfhowl Manor in hopes of breaking the curse, but each time the Port Braseham Historical Society, now led by popular resident Seamus Quinn, intercedes and prevents it. Turns out the eyesore is a historical landmark. More than once the town council has been urged by outsiders to create a tourism campaign around the curse of Wolfhowl – Ghost Hunters *anyone? – But they refuse. They do not believe in profiting off of a story so full of sorrow – but they don't believe in going anywhere near it either. Aside from a locally assigned caretaker to handle the land, the house is off limits. However, the house is owned by the Historical Society and so long as you promise not to knock the house down or make any major structural changes, you could own Wolfhowl Manor. It's up for sale. The cost? According to the locals… your life.*

This is what the tight-knit community of Port Braseham doesn't want you to know. They just want you to forget about it, and it isn't in the interest of tourism. They'd like you to forget all about them too. Just wipe Port Braseham off the map and let them live their lives simply, and in the shadowy burden of their house on the hill.

"Hey."

I nearly fall off my bed when Beckan, who's standing in my bedroom doorway, greets me, but I do manage not to scream this time. "You scared me!"

"Sorry." He holds up his hands innocently. One holds a bulky plastic bag.

"What's in the bag?"

"These are your safety mechanisms miss," he says with a bow. "I have your deadbolt locks as requested."

"Thanks," I laugh. "It only took you a month!"

"Well, you know, the busy small town life," he says sarcastically.

"I know it's silly, because I'm sure no one around here even locks their doors, but it sure would make a city girl like myself feel better." I play up the damsel in distress accent as I clasp my hands under my chin and bat my long eyelashes.

Beckan laughs and juts his chin toward the mess of papers on my bed. "What're you up tah?"

"Doing some research on the house," I say and motion to the pieces of the file around me. "I snagged the file the realtor gave Mother. I've been curious about the whole curse thing."

"Oh?" Beckan sits next to me on the bed, close. The hair on my arm prickles with electricity. He smells like pine trees and fresh air. "No plans tonight?"

"Only avoiding my calculus homework."

"Ah," he nods knowingly as his eyes search the articles and zero in on the one about the woman who died here in the nineties.

"Oh yeah!" I scoot closer as he picks up the article. "I want to ask you about that one. It's about a woman who died here in 1996, but it didn't give any details. It wasn't that long ago. I thought maybe you or your dad might know who she was and what happened."

Beckan's smile fades. "Yes," he says. "I knew her, and I know what happened."

"You do?" I say, powerless to hide my excitement.

"Yes," he says somberly. He holds the article between two fingers, rubbing the recycled paper gently between them. "The woman this article's about, the woman who died here...was my muthah."

Hagan and Alison Boyle
The Second Owners: 1933-1934

Hagan and Alison Boyle deserved every bit of the romantic story they were capable of. She was heiress to a great fortune who deigned to take notice of a poor city boy in the family's clothing factory. But they didn't have the happy ending one would imagine. Quite the opposite in fact. Alison's family took Hagan under their wing. They turned him from a pitiable custodian struggling to make ends meet into a successful businessman who eventually ran a factory of his own.

Alison and Hagan were married six months after their first date, but the marriage was over by their fifth anniversary. Under the stress of infertility and the daily stresses of the family business, their passion for one another failed. If only they'd left each other, they might have avoided their fate inside Wolfhowl Manor.

The more successful Hagan became, the more captivated with the world of business – and money – he was. After two hard years working his way to the top, he was able to hire a manager to take care of the daily factory business. He then spent the majority of his time making lucrative business deals over martinis and Alison whiled away her hours as a rich but bored housewife over double martinis. Though the couple did spend time together, it was usually in the company of several friends over many double martinis. Eventually this lifestyle led them both to stray into the arms of lovers, but alas, did not lead them to divorce.

In 1933, Hagan decided they needed to get away from the city lifestyle, away from their nightly parties and drinking binges, and grow up a little. He thought they might dry out in a nice summerhouse, which if nice enough, would become their full time quarters. Perhaps they could find a way to rekindle their love and youth. Through a friend, Hagan learned of the property on Wolfhowl Mountain. Although the house had been unoccupied for thirty years, there was a caretaker and Hagan was assured it was perfect for the couple to use as a city escape for a while. There was plenty of room to entertain guests and being so close to the water, Hagan's eyes were full of yachts and beach parties. Hagan bought the property sight unseen, and without consulting his wife, in April 1933.

Alison didn't spend much time involved in her husband's monetary affairs. As long as she didn't have to lift a pretty little finger and they had enough money for her pretty little things, she was sated. It was this that kept her from protesting when Hagan announced he was packing them up and moving them to Port Braseham, Maine to take up residence in their new summer home out of the city. She idly hoped she'd find the caretaker attractive and Hagan would find something to do with himself, like a hobby.

It wasn't until they arrived at Wolfhowl Manor they realized their terrible mistake. The original construction had begun to rot, creating gaps for drafts and holes for rats. There was no hot water, when there was water at all. Though the view was stunning, the sea was hardly accessible from the house. Hagan's dreams of reconnecting with his still beautiful yet emotionally unavailable wife through balmy jaunts on the beach and leisurely sails along the shore were dashed. The way she glared at him that first night sealed the fate of their fractured marriage. Once they settled in, Alison was more interested in the view at the bottom of her martini glass than her once doting husband and was bored to the point of lethargy.

It didn't take long for their partying lifestyle to find the Boyles in Port Braseham. A month after their arrival, friends started arriving unannounced. Hagan had greatly missed the empty interactions of his friends, with whom he had nothing in common but money, and craved an alcohol-fueled adventure in the absence of his wife's love.

Speaking to police after the couple's death, their friends would reflect that they'd seen quite a change in the fun loving couple after they left the city. Though it was true they often did their loving separately, there was no actual discord between them. Hagan and Alison were perfectly aware of each other's transgressions and, though they may not have approved of them, accepted them. They still knew how to throw a party and have a good time. However, the couple who fought over almost nothing prior to the move, fought over nearly everything afterward. Alison kept track of every dime Hagan spent. Hagan kept track of every drink Alison consumed. Alison complained about every failing of the house and the caretaker's failure to keep the house up to her par while Hagan complained it was her fault for spending so much time in the caretaker's cabin. Things between the couple had been unbearable since at least July 1933, a fact confirmed by some of the townspeople who occasionally saw them in town.

As near as anyone could tell, the Boyles hadn't actually been seen in town or visited by any friends since Christmas 1933. They became recluses, refusing to leave the house and sending the caretaker on their errands.

On the early morning of New Year's Day 1934 the townspeople saw, first a spiral of smoke drifting from Wolfhowl Mountain, and then great billows of black smoke sullying the pink sky. By the time the Bar Harbor Fire Department arrived, the entire north wing of the house was engulfed. It took hours to beat the flames into dying embers. The bodies were found a few days later as investigators sifted through the ashes.

The original police report showed Alison Boyle shot her husband and then set the fire in a bedroom. She died of smoke inhalation while holding Hagan's lifeless, blood-covered body. The cause of the fire is listed as unknown and the official cause of death for both parties was reported to be smoke inhalation. That's what a lot of money can buy you if your daughter is heir to your fortune.

Chapter Fourteen
Mrs. O'Dwyre

An unbearably long silence passes between us, Beckan still glaring at the article intently, as if he's hoping to set it on fire with his mind and erase the terrible event. His green eyes flick slightly from side to side, reading the article over and over. I try to think of something to say. I'm sure Beckan doesn't want to talk about it, and I don't know if I want the details anymore. It's too grotesque for it to be so closely related to someone I know, to a friend. I haven't had much interaction with death in my life and don't respond to it well myself.

"I'm sorry, Beckan," I say finally. My words feel sharp and awkward in my mouth. "I-I didn't know."

Beckan shrugs, finally looking at me. "How could you? It happened a long time ago." I watch his glassy eyes quickly dry up, without so much as a sniff.

"You don't have to tell me about it."

"No, it's okay." Beckan hands the article back to me. "You're going tah heeah 'bout it soonah or latah. She's part of the history of the house now I guess. One of its many victims."

"What happened?" I ask tentatively.

"The details are still pretty fuzzy," he says, pushing himself off of the bed. He paces between the door and the closet in long strides. "What we know 'bout that day we've mostly guessed at. My parents were always a happy couple. They were high school sweetahahts, even though Pop didn't graduate. Pop had been livin' heeah on the property his whole life and Ma moved in with him. Pop doesn't talk 'bout it a lot, but he always said thins were 'peaches an' sunshine' until the Hollisters."

"The Hollisters?"

"Owners of Wolfhowl back in the eighties," he says. "Last owners before you. They weren't heeah for long, but Ma took a likin' tah the wife. They were newlyweds. Moved up heeah tah staht a family. They seemed happy."

"What happened to them?" I'm a little afraid of the answer.

"Nothin' actually," Beckan says, pulling a pack of cigarettes from his back pocket. He almost lights it, but then realizes where he is. "D'ya mind?"

I don't like smoking. It smells awful and looks stupid. But I figure Beckan needs it, and since he's about to bare his soul to me, I point to the balcony. "Let's go outside. But if Mother says anything, I'm throwin' you under the bus."

"Fair enough," he says with a smirk.

We step onto the balcony. Port Braseham explodes with light across the bottomless pit of the hill as the sun slips below the horizon. I close the doors to block out some of the bedroom light so I can watch the town twinkle as I listen.

"So the Hollisters?" I say.

Beckan lights his cigarette and takes several therapeutic drags before he replies. "They just picked up and left one day," he says, the smoke flowing out of his mouth as he talks. "They'd been tryin' tah staht their family, but the wife had a couplah miscarriages I think. Havin' children's always been kinda a problem 'round heeah."

"So I've heard."

"Anyway," he sighs, "the wife got wicked depressed 'bout it and they eventually left. They put it up for sale, but it ultimately went back tah the historical society. It wasn't long aftah the Hollister's abandoned the place that Ma became obsessed with it."

"Obsessed?"

"Yeah. Pop and I caught her starin' at it a lot, just thinkin' or... list'nin'."

"Listening? What do you mean?"

He shrugs again. "Dunno. When Pop would ask her what she was doin', that's what she'd say. She was list'nin'." He pauses to use his burned down cigarette but to light another, and then flicks the dying ember into the darkness below.

"I think she felt a lot like the Hollister wife," he continues. "She and Pop wanted more children aftah me, but they couldn't make it happen. Doctor told her she was barren when I was real little. Said she was lucky tah even have me."

"That's harsh."

"Aftah the Hollisters left, it seemed tah hit her pretty hard there'd never be anothah baby 'round. She talked a lot 'bout babies, 'bout havin' more, even though she knew it was impossible. There were a lot of conversations that began with 'I wish...' I can't say it made me feel real warm and fuzzy. It was hard tah understand as a kid." He falls quiet, staring off into the night.

"What happened in the house?"

Beckan clears his throat, takes another drag of his cigarette. "Ma liked tah take long walks. Said it helped her clear her head. So, when she disappeared the afternoon of Christmas Eve, we didn't think much of it. It wasn't until dark we really stated worryin' because we knew the storm was comin'. We walked the property and called friends, but we couldn't find her. We called the police department, but they don't spend much time worrying' about us up heeah on the hill. They couldn't do much until the storm was ovah anyway." His voice betrays a hint of bitterness.

"Pop went out early the next mornin', soon as the rain stopped, and walked the property again. He thought he saw somethin' in one of the upper windows, so he went in. He found her up in the other bedroom," he motions toward the fire room with his cigarette, "hanging' from the rafters. Been dead a while, all night probably."

"Oh Beckan, that's terrible," I whisper. "I'm so sorry – I shouldn't have asked. I –" I falter, unsure what to do or say. Is this a hug moment? Would he even want a hug from me? I study his face, barely visible now in the darkness, but the glowing coal of his cigarette reflects in his glassy eyes. I reach out and squeeze Beckan's hand, an instinctual response. His rough fingers rub against my soft skin like sandpaper as they squeeze mine gently back.

"I don't pretend tah understand why she did what she did," he says, "but I've made peace with it. Pop hasn't been in the house since. I think he's afraid of what he'll see."

"He thinks it's the curse, doesn't he?" I ask, trying to keep the skepticism out of my voice, and Beckan nods. "What about you?"

"Undecided," he shrugs. "Sometimes when I'm in heeah, I think I hear her... Look, I'm not crazy," he adds when he sees my skeptical expression. "She liked tah hum a lot. There was never an ounce of silence in our house unless Ma was asleep. And when I'm up here, turning screws, fixing doorknobs... sometimes I think I hear her hummin'. But other times I'm heeah...and thins seem normal. Quiet. Like it's any othah house. And then I staht tah think I made it all up because I miss her."

"Do you...hear her a lot?"

Beckan hesitates, but then nods slowly.

"Have you…" I shiver suddenly, momentarily losing my breath. "Have you heard her since we moved in?"

Beckon nods again.

"You aren't afraid?"

"I don't scare so easy," he says. "Even if the house is cursed, what am I supposed tah do?"

"Exorcism?"

He laughs. "Been tried before, believe it or not. You just have tah accept it and hope it doesn't come aftah you."

His tone frightens me and I hug myself. The air is damp and chilly. All light has disappeared below the horizon, leaving us in the small bronze light filtering through the curtains. I feel weird. Something Beckan said has my guts churning, and something is rising to the surface faster than I can control it, like vomit. My mouth starts moving without my permission and I realize I'm about to tell Beckan something I haven't shared with anyone other than my anger counselor. Something I vowed never to speak of again.

Sensing my inner turmoil, Beckan flicks his cigarette over the edge of the balcony and leans on the railing. "Spit it out, girl."

"My dad is dead." The words tumble out so quickly, and my hands fly to my mouth, as if stuffing them back down my throat would make it untrue.

Beckan stays quiet, but puts a heavy arm around my shoulders. He squeezes my body into a half-hug and simply says, "I'm sorry."

A sob explodes from my throat, but I quickly stifle it. "I'm sorry," I say, wiping at my watery eyes. "It just came out. I don't mean to take away from what happened to your mom, but… I guess I'm trying to say I've been through what you've been through. I understand." I've tried to deny it for so long, told myself Dad is back in Texas missing us, but saying it out loud makes it real. I let my weight slip a little and lean into Beckan, allowing him to comfort me in a way I've never let anyone.

"D'ya want tah tell me what happened?" he asks gently.

"I dunno," I say honestly.

The silence grows awkward and I feel the need to fill it with my voice. "My parents split about a year ago. Nothing had been finalized, but they were separated and moving forward with the divorce. It was toughest on Liam and Dad. They were so close, but Mother won temporary custody. Dad really went off the deep end after that I guess. It was hard for him. He really wanted to work it out, but Mother already had a foot out the door when she filed."

"And you?" Beckan asks. "How did you feel 'bout it?"

"Um..." Anger is all that comes to mind – blinding, white hot, all-consuming anger – which I beat down with every ounce of my self-control. "I dunno... I don't want to talk about me anymore."

"Okay."

"He was basically living in a hotel," I continue. "My dad, I mean. Mother commandeered the house. She didn't want to see him, so she'd drop us off for visits. I let Liam run ahead of me one day. The door was unlocked..."

"Poor Liam."

"Yeah. He found Dad in the bathroom."

"Bathroom?"

"Yeah, in a tub full of red water," I explain. "I don't think Liam understood at first. He thought Dad was playing a game. It was a few days before he could really be made to understand, and even then... I don't know if he really understands Dad killed himself."

"Sounds bad," Beckan says sympathetically. "But Liam is doing okay. He's a good kid. He'll be alright." His voice is calm and confident, as if saying it makes it true.

"I hope so.

"And you?" Beckan asks again.

"I'm just...angry," I say. I grit my teeth and fight back the tears. I shake my head.

"That's okay," he says. "But you can talk tah me in the future, if you want. And honestly, I know this is a serious moment and all, but I'm glad tah see your frosty exterior thaw a little bit."

"Gee thanks." I smile up at him, and for a moment, we stand together, his arm around me, and it's like I can feel a static charge between us. As I look into his dark eyes reflecting the bedroom light, I feel it build and build. And then –

There's a crunching of gravel as Mother's station wagon pulls into the driveway and I pull away from Beckan a little too quickly.

"She's getting home late tonight," Beckan says, glancing at his watch. "It's nearly eight."

"Oh crap! Liam! I didn't make him dinner! He's probably died of starvation." I reach for the doorknob, but turn back to Beckan and add, "Thanks. For talking."

"Anytime, Rose." His eyes hold mine a beat too long and I know he means it, but there's something hidden in his tone. I look away awkwardly, twisting the knob and pulling the door open as Mother gets out of the car. When my eyes hit my bedroom, I'm shocked.

My room is an explosion of my belongings. The closet door is nearly torn off the hinges and all of my clothes are strewn across the room. The canopy of the bed is hanging down with a deep slash down the center. The sheets are ripped from the mattress and hanging down over the edges. Something tore my bedroom to bits.

All I can do is scream. *"Mom!"*

Chapter Fifteen
Let Me In

"Mom!" My fingers dig into Beckan's arm. He's silent, his mouth agape and his eyebrows nearly meeting his hairline. I hear Mother's clumsy stomps on the stairs before she breathlessly bursts into the room. I run and cling to her. At once I'm met with the stench of alcohol and cigarettes.

"What's wrong?" Mother's slur is barely perceptible to anyone besides me.

"Where've you been?" I temporarily forget my panic. I'm focused on my flaring anger. "Are you drunk?"

Mother meets my disapproving glare with a raised eyebrow. "Don't you question me like that, young lady. If I want to go to happy hour with my coworkers, then that's my business."

"Without even telling anyone?"

"I would've texted your cell phone, dear," Mother says sarcastically, "but I can't do that now can I? Now, tell me what's going on. What in the world happened in here?"

"I don't know! Beckan and I were on the balcony. This is what we found when we came in."

Mother's eyes, narrowed with suspicion, dart between us. "On the balcony? Why? And why weren't you watching your brother?"

As if on cue, Liam's curly head pops into the room. "Why's everyone yellin'?" He's rubbing his eyes as if waking up from a nap. "What's happening?"

"That's what I'd like to know right now young lady," Mother says without taking her beady eyes off me, hands on her hips.

"Why wasn't *I* watching Liam?" I throw my hands up. "Why weren't *you?* You should've been home *two hours* ago!"

"Don't turn this around on me, Rose!" Mother huffs around the room and jabs a finger in the air. "Look at this mess! Tell me what happened right now!"

"I. Don't. Know." I say like I'm talking to an idiot. "That's what I'm telling you! I was up here looking over my homework when Beckan stopped by. We started talking, but he wanted to smoke, so I took him to the balcony. We weren't out there more than ten minutes. I swear the room was fine when we left!"

Mother's eyes survey the maelstrom. They freeze on one of the articles lying under a shoe on the bed. She grabs it, recognizes it immediately. She begins rifling around on the bed, finding several of the articles and their folder in the tangle of bedclothes. "And what's this? What are you doing with this? How dare you go through my things!"

I clamp my hands on my hips. "Well someone had to! You certainly weren't going to tell us anything!"

"None of this matters, Rose!" Mother shakes the papers at me. "This is *my* business and mine alone. It's nothing for you to be concerned about!"

Behind Mother, Liam's eyes tear up, but neither of us notices.

"Nothing to be concerned about? Are you crazy? Look at my room! What do you think did this, huh?"

"Don't you take that tone with me!"

"Mother! People *died* here! A lot of them!"

"Died?" Liam says, his eyes growing wide.

"Why don't we try tah calm down, ladies." Beckan says, but he may as well be invisible.

"It's nothing," Mother says. "So a few people died? So what?"

"So what? Mother, those people died in this house because something killed them!"

"Stop yelling!" Liam shouts, putting his hands over his ears.

"Something *killed* them?" Mother rolls her eyes and laughs. "Really, Rose? Listen to yourself! I thought you were smarter than this. There's no such thing as ghosts! Those poor people died, yes, but they were depressed. Depressed people do..." She falters, dropping her hands to her sides. "Depressed people do sad things."

"Mother, look around you!" I say, frustrated. "Look at my room! Do you think this is my way of unpacking?"

"I've about had it with your attitude," Mother says firmly. She gathers the rest of the articles and papers from my bed and shoves them into the folder. "These articles mean nothing. Nothing! Now, I know you don't want to be here. You've made that perfectly clear. But to orchestrate something so ridiculous to scare me into going back to Texas? And to involve a nice boy like Beckan in this scam of yours? Now that's a new low."

"What? You think *I* did this? Mom – "

"Really, Rose. Ghosts?" Mother sighs and shakes her head. "I've had enough out of you for tonight and I have a terrible headache."

"Gee. I wonder *why*," I mutter under my breath.

Mother shoots me her last warning glance. I know the old Mrs. Delaney would've flown off the handle, maybe even smacked me, but she wouldn't dare do something like that in front of Beckan. Instead, the new Mrs. Delaney lets out a long, controlled sigh and puts a delicate hand on her forehead before she replies.

"I'm going to bed. You're to get your brother some dinner, as I'm sure he's starving, and then you're to clean up your room. Is that clear?" I stay silent, grinding my teeth to powder. To Beckan, she says, "I'm sorry you had to be a party to this, Beckan. I appreciate you coming up here, but you can go home now. Whatever it is can wait until tomorrow."

"Yes, ma'am," Beckan nods.

Liam's tiny form has vanished. Mother looks around. "Now where'd your brother get to?"

"Liam?" I call.

"I think he went tah his room," Beckan says, still standing awkwardly behind me, worrying his hands together while waiting for his chance to escape.

I feel foolish. Embarrassed. The heat of my anger fades in the wake of my concern for Liam, but my cheeks stay red. Liam hates yelling, and he especially hates it when Mother and I argue because it reminds him of Dad and the troubling months before our parents split up. Even worse, for weeks after Dad's death, Liam was convinced all arguing people would die any moment. It took a lot of crying nights and multiple therapy sessions to calm this intense panic. And here I am, his big sister and protector, screaming at Mother about ghosts and murder right in front of him, acting like a jackass instead of Big Sis.

"I'll go get him since you aren't *well*." I start out of the room.

Beckan follows, heading down the closest staircase. "I'll get stahted on the door locks tomorrow. Goodnight, Rose." He waits for me to turn around.

"Goodnight." Something flickers behind those green marble eyes. Is it sympathy? Or judgment? He turns away before I figure it out.

"Mrs. Delaney." He nods at Mother and then continues his descent.

In the doorway to her own bedroom, Mother stands with her arms crossed, glaring at my back. She's no doubt thinking about how she would have punished me if there weren't any witnesses.

I knock on Liam's closed door. "Liam? It's me." I try turning the knob, but it doesn't twist. Confused, I try again. "Liam? Did you lock the door? Let me in please." I hear sniveling behind his door and then the sound of the jiggling knob.

"Let me in, Liam," I repeat sternly.

"I'm trying," he says, his voice muffled by the door. "I didn't lock it."

"Maybe you locked it by accident." Mother straightens in the corner of my eye.

Beckan stops about halfway down the stairs. "Those doors don't have locks."

I whirl around. "What do you mean?"

"There aren't any locks on the bedroom doors," Beckan repeats as he heads back up the stairs. "Maybe the door's jammed?"

"But the knob won't turn." I'm barely keeping my panic at bay. I try turning the knob again and push against the door, willing it to open, but it doesn't budge.

"Rosie, I want to come out," Liam says. "I want out now!"

"I know squiggle worm," I say as calmly as I can. "The door's just stuck. Don't worry. We'll get you out in a minute."

"Let me try," Beckan says. I move out of his way, glancing at Mother. Her sweater is wrapped tightly around her body and her lips are sealed in a straight line. Her worry is carefully controlled on the outside, but I know panic rules on the inside.

Beckan tries turning the knob, but it doesn't give even the slightest bit. Not one to give up easily, he tries a few more times, even pushing his weight into the old wooden door, before taking a step back and staring at it, perplexed.

"I want out!" Liam cries.

"Sit tight, buddy," Beckan says reassuringly.

"What do you think?"

"It's like every time I try to turn the knob or push on the door… it pushes back." I see the worry in his eyes. We both know the door isn't stuck. Something is holding my brother hostage in his room.

"Liam?" Beckan says.

"Yeah?" I can hear the tears in Liam's voice and my heart sinks further into the chasm of my soul. I'm a terrible sister.

"Go sit on your bed okay?" Beckan says. "I'm goin' tah push on the door real hard, but I don't want you tah get hit when it opens."

"Okay." Liam's heavy footsteps retreat.

Beckan steps back to the railing and then throws his weight into the door as hard as he can. I flinch at the thump of his shoulder beating the door, but it doesn't give. He throws his weight into the door again and again, each time my body twitching from the sheer force he's applying. Why isn't the door opening?

The sound of splitting wood fills the air. Beckan throws his body into the door with renewed energy. Sweat breaks out on his forehead. He's throwing every pound of his body into the door as hard as he can but it doesn't yield to his strength. He hits it ten or eleven times before the wood finally gives, but the door doesn't open. Instead, Beckan punches a hole the size of his shoulder in it ala Jack Nicolson in *The Shining*.

"Hey buddy," Beckan says, looking at Liam though the hole. "Don't worry. We're going tah get you out." He reaches an arm in through the opening and tries to turn the knob from the inside, but it still won't turn. "You just sit tight, Liam. We're right heeah."

"Okay," Liam says, quietly wiping snot on his sleeve.

Beckan turns to me. "I'm goin' tah have tah get my tools. We'll have tah take it off the hinges."

"What?" Mother finally remembers her voice. "Are you kidding?"

"I'm sorry Mrs. Delaney," he says with a shrug. "I don't see what else we can do without destroyin' the door completely." Beckan disappears briefly and returns, working on the hinges, unscrewing each one as quickly as he can.

Beckan removes the last screw. The door abruptly flies downward with a deafening *SLAM* against the wood floor, the sound reverberating through the foyer like a crack of thunder. Beckan barely gets out of the way before he's swatted like a housefly.

"Must've been a draft," Mother offers quietly.

Liam sits on his bed, dried tear tracks trailing down his face, as Beckan approaches him. "You okay buddy?"

Liam nods silently.

I'm close behind Beckan and wrap Liam in a tight hug, more to comfort myself than him. "I'm sorry about all the yelling. Mommy and I, we just lost our tempers for a minute, but everything's okay. Mommy isn't going anywhere. I'm not going anywhere. I'm really sorry." I kiss his forehead and squeeze him a little tighter.

"What about Beckan?" Liam asks.

"Beckan?" I release Liam and glance at Beckan. He stands awkwardly in the doorway.

"Yeah. Is he going anywhere?"

"Of course not," Beckan answers. "I mean, I do have tah get home tah my own bed, but I'll be back tomorrow. I promise." Our eyes meet but I look away as my cheeks burn.

"Okay kiddo?" I say, squeezing Liam's shoulders.

"I'm hungry."

$$*\qquad\qquad *\qquad\qquad *$$

After all the excitement dies down and Beckan leaves, I make Liam a quick snack before putting him to bed. As it turns out, he's not starving. He apparently ate dinner while Mother was downing shots and I was putzing around on the Internet. I'm both surprised and unnerved by how easily my brother, a mere five years old, is able to get on without me all of a sudden.

For once, Liam doesn't fight bedtime. Crying always saps the energy out of him and so far as he knows, the earlier incident is as simple as a swollen door and a drafty house, which will hopefully keep the nightmares away.

I make a perfunctory attempt to clean my room, all the while mulling over my eventful evening. I can't believe Beckan's mother died in my house. It's impossible to believe I told Beckan about Dad. I hadn't even talked about it with my best friend back in Texas when it happened. I closed myself up like a fan, keeping the outside world on the other side of an imaginary wall. If it weren't for Liam, I would've retreated into myself completely.

I try explaining away both incidents – my ransacked room and Liam's door – but nothing makes sense. A strong draft? Only if my bedroom has its own atmosphere. Did Liam ransack my room, maybe angry for not paying him more attention? Could a draft really be responsible for Liam's door? I don't think so; even the kind of draft that occasionally pushes a door closed wouldn't have kept Liam's door sealed so tightly that it couldn't be opened. What did Beckan say? Every time he pushed against the door, he felt something *pushing back*. Liam couldn't have done that, no matter how tubby he is. Besides, he's more marshmallow than muscle anyway.

When I see it's after eleven thirty, I sigh with exasperation. I haven't made so much as a dent in the mess around me, but I'm exhausted. I clear space on the bed and fall asleep almost instantly.

I dream of the house in black and white; the way I've always felt I should see it since I first laid eyes on it. I see it from outside. I'm standing a little ways down the mountain.

Rose...

Great storm clouds fill the emptiness behind it with flashes of white lightning and cracks of thunder.

Rose...

The great turrets loom over me, giant knives on the hill.

Rose, let me in.

The stained glass windows, lit with a flickering glow, glower down at me like angry eyes.

Let me in... Let. Me. In.

The rotting front steps frown at me like a toothless black bear.

LET ME IN.

The red doors, the only part of my dream in color, glare down at me. They're a bright, vibrant crimson that melts onto the porch, blood spilling toward me.

LET. ME. IN.

The porch lights on either side of the doors come to life. Slowly the doors begin to part. They *grrrrooooaaann* open, revealing the impenetrable darkness that rules within.

LET. ME. IN. ROSE.

I wake with a start. My breath is caught in my throat. My shirt clings to my sweaty skin. It's after three a.m. and my room is bathed in the faint moonlight drifting through the windows.

I'm cold and wrap my arms around myself, realizing I'm still fully dressed.

From the foyer, comes a startling sound.

Thump, thump, thump.

A cold chill raises goose bumps along my arms and legs. I get up. I edge toward my closed bedroom door, carefully navigating around my belongings still strewn around.

Thump, thump, thump.

I open the door with a slow *creeeeeaaaak* and peer into the dark hall. No, it isn't dark. Where I expect darkness is a soft yellow light. Where's the light coming from?

Thump, thump, thump.

The further into the hall I venture, the louder the sound becomes. Peering around the corner and down the staircase, all of my questions are answered.

At the bottom of the stairs, the two blood red doors stand wide open, bouncing back into the walls in a breeze with a *thump, thump, thump.* The porch lights emit the yellow light spilling through the doorway. Beyond them, all is impervious darkness.

Chapter Sixteen
Ghost Hunters

"Would you like a ride?" Beckan meets us on the porch the next morning. His eyes lock on me as I zip Liam's jacket and send him into the cool morning mist.

"Sure." I allow Beckan a small smile, still embarrassed about his window into the dysfunctional Delaney household last night.

"How are you?" He picks up Liam's bookbag and lets him run ahead to the truck, keeping his eyes trained on mine.

"Okay, I guess." I say, stifling a yawn. "Tired." Lifting my backpack and closing the heavy door behind me takes more effort than usual.

"You look it," he says. When I raise an eyebrow, he backpedals. "No offense. I didn't mean that th-the way it s-sounded." He laughs. "Sorry."

"It's okay. I'm a little irritable anyway," I say with a wave of my hand. "I'm sorry about all that business last night between me and Mother. It's been a while since we had a good screaming match. I guess we were due." A blast of icy wind nearly knocks me off of my feet as I descend the front steps. "Thanks for the lift today. It got cold!"

The chill arrived suddenly overnight. I'm wearing pants for the first time in months, and a jacket for the first time in recent memory.

"Yeah, we'll be gettin' a storm in the next day or so I suppose. No worries 'bout all the othah stuff. Everythin' okay aftah I left?" Beckan pulls the passenger door open.

I look at Liam, all smiles after a tough night, and shake my head. I haven't decided if I want to tell anyone about my dream or the strangeness of the open doors – which I know I locked behind Beckan last night – and I'm certainly not going to talk about it in front of Liam. Beckan doesn't push it.

Silence floods the cab of the truck until we reach the bottom of the hill, where Letta waits for me. Her dark hair is loose today, blowing around her like a black tornado. I look at the small bench seat in the truck. There isn't much room left, but Letta's petite.

"Can we pick up Letta?" I ask. "She looks cold."

"It'll be a tight squeeze." Beckan slows to a stop next to her and rolls down his window. "Want tah hop in?"

"There's room!" I shout over the roar of the diesel engine.

Letta smiles and runs around to the passenger side as Beckan rolls up his window. I scoot over, feeling Beckan's warmth through the sleeve of my thin jacket. Though it's cooler today, I notice he wears only a short-sleeved flannel shirt. Liam squeezes close to me on the other side as Letta hops in.

"Thanks!" She swings the door closed and pushes several wild strands of hair out of her face. "The wind's really picked up. I guess we're about due for a storm."

"I love thunderstorms!" Liam shouts, his angelic voice loud in the small cab.

"Me too!" Letta gives Liam a high five and he giggles. "So, how's it going?"

"Erm..." I say.

"Aah..." says Beckan.

"I got locked in my room!" Liam shouts with such exuberance one might think he actually enjoyed it.

Letta smiles at Liam, then looks at me and then Beckan, while we both concentrate on the road. Sensing the sudden tenseness in the air, she changes the subject. "Um... So have you decided about cheerleading tryouts? They're only a day away..."

"Crap!" I smack my forehead. "I didn't talk to Mother about it yet. Maybe tonight." The cheerleading tryout information has been on the announcements every week since school started. I've been meaning to ask Mother for weeks, but don't know how to bring it up. With all the excitement last night, I'd completely forgotten about it.

"Cheerleadin'?" Beckan sounds surprised. Or disappointed. I can't tell which, and I'm bothered.

"Yeah. Why? Are Port Braseham's cheerleaders really bad?"

He shrugs. "I've no idear. They're like cheerleaders anywhere else, I guess: shallow, dramatic followahs. They're just pretty attention hogs with too much makeup. You don't seem the type." He couldn't have sounded more condescending if he tried.

"Tell me how you really feel," Letta laughs.

I prickle, careful to keep my own heavily painted face blank, if only because everything Beckan says is true. But cheerleading is more than that to me. It's a sport; it requires talent and adrenaline, practice and determination. It makes me feel alive, being tossed into the air and flipping across a field like a skipped stone.

"Not all cheerleaders fall into your neat little stereotype," I snap. When our eyes meet as he glances away from the road, anger flares up inside me. "It's a sport, like any other." I'm not about to admit to him I'd been every bit of the stereotypical cheerleader he describes. I'm almost more determined to join the team now, just to spite him.

He snorts. "Maybe back in Texas. I just don't think you're goin' tah like it as much heeah."

"I'll be the judge of that if you don't mind." I cross my arms and look away from him. From the corner of my eye, I see Letta stifling laughter.

The frosty silence becomes another passenger in the crowded cab. The truck comes up on three figures stalking along the edge of the road. They huddle together, trying to protect themselves from the wind.

"Hey, it's Shane, Eileen and Patty," Letta says. "Wave at the icicles everyone!"

We wave at the three red faces scrunched close together. Shane smiles and gives us the finger.

"They're sooo jealous," Letta laughs.

A minute later we're turning into the school's parking lot. Liam is the first one out as Beckan screeches to a halt, crawling over Letta in his unapologetic and monkey-like manner. I grab the hood of his jacket before I let him totter off. I double-check his jacket is zipped and advise him there's no reason to go telling everyone he was locked in his room last night. The last thing we need is more strange stares from people who feel their beliefs in ghouls are confirmed by my brother's exaggerated version of events.

I ignore Beckan as he waves us off, and we take shelter from the stinging wind inside. Letta saves her attack until I'm bent over inside my locker.

"Alright, spill it!"

"Huh? Spill what?" I try to concentrate on my schedule. What do I have today? History or math? Both?

"You made out with Beckan didn't you!" Letta shouts.

I smile awkwardly at a couple of other early arrivals, looking curiously in our direction. "First of all, keep your voice down.

Second of all, I most certainly did not!" I feel the heat of a blush coming to my cheeks as I stuff a binder into my bookbag.

"Well something's going on," Letta insists with a jabbing finger. "There was way too much tension in that truck for there to be nothing going on between you two. Don't tell me he's finally melted that icy exterior of yours."

"It's personal." I want to tell Letta what happened, but I don't want to tell her in front of all the prying eyes and ears of my classmates. When I finally close my locker, Letta's wearing her best puppy-dog-face, withering away my resolve.

"Alright, come on." I grab Letta's arm and drag her into the nearest girls' bathroom.

"Out with it," Letta says the second the door falls shut, "or I'm going to die of impatience."

"Don't repeat this okay?" Letta nods encouragingly, pretending to lock her lips with an invisible key, which she then places in a pocket.

"Remember the file I told you about a while ago?" I say. "There was an article in there about a woman who died in my house several years ago, but there weren't any details. I asked Beckan about it last night, and he told me it was *his mother.*"

"Shut up!"

"Yeah. Anyway, so I dunno, I had a moment of sympathy I guess." I roll my eyes. "A moment of weakness."

"And you kissed him!" Letta hisses. "I knew it!"

"What? No! No. What's your obsession with making out with Beckan?"

"You have to ask?"

"Anyway," I continue, "after he told me what happened to his mother, I told him..." I sigh. Am I really about to talk about Dad's suicide to another person in the same twenty-four hour period? "I told him what happened to my dad."

In a hushed tone, I tell Letta about Dad and the conversation between me and Beckan. Once I start, I can't stop, and I tell Letta all about the argument with Mother and my near death of embarrassment that it happened in front of Beckan. I tell Letta how my room was ransacked, how Liam was locked in his room, and last of all, I relate my dream and the open doors in the middle of the night. Letta frowns and gasps and throws her hands over her mouth in all the right places.

"Well, you had a quite a night," she says when I'm finally done.

"That's an understatement."

"Do you really think a ghost ransacked your room and locked Liam in his?"

"Ugh! I wish I knew what I believed! Every time I'm determined to believe it's just a drafty old house, something crazy happens and I question reality. What am I *supposed* to believe?"

Letta shrugs. "What about the doors? Your dream?"

I shrug back. "I *know* I locked the doors. I'm positive. How they opened–"

"After a creepy dream about something trying to get in..."

"–I have no idea." I stifle a shiver. "I don't know what happened and I don't know what to do."

"Obviously, it's time for a more thorough investigation," Letta says.

"What do you mean?"

Letta begins to list off items. "Search the house from top to bottom. Research. Ouija Boards. A séance or something. A conversation with all the superstitious old people living around here. They've gotta know something."

I remember the cool hand on my shoulder my first week in the house. It still feels fresh. "I don't know, Letta. What if we stir something up?"

"That's the fun part," Letta says. "Come on. I'll help. We can do it this weekend. It'll be like an episode of *Ghost Hunters!*"

I can't help but laugh at Letta's enthusiasm, but as I do, I notice I'm not the only one.

We turn around to find Mary Donovan exiting the last stall. She smiles at us with mock sweetness, her perfect teeth nearly blinding me. "Ghost hunters? Not enough going on in your social life, huh, Ghost Slut? How sad." She's distracted by her reflection, admiring it in the dingy mirror. Not a hair, eyelash, or eyebrow is out of place.

I hate her.

When Mary's finished congratulating herself on her own beauty, she eyes me carefully, as if evaluating me, and I feel naked.

"Have a nice day, ladies," Mary says sweetly, brushing by us, bumping into my shoulder on the way out. I glare after her.

"Well," Letta says. "Shit."

Chapter Seventeen
The Sullen Boy

I slink to homeroom and sit as far away from Mary as possible. Unfortunately, this doesn't hide the giggles and stares of Mary's girlfriends, whom she's obviously told what she overheard in the bathroom. I can only imagine the rumors she's starting.

Ghost Slut loves the O'Dwyre boy.
Ghost Slut thinks she's a detective.
Ghost Slut thinks she can get rid of the ghouls.
Ghost Slut, what an idiot!

The news spreads like a wild fire, and like a game of telephone, none of the rumors remotely resemble the truth by the time Mary and her friends are finished. The only blessing so far is Ms. Brennan's lack of comment suggests she approves of my skinny jeans and long sleeved t-shirt. After attendance and announcements, I bolt from the room and head straight to English.

The sullen blonde boy from homeroom and history – Adam – sits by the window again. Every day, he gazes out as if lost in the midst of a bad memory he can't escape. He's an outcast, never interacting with anyone, although I can't be sure if his status is voluntary or not. I really don't feel like being surrounded by people who keep staring at me or treating me like I have something contagious today. Maybe Adam will let me sit near him and I can some have peace for once.

"Is it okay if I sit here?" I ask, pointing to the seat in front of him. I'm not sure why I'm asking his permission. Texas Rose would've just sat down, flung her hair in his face and ignored him. Who am I turning into? Adam doesn't answer me, doesn't even acknowledge me. The room is filling up with other students, so I take the seat.

I make it through English easily. I even raise my hand and offer my thoughts during a discussion on the greatest authors of all time. Of course I found a way to bring up Jane Austen and Shakespeare. Another girl raises her hand to say Suzanne Collins, a modern author who's changing the face of young adult literature, should be considered for the list. It starts a fun little debate and Mrs. Clancy seems to appreciate my contributions, which makes me feel a little better.

I'm gathering my things after the bell when Adam mutters behind me. I have no idea if he's talking to me or to himself because he stares at the floor, like he's talking to his shoes.

"I don't talk to anyone and no one talks to me." His voice is so soft and quiet I barely hear him. "And that's the way I like it." He zips out of the room the second his mouth closes, leaving me confused.

Chemistry is about as boring as it can get. Mr. McLoughlin presents information about stoichiometry in a mindless drone so monotonous that he nearly lulls me to sleep.

I'm glad to see Letta and the others at lunch. The wind outside has picked up and the temperature has dropped, so I can't hide from Mary or Ronan outside today.

"Uh-oh." Shane has a French fry perched on his bottom lip. He's peering over my head from his seat between Eileen and Patty. "Make sure you get him in the face this time. Heeah, take my cherry cobblah."

Letta turns. "Uh, great." I don't have to turn around to know who's approaching, but I do anyway.

Ronan strides across the cafeteria with Mary strutting on his arm like royalty. He looks good today. His shaggy hair has a little gel in it and it's combed just right, so it looks like he's just rolled out of bed and styled it perfectly at the same time. Mary, of course, is stunning standing next to him. Obviously, they're a couple. How could they not be? Zeus and his Aphrodite. Darcy and his Elizabeth. The certain Prom King and his Queen.

They're both throwing fake smiles at me, and I'm immediately wary. I haven't talked to Ronan since I painted his shirt with my lunch. They'd let me rest for a few weeks, but now it's their turn in this little game of high school politics we play.

"Hi, Rose," Ronan says. "Mind if we sit?" Asking is a formality; he's already sitting as he asks, shoving Patty into Shane and Eileen, forcing them to scoot down to make room for Ronan and Mary, looking perturbed.

"How are you today?" Mary asks with a knowing smile.

"What do you want?" I ask bluntly. I almost cross my arms, but remembering how Beckan mocked my body language, keep my hands in my lap.

Ronan laughs. "Straight to the point," he says. "I like that." If I hadn't been carefully watching Mary, I would've missed the tiny daggers behind her big brown eyes.

"Really, Ronan," Letta says. "Spit it out before we vomit over all this fake sweetness."

"Shut up, Anne Frank," he says so venomously, I'm a little taken aback. He checks himself quickly, and the ugly anger that had suddenly overcome his features relaxes into a serene calm.

"Look," Ronan smiles again. "Let's start over okay? I'll forget about my dry cleaning bill if you forget about my rude behavior. There's no reason we can't get along."

"Wanna bet?" Shane whispers under his breath.

"What he's trying to say," Mary says, finally breaking her curt silence, "is we'd like to invite you to the Storm Party." I notice Mary and Ronan don't suffer from the same accent as everyone else around here. Each word is carefully enunciated, like the automated voice telling you not to leave your bags unattended at the airport. Mary sounds like the realtor, Mrs. Carroll. I wonder how many diction lessons she'd needed. I'm betting the reason has something to do with beauty pageants. She's probably Miss Maine Maple Moose three years running.

"Storm party?"

"We throw a little party every year just before the first big storm leading up to Christmas," says Mary.

"We?"

"The kids in town," Ronan says. "The adults always treat the storms as some kind of bad omen, but we use it as an excuse to throw a wicked party."

The nods of my friends confirm this isn't a trap for Stephen King's *Carrie*, as I'd suspected. "Alright," I say. "Where and when is this *wicked* party supposed to be?" The thought of attending nauseates me, but it's the perfect place to be seen. Hopefully, it'll help others realize I'm not a leper.

"Midnight Friday," Mary says, "but the location stays secret until right before so the parents don't find out."

Ronan pulls out his cell phone and my face immediately flushes. "Give me your number. I'll text you the location Friday night."

"I don't have a cell phone," I say, embarrassed. Mary finds this humorous, but Ronan smiles.

"An old fashioned girl," he says. "Ain't that cunnin'."

"Here." Letta throws a balled up napkin at Ronan and Mary. "There's *my* number. Text me. We already have plans," she says as she puts an arm around my shoulders, "but we'll try to make it if we can. I assume all of the kingdom's subjects are invited."

"The more the merrier," Mary says, but her tone clearly indicates the opposite.

"Lookin' forward to it." Ronan stands and takes Mary's hand.

"Oh, by the way," Mary says as she gets up, "rumor has it you were a cheerleader in Texas. True?"

"True," I say confidently.

"I assume I'll see you at tryouts tomorrow then? Should be…interesting," she says, eying me critically. "Don't forget to hide your cankles."

They strut back to their table, but Ronan chances a smile and a wink over his shoulder.

"Chumps." Shane says, curling his lip in disgust.

"You don't want tah go tah the party?" Patty asks, disappointed.

"Oh, of course I'm goin'," he says simply.

"Have you guys been before?" I ask.

"Of course," Eileen says with a wave of her hand. "It's not that exclusive. It's just a bunch of kids partyin' in someone's barn. Anyone can go."

"And what plans will I be breaking to attend said storm party?" I raise an eyebrow at Letta.

"Oh I dunno," Letta says. "I just didn't want him to think you were so easily available."

"And?" I say, sensing there's more.

"We thought Friday night might be a good time tah play detectives at your house," Patty says. "What's more fun than a ghost search the night of the first storm?"

"Ah," I say as the other shoe drops. "Sure. I guess. I'm sure Mother'll be out. I don't know what to do with Liam though. I don't want him around for that."

"Let me talk to my parents," Letta offers. "I bet I can get them to babysit. They love kids."

And just like that, I'm ready to celebrate a weekend in Port Braseham with my new friends, a few ghosts, and maybe a party. I'm finally starting to feel a little less out of my element. About damn time.

*　　　　　*　　　　　*

Walking home with my friends, I remember the sullen boy, Adam, and what he said in English.

"Hey, do you guys know that blonde boy, Adam? Looks kinda sad all the time?"

"The lost puppy?" Shane says. "What 'bout him?"

"What's his story?"

"What do you mean?" Patty asks.

"Well, he's a little odd, isn't he?" I say. "Today in English, I asked if I could sit next to him."

"And he ignored you right?" Eileen says. "That's normal. He keeps tah himself. Kids used tah bully him a lot, but then he just stopped respondin' and ignored them completely. The other kids got bored. I guess he figured it worked so well, he'd ignore everythin' all the time."

"When was that?"

"Two years ago maybe?" Eileen replies.

"Wow." I feel bad for him. "Is that why he's so miserable?"

"I'm sure that's part of it," Patty says, "but I think there's more tah it."

"You mean about the house?" Letta says and Patty nods.

I feel the pit reopening in my belly. "Please tell me you aren't talking about my house."

"Sorry," Patty frowns. "His grandmother tried tah burn it down back in the seventies."

"Really?" I'm surprised by the connection. "Enit or something?"

"Yeah, Enit O'Sullivan. She was a stranger 'round heeah so far as anyone knew – until she tried tah burn the house down," Patty explains. "Then, when they tried to commit her, her daughter, Adam's mother, moved up heeah tah take care of her. The townspeople didn't like that much. They wanted her out of town, but for whatevah reason, she's been determined tah stay evah since."

"What about Adam's dad?"

Eileen shrugs. "He's out of the picture."

"Huh." I hug myself in my light jacket to keep the cold out. "I wonder what Ol' Enit's story is."

"You could ask her." Letta nods across the street. "She's over there, staring right at us."

I follow Letta's eyes to a strange old woman with milky eyes. With a gasp of recognition, I realize Enit O'Sullivan was the woman in The Wharf Rat. She's walking down the sidewalk, back into town.

"Can she see us?"

"I doubt it," Shane says. "She's been blind for years. Even if she could, nothin' lucid has made it out of her mouth since the fire. At least that's what Pop says."

"She comes intah town all the time," Eileen says knowingly. "Likes tah stop people and say crazy things."

"Like what?"

"The end is nigh Rose Delaney!" Letta's voice is low and ghostly, and she holds out her hands like a zombie. Then she laughs. "She just likes to stir up trouble. I feel bad for her though. I think she really believes she's psychic somehow. That's why they say she tried to burn the house down. She knew all the evil it had done and all the evil it would do."

The conversation dies down after that, and we walk on in silence. I don't have to turn around to know Enit's cloudy eyes are looking at my back. I can feel them looking right through me.

Chapter Eighteen
It's On

The O'Dwyre cabin is dark and their truck is gone. When I get home, there's a shiny new deadbolt on the front door. Liam is at the kitchen table with a coloring book and a snack while Beckan kneels at the backdoor, installing another lock. He looks up and smiles when at me.

Seeing Beckan reminds me how he insulted cheerleading this morning. Boy-crazy sheep painted up like prostitutes. Well, those weren't his actual words, but that's what he meant. His attack on cheerleading feels like an attack on me. The door I'd opened last night slams shut, and I shove the emotions I shared with him back down into the abyss where they belong. He insulted the only thing I'm any good at besides ballet, and I don't see any ballet troops hanging around school. I haven't even seen a dance studio around town.

"Hey squiggle worm." I say, tousling Liam's reddish brown mop and glancing down at his coloring book. "What're you coloring?"

Liam shrugs. "I dunno." Looking down at Liam's messy colors outside the lines, I'm not sure what he's coloring either. It looks an awful lot like Jesus holding Aladdin's lamp. I flip the coloring book to the front and read the title.

"The Parables of Jesus?"

"They gave it to me at school."

"Of course they did," I mutter. Haven't these people heard of separation of church and state?

"Did you manage to keep your food on your plate today?" Beckan calls over from the back door. A strong gust of wind pushes its way into the kitchen, slapping the screen door open and closed. "I heard the local royalty joined you for lunch again."

"You almost done?" I say impatiently, ignoring his question. "It's freezing in here."

Beckan bristles and huffs into his five o'clock shadow. He picks up a few tools, sliding them back into his tool bag, and stands. "Your locks have been installed, your highness." He slams several keys on the counter. "You're welcome." He looks me over, a little hurt and a little mad, but says nothing more. He waves goodbye to Liam before stalking out the back door.

"Are you fighting?" Liam asks without looking up from his book, his voice sullen.

"No," I reply in a clipped voice.

"You're both mad," he says. "I can tell."

"It's nothing to worry about." I hug him loosely from behind his chair. "We're not fighting. I promise." It's not really a lie. It isn't a real fight until someone starts yelling or throws something; at least that's how fights work in the Delaney family.

There's still a few hours until Mother gets home (unless there's another "happy hour"). I drop my backpack, still slung over my shoulder, into one of the kitchen chairs.

"Mind if I join you?" I slide out the chair across from Liam and set to work on some Latin conjugations.

I work intently, moving on to English and then math. I'm doing everything I can to get cheerleading off my brain, although Beckan keeps popping up more than cheers and pom-poms. I hardly notice when Liam disappears to watch television and don't hear Mother come in.

"Hi honey."

I jump and turn to see Mother setting her purse on the counter. Glancing at my watch, I see she's home right on time, and my muscles loosen. If Mother's home instead of at the bar, she probably had a good day.

My customary behavior toward Mother after an argument like last night's is an icy silence and dirty looks, but tonight I want something, so I force a smile and play nice, testing the waters.

"How was your day?"

"Okay," Mother says, sighing. For a minute, she puts her head in her hands and closes her eyes.

"Really?" I ask, an eyebrow raised.

"Another headache." She smiles at me wearily. "How was your day?"

So, Mother's choosing to forget about last night. Fine by me. "Fine. Plenty of homework to keep me busy." I motion to the papers and books spread across the table.

"Well, let's do something about dinner, shall we?" Mother brightens up. "I'm feeling some homemade pizza tonight. How 'bout it?"

"Sure." I gather my things and slide them back into my bag. "I'll help."

Mother and I work in the kitchen, rolling the dough and making the sauce. Liam, drawn by the aroma, comes in and helps too. He giggles as Mother, in a rare moment of silliness, throws the dough into the air a few times. She doesn't even get angry when she drops it on the floor. She just picks it up and dusts it off with a light "Oops!" The air in the house is so light and happy. I almost change my mind about cheerleading just so it can stay that way.

As we sit to eat, I'm trying to decide what to bring up first, cheerleading or Friday night.

"So, um, Mother," I say as I chew a bite of pizza. She looks at me with a smile, waiting. "I was invited to a party on Friday."

"Oh?" Mother sounds pleased her disgruntled daughter has made friends. "That's good news!"

I stare at Mother and she stares back. I don't want to ask her if she'll be out on Friday. The implications are obvious; Mother'll be out at a bar if she's out at all. I don't want to offend her, but I don't want to invoke my own anger if Mother does plan to be out drinking. And what about Letta and the others coming over? I can't snoop around if Mother's home. I flick my eyes to Liam, happily playing with his food.

"Well, as it happens, I've been invited out on Friday as well." Mother puts her arm around Liam. "What are we going to do with you, kiddo?" She tickles his neck lightly, trying to keep him from realizing his whole family will be out without him. Since Dad died, we're always careful to make sure Liam never feels abandoned.

"Actually, my friend Letta," I say, "lives at the bottom of the hill. She said her parents like kids and maybe they could babysit Liam on Friday."

"Oh, so you've planned this all out already, have you?" Mother's irritation is carefully hidden inside the lightness of her voice, her arm still around Liam's shoulders. I don't reply.

"Well," she says, "I'll have to meet Letta's parents. We can't leave Liam with perfect strangers."

But it's totally okay to leave him for hours with the O'Dwyres, two people we barely know, one of them an incoherent ape, and the other an inconsiderate jerk.

"Maybe we can take a walk down the hill when I get home tomorrow if it isn't too cold." Mother forces a tight smile. She doesn't like what I've arranged, but it doesn't' bother her enough to cancel her plans – or mine. "Make introductions and such."

"Well, actually..." I hesitate. I've already scored one win; is it worth trying for two? Do I want to be on the cheerleading team badly enough to risk another fight and upset Liam again? I decide I do. I've been dragged to this stupid town, but that doesn't mean I have to give up who I am or what I enjoy.

"Out with it," Mother says, and this time Liam perks up, looking at me instead of his plate.

"Cheerleading try outs are tom –"

"No." Mother interrupts. "Absolutely not." Her sharp look tells me arguing is useless, but I'm not giving up so easily.

"Why not?"

"What do you mean why not, Rose?" Mother says incredulously. She sets her pizza slice down so she can lecture me properly. "Have you forgotten what happened?"

"Of course not," I say as my cheeks get hot. "But that was different. It was a fight. It wasn't about cheerleading."

"It doesn't matter what it was about, Rose. You knocked a girl to the ground and stomped on her head over a boy. Just thinking about it reminds me how ridiculous – The poor girl was in the hospital with a serious concussion for nearly a week. I had to pay her medical bills!"

Actually, it wasn't *just* about a boy. It was about Jack Sterne, the quarterback, my desire to be his prom queen, and that slut, Isabella Brown, I'd had to compete with for what was certainly my head cheerleader right. Isabella was the one who made a pass at Jack right in front of me at a party the night before The Incident, shooting me a coy smile and winking her fake eyelashes at me. Isabella started the cattiness and she deserved what she got as far as I'm concerned. Also, *I'm* the one who paid the girl's medical bills from the small savings I'd made teaching ballet at the community center. I don't have a dime left – but now isn't the time to point out these distinctions.

"Mother," I plead, "I don't disagree that my behavior was...regrettable." I've always regretted the consequences of that famous stomp, but I still feel a certain satisfaction when I remember the sensation of Isabella's skull under my sneaker. It's an impulse my anger management counselor said was unhealthy, and I should do my best to quash it, but in this moment, I allow myself this one small satisfaction. "You can't keep holding that against me. It was one incident totally separated from cheerleading. A mistake. It just *happened* to occur at a cheerleading event, and the other girl just *happened* to be a cheerleader."

"That may be, but I'm not letting you get back into that whole scene," Mother says. "Those cheerleaders were snotty, selfish drama queens who liked making you squirm. And you were the same way. You've always been drawn to drama, and cheerleading fed that. The point in coming here, to this," she rolls her eyes toward the ceiling, "this pinhead of a place was for you – for all of us – to start fresh. And I'm not risking that just for you to shake your but around at football games."

"Mother –"

"Rose, this isn't a debate. The answer is no." She sighs and forces a smile. "Why can't you get back into ballet? You're such a beautiful dancer."

I laugh. "And where exactly should I do that, Mother? There aren't any dance studios in this hellhole!"

"Watch your language." For a moment, I see the old Mrs. Delaney trying to take over. I watch Mother's finger twitch and begin tapping, like she's stifling the urge to reach out and slap me. She probably is. "Maybe there's a studio in a neighboring town."

"And how would I get there?" I'm struggling to control my voice and my anger. "You plannin' to give me the keys to the car?"

"Not with that attitude, young lady." She sighs again, calming herself. "This discussion is over. I'm sorry, but my answer is no to cheerleading, and that's final. Maybe if you weren't such a hothead, and were more responsible with your decisions, you wouldn't be in this mess. Food for thought, honey." Mother picks up her pizza slice and nudges Liam with an elbow. "How was your day, kiddo?"

Dismissing me like that only makes me angrier. I listen to Mother coax Liam out of his pout without actually hearing her words. *And that's final.* Those words keep appearing in front of my eyes as red mist. *Final.* Something about those words flips a switch somewhere deep inside me. The heat of my anger wells up and I think, Final my ass. I'm going to those tryouts, dammit. I'm going to make the team and show these small town snots what real cheerleading looks like.

Oh, it's *on,* Mother, I think as I push a piece of pepperoni around my plate. It's *so* on.

I leave Liam and Mother at the table and stomp up to my room, making as much noise as possible, and slam the door behind me. I almost forgot about my tornado-damaged room, and now I moan in frustration.

I bend down to pick up some clothes and slowly begin putting my room back together, hoping it'll distract me. I have the great desire to vent, but I'm not going to call Letta from the hall phone and risk being overheard. I know Beckan would have something encouraging or reassuring to tell me, but I'm also certain he's in no mood to say it, and I don't care to hear it from him anyway. I desperately wish I had my cell phone. The desire is almost strong enough to make me wish I hadn't knocked Isabella down and smashed her face into the squeaky clean wood of the basketball court. Almost.

Chapter Nineteen
Some Days Just Aren't Your Day

Mother gives Liam his bath and puts him to bed because I refuse to leave my room or even open the door when she knocks. After they're both in their rooms, I walk through the darkened house and triple check that everything's locked up tight, especially the front doors. I slide the stiff new deadbolt into place myself, and turn off the porch lights. When I go up to bed, there's only the faint glow of the light over the stove in the kitchen to show me the way.

I have the dream again. This time the house is larger, more imposing on my antlike size. The rumble of the thunder is a freight train in my ears and the explosion of lightning burns my retinas.

The red doors invite me closer, pull my feet up the mountain. The porch light winks on and beckons to me. My tangled black hair is thrown back in a burst of wind, and suddenly I'm standing before the glaring red doors, bathed in the black and white light of the porch light.

Let me in, Rose.

My hand reaches for one of the gleaming handles.

Open the doors, Rose. Let me in.

I start awake, sitting up in bed and looking around. As my eyes adjust, I see everything is as it should be. In my room...

I get up and go into the hall, the wood floors cold on my bare feet. Peering down into the foyer, I see the front doors are still closed, the deadbolt keeping the inside in – and the outside out. As I'm about to retreat to my room, I hear Liam's sweet voice from behind his door. I can't hear what he's saying, but I hear his laughter clearly.

"Liam?"

Beckan had also installed a new door on Liam's room while we were at school. It's a lighter wood and it doesn't match the rest of the house. I now find myself tapping lightly on it. It sounds hollow, less sturdy than the solid oak of my door. "Liam, are you awake?" I call, opening the door.

Liam's marshmallow shape is tucked neatly under the covers. He lays on his side, his back to the door. I can barely make out the rise and fall of his breaths as he sleeps. Although everything seems normal, I have the distinct feeling I've just missed something. Like maybe Liam was sitting up in his bed right before I opened the door, and is only feigning sleep now. I can't quite put my finger on why. Are his breaths too close together for sleep? Are his covers pulled a little too tightly under his chin? With the uneasy feeling dogging me, I close the door and return to my room.

I lay awake for the next hour, trying to sleep and failing, and a terrible feeling creeps over me. My anger tightens in my throat. A wave of depression comes over me and with it the fleeting image of my father, lifeless under a tub full of bloody water, fills my eyes. I cry myself to sleep.

*   *   *

I can't shake sleep off the next morning. My eyes feel swollen. My tongue is a dry beached whale on the sands of my mouth, and my muscles protest with aches and pains, like my body was up to no good while I was asleep. I don't budge when my alarm goes off and it's Liam who eventually rouses me.

"Rosie!" He yanks my covers. "Rosie, get up!"

"Go get ready," I slur and pull a pillow over my head. "Ask Mommy to get you breakfast. I need a few more minutes."

"Mommy isn't here."

"What?" I squint in the light coming through the windows. "Why not?"

"Because she had to go to work."

I shoot out of bed. "Oh my God! What time is it? Dammit! I can't believe–" I'm searching for a reason to blame Mother, but can't find one. I look at Liam. He's dressed himself in a t-shirt with a muddied brown chocolate stain down the front, shorts despite the cold weather, and two different shoes, but matching socks. "We're so late! Quick, go and change. I'll be right there to help you."

"What's wrong with these clothes?"

"Go, Liam!" Liam runs out of the room and I throw on the first outfit I find and run down the hall as the phone starts ringing.

I grab the phone with annoyance. "Hello?"

"Hey, it's Letta. I'm down at the bottom of the hill. I was starting to worry. You really need a cell phone."

"Hey, sorry. I overslept. I'm so late. You'll have to go without me if you don't want to be late too."

"What about you?"

"I'll figure it out, I guess." I drop the phone without saying goodbye and go help Liam, who's now trying to pull on his Spiderman Halloween costume.

I manage to get Liam suitably dressed, throw a Pop-Tart in his mouth, and get out the door five minutes before we're due in class. Unfortunately, it's nearly a twenty-minute walk to school, Beckan's nowhere to be seen – not that I'd even accept a ride from him at this point – and obviously, Mother took the car to work – not that I would've been allowed to drive it anyway. I don't even have a Maine driver's license.

I yank Liam along by the arm and he huffs and puffs, trying to keep up. I'm still fuming with silent rage. I didn't even hear my alarm go off. Why does today have to be the day I'm late? Today's the day I need to be perfect. Today's the day I have to get that red lipstick just right. Today's the day that I have to blow-dry my hair and get it into that flawless ponytail. Today's the day I have to shove that fake smile down Mary Donovan's throat at cheerleading tryouts. How can I do that looking like this? I want to scream.

My oily tangled hair is in a loose messy bun at the back of my neck, several strands flying out behind me. I'd paused in the bathroom long enough to get some cover-up on my emerging stress acne, which leaves me looking tired and a little bit sick. I'm wearing a wrinkled, long-sleeved t-shirt, perfectly accentuating the wide hips I hate so much, and jeans. I feel hideous. I'm doomed.

The wind picks up at the bottom of the hill and the cold goes right through our light jackets with the ease of a chainsaw through twigs. "Ugh!" I shout. "This is the longest walk of my life!"

"I-I'm s-s-sorry, Rosie." Liam says through chattering teeth.

"Oh it's not your fault, Liam," I say, slowing down. It's Mother's, I think venomously. How could she leave us like that, without even making sure I'm up to take care of everything? "It's my fault. I overslept. I'm sorry I'm acting like a drill sergeant today. I just feel bad you're going to be late."

"You're going to be late too!" He says helpfully.

"I know. C'mon," I pull him closer and put my arm around him. "Walk closer to me. Maybe I can keep you a little warmer."

When we're about halfway to school, we hear the rumble of a car engine creeping up behind us. A sleek black BMW SUV pulls up on the curb next to us. Behind the slowly receding tinted window is not exactly my worst nightmare, but it's close.

"Hey," Ronan shouts. "D'ya need a lift?" His hair has that perfect bed-head style again, and appears to have subtle red highlights in the early morning sunlight. His smile nearly dazzles me speechless. He's wearing a white collared shirt under a preppy blue sweater.

"Sure," I say, hoping I can blame my reddened cheeks on the wind. I open the back driver's side door for Liam and help him into the back seat. I'm about to follow him, but Ronan stops me.

"Sit up front, Rose," he says. "Keep me company."

"Oh. Okay." I strap Liam in, ignoring his anxious look.

I run around the front of the SUV and climb into the passenger seat. I tuck a loose strand of hair behind my ear and try to feel like my pretty self and not a greaseball.

Ronan smiles his glossy smile at me, and this time, it looks genuine. "I'm glad tah see you."

"Oh?" I hear more inflection in his Maine accent than I've noticed before.

"Yeah. All the girls were convinced you'd stay home sick," he says as he pulls back out into the road without a turn signal, flipping the wheel around with flair.

"I wouldn't give them the satisfaction," I say with a smile. "I'm looking forward to showing them what cheerleading is supposed to look like."

And there she is, the old me, just for a second. The me who knows what it's like to make girls cry at the sound of my catty barbs, who knows what it's like to pretend to avoid the drama, all the while making my way directly toward the headlights. The drama is so tightly woven together with the adrenaline of the competition. And it isn't just the competition between teams that calls to me. It's the competition between the girls. Who's the prettiest? Who's the bitchiest? Who's the easiest? Who has the hottest boyfriend? Which superlative should I have? Which one could I get? Which one do I *deserve?*

Back in Texas, it seemed so important to be in that scene because it was those people who mattered. That's all I really wanted – to matter, if not to someone special, then to anyone, everyone. But it's different here, because I certainly do matter– but I'm not happy about it at all. It's all wrong. I'm hoping that joining the cheerleading team will somehow right things for me.

Ronan's laughter brings me back to attention. "Well I've no doubt you'll give them a run for their money. That's good," he says. "Mary's had it pretty easy for a while. She could use a good scare. Keep her on her toes." He looks away from the road long enough to smile at me and I blush again.

"So, is this your brothah?" Ronan looks at Liam through the rearview mirror. "Hi, little man. How are you?"

"I'm not little," Liam mumbles, pouting.

"You sound different today," I say.

Ronan smiles knowingly. "Mary doesn't like the accent very much."

"Why?" I say proudly in my best southern drawl. "Your accent tells where you're from. You should embrace it."

"She thinks it makes us sound like idiots or somethin'. I have to hide it when she's 'round or she gets her panties in a wad." He rolls his eyes and I laugh.

Ronan pulls into the school's parking lot. We're only ten minutes late thanks to his ride. Together, we walk Liam to the elementary doors.

"Have a good day squiggle worm," I say and ruffle his hair. "And say thank you to Ronan for giving us a ride. That was nice of him."

Liam mumbles a thank you to his feet, and then as he's about to go inside says, "Beckan's truck is better." Then he disappears.

I gasp. "That little –"

"It's okay," Ronan says as we walk to the other side of the building. "I get it. I have a couplah little brothahs myself."

"Yeah?" I smile as our pace naturally slows. "How old?" A gust of wind twists around us and I inhale Ronan's sweet cologne. It's a sharp contrast to Beckan's musk and cigarettes.

"Eight and ten," he says, jamming his hands into the pockets of his expensive leather jacket. "They can be real pains sometimes."

A few seconds of silence pass as we approach the high school doors.

"So, I know why I'm late," I say. "I overslept. Why are you late?"

Ronan looks away for a second and then turns back to me with an embarrassed smile.

"What?" I fiddle with a backpack strap. I can't remember the last time I'd been nervous in front of a guy.

"Well," he says, "I was lookin' for you."

"Really?" I say because I can think of nothing else, but I must've sounded threatened, because Ronan begins struggling for an explanation.

"Look, I'm not stalkin' you, I swear." He pauses in front of the doors, blocking them to me. "I'm curious 'bout you, Rose. You're just... you're different. Somethin' 'bout you..." He shrugs, as if shaking the thought away. "Anyway, don't tell Mary. She's wicked jealous of you already." He pulls open one of the doors and gestures with an open hand. "Aftah you."

*   *   *

"What a pig," Letta says. "Mary *would* kill you if she found out, Rose. She's vicious. Last year she caught Ronan under the bleachers with another girl and went ballistic. Beat the crap out of her."

I snort. Mary isn't so different from me – which is probably why I hate her so much. "Why are they even together?" I ask, even though I already know the answer.

"Because they're supposed to be," Letta shrugs. "They're like a local monarchy. Two people, who might care about each other in some deep, dark place, and have to be together for the good of the kingdom. They have their little not-so-secrets, just like anyone else." Her voice quiets and her eyes go to her feet, but I don't notice, preoccupied as I am with what's about to happen.

The last bell rang only moments ago and we're slowly walking toward the gym. With each step, my pulse quickens. I try to laugh off the nervousness, reminding myself this is what I enjoy, this is what I want, but the pep talk isn't sticking.

"Are you ready?" Letta asks as we approach the gym doors.

"Of course." I try to sound confident.

"Alright, well you don't want to be late. Here." Letta stoops over her bookbag and pulls out an old set of gym clothes. "I know my dwarf clothes won't fit you quite the same, but it's better than nothing. Anyway, the shorts will show off your nice ass."

"Letta!"

"Just sayin'. Anyway, I'm gonna head home. Call me when you can and let me know how it goes – if you aren't grounded. Maybe I can finagle some arrangement with my parents and hold your mom up."

"Okay. Thanks, Letta," I give her a quick hug. "You're the best."

"You know it. Go get 'em tiger!" She shouts as she walks away.

I change clothes in the girls' locker room. The shirt is only a little short on me, just hitting the top of my hips. The shorts turn out to be perfect. Letta's right; they do show off my butt, and they make my legs look like long, lithe totems. As I pull my hair tightly behind my head and catch a glance of my striking looks in the mirror, I feel more confident. I pull a tube of lipstick from my bag and press the crimson to my lips, painting them generously. With a wicked smile and a tug on an eyebrow I think, Oh, I *got* this. I throw my shoulders back, give my reflection a wink, and strut out of the locker room.

There are more people in the gym than I expected. Somehow I pictured my tryout to be more personal: four severe looking girls with plucked eyebrows and hair-sprayed ponytails glaring me down in an empty gym. After all, how many cheerleaders can a pathetic school this size really need?

A group of boys in basketball uniforms dribble at the other end of the gym. Several people sit in the bleachers watching the practice, most of them parents. On this end, Mary and five other girls in cheerleading uniforms are talking to each other with their hands on their hips. There are ten other girls waiting to try out for the team, eyeing Mary and her cohorts jealously. Some of them don't have a shot in hell of making the team. They're too heavy, too plain, too short, too ugly, too desperate. I give them credit for having the guts to try out though.

I walk toward the bleachers to sit with the possibles, aware several people are staring at me. As I sit, a group of students enter the gym and climb into to the bleachers behind me. I recognize them as the rest of the popular kids, mostly girls, who hang out with Ronan and Mary at lunch. At the tail end of the group is Ronan. He walks up behind Mary and pinches her on the rear. She jumps, at first annoyed, but then Ronan a lays thick kiss on her lips and she hugs him. Then he leaves Mary to get organized with her teammates, and makes his way to the top of the bleachers. As he passes me, he winks.

"Good luck, Ghost Girl." His voice is clearly mocking and I hear laughter behind me. I shoot him a dirty look, feeling betrayed after our encounter this morning. Didn't he seek me out? Basically told me he's interested in me? Then it dawns on me – Ronan's just playing games.

I sit patiently and watch each of the other girls try out, putting boys out of my mind. A few are okay, but most are terrible. I watch Mary and her teammates laugh, sometimes trying to hide it, sometimes not. The audience behind me is even crueler, shouting jeers and insults mid-cheer. More than one girl runs out of the gym in tears.

I should've known I'd be the last to go. There's a certain amount of acid in Mary's tone when she calls "Ghost Girl – oops. I mean, Rose Delaney" to the floor. She smirks at me and the audience whistles and catcalls, but I refuse to let it get to me. I stand before my audience with a wide, bright smile, conscious of my perfect posture.

But I should've known today just wasn't going to be my day.

Chapter Twenty
The Twilight Zone

I lumber home at a snail's pace, nursing a bloody nose with a gym towel and reliving my nightmare afternoon. The sun slinks below the trees and the cold air bites at my fingertips. Unlike a good Catholic girl, I'm currently cursing my existence, my stupid mother, this whole stupid town, and most of all, that evil bitch Mary Donovan.

At tryouts, things initially went my way. The other girls were relatively talentless. My own audition, using an award winning cheer from my days in Texas, was the best by far. I completed it with confidence, charm, and grace. But of course, this hadn't been enough for Mary and her cronies. They wanted the girls trying out to form a pyramid.

I wasn't worried about my own performance in the pyramid. I'm a tall girl and have been on the bottom of many a pyramid. It's the other girls I was worried about. If they weren't good at balancing, or didn't know how to dismount properly, someone could get seriously injured. Someone like me.

As Mary directed the other girls, all I could think was, Of course! *Of course,* I would be the one responsible for the heaviest wannabe. One of the smaller girls was lifting the other half of this whale, while another top-heavy girl with D-cups climbed to the top. Either Mary had no idea how to form a pyramid, or she was toying with the new recruits.

Just as I was complaining to myself and rolling my eyes at the sheer absurdity of such a pyramid, the girl at the top lost her balance. The whole pyramid toppled, and I ended up at the bottom of the pile in a tangle of elbows and knees, with the whale's foot on my snout.

I pull the gym towel away from my nose. The blood flow has finally stopped, but my nose smarts something awful. I'll have a black eye for sure. Even if I manage to make it home and change before Mother gets home, I'll never be able to explain my Marsha Brady beak. I'm definitely grounded. Again.

Goodbye storm party. Goodbye cheerleading. Goodbye Texas Rose.

"Dammit!" I yell, stomping my feet on the sidewalk. Oh, I'm going to get back at Mary Donovan for this one. I don't know how or when, but it's going to be *good*.

I hear the familiar rumble of the O'Dwyre's diesel as Beckan pulls up to the curb. He glances through the dirty passenger window, sees my bloody towel, and hurriedly waves me into the cabin, concerned.

Still shivering in Letta's tiny gym clothes, I don't hesitate.

"Good Lord, girl!" Beckan says. "What happened?"

I look at my steadily swelling nose in the mirror on the sun visor. "I got stomped on by a fat chick. Sort of."

"Come heeah," he says. "Let me see."

Beckan pulls up on the parking brake lever and slides across the seat to get a better look at my nose. For the first time since we met, I'm not fighting an urge to pull away. His rough hands touch my cheeks gently, which begin to warm underneath them, and I get a good look at his green eyes while they survey me. They have little flecks of gold strewn throughout, making them sparkle like coins at the bottom of a fountain. A warm feeling spreads through my chest and I bite my lip.

He turns my chin gently and inspects my nose from different angles. I pray there isn't a giant booger hiding up there. "Well, at least it isn't broken," he says finally. He lets his hands drop, but doesn't slide back behind the wheel.

"It feels like it." I ignore the heat rising off my body. "How do you know anyway?"

He laughs. "Get in enough fights and you know what a broken nose looks like."

There's a moment of awkward silence between us. Beckan looks like he wants to say something, or is expecting me to. His lips look about to part when he breaks away from my gaze and returns to the steering wheel. Without another word, he releases the parking brake and puts the truck back in gear.

I glance at the dashboard clock. I still have half an hour before Mother gets home. I'm deciding whether I should bother concocting a lie about my nose as Beckan pulls up in front of the cottage and shuts off the engine. When he doesn't get out, I look at him.

"I'm sorry 'bout before," he says. "I didn't mean tah hurt your feelings 'bout cheerleadin'."

My cheeks redden, but not in anger – in embarrassment. All of my anger at Beckan over what he'd said about cheerleading and I didn't even make the team. Seeing myself through the lens of his apology makes me feel silly and immature.

"I'm sorry too." I avoid his eyes. "When you said all that stuff about cheerleaders being shallow and dramatic attention whores, it was like you were insulting me, not just the sport. I lived for cheerleading. That's who I was back in Texas. That's who I am. That's the real me."

"Rose?"

"What?"

"Did you evah stop tah think that *this* is the real you?"

"What do you mean?"

"I mean," he points at me, "the messy hair, the carefree outfit, the less-is-more makeup. The nice girl who smiles when I make a joke. The one who worries less 'bout standin' out and more 'bout her little brothah. The girl who cares more 'bout her family than bein' head cheerleadah."

I don't respond. I can't. I'm too stunned.

"Think 'bout it," he says as he opens his door. "I like this Rose more." He only makes it a few steps before Liam bounds out of the cabin with Lady right behind him, and wraps himself around Beckan's legs. I stay in the cab, feeling like a heel.

*   *   *

In the end, I decide not to lie, partly because there's no makeup in the world that'll hide this injury. It hurts something awful and I'm going to have to keep ice on my face all night if I want to look remotely normal tomorrow.

The other part is what Beckan said. Is he right? I miss the status and popularity that came with being on the cheerleading team, but maybe he has a point. Maybe Mother is right too (not that I'll tell her that). This move is a chance at a fresh start, a chance to change for the better. The trouble is, I'm not sure if I'm ready for change, or for any *more* change. I'm not sure I can handle it. I might just crumble under the anxiety of it all. *What should I do? Who am I? Am I doing the right thing?* Questions I've pushed to the back of my mind for months are suddenly unavoidable.

Mother's a little late getting home, but as it turns out, she'd run into Letta's parents at the mailbox, conveniently located at the bottom of the hill where our driveway meets Letta's street.

Although I'm sure the encounter is no coincidence, and Letta successfully bought me a little extra time as promised, Mother doesn't give it a second thought. She finds me at the kitchen table with my homework.

"They're lovely people," she gushes. Mr. Bauer runs the local dry cleaning shop, and Mrs. Bauer gives piano lessons. They'd love to watch Liam tomorrow night so Mother and I can have a little fun. And, Mother hopes, Liam can spend each afternoon there, for a fee of course, so he isn't spending so much time with such uncivilized company as Derry. Maybe he can even get some piano lessons.

Mother manages to relate all of this information before she notices my swollen nose and black eye.

"My God Rose!" She says when she finally stops to take a breath. "What happened? Let me see." Mother gives me one of her quick nurse-mom examinations. She lets go of my chin with irritation when she's finished. Her touch isn't nearly as gentle as Beckan's.

"You're lucky it's not broken," she snaps. "You'll have to keep ice on it to keep the swelling down."

I hold up a half-melted bag of ice.

Mother sighs and slides into the chair across from me. "Well, what were you on the wrong end of this time? A fist or a pompom?"

"Does it matter?"

Mother puts her head in her hands and rubs her eyes before she replies. "I suppose not. Did you at least make the team?"

I shake my head.

"Well, honey, I'm not gonna lie, but I'm glad." Mother leans back in her chair. "I don't know if I could've gone through another year of all the drama and tears. Not after..." Her voice trails off and she looks away. I will her not to cry.

"Am I grounded?" I ask.

"You know what, Rose? No."

"*No?*"

"No," Mother says. "I always ground you and take things away from you and what happens? Nothing. You defy me anyway. I'm tired of fighting with you, Rose. I'm tired of fighting, period. This family has been through too much. So no, I'm not going to ground you."

I stare at Mother like she's sprouted three heads. What happened to her angry Irish temper? What happened to the woman who screams over a late homework assignment? What happened to the woman who spanked me as a child for spilling a cup of juice on the carpet? Where's the woman who once sent me into the trees behind our house, looking for my own switch?

"Oh, stop looking at me like that," Mother says finally, getting up. "I'm still your mother. I'm not possessed. Now, get a fresh bag of ice for that honker and help me with dinner."

"Mom, are you sure you don't want to punish me?"

She lets out a bizarre, humorless laugh. "Would you feel better if I did?"

"Well, no. It's just weird."

Mother puts her arm around me and kisses my forehead. "A fresh start, Rose. For all of us."

I nod, but I don't feel any better. What's going on today? First cheerleading tryouts are a disaster, then I fall into an identity crisis, and now Mother's been replaced by some caring, compassionate being. What episode of *The Twilight Zone* am I in?

After dinner, Mother washes the dishes and I try coaxing Liam into doing a bit of spelling homework. He'd disappeared from the table before he was finished chewing his last bite of mac n' cheese, and I find him plopped on the floor in the living room, about three feet from the television.

"What are you watching?" I ask.

"SpongeBob!"

I sit on the couch and pull the coffee table closer, setting Liam's spelling in front of me. "Let's turn off the T.V. for a bit and get this homework out of the way."

"No."

I look up. "Excuse me?"

Liam doesn't turn away from the television. His eyes are glued to the bright yellows and pinks of a pineapple under the sea.

"Liam, get over here this instant," I say, incredulous. I'm not used to defiance from sweet little Liam. "You need to get this done. Then you can watch cartoons until bath time."

"I don't want to."

I can't wrap my brain around what's happening. First Mother, and now Liam? "Liam, what's gotten into you?" He doesn't reply.

I snatch the remote control from an end table and turn the television off. I don't realize how loud the cacophony of the cartoon music and sound effects are until my ears have the relief of silence. I hear Mother, clanking silverware together as she

cleans at the kitchen sink. She's humming something...
something new and different yet somehow familiar.

"Hey!" Liam whirls around on me. "Why'd you do that?"

"I told you," I say. "You need to do your homework. Now
c'mon. It won't take long."

"No!" Liam shouts. "I wanna watch TV!"

Suddenly the noise of the cartoon returns and the darkened
room is aglow with the eerie light of the television once more. I
look down at my hand griping the remote control, my thumb
hovering over the power button. Did I accidentally push it?

"No, Liam," I say sternly and turn the television off again. I
put the remote down on the table and pick up a pencil.
"Homework," I say, offering the pencil to him. "Now."

"TV!" He shouts again, and it's as if the mere sound of his
voice brings the television back to life.

"SpongeBob Squarepants! SpongeBob Squarepants!"

"What the hell..."

Liam glares at me until he realizes the television is back on.
With a trance-like smile, he turns around and sits in front of the
TV again, chin in his hands and legs folded neatly beneath him.
It's as if nothing about this situation is strange to him at all.

"That's it! I stomp across the room and yank the television's
plug from the wall.

And then I panic. Because the television is still blaring. And
Liam, the sweetest boy on the planet, is defiantly sitting there in
front of it, oblivious, eyes glued to his favorite cartoon.

"Alright. I'm out." I leave the room as fast as I can and start
up the stairs. Mother's humming assaults my ears with that new,
yet familiar, tune.

I seek refuge in my room, closing the door behind me.
What the hell is going on in this house? My small family feels like
aliens, myself included. I lean my back against the door. I want
to block out the noise. No more cartoons. No more strange
music. No more whirling thoughts. Only me and the silence.

Even though it's still early, I put on my pajamas, grab *Pride
and Prejudice*, and climb into bed. I'm determined to put today
behind me as fast as I can.

*   *   *

The dream is more persistent than ever. The voice no
longer asks to be let in; it demands it. The blood red doors bulge
out toward me. The thunder deafens me and the lightning makes

it impossible to keep my eyes open but for a few fleeting blinks of my hand twisting the knob.

It isn't until I wake drenched in sweat that I realize why Mother's song is so familiar. She was humming the music from my dream.

Chapter Twenty-One
Wolfhowl Manor

Of course I'm up on time the one day I desperately want to stay home and bury my head in the sand. Fortunately the swelling in my nose went down overnight, but my head aches and my eye is black as coal. Just what I need, something else to make me feel like a leper around here. I do my best to cover it with makeup, but it remains a glaring reminder of my failure. I dry my hair and twist it into a fancy bun with several curled strands framing my face, hoping the fancy up-do will detract attention from my eye. For the first time in my life, I wish I had a pair of those dorky, thickly framed glasses to hide behind.

The temperature dropped into the thirties overnight and the wind has picked up to gale forces, prompting Derry to grump "The storm, she's a'comin'," when Beckan offers us a ride to school.

Derry sits behind the wheel and Beckan is in the middle. I climb in next to him. Liam, the devilish behavior of last night merely a memory, hops into my lap, and I strap the belt across both of our bodies.

I try to ignore the weird feeling between us after what Beckan said last night. It's like there's this electric current, an annoying vibration, connecting us. I avoid his eyes, but say a quiet hello to his good morning.

I go through the school day trying to keep a low profile, which is difficult after Ms. Brennan exclaims "Oh deah! That's quite a shinah!" in homeroom. Anyone who hadn't already noticed, turns to stare at me, and the rest of my day is full of jeers like, "Hey Ghost Girl, did you get into a fight with a ghost?" followed by laughter.

I eat lunch with Letta and company, as usual. Tonight, Letta declares, we're on the hunt for something ghostly. With her as our leader, we make plans to meet at Wolfhowl after dinner. Ronan swings by toward the end of lunch to remind me about the party. This time I play coy, still unsure of him.

Mother comes home from work and immediately goes upstairs without a word. I watch the clock from my perch on the couch. It takes her over an hour to finish primping for whatever excuse to drink she's headed to. In her haste, she of course forgets to do something about dinner. I make a couple of sandwiches for Liam and me, which we eat in the living room by the eerie blue-green light of the television.

I stare at Liam's pudgy silhouette sitting so close to the screen. His back rounds as he hunches over, his head in one hand and the last bite of his sandwich in the other. I think about all the positive changes I've witnessed in him since we moved here. I'd felt so sure he was getting better, happier, more well adjusted. Is that still true? What about last night? I guess it could be delayed backlash over the move. Or maybe it's about Dad. Does he belong back in therapy? I feel like I'm staring at a stranger.

I get off the couch and sit next to Liam. "Hey, squiggle worm."

Liam grunts without looking away from the television.

"How're you doing?" I ask. "Do you like it here?"

He shrugs. "It's okay, I guess. Beckan's pretty cool."

"Yeah..." I say awkwardly. "You aren't having bad dreams again are you?"

"Bad dreams?" Now he turns to look at me.

"Yeah, like when..." My voice trails off. I don't want to upset him by bringing up the nightmares he had after Dad died, about what he'd seen in that hotel bathroom. I had nightmares too, and they were terrible for me, but I'm at least able to understand them. The frightening dreams were awful for Liam, who couldn't understand them at all. Terrible images of Dad trying to drown him in a tub of red water, his eyes crazy with anger.

"You know, um, about Daddy?"

Liam shakes his head. "I haven't had a dream about Daddy since we moved here."

"So you're sleepin' okay?"

"Sure. Why?"

I shrug.

"What about you, Rosie?" Liam asks. "You're the one who looks tired."

I laugh at Liam's total lack of brain to mouth filter. "Actually I *am* pretty tired."

"Are you having nightmares?" He asks, for the first time seeming to really look at me, to see me sitting there beside him.

"No, not exactly," I say, "but I have been having this really strange dream ever since we got here. It's about the house."

"Is it about the red doors?" Liam asks.

I freeze and words fail me. It takes some time to gather my thoughts, and I finally whisper, "How'd you know?"

"I had the same dream," he says nonchalantly, as if it's nothing to worry about. "I was standin' in front of the doors and they were locked. I kept hearing a voice. It said to let them in." He imitates a deep voice and grimaces. "Let me in, Liam." He smiles. "Just like that." Then he giggles, like we're playing a silly game rather than talking about a nightmare.

"And?" I ask intently. "Then what?"

Liam furrows his eyebrows and shrugs, as if there's no other logical response. "I let Her in. Duh."

I stare at him in disbelief. Liam's been having the same strange dream, only he isn't bothered by it in the slightest. I don't know what to think. I'd been trying so hard to keep the menacing voice – and whoever it belonged to – out, and my little brother just let them right in.

A chill races down my spine. "Who, Liam?" I grab his shoulders with my fingernails. *"Who* did you let in?"

"Tada!" Mother enters the room with a flourish. She flips on the lights and we blink as our eyes adjust.

Mother looks absolutely ravishing. Her pale skin is ivory smooth. Her long red hair is curled and flows over her shoulders like a spilled glass of red wine. Her slinky emerald dress matches her sparkling eyes. The dress wraps her torso in a tight hug, loosening at the hips and falling weightlessly several inches shy of her knees.

"Well?" She asks when we don't immediately reply.

"You look pretty, Mommy!" Liam says.

"Um, yeah, Mother," I say, trying to shake the strange feeling that had come over me. "You look great." And I mean it. Mother hasn't looked this good in a long time. But instead of feeling happy for her, I'm mad. It's too soon. It's too soon for her go out partying, looking like this, all painted up like a doll, trolling for a man. A new man. A replacement. But I say none of these things, pushing them down to steep a little longer.

"Alright, kiddo," Mother says to Liam. "Grab your bag. We're out the door."

"Aww, why can't I stay home?" Liam whines.

"Let your sister have fun with her friends, sweetie," she says, winking at me. "You'll have fun with the Bauers. It'll be just like when you see Grandma and Grandpa."

Liam's face brightens. "Does Mrs. Bauer know how to make chocolate chip cookies?"

"I'm sure she does, but you know if she doesn't, I bet she'd love to have you teach her."

"See ya, Rosie!" Liam grabs his overnight bag and bolts out the door.

"Wait, Liam! Your jacket!" Mother chases after him and the door swings shut behind her with a loud, echoing slam.

For the first time since that ghostly hand on my shoulder, I'm utterly alone in the house. And I don't like it one bit.

*   *   *

A crack of thunder jolts me awake right before the doorbell rings. The hard rain beats down on the house like a timpani. Aside from the lights in the living room, were I'd fallen asleep on the couch, the house is completely dark. I feel my way along the wall to the light switch in the foyer and the door handle with a few flashes of lightning to help me.

Four soggy dogs stand on the other side of the door as the sheeting, horizontal rain pelts their backs. Letta, Eileen, Patty, and Shane are thrown through the doorway with a strong gust of wind and I close and latch the door behind them with difficulty.

"Holy cow!" I practically have to shout over the creaks and groans of the house in the wind. "How long has it been raining?"

"You're kiddin' right?" Shane asks. "It's been comin' down like that for at least an hour."

"I fell asleep. Are you guys okay? Do you want something warm to drink, or some dry clothes?"

"I think we're okay," Letta says, shaking off her raincoat as the others do the same.

"We Mainahs are prepared for weather like this," Patty smirks, hanging her coat on the old fashioned coat rack by the door. Mother found it at a flea market on one of our excursions a few weeks ago. The others follow suit.

"It looks like it," I say. Letta bends over her bookbag, pulling out flashlights, disposable cameras, and cookies.

152

"Cookies?"

Letta shrugs. "I was hungry. I grabbed them on the way out. They're really good. Mom made them this afternoon."

I bite into a chocolate chip cookie. It's the best cookie I've ever had.

"Wow, right?" Patty winks as she bites into one herself.

"Don't worry," Letta assures me, "I left plenty for Liam. Mom was so happy to have a kid around again that she made, like, four batches. Don't worry about him. He's in Heaven tonight."

"Thanks. I owe you one." Letta's assurance makes me feel less guilty that Mother and I basically abandoned Liam for the evening.

After everyone eats a cookie or three, Letta gets down to business. She hands each of us a flashlight.

"What's with the flashlights?" I ask.

"Oh, the power is most certainly going to go out," she replies. "Always does when the storms come. Anyway, I figured this is a pretty big place, so we should split up."

"I think as the man of this little committee heeah," Shane says with mock importance, pulling on the waist of his pants, "I should naturally investigate the basement. If there's a ghost or a body tah be found, that's where it'll be." I don't tell him how right he might be.

"I've always been curious 'bout the basement of this place. I'll go with you!" Patty says, a little too eagerly, and her cheeks redden.

"I'll come with you too," Eileen says. Her face is emotionless, but I detect a note of jealousy in her tone.

"Okay," Letta says, rubbing her hands together. "It's Team Rosetta then! Where should we start, Rose?"

"Well," I pause, the silence filling with the *rat-a-tat* of the rain on the windows, "There's not really much on the main level. It's pretty boring down here. I actually haven't been to the third floor at all. I don't think any of us have. Isn't that strange?"

"Great!" Letta's excited. "We'll take the third floor while you guys check out the basement. Oh! One more thing." From the depths of her bookbag, Letta extracts two walkie-talkies. "Use these to communicate any interesting findings." She turns them both on, hooks one onto a pocket and hands the other to Patty.

There's an uncomfortable silence as a miasma of anxiety permeates the air. Though we'd thoroughly talked about this moment, and even laughed at the idea, actually carrying it out makes it real. It makes Wolfhowl Manor real. It makes the idea there is something sinister here real. It makes our *fear* real.

It takes a burst of lightning and thunder to bring us back to reality. Patty lets out a burst of nervous laughter.

"Alright," Shane says ominously, shining the flashlight under his chin. "Let's see what Wolfhowl Manor's all 'bout. We'll be riiiiight baaaaack! Mwahahaha!"

Chapter Twenty-Two
The Diaries

"Oh, stop bein' silly. C'mon." Eileen tugs on Shane's arm and Patty follows.

"Good luck," I say as I pass by them. I lead Letta into the kitchen and show her the skinny, rickety staircase leading up into inky darkness.

"I haven't been up here before," I say. "I think they must have been meant as servants' stairs or something."

"Why not?" Letta asks, sticking her head into the shadows of the stairwell, which envelopes her up to her shoulders, turning her into a headless ghost.

"I mostly just take care of Liam or hang out in my room. This staircase only goes to the third floor, and the stairs in the foyer go only to the second floor. Isn't that weird? This is such an odd house. Aside from the fact that it's probably haunted, I mean."

Letta nods. "I don't see a light switch. We'll have to use the flashlights. Ready?"

"As ever," I say without enthusiasm.

Letta takes the lead up the stairs, each footfall accompanied by a loud echoing groan that begins at our feet and reverberates throughout the house. Under the beam of the flashlight the wood is dusty and some of the slats are rotting away. I keep my feet to the outside of each stair, avoiding the iffy middle parts, afraid they might swallow my feet whole.

We make three tight turns before emerging into a vast, dark space on the third floor. Letta waves her flashlight around the walls until she finds a light switch. One dingy light bulb in the center of the ceiling barely illuminates the long, rectangular space.

At the top of the stairs stands a weathered door. Peering through a nearby window, we glimpse another balcony on this level, snaking around the back of the house toward my bedroom. Another set of windowed doors are set into the adjacent wall, allowing access to the balcony. Three windows look out onto the backyard and cliff, both invisible in the stormy darkness. A fourth lay in the far corner next to the balcony doors. The rain and wind rattle the glass panes in their decaying frames and the distinct sound of leaking air comes from the cracked caulking. The space is unremarkable; it's just as rotten and dilapidated as the rest of the house.

"Well this is disappointing." Letta turns around and uses her flashlight to walk her eyes around the room. "Oho! What's this?"

"What?" I follow Letta's gaze. Her light reveals several doors leading off of the space we stand in. I count four, three on the long wall and one off in the far corner that turns out to be a small, old-fashioned bathroom similar to the one by the kitchen.

"Which door shall we try first?" Letta asks.

I shrug and head for the door opposite the balcony. I reveal a small room that was probably intended as a second nursery. It's fairly small and finished in light green wallpaper with tiny pink bunnies hopping along a chair rail. It has three dormer windows and a door leading to a balcony. It has the turret cutout, but there's no door in it like the one in my room.

Trying the middle room, we find the mirror image of the first. This time the wallpaper is light blue with little trees sprouting from the corners. This room has a dormer window on the front and a door to the outside, sharing the balcony with the first room.

Closing the door, we make our way to the far room, catty-corner to the bathroom. We notice a small hallway between the second and third rooms. It's pitch black and a cold draft wafts toward us.

"I wonder where that leads," I say, my voice trembling slightly.

"We'll check there next… maybe. Let's see what's in here first."

The last room has a set of ornately carved double doors, similar to the front doors of the house. They are tall and painted in the same blood red, although not as recently; the paint has chipped away in places to reveal the original wood.

"This room is special," Letta says excitedly. "I can tell." She pushes through the doors and flips a switch. When the room lights up, I'm amazed at what I see.

*   *   *

Downstairs, Shane and the girls creep down the basement stairs as one. Shane is at the front, hunching down so his head doesn't scrape the exposed ceiling. Patty crouches behind him, with her head poking out to the side so she can see where her feet are going. Eileen brings up the rear, clutching the walkie-talkie in one hand and Patty's cold paw tightly in the other.

"Don't you gals need a scrid more space?" Shane says, stumbling near the bottom of the steps. "If we keep treadin' the same steps, we're gonna fall straight through."

"Nope," Patty and Eileen say in unison.

"It smells wicked gross down heeah," Eileen adds.

"It's damp," Patty says as they reach the bottom, and Shane flips the light switch.

They find the basement as Rose left it weeks before: dark and cold, the walls shrinking away from one lonely light bulb.

"Creepy." Eileen lets go of Patty's hand. "What's back heeah?" Eileen finds the small bathroom with the black and white tiles.

"This door looks a mite bit more interestin'," Shane says, pointing his flashlight at the small, rotten door of the mudroom.

"I don't think we should go in there," Patty squeaks, holding onto Shane as if he were a lifejacket.

"Don't be stupid, Patty. That's what we're heeah for." Eileen joins them. "Well," she looks at Shane. "What're you waitin' for?"

"Me?" The small hairs on the back of Shane's neck stand on end, every one of them silently telling him not to open the door, but he doesn't want to look like a coward in front of the girls. He hands his flashlight to Patty and steps closer to the door. He tries to twist the knob and is met with the same resistance Rose struggled with. "It's warped," he says. "Stand back."

Patty and Eileen take a few steps back, cowering close together as they watch Shane push his body against the door. After a few minutes of brute force and jiggling of the knob, Shane is able to push the door open.

Patty wrinkles her nose. "It smells like dirt."

Shane hunches and passes through the short, misshapen doorframe. He walks to the center of the room and pulls the chain for the ceiling light. Patty and Eileen follow him, looking around cautiously.

"You look like a giant," Eileen laughs.

But Shane isn't paying attention to the low ceiling. He's surveying the room with curiosity. "Look at all these toys," he says. "They look like they've been heeah a long, long time."

"They're so dirty." Patty creeps up next to Shane and the hairs of their arms mingle.

"Well, look at the floor," Eileen says, "if that's what you can call it. It's nothin' but dirt. Why?"

"Why would you put in the concrete for part of the basement, but not all?" Patty bends down and picks up a wooden alphabet block. It's so caked with mud she can only make out one letter, an E.

"You wouldn't," Shane says, taking his flashlight back from Patty. "Look." His long, slightly trembling finger points to the same back corner of the room that Rose noticed, where the dirt is uncluttered and seems particularly churned. "Look at the concrete there. See the edges by the wall? You can see where it's been taken away with a jackhammer or somethin'."

"What are you sayin'?" Eileen asks.

"Someone made this room for a purpose," Shane says ominously.

Together, they advance to the corner, stepping gingerly over the forgotten dolls, teddy bears, blocks, a train set. Shane bends down in the corner and puts his hand to the dirt.

"What's this?" Eileen finds a door in the back corner. Her light touch pushes it open. "Oh, hey, it's the bathroom again. Here, hold this." She passes the walkie-talkie to Patty and disappears through the doorway.

Patty watches Shane methodically investigate the dirt. He puts some in his hand and smells it. He rubs it between two fingers.

"Why would you do that," he says to Patty, thinking aloud. He puts his chin in his hand, smearing dirt on his face. "Why would you cut away the floor and then pile it with all this junk?"

"I think the more important question," says Patty as she crouches next to him, "is why is *this* corner so clear?"

"Why does it seem..."

"Recently dug?"

"Yeah…" Shane nods and puts his hand back on the wintry dirt. He closes his eyes and concentrates. A clap of thunder pries his eyes open and he looks at Patty, alarmed.

"Do you feel that?"

"Feel what?"

Shane grabs Patty's cold hand in his and places it flat on the ground next to his. *"That."*

Patty stares into Shane's blue eyes, feeling the ground beneath their hands. "That's so weird," she says. "It's like the ground is..."

"Pulsin'," Shane finishes.

"D'you think there's somethin' under there?" Patty asks, beginning to feel a little excited.

"Let's find out. We need somethin' tah dig with." He turns around and paws through some of the nearby toys until he finds a small beach shovel. He laughs. "Hey, look at that!"

"Convenient."

Shane begins to dig with the tiny shovel and Patty helps, clipping the walkie-talkie to her belt and pushing the dirt away with her hands. The dingy light above them flickers a few times and then goes out.

"Perfect," Shane says sarcastically.

"Heeah," Patty stops digging and aims her flashlight into the small hole they've made. It's only about six inches deep but something's definitely there.

"What is it?" Patty asks.

Shane pulls the small object out of the hole. He clears the grime away with his hands. "It's a book," he says, dumbfounded. He turns it over a few times, trying to make sense of this discovery.

"That's not just any book," Patty says, snatching it from him. "It's a diary! And look! It has initials. A. B."

Shane reaches his hand into the hole again. "Here's another one." He wipes off the cover and reads, "B. O."

"Look, there's one more." Patty retrieves it and sets it on top of the other in her hand. Swiping the dirt away with her shirtsleeve, she reads, "E. L."

"Bizarre," Shane says. He opens the one still in his hand and staring at the old-fashioned cursive writing inside. "Why so many?"

"And why are they buried?" Patty's uneasiness returns.

"Lonely Jew to Three Kings." Patty and Shane both start as Letta's voice crackles through the walkie-talkie.

Patty puts a hand on her chest to stifle a yelp. She hands the diaries to Shane and reaches for the radio.

"Lonely Jew to Three Kings, over."

"Three Kings tah Lonely Jew," Patty says. "What's up?"

"You'll never guess what we found up here!"

"She sounds excited," Shane says.

Patty nods. "We've found some interestin' thins down heeah ourselves."

"Are you about done down there? You should join us in the kitchen for a nightcap," Letta says.

"Think we're done?"

Shane nods as they get to their feet. "Where's Eileen?"

"She went through that door, into the bathroom I think."

"She's been in there a while – "

A bone-chilling scream rips through the basement, in perfect time with a clap of thunder and a flash of lighting.

*   *   *

"I can't believe this!" My voice echoes in the vast space. "I'm in heaven! I can't believe this sanctuary has been up here all this time and I had *no* idea."

"It is impressive," Letta says.

The double doors opened onto a huge library. All four walls are covered floor to ceiling with books – ancient volumes and first editions. The chestnut shelves are only interrupted by a couple of dormer windows on the front of the house. Voltaire, Shakespeare, Milton, Hemingway, Homer, Rand, and yes, even several first editions of Jane Austen's works. It's quite an eclectic collection. The books are dusty and worn from eagerly reading hands, but are otherwise in good condition. This room feels different, special somehow. It must've been well maintained by some, or possibly all, of the previous owners; some of the titles are too recent to come to any other conclusion.

The library is directly above the fire room. I feel its energy pulsating beneath my feet. The far wall of library shelves are charred and burned. Here, the books lay carelessly heaped on the floor, some covered in soot.

"Wow," Letta says, staring up. "That's pretty."

I follow her gaze to the ornate chandelier shining its soft light down into the room. Each flash of lightning throws rainbow refractions against the shelves, as if showing off each book. As if saying, *Look! Look! These are here for you! Read them!*

I sigh and smile. "What a wonderful place."

"Check this out," Letta calls from the corner with the octagonal cut running through it. Instead of a funny little room being blocked off by a tiny door, it opens into a cozy little reading alcove. There's a small table with a dusty stained glass lamp on it, and a plush, wing-backed chair.

I plop into the chair, sending a plume of dust airborne. Letta coughs, waving away the dust motes. I feel something hard underneath me and, reaching into the crease between the cushion and an arm of the chair, I pull out a small book with yellowed pages.

"What is it?" Letta asks.

"I think," I say as I open it, revealing tiny print in smudged ink, "it's a diary." I wipe the front of the diary on the arm of the chair to dust it off and discover initials. "A. C. It looks really old."

"Interesting. What does it say on the inside?"

As I'm about to reply, a deafening crack of thunder echoes throughout the house and we're thrown into a sudden and eerie darkness, broken only by the dimming swath of Letta's flashlight. The beam wavers as Letta shakes like a leaf. The darkness weighs down the air, making it hard to breathe.

"Do you want to check out that hall?" I ask tentatively.

"Uh, sure." Letta wastes no time leaving the library and I quickly follow her with the diary, closing the doors behind me. We round the corner and find ourselves in a short, dark hallway. The flashlight reveals an open door, stairs beyond.

"Sheesh!" Letta says. "This place has more stairs than The Washington Monument. Where do you think these go?"

"The attic. Should we check it out?"

Letta rallies her courage. "Of course!" She wraps her arm through mine and we proceed as one.

Several portraits hang on the walls, each of a different married couple. The first looks to be the oldest, with two severe looking people in black and white, wearing clothing from the late eighteen hundreds. The man is clearly older than the woman, who looks miserable. His beard makes him look like a wild bear. Her belly is swollen with life and ready to burst. His stiff hands rest on her shoulders and she clasps hers under her belly.

"Look," Letta says, pointing at the baby bump. "She's gotta be nine months pregnant, but she looks so…sad."

Another portrait shows a similar looking couple. Judging by the clothes, this photo isn't much older than the first. This man looks even more severe than the first with his deep, wrinkly frown and a thick unibrow. But the woman is pretty and wears a small smile, like she knows something her husband doesn't.

The next portrait shows a much younger couple, again in black and white, but twenty or thirty years later. The woman is beautiful and wears a short, sparkling flapper era dress, and holds a long cigarette holder, a curl of smoke wafting from the tip. The man, wearing a tuxedo, smiles with her, a glass of liquor in one hand, his wife's shoulder in the other. They look like the kind of fun-loving people Mother would like. Something's off about their smiles though. They're too tight, like two people who've been forced to say "Cheese!" in the middle of an argument. It reminds me of the months leading up to my parents' split, when they put on fake smiles for everyone, but their false smiles always betrayed them.

"These must be some of the old owners," Letta says. "I wonder which one is A. C.?"

"Hey," I say, realizing something, "hold on a minute." I use the flashlight to review all three photos again.

"What?" Letta asks.

"These were all taken in the drawing room," I say. "I recognize the fireplace."

"So?"

I shrug. Something about these photos nags at me.

At the end of the hall, we approach the open door with trepidation. Here, the howl of the wind and tatting drum of rain is so loud that having a conversation is nearly impossible.

"Maybe we should leave the attic for another day, when it isn't raining," Letta says, nearly shouting. "It could be cold and leaky."

A shiver crawls up my spine. "Fine with me. Let's check in with the others."

We find our way back to the staircase. The weather isn't quite as loud here, but we still have to turn the volume on the radio all the way up to hear Patty.

"Lonely Jew to Three Kings, over."

I laugh. "What?"

Letta shrugs and calls over the radio again as I shake my head. *"Three Kings to Lonely Jew,"* Patty responds. *"What's up?"*

"You'll never guess what we found up here," Letta says, thinking of the photos and the diary.

"We've found some interestin' thins down heeah ourselves."

"Are you about done down there? You should join us in the kitchen for a nightcap."

We're just wondering what's taking Patty so long to reply when Eileen's scream comes over the walkie-talkie, loud and clear.

Chapter Twenty-Three
The Doors Open

Shane and Patty hear Eileen's frantic footsteps race from the bathroom through the other door and they run after her.

"Eileen!" Patty says. "Wait!"

Eileen is already at the top of the stairs by the time Shane and Patty scramble to the bottom. Eileen's sheer panic gives them the sensation of being pursued from behind, as if the darkness chases them. They run.

Shane and Patty burst out of the basement door. Eileen is already tugging open one of the front doors, preparing to run into the wailing storm.

"Eileen!" Shane shouts. "Stop!"

Eileen ignores him. She opens the door, but freezes in her panicked tracks. There, on the other side of the doors, is the shadow of a monster backlit by lightning. She screams again.

"What is all the screamin' about?" I say as Letta and I run into the foyer. "What's going on?" I see the shadowy figure on the porch, but recognize him immediately.

Beckan rushes into the foyer, slamming the door and locking it behind him. "What the hell is goin' on up heeah?" Rain drips from his soaked hair to his drenched coat and pants. He looks like a drowned cat.

Eileen breaks into tears and throws herself at Beckan, burying her pretty face in his chest, her sobs muffled by his flannel jacket.

"Get the lights," Shane says.

"The power's out," Beckan and Letta say in unison.

"That's why I'm up heeah," Beckan says, looking at me. "I came tah check on you. Now, would someone mind tellin' me why Eileen Patton, who hasn't said two words tah me in her entire life, is clingin' tah me like grim death?" Eileen grips Beckan with all her strength and quietly sobs into his armpit. He awkwardly holds his hands away from his body, as if he's thinking of shaking her off like a wet dog.

"We don't know," Patty says, sounding panicked herself and worrying her fingers along the edges of the diaries.

"We were in the basement," Shane says, turning to me. "Patty and I were in that weird room with the dirt floor and Eileen went into the bathroom next tah it. Next thin we know, she's screamin'."

"What are those?" I ask, eyeing the diaries in Patty's hand.

"We found these buried in the basement," she replies, holding them out to me. "We think they're diaries."

"Buried?" Letta says, and Patty nods. "Weird."

I ask, "Were they in that weird corner, where there was nothing on top of the dirt?"

"Yeah," Shane says. "What 'bout you? What'd you find?"

I take the diaries from Patty and then pull the diary I found from a back pocket, setting it on top of the others, making a stack.

"They're identical!" Letta exclaims.

Letta's right. Aside from the dirt on the ones from the basement, the diaries are exactly the same in size, shape, and design. I read the initials on the cover of each and wonder what it means.

"Um, hello?" Beckan says. "Crazy cryin' girl still attached."

"Sorry." I hand the diaries to Letta. "Here. Can you guys take Eileen into the kitchen? I set some mugs and hot cocoa packets out before you got here. Maybe that'll calm her down. I'll be there in a minute"

"Sure." Letta and Patty go into the kitchen while Shane pries Eileen off of Beckan with a gentle "Shh" and rubs her head. "Just relax. Let's go sit."

Beckan waits until the others are out of earshot before he echoes his earlier question more firmly. "What the hell is goin' on, Rose?"

"Sleuthing," I say as innocently as I can.

"Sleuthin'?"

"Yeah," I shrug. "I wanted to know more about the house. They offered to come over and help. We were just lookin' around. What's wrong with that?"

"Nothin' good evah comes of that, that's what."

"What do you mean?"

Beckan cusses to himself. "Nothin'. It means nothin'. Have you satisfied your curiosity now?"

"Actually," I say carefully, "there was one more room I wanted to check out."

"Oh?" Beckan says unenthusiastically, hands on his hips. "Which one?"

"The fire room," I reply. "The one that hasn't been restored up at the top of the steps."

He shakes his head, exasperated. "Why?"

"It's the only room left," I shrug. The silence between us grows and we hear the clinking of spoons and susurrus of subdued voices from the kitchen.

Beckan sighs. "I suppose you're gonna go whethah I go with you or not?"

I nod.

"Fine. I'll go up there with you. But let the record show it's under duress."

"Noted." I grab the flashlight Letta had set on the floor to make room for the diaries in her tiny hands, and we ascend the staircase.

I hesitate at the door long enough for Beckan to ask if I'm sure I want to go in. I rally my strength with a nod, and push through the door.

The same miserable feeling that had overtaken me that first day sweeps over me again. The sadness, anger, and desperation hit me like a tidal wave and I fall back into Beckan.

"Are you okay?"

"Yeah," I lie, refusing to admit I'm suddenly light-headed.

I shine the light on all four of the blackened and charred walls. The far wall leaks from the force of the wind and rain, but I can barely hear the trickle above the din of the storm. There's another loud crack of thunder and a flare of lightning on top of each other.

"What is it you're expectin' tah find up heeah?" Beckan asks, sounding nervous.

I focus the flashlight on the octagonal cutout identical to the one in my bedroom. Even in the scarred blackness, I can see the small square door. "I want to know what's behind that door." I look up at Beckan and his eyes meet mine in the dark, intense and irritated.

"Alright," he says reluctantly. "Let me see if I can get it open." He follows the beam of light and I move so the door isn't lost in Beckan's shadow.

Beckan crouches down and surveys the door. He puts his fingers around the edges. Just as he's about to pull, the door crumbles into ash at his feet, and I gasp.

"Well that was easy," Beckan says.

"What's back there?"

"Nothin' that I can see."

"Look harder."

"Flashlight," he demands with an open hand. I hand it over and he shines the light into the shadowy abyss of the turret. "I still don't see –"

"What?" Every hair stands at attention. "What is it?"

Beckan's body ices over on the spot. "You aren't going to believe this."

"What?"

Beckan reaches into the turret and pulls something out, something small in his bear paws. I take the flashlight back from him and point it at his hand. He blows on the object and ash flutters into the air like mini feathers. In his hands he holds a small, red diary.

"What's in it?"

"Nothin'." To prove it, he flips through the diary's pages. They're all white. Pristine. Blank.

I reach out a hand to take the diary. I feel the air pulsating around the small book. This diary is important, I know it. The house wanted me to find it, wants me to have it. My fingers are only millimeters from the red leather when –

Boom. The sound rings through the house, loud and hollow.

"What was that?" I say, alarmed.

Beckan shrugs as the sound echoes again, louder. *BOOM.* We race into the hall.

BOOM. The sound is loud and deafening in the cavernous foyer.

"What is it?" I shout, covering my ears.

Beckan puts an arm around me as Eileen, Shane, and Patty burst into view below.

BOOM.

Shane looks up at us and points, shouting. What's he saying? I can't hear him over the storm.

BOOM.

"What?" I keep my ears covered, but come closer to the banister, trying to read Shane's lips as he gesticulates. *It's what?*

BOOM.

"It's the doors," Shane is saying. "The doors!"

I follow Shane's finger and look at the blood red doors.

BOOM.

It's as if something is outside in the storm, trying to get in. It's more than the knock of a stranded stranger.

BOOM.

It's more than the bang of a battering ram.

BOOM.

With each bang, the doors bulge inward and Letta yelps.

BOOM.

I'm coming in, Rose. I'm coming in.

"No!" I back away from the banister. How's this possible? I'm awake.

Beckan grabs my arm to steady me.

BOOM.

"It's not possible!" I look at Beckan for help, but see my own fear reflected back.

I'M COMING IN, ROSE. YOU CAN'T STOP ME.

"I'm awake!" I'm still covering my ears. I back up until I feel the wall behind me. *"I'm awake!"* I scream.

BOOM.

Suddenly, both doors fly open and Eileen screams. They slam all the way back on their hinges as rain, wind, and debris whirls into the foyer. The storm roars into the house like a hungry lion, attacking our faces with the teeth of twigs and leaves and whatever else is picked up by the wind's clutches.

The world begins to darken and the floor starts to fall away from my feet. I scream again, tears streaming down my face, "I'm awake! I'm awake!"

"Rose!" Beckan shouts over the snarl of the storm.

I'm falling. The world gets dimmer and dimmer. Beckan's face fades. I hear my own scream, as if from at the bottom of a well.

"But I'm awake!"

And then, nothing.

PART TWO

Jason McBride
The Third Owner: 1961-1963

Jason McBride, by all accounts, was a good man. He made his money and reputation early and young, and all without the help of a college degree. He went straight into the successful family construction business, McBride and Sons, the day after his high school graduation. He'd never wanted to do anything else. He'd never considered doing anything else, and even if he had, he would have ended up in the same place anyway. Jason was the youngest of four boys and all three of his elder brothers had joined the family business. It was a family tradition no one opposed.

McBride and Sons' specialty was restoration. They rebuilt dilapidated houses. They brought glory back to crumbling brownstones, strength back to bowing frames, warmth back to the cold coal-caked hearths. When business was slow or it was too cold to do some of the more intensive work, they got by restoring antiques and other aged wooden furniture. The McBrides were a family of artists when it came to wood and Jason greatly enjoyed working alongside his aging father and maturing brothers. Although he was often treated like the baby of the family that he was, and teased endlessly, he wouldn't have traded his job for any other in the world.

As far as Jason was concerned, his life was good and he was exceedingly happy. This lasted for five years. Living and working was fun and easy. He was learning from the University of Life. He learned math by building with his hands. He learned architecture through trial and error. He learned literature through conversation with others. What did he need college for?

Then the unthinkable happened. Jason hereafter only referred to that day as The Incident, and The Incident was only referred to if absolutely necessary.

The day of The Incident, Jason stayed home with a hangover. His oldest brother was getting married the next week and they had celebrated a little too hard the night before. His three brothers could hold their liquor fine, but Jason, always the baby of the family, was easily weakened by the wiles of alcohol. When he wasn't vomiting, he was thinking about vomiting.

Mrs. McBride, a lifetime stay at home mom who enjoyed spoiling all of her boys, did what she always did around lunchtime. She packed lunches for her husband and sons, always something homemade. She served Jason before she left for the construction site that was the Otto family home on the other side of town. Lunch, Jason would always remember, was a roast beef sandwich made from the leftover seasoned meat the night before and a piece of his mom's famous blueberry cobbler. He was lying in his bed, letting the wafting smell of lunch churn his stomach, when his life, as far as he knew it, ended.

Mrs. McBride arrived at the Otto home promptly at noon. The Otto family had recently welcomed their fifth child and needed to make some accommodations to their house in order for the family to be comfortable. While the family stayed at a nearby hotel, the McBride men were swinging sledgehammers and gutting the structure. After making some inquiries of the bricklayers lounging in the shade by the curb, Mrs. McBride found her husband and sons in what used to be a small kitchen nook, hungrily awaiting their lunch and telling dirty jokes. Jason's brothers greeted their mother with a group hug and a loud "Ma!" That was the last thing anyone heard before the explosion.

A leaking gas line. That's how the fire marshal explained it to Jason a few days later. It was his father lighting his regular pre-lunch cigarette that set the blast off. How his father, brothers, or mother could have missed the telltale smell of the leaking gas, Jason would never be able to ask. Nor would he ever be able to ask how his experienced father or brothers could have let something so avoidable happen. How could they have let this happen? How could they so carelessly abandon him like that?

There were no coffins at the McBride funeral. Five gold urns sat side by side at the front of the funeral parlor, not that Jason would ever remember that. His days were dark and the many condolences were a blur. After the news truly hit him, and after he was done cursing God and the world for turning him into nothing better than a stray dog, all he would remember were the roast beef sandwich and the blueberry cobbler rotting on his bedside table.

McBride and Sons was left to the only surviving son, but how could he continue his family's work, his family's art, all on his own? The old rocking chair in need of sanding and a new coat of stain made him think of his father's hands, rough with years of experience. Swinging a sledgehammer to knock down drywall made him think of his eldest brother's brawny form. A lunch pail, no matter what the contents, brought back the fragrant pastry smell of his mother's apron. No, he couldn't return to that life. That Jason was dead, separated into pieces, a little bit of him in each golden urn. The new Jason, the hollow-shelled orphan that remained, sold the business of McBride and Sons and left town a very rich, but very lost, twenty-five year old.

Jason's devastation couldn't be understood by anyone. In an unexplainable instant, he became an orphan. Son to no one. Brother of no one. It seemed he was the last man on Earth, and that's how he lived for a few years. He walked from city to city, listlessly wandering in search of a new life. He let the wind alter his course like a kite, camping outside as long as there was no risk of hypothermia. In the dead of late Decembers and Januarys, he found an abandoned hovel somewhere to curl up in, made a fire, and moved on the next day.

How odd that this nomadic habit of his was exactly how he came to be in possession of Wolfhowl Manor. It was late on an icy January evening of 1961 when his eye caught sight of the looming dark shadow on the hill. A hard rain had been pelting him for miles. He was chilled to the bone and desperate to lie down and fall into a coma. The apparently deserted mansion would be perfect.

Jason managed to spend a peaceful and warm night in the drawing room of Wolfhowl Manor, despite the creaks and groans of the aging wood under the weight of the storm. Many children had run screaming from the very same sounds, certain a ghost had breathed by them or a monster had brushed their ankle. But these sounds were familiar to Jason, comforting even. Just the lonely low cries of a house in need of a little love and a lot of work.

The O'Dwyre's, catching sight of the smoke curling out of the long cold chimney, wandered up the hill and found the stranger cooking his breakfast over the fire. But there was no trouble here. There was no trespassing argument. Jason even made Derry, a bright twelve year old at the time, a cup of hot cocoa, and his father a strong cup of coffee, which they consumed together on the back porch as they drank in the predawn sky off the edge of the cliff. Though the O'Dwyre's had not been the warmest people he'd ever met, Jason realized he enjoyed a little company. The conversation was light, but all Jason heard that mattered was "for sale."

It took less than a week for the sale to go through. The historical society was elated to have a young handyman moving into the home, who would hopefully restore its previous grandeur and perhaps create a nice site for a bed and breakfast to bring some tourism to their troubled town. Oh, there were many who wished Jason gone as well, who warned him to leave well enough alone and to get out of Port Braseham while he still could, for nothing but death and sorrow awaited him here. But Jason was undeterred. He'd left a lifetime of death and sorrow behind him. He was immune. He went from one day to the next with no purpose, no plan, no want. But the second he took possession of Wolfhowl Manor, Jason felt a switch flip inside of him. For the first time in many years, he felt alive with hope.

Jason's plans for the house were grand. He would heal the house. He would complete what the original owners did not. He would close up the scars of the previous fire. He would strengthen all signs of age until everything was shiny and new and strong. He would breathe in the fresh smell of new wood and remember his father. He would cook grand meals in the gourmet kitchen and remember his mother. Then he would find a partner, a wife, and start a new family, and this was how he would remember his rough and tumble brothers. This was how he would honor his family lost.

Jason started small at first. The drawing room had been completed with the original construction, but the floors were dull and scratched and the walls were bare and plain. He polished the floors and replaced the splintered beams. He added carved trims to the windows and to the back door. He sanded the original delicate carvings of the fireplace mantle and created window seats in the two bay windows overlooking the garden. He put in porch swings at the bottom of the front turrets, thinking fondly of sitting there one day with a nice woman and rocking quietly, sitting close with their heads bent together. He even hired a pretty interior designer from town to help with the finishing touches. Jason was a true builder, but knew nothing about interior design unless it involved carving wood.

One room at a time, Jason made his way through the house. Completing, restoring, creating anew. He began to thrive. He began to feel alive again. He opened himself up to the world. When he wasn't working up on the mountain, Jason was a frequent and giving guest at church and was often seen around town, not only stocking up on materials, but chatting up young women of marrying age and helping older citizens with their chores. He became the most eligible bachelor in town, and to many, he was known as the Handsome Boy Scout.

Port Braseham itself entered a period of prosperous calm while Jason worked up on the mountain, as a kingdom would prosper under a fair and just monarch. The town began to grow, to make money, and yes, even take in some tourists from bed and breakfasts in the neighboring towns. The fish were returning. The crops were growing. The weather was fair and calm.

By the summer of 1963 the house was looking more remarkable than ever inside and out, and the townspeople began to wonder if their notion of a curse had just been some silly superstition after all. No tragedy had befallen this nice man. Flatlander he may have been, but to many, he was the savior of their town. He was the one who was finally able to bring happiness to the house, to the town. He broke the curse.

There was only one who remained staunchly convinced the curse lived on, lying dormant, waiting - waiting for the right moment to strike, the right moment to take all the townspeople had earned in one fell swoop. Oh, the storm was coming alright, and it was coming very soon.

Her name was Enit O'Sullivan.

Jason knew of strange ol' Enit. They had met many times at church and she was always staring at him with those icy eyes, as if she were trying to look right through him, convinced his soul was dammed. He tried to be friendly to her, but she never did seem to warm to him. This is why, when Enit showed up on his doorstep on a nice afternoon in late April to ask him to dinner at her home, Jason was quite surprised. Perhaps the old maid had decided to bury the hatchet and get to know him, he thought. But if Jason had been hoping for a peaceful get-to-know-you dinner conversation, he was disappointed. What he got was more like a tarot reading. He had heard stories of the curse, sure. And he had even heard stories of Enit's psychic babble. Had he actually considered any of it to be true? Of course not! His parents had raised a levelheaded and God-fearing son. This curse was nonsense, conjured up out of coincidence and accident. And this is exactly what he told Ol' Enit.

Inviting Jason to dinner at her home had been a pretense. Instead of a nice seafood stew, what Jason received was a psychic warning about the curse and his impending death.

174

Doomed, Enit had said in that spooky voice of hers. His soul was doomed. Just as Alva and Eamonn had been doomed. Just as Barbara and Robert, and just as Hagan and Alison. No, Jason would fare no better than these other fools. His only chance was to flee, and to do it straight away. If he was lucky, the house would let him free of its grasp.

Walking home from Enit's, shoulders held high and chuckling to himself, was the last time anyone saw Jason.

Three weeks went by without the charming young man coming into town, but no one worried at first. Jason was close to completing his renovation of Wolfhowl Manor and all talk revolved around the party that would follow the completion. No one aside from the O'Dwyre's and a few members of the historical society had been inside of the house for years. Surely, the townspeople told themselves, he was just being diligent in his efforts.

It was after his fourth absence from church that three of the local old biddies decided to check on him. Who was feeding him? Who was making sure he was taking care of himself the way a young man should? His mother was dead after all. He was working too hard. He needed a decent meal and some rest. Such a nice man like him should really think about settling down with a nice young woman from town, Catholic of course.

It was a sweet and dry late July afternoon when the three women made their way to the front doors. They knocked, of course, but were not surprised when Jason didn't come to the door. The sound of a knock in such a cavernous old place was sure to be swallowed up quickly. It was no surprise to find the door unlocked either; this was Port Braseham after all. What was a surprise, however, was the discovery of Jason's body in the bedroom at the top of the right grand staircase, recently re-carpeted in a lovely crimson. It appeared that, after securing the chandelier in the third floor library (he had taken it down to replace some of the missing crystals and dust the rest), Jason had stumbled off the ladder. His sturdy form fell easily through the fire-eaten floor of the library and into the room where all of the previous owners had met their deaths. But Jason had not hung himself, no. There was no suicide for this reformed man. Instead, he was impaled on his own saw.

"I warned him," Old Enit said at his well-attended funeral. She pressed her lips tight as she leaned toward the person next to her with a nod. "He should have listened to me."

Chapter Twenty-Four
The First Diary

*Y*ou aren't good enough for him.

I start awake in the darkness, and my head connects with something small and hard.

"Ow!" Letta falls backward onto the end of my mattress, a hand on her forehead.

"What are you doing?" I'm rubbing my own forehead. "What happened?"

"Making sure you're still breathing." Letta folds her legs beneath her as she explains. "You passed out. You've been out for over an hour."

"Really?" I'm surprised, although my head *does* feel a little foggy.

"Don't you remember?"

I try to remember, looking around in the dim light of the flashlights aimed at my bedroom ceiling. Beckan is hunched up in the bay window, asleep. I remember the search upstairs, finding the diaries, the power outage, and meeting Beckan in the foyer. Then I see the doors in front of me, and my heart sinks. "The doors…" My voice is barely a whisper, but Letta hears me.

"Yeah, they opened," Letta says, quickly adding, "in the wind."

"That's not possible. Beckan locked them when he came in, remember? I watched him do it."

"I know," Letta says quietly. "You know… Beckan said you were screaming. I mean, we couldn't hear anything from below, not over the storm, but…"

"I'm awake."

"What?"

"That's what I was screaming," I say. "I screamed *I'm awake.*"

"Your dream?" Letta asks.

I nod as the terror returns, fresh and potent. That dream is where reality and ghosts collide. Is it real? How else can I explain the doors opening the first night I had the dream? And again tonight? The doors were deadbolted, I'm *positive*.

"I've had the dream several times now," I say. "Each time it's more vivid, more real. And each time I wake up right before I open the doors."

"So you're saying your dream came true?" Letta raises an eyebrow, dubious.

I shrug. "I don't know. I just know what I heard."

"What do you mean?"

"I heard a voice demanding to be let in, just like in my dream. And then… the doors opened."

"Who do you think it was?"

"I'm not sure," I say. "But Liam's had the same dream. He told me earlier."

Letta sits up straighter. "Yeah? What'd he say about it?"

"He let it, whatever *it* is, in," I said. "And he's been acting weird lately. He kinda does what he wants. He doesn't listen to me. Neither does Mom. I feel like they've teamed up against me or something."

"Yeah, but that could be the stress of the move," Letta says. I appreciate her half-full glass, even though we've been in the house nearly three months now. "He probably just misses Texas and stuff. It's all part of adjusting – new friends, new routine, a strange new house. Real life always pops up in your dreams in weird ways. Who knows what dreams really mean anyway? Am I right?"

"Maybe." Neither of us believes what happened tonight can be rationalized away so easily. Something made those doors open, but it sure as hell wasn't the wind. Silently, we're going through a door together, a door that leads to the other side. Walking through this door means we believe in something other. Something supernatural, something evil. And there's no going back from that.

Letta smiles and squeezes my hand. "Don't worry."

Beckan lets out a loud snore and we both start. His eyes open, narrowly at first, but when he sees me sitting up, they burst open and he sits up. "Hey. What time is it?"

"After midnight," Letta says.

Beckan comes over to sit beside me. "Are you okay?" His voice is laced with concern.

"Yeah," I say, feeling my cheeks burn. "I'm fine. Embarrassed I'm such a chicken. I can't believe I fainted."

"Don't worry 'bout it," he says. "I'm pretty good at carryin' damsels in distress tah bed."

Letta guffaws loudly, and Beckan blushes. I change the subject.

"I'm sorry you missed the storm party," I say to Letta.

"Don't worry, we didn't miss anything. Ronan sent me a text while you were out. Lightning struck the Carrey's barn, which is where we were supposed to go," Letta says. "Set it on fire, despite the rain. They're rescheduling it for tomorrow night at the park. It'll be more fun there anyway."

"Oh. Where's everyone else?"

"Eileen bolted out the back door, running into the storm like an idiot when the doors opened," Letta says. "Don't worry – Shane and Patty caught up to her. She was a cold soggy mess when they found her, but they got her home. She still won't say what happened in the basement."

Beckan gives me a withering look dripping in I-told-you-so smugness.

"I'm glad no one got hurt," I say, "besides myself, I mean." Neither Beckan nor Letta smile. "Come on, guys. Stop being so serious. You're freakin' me out." In truth, I'm still scared – scared of the doors, scared of this house, and scared for my family. I don't understand what's going on, but I've been counting on Beckan and Letta to be the voices of reason, not to encourage my ghostly fears.

"Listen, 'bout what you said before you fainted –" Beckan starts.

"Alright," I interrupt. "I know I freaked out. It's not that big of a deal. Can we not relive this please?"

"I want to know why you said that," Beckan says. "I'm awake. You said it over and over. You were screamin', Rose. It scared me."

I sigh. I want to tell him I'm scared too. Instead, I tell him about the dream. It's a long time before Beckan responds. His face is unreadable at first, but then something seems to dawn on him, and whatever it is, it's not good.

"What?" I finally ask, the pit in my stomach growing colder. "What is it?"

"My muthah," Beckan says. "She, ah, had the same dream. Before she died."

"Holy shit!" Letta exclaims, voicing my own shock. When Beckan and I jump, startled by her shout, she covers her mouth. "Sorry."

The silence weighs us down, keeps us quiet. The storm has died down to a tiny *pitter-patter* on the windows and roof. The house itself creaks and groans less, having survived the worst of the squall. Beckan gets up and walks to the balcony doors. He pulls the curtain aside and stares into the darkness for a while.

"You can see the smoke from the Carrey's barn," he says finally. I can tell from the way he licks his lips he wants a cigarette.

Letta glances at the clock. "It's getting pretty late."

"Yeah," Beckan turns around. "You should get some sleep," he says to me, his serious green eyes boring into mine. "I'll take you home, Letta."

"No!" It comes out louder than I mean it to. "Don't go, I mean. It's just I…" I don't want to admit how terrified I am to be in this house alone. "What if I have a concussion, or gave Letta one when we conked heads?" I try to laugh, but my throat tightens and chokes it off. "Can't you stay the night?"

"Sure," Letta says. "I'll text Mom I'm staying here. I'm sure it'll be fine." She crawls up on the bed next to me and leans against the headboard. "Oh hey, I meant to tell you," she says, staring at the canopy, "My dad can fix that rip for you. He's pretty awesome with a needle and thread thanks to his dry cleaning business. He does alterations too."

"Thanks." I'd almost forgotten about the ripped canopy and the attack on my room. It seems like forever ago.

Beckan stands anxiously near the door, wrestling with something inside his head. "Alright," he says, rubbing the back of his neck. "I'll stay too. Just tah make sure you're both alright." He comes over to the other side of my bed. His heavy frame sinks into the mattress and I fall slightly toward him. As if taking an unspoken cue, Beckan lifts his arm behind me and Letta huddles close to me on the other side so that Beckan's hand grazes her soft, dark hair.

"You guys get some rest," he says. "I'll keep an eye on…thins."

I don't think I'll be able to sleep after what happened, but I surprise myself by sleeping a deep, dreamless sleep.

*   *   *

I wake around eight Saturday morning to the sound of the heavy knockers coming down heavily on the front doors. Beckan's disappeared but Letta lays on her side, curled up under

179

my comforter. When the loud echoing knock sounds again, she starts awake.

"Someone's at the door," I say. I'm groggy and my limbs are still heavy with sleep.

"Okay!" Letta shoots up with her usual pep, as if she's been awake for hours. "I'm sure it's my parents with Liam." She skips down the stairs. I follow slowly, still rubbing sleep out of my eyes.

As predicted, Letta's parents stand on the porch in the frigid morning air, all bright smiles and ruddy cheeks. They look exactly like Letta; small, pale, and cloaked in dark black hair.

"Sorry we're so early, Rose," says Mrs. Bauer, "but Liam was missing home this morning." She puts a hand out toward me. "And it's also nice to meet you!"

"Oh, yeah, of course!" I shake hands with both of them.

"Did you have a good time last night?" Mr. Bauer asks, winking at Letta.

"You bet!" Letta says. "Listen Rose, you get some rest and relax today. I'll give you a call later." She winks and grabs her backpack and coat, heading out the door before I can even say goodbye as Liam dashes inside. He's so quick that my goodbye to the Bauers borders on rude. I close the door and grab Liam by the hood of his jacket before he can disappear into the bowels of the house.

"Hold it, squiggle worm," I say, pulling him into a tight hug. "I missed you!" Liam doesn't hug me back, and when I look at him, I notice tear stains trickling down his face. "Hey," I say gently as I take off his jacket and he sets down his overnight bag, "what's wrong?"

He shrugs. "Nothin'."

"Don't you lie to me, Liam Andrew Delaney," I say. "Now out with it. What's going on?"

"I just wanted to come home," he says. "It was just time for me to come home."

"Why? You could have stayed with the Bauers a little longer if you wanted. Letta told me Mrs. Bauer makes great cookies." I smile at him and pinch his cheek. "I bet she makes pancakes pretty good too."

"I missed home."

"Texas?" I ask, confused.

"No," he says with exasperation. "It was just time for me to come home. She wanted me to come home. Okay?"

"Who? Mrs. Bauer?"

He sighs heavily. "Nevermind. I'm hungry." He goes into the kitchen without another word. I don't stop him.

*   *   *

I'm not going to analyze Liam's behavior. It'll only make my anxiety worse, and it's already skyrocketed after last night. I wander around the house for a while, picking up here and there, to distract myself from the feeling of being watched no matter what room I'm in. After a while, I check in on Mother, who's snoring off last night's alcohol, still wearing her cocktail dress. I'm not sure what time she came home, but the Volvo is parked crookedly out front and I'm just relieved she came home alone.

Returning to my bedroom, I take down my torn canopy, fold it, and set it on the floor by the door so I'll remember to give it to Letta later. Maybe I'll walk it down there myself and apologize for my rude goodbye…and ask how things went with Liam last night. Maybe the Bauers can tell me why Liam wanted to come home so badly.

Depressed, I curl up on the window seat and stare out at the darkening sky. The rain is in a lull for the time being, but judging by the clouds rolling in off the horizon, it won't be long before the encore begins. Uncomfortable, I rearrange the throw pillows when I feel something quite unlike a pillow; in fact, there are five quite unlike-a-pillows digging into my back.

The diaries! I forgot all about them. I grab a dirty t-shirt from my hamper and wipe each of the little books down. Each diary is leather-bound with a red cover and a pair of initials scrawled inside a small framed rectangle on the front. A. C., A. B., B. O., E. L., and the one from the fire room, left blank. I flip through each of the diaries, setting the blank one to the side, trying to decide which one to read first. Reading the diaries in chronological order is the only thing that makes sense, and A. C. has the oldest entries, beginning in 1849, so I start there.

The diary belonged to Alva Callaghan, a seventeen-year-old girl who emigrated from Ireland with her husband, Eamonn, just before starting the diary. Alva's neat cursive describes the heart-wrenching goodbyes to her family after Eamonn decided their future lay in America. She wasn't sure Eamonn was making the right decision, but she loved him and had pledged her life to him, so she'd follow his footsteps wherever they took her.

The journey from Ireland was a long and difficult one for the couple. Alva was seasick the entire journey while Eamonn

181

worked as a deckhand to pay for their passage. They eventually arrived in America and found their way to Maine, where some of Eamonn's extended family had settled a few years earlier. The Callaghans established themselves in the then relatively new town of Port Braseham. In late October 1849, Alva wrote:

Everywhere I look, I am reminded of home and all of the things I miss. In many ways, life in Port Braseham is very similar to Ireland. Everything is green. The grass is green. The trees are green. The houses are green. I should wish that my favorite color were green!

There is the wonderful salty smell of the sea so near, which reminds me of home... I wonder how Mama is holding up without me. I wonder how my sisters are doing. Has Laura had her baby? Has Roisin married that dreadful James? I hope she chose Dylan instead! And is my dear brother, Keagan, being nice to his sisters? Oh, how I miss them!

The move is made easier by Eamonn's cousins, who have been so very kind. Although their house is small and they barely know us, they welcomed us into their home with open arms. Eamonn helps his cousin Seamus on his fishing boat, while I stay home to help Seamus' wife, Rebecca, with their three energetic children, all boys: Thomas, Stephen, and Joseph – all under the age of eight. How Rebecca managed to keep up with them before I arrived, I shall never know! They are quite clever and mischievous. Just the other day I found all three of them on the roof with no idea how they got up there or how to get them down! I had to call over the pastor and his ladder, as Seamus and Eamonn were not due back for several hours and Rebecca, trusting me, went to the market and left the boys in my care.

I enjoy Rebecca very much. She is nearly twice my age, but she doesn't talk to me like I am a child. She treats me like a woman, which I like very much. Being the youngest of seven, I was always treated as the baby of the family, and it is nice to feel independent. And, thank goodness, Rebecca is not quick to anger! When she arrived home to find the pastor and the boys on the roof, she merely laughed and patted me on the back.

Caring for the boys has reminded me how very much I want my own children. Two boys and two girls; Joshua and Darren (after Father), and Holly and Emily (after Mother). I try not to bring it up too much as it bothers Eamonn to talk about wishes. I think he still feels like a young man, but he is nearly 37!

Wow, seventeen and thirty-seven? I suppose it wasn't a big deal back then, but something like that could get you arrested today. I flip ahead, looking for something interesting, and find a short entry with the first mention of Wolfhowl Manor in mid-December.

We have just purchased land on the most beautiful hill in town! I can hardly wait, but wait I must. All we have is the land, but Eamonn has promised to build the most wonderful house to my specifications. It will truly be the House of Our Dreams! And to know it was lovingly built with my husband's own hands fills me with great joy! How very lucky I am! I must write to Mother and tell her straight away!

January through May are pretty mundane. Eamonn was a busy man, constantly on the fishing boat or working on the couple's new house, but Alva could only lavish her hard-working husband with compliments, worshiping the ground he walked on. They moved into the incomplete house in April to give Eamonn's cousin their house, and space, back. Seamus and Rebecca were expecting another child and Alva desperately hoped it was a girl for Rebecca's sake.

Alva continued helping Rebecca and began teaching piano lessons to help make ends meet. Then, something interesting – the first storm Mr. Lindsay mentioned in class. It was a severe thunderstorm in late May 1850. The storm had hail and waterspouts that, according to Alva, "ripped the corn crops straight out of the ground and into the sky." It's after this Alva's diary starts documenting not only the decline of Port Braseham, but also her own descent into madness, and it's such a deeply dark romance, I can't put it down. As in many of the old romantic tales, it's just as the couple nearly achieves complete happiness that their descent begins.

Alva's diary walks through the small events of summer and winter in Port Braseham. Through Alva's thoughts, I begin to understand the devastation that first storm had caused to the town. It's almost as if the residents of Port Braseham were experiencing their own little Great Depression. The town had built itself on farming and fishing, the only two things that didn't seem to be available to them all of a sudden. People weren't starving exactly, but times were difficult. As the months dragged along, Alva's outlook on life became bleak.

I'd been so excited to move into our own house all those months ago. But I never dreamed how much would change, how alone I would feel.

Being with Rebecca and the boys is wonderful and exciting. There is always talking and laughing and the noise of the boys playing somewhere. Neighbors visit and there are teas and strolls downtown. I am surrounded by an aura of contentment when we are together.

But it is different up on this hill. Eamonn is gone more than ever, and I'm left with nothing but the constant lonely whistle of a breeze leaking through the unfinished frame of our 'house' and a silence so heavy it feels like its own presence. It gives one the feeling of being followed, shadowed from room to room by something that always lurks in the shadows.

We are far enough from town that no one visits, not even Rebecca. She came up with the boys just once, but left almost immediately after, feigning illness. The boys themselves refused to even enter the house, looking at it as if it were some… well, some monster, something to fear. I tried to reassure them, but they would only hide behind Rebecca's skirts, as if they were all toddlers again. I tried to talk to Rebecca about it once, but her face became so pale and rigid that I let it go for fear she would faint.

The loneliness I feel here is of the deepest kind I have ever felt. I truly feel that I am alone. From the windows, looking down on the town in the dark, one could almost be convinced it is deserted. That you are alone. Each day I feel a little more isolated from the world and a little more afraid of the future.

But then, you know that, don't you?

The only subject that seemed to bring life and joy to Alva's writing was the thought of children. During the long days that Eamonn and Seamus were out on the boat, Alva spent much of her time playing with Rebecca's children. The seed of motherhood had been planted deeply, and there would be nothing to stop her from having a child of her own very soon. She even began to imagine what such a child would look like.

Thomas has the loveliest green eyes. Every time I see him, his magnificent eyes spill over with warmth and joy. If only our child could have such wonderful eyes, but Eamonn is very dark in complexion. There shall be none of Stephen's fiery hair or Joseph's porcelain skin – well, perhaps the porcelain skin. I am quite pale myself.

Oh, each day I think of being a mother more and more. It scarcely leaves my mind for a moment! 'Why must you always hurry things?' is what Eamonn always says, but I can only smile. Just wait until he hears that he is to be a father! Then he will understand! He will begin to think as I think: What will my son or daughter be like? Will they be warm and laugh often like Stephen? Or will they brood and cry like Joseph? If it is a girl, will she like pink? Will I have to force her to wear the little lavender dresses I will make for her? Will my son love being doted on and carried along atop his father's shoulders?

I will drive myself crazy with anticipation if we do not conceive soon! Or perhaps it is you that I will drive crazy!

I keep reading about Alva's visions of her child, of motherhood, of life in Port Braseham with her handsome family. Each entry is more detailed, more urgent, more desperate.

Alva and Eamonn became pregnant in May 1851, exactly a year after the famous storm. At first, both were elated. Alva planned the nursery and did all of the things a young mother-to-be would do. Eamonn's reaction was different. He was happy at first, but by August, Alva had decided Eamonn didn't want a baby at all. He was always in a bad mood and snapped at her with the slightest provocation. She became depressed, but even in her depression, she made excuses for her husband. He worked hard, both on the house and on Seamus' boat, but the fishing industry was suffering and he worried the house wouldn't be done in time for the baby. In late August, she wrote:

It isn't his fault. It is perhaps mine, for asking so much of him during such a difficult time. It isn't only Eamonn who suffers, but the town, for that strange storm last May – yes over a year ago now! – seems to have destroyed not only the crops, but also the soil to plant them in, and it has carried away every last fish. Every Sunday at church, I pray for the relief of the town. Rebecca says I am being too sensitive. There is 'a normal ebb and flow to things,' she tells me. 'All will be well in the end.'

I could almost believe Rebecca were it not for Eamonn's strange behavior. He is always away from the house, either on the fishing boat praying for a catch or in town on an errand. When he is here, he stomps around as if he were carrying an elephant! He seems always to wear a frown and is more reserved than the man I married. It seems I can do no right by him. Dinner is never made properly. The house is always dirty and covered in sawdust – as if that were my fault! And to have seen the look he gave me when I came home yesterday with a small basket for the baby's room! He must have thought it cost a fortune! I have asked him many times what is wrong, but he always says it is nothing.

Perhaps I am only being paranoid. I know Eamonn thinks so. When I'm here all by myself, in this monstrous house, I feel odd. I feel strange. I have the sensation of being watched. Ha! I am laughing at myself. I know it is not possible, but it almost seems as if a ghost were here, shadowing me as I complete my daily duties, as I sweep or teach little Joseph to play piano. I have ventured so far as to ask Eamonn to try to be home before dark, but he feels I am acting a 'foolish little girl. You take Seamus' ghost stories for the boys too seriously!'

As the weeks and months passed in Alva's diary, it feels less and less like a diary. It's more like she was writing a letter home to a sister or best friend. She told stories to a mysterious "you" and asked questions as if she truly expected an answer, and even sometimes, as if she'd gotten one. It increased as her pregnancy developed and her relationship with Eamonn became more strained.

In September:

Eamonn continues to be gone most of the day. He leaves before sunrise and gets home hours after sunset. I miss him even when he is right in front of me. He barely speaks anymore. I'm so lonely for conversation that I've started to talk to myself! Of course, I spend time at church and with Rebecca and the boys, but even Seamus is home more than Eamonn. I worry there is something he has not told me.

Am I paranoid? And if not, what can I do? What would you have me do?

In October:

Eamonn is as frigid as the air outside. He only tells me he loves me when I protest he has grown tired of me. He no longer asks how I feel or after the baby. It is as if he doesn't care for us at all.

My heart is breaking, I tell you, just breaking.

I wish you wouldn't say such things, but perhaps... Perhaps you are right.

By November, Alva's depression equaled the size of her swollen belly.

The baby moves inside me, but I feel nothing. I do not deserve this gift from God. I will be as much a failure at mothering as I have been at being a wife. I am not good enough for this child. We are not good enough for this child. We cannot even finish a house, much less raise a child! No, we are not parents. How could I have been so blind?

This child deserves better. But who? Tell me, who will be the mother this child deserves?

That entry sends chills racing down my spine.

The baby was born a year to the day after Eamonn and Alva purchased their land. The first floor of Wolfhowl Manor was complete, and Eamonn finished the nursery and master suite, but only just. The third floor and the attic were coming along.

Eamonn had been rushing to finish the necessary rooms before the baby's arrival. For this reason, many of the rooms on the north side of the house were incomplete, including the room next to the nursery. The room next to Liam's. The fire room.

Alva's depression worsened after the birth of their daughter, Emily Lenore. Convinced as she was that they were undeserving of such a wonderful child, Alva had a difficult time caring for her. She did all she could to avoid bonding with Emily Lenore, convinced the girl's true mother would soon arrive and whisk her away to the life she deserved.

Eamonn, distant though he was, became concerned by Alva's deep depression. He called the doctor to visit them several times in the two weeks following the birth of Emily Lenore.

The doctor! Can you imagine? The doctor cannot help us, because there is no help for us. Yes, I am certain now. So undeserving, as you've been kind enough to remind me. I'm merely a vessel. Emily Lenore's true mother will come soon. I am sure of it. I can feel it inside me.

Yes, her true mother is close.

That's the last entry in Alva's diary, on Christmas Eve 1851. That rings a bell somewhere. What was it Mr. Lindsay told our class? The first annual Christmas Eve storm was in 1851. Yes, but something else still nags at me. Christmas Eve of 1851 is also the night the builders of Wolfhowl Manor, died. Yes, that's what it is.

Chapter Twenty-Five
The Storm Party

Mother hasn't come out of her room, clearly still recovering from a night of hard partying. She doesn't protest when I ask about going out, but I hear the sadness in her voice. I wonder if the dark circles under her eyes are from a late night, or from crying. I feel a little guilty for being so wrapped up in myself. I guess I assumed the move would be easy on Mother because *she* was the one who wanted to move. Am I wrong?

Liam spends all day in his playroom. I check in on him a few times to make sure he's behaving and that his needs are met, but clearly my care isn't required. When I check on him for lunch, he already has a sandwich in his hand. Sitting in front of his pudgy form on the floor is a set of dirty miniature soldier figurines I've never seen before.

"Hey, where'd you find those?" I ask, but Liam merely shrugs and goes back to his little warring men. I wait for an answer, but when it's clear I'll get none, I leave him to his own devices.

Around eight, right before Letta's due to arrive to look at Alva's diary and get ready for the storm party, I go back up to Liam's room to help him get ready for bed. I find him in his bed, already washed, teeth brushed, and in his pajamas. He's sitting Indian style with his chin in his hands and staring into Mother's old rocking chair in the corner, as if something there holds his attention.

"Holy cow, squiggle worm," I say. "I'm impressed! Look at you gettin' ready for bed all by yourself!" I sit next to him with a smile. "So what'll it be tonight? The princess and her knight? The goblin and the gremlins?"

"No."

"No?"

"I don't need one of your stories tonight," he says simply. His voice is so moderate and unreadable, it's unnerving.

I try not to sound offended. I mean, he has to outgrow story time someday right? "Oh. Okay. Well, are you going to bed then?"

Liam glances back toward the rocking chair, as if awaiting some invisible cue, then looks back to me with a nod. "Yup!" He crawls up to the head of his bed and lays down, his head on the pillow and his perfect little curls spilling around his halo-shaped face.

Where is my little brother? I wonder. I hear him say goodnight as I close his door, but somehow I know he isn't talking to me.

*   *   *

Letta and I primp for the party. While I'm creating perfect curls in my ponytail with a curling iron, Letta sits on the toilet looking through Alva's diary. She's cute in a floral print dress and stylish ankle boots. Her short straight hair has a few well-placed curls of her own and she's applied a light layer of lavender eye shadow that brings out her dark eyes. I'm so used to seeing Letta in her plain Jane style, I almost didn't recognize her when I opened the door.

I've paired my tightest skinny jeans with my three-inch heeled knee-high black boots. I especially like my skin tight red top because the low cut v-neck accentuates my cleavage without actually showing any of it. (Always leave them wanting more right?) I'm sans necklace, but pull at my dangling silver earrings to make sure they won't fall out. As I focus on my reflection in the mirror, I feel the energy of the fire room on the other side of the wall, pulsating out toward me. Calling to me.

"What do you think happened to them?" I ask Letta as a distraction.

"I'm not sure," Letta says, closing the diary and putting it on the counter. "The only common knowledge is that the Callaghans' deaths supposedly started the curse. There's all sorts of twisted rumors of course, but who knows what really happened? We just have the based-on-a-true-story version, you know? It barely resembles the truth anymore."

"It's so chilling to read her words," I say, giving orders to some rebellious strands of hair with gel. "She really did lose it there at the end."

"Yeah, I feel bad for her," Letta says. "Cleary, she was lonely. To want children so badly, but then realize you can't handle it? It's tragic."

I snort. "Is there anything associated with this place that *isn't* tragic?"

"Well, maybe I can pump some people for information at the party tonight. It's the perfect place to gossip, talk about the taboo, kiss a fool..."

I laugh. "What fool will you be kissing this evening?"

Letta shrugs and winks. "You never know." She looks at her watch. "Are you almost ready? Shane'll be here any minute."

"Almost."

"And what fool are you trying to look so beautiful for anyway?" Letta asks slyly. "Beckan or Ronan?"

I start. When did Ronan enter the picture? And although I can't deny the developing electricity between us, I don't think a party is really Beckan's scene.

"Oh come on," Letta nudges me. "Ronan's obviously trying to start trouble, and Beckan staying last night? Clearly he was staying for your benefit, not mine."

"Listen, I'm in no need of a knight in shining armor. And Ronan's with Mary."

"Never stopped him before."

I'm beginning to form a question when I hear the heavy knockers on the front door echoing throughout the house. Letta gets the door for Shane while I tell Mother I'm leaving.

I find her exactly as I left her hours earlier, lying in her bed under the covers, but she isn't asleep. She's just staring off into space. Her mouth almost seems to be moving, but no sound comes out. At least she's finally changed out of her cocktail dress.

"Mom?" Mother's eyes slowly move around the room until they find me. "Letta and I are leaving now. I'm not sure what time I'll be home. Is that okay?" Asking for permission feels ridiculous; I'm so used to doing whatever I want. But seeing Mother like this makes me treat her more gingerly. She looks like a delicate flower that's been left in the sun without water – wilted, pale, and dry. She might fall apart in the lightest wind. As I wait for some kind of reply, I feel a certain fear, a fear I'm not familiar with and can't identify.

"Yes, Rose, that's fine," Mother says evenly. "Have fun with your friends. Is Liam in bed?"

"Yeah."

"Good," Mother says. "Good." She closes her eyes.

I quietly back out of the room. I've never seen Mother so docile and agreeable. It's bizarre. Maybe she has more than a hangover.

Shane, Letta, and Patty talk quietly downstairs. Shane, in typical guy style, looks about the same as he always does, but he's wearing a sweet cologne and has used a little hair gel.

Unlike Letta, Patty usually puts a lot of thought into her outfit choices. There's always something bold about her, either in pattern, hairstyle, or small accents, like brightly colored feather earrings or a quirky, colorful necklace. Tonight she's upped the ante with a pair of yellow skinny jeans and a tight fitting red top the same flaming red as her hair. The only thing that's usually plain about her is her face. A little face powder and mascara are the norm, but tonight she's wearing bright pink lipstick and a swath of yellow over each eye. It's like she paged through a fashion magazine and picked out her outfit, but she's done it well. She certainly won't be missed in the semi-darkness of a high school party.

"How are you feelin'?" Shane asks as I join them.

"We were worried 'bout you," Patty adds.

"Uh, I'm okay, thanks," I say nonchalantly. "Fainting is pretty normal for me when I get freaked out," I lie. "I'm just lucky I didn't hit my head. I was worried about you guys when I woke up. Where's Eileen?"

Patty shrugs. "Haven't heard from her since last night, but I'm sure she'll be at the party."

"Yeah," Shane says. "She drops off the radar sometimes. I wouldn't be surprised if her phone was destroyed in the storm last night anyway. She was soaked when we found her."

"I'm just glad she wasn't hurt. Do you have any idea what happened?" I feel silly even asking. Obviously, the girl had been terrified, and instead of fainting like I did, she panicked and ran.

"She was in that little bathroom in the basement," Shane shrugs. "We didn't heeah anythin' until she stahted screamin'."

There's a pause as each of us recalls last night in our own mental images.

"Alright," Letta says suddenly, "let's go! If we're lucky, we'll get there before the rain starts back up."

As if hearing Letta, Zeus himself unleashes a bright flash of lightning eventually followed by a low and distant rumble of thunder.

"And," Letta says with excitement as we put on our jackets, "Rose read one of the diaries!"

"Ooh," Patty says, clapping her hands together. "Do tell!"

Letta and I share what we learned as we trundle along in Shane's old clunker. Unfortunately, neither Shane nor Patty has any ideas about the deaths of Alva or Eamonn. That subject is strictly taboo. In fact, they tell me Principal Flynn gave Mr. Lindsay a stern warning in regards to the information he'd given my class about the first Christmas Eve storm. I feel guilty I'd asked the question that started it all.

Shane pulls up near the sign for Penobscot Park and turns off his headlights. Several cars already litter the side of the road. The party itself isn't forbidden, but to have it on state property after dark certainly is. There's a casual recklessness by the partygoers, however. They shouldn't be here, yet their cars are easily visible to anyone who drives by on the well traveled thoroughfare. Shane finds a space between a familiar BMW SUV and an old Ford Taurus.

"It's a bit of a hike from heeah," Shane says as we gather on the side of the road. He and Patty take the lead, walking close together, and Letta and I walk carefully in their wake. We aren't exactly wearing footwear conducive to a walk through a muddy and heavily wooded area, and Shane is obliged to help each of us at one point or another to prevent anyone spraining an ankle.

After a ten-minute walk, we begin to hear the telltale signs of a party. There's the deep bass thump of dance music, the sounds of happy screams and laughter. Light begins to pierce the tree line and we come upon a large modern cabin in a clearing.

People are everywhere. It's mostly high school students, but I catch sight of a few older looking eighth graders and some twentysomethings. Most of the attendees are making their way inside, unwilling to brave the chill outside, but there's a group gathered on a second level balcony smoking cigarettes. To my surprise, one of them is Beckan, who leans on the railing as he talks to a girl about his age. They're both smiling and he laughs at something she says. It's the most emotion I've ever seen him display. Who is this girl? An uncomfortable warmth spreads through my chest.

The interior of the cabin is contemporary with a floor plan that opens wide below a second level loft. The wood is sturdy but made to look rustic. There's wooden furniture everywhere, covered with colorful cushions. A large fireplace dominates one wall with a stone mantle going all the way up to the exposed ceiling, a roaring fire burning within. Loud music pours from speakers on a shelf near a fancy kitchenette. Several people have gathered here around a group of kegs. To my surprise, I see Eileen coming out of a keg stand to a round of loud cheers.

Yep, all the signs are here; it's a party alright.

Shane throws our jackets into a bedroom off of the main living area. They land on the mountain of coats already gathered on the bed next to a couple making out. Our group is separated almost immediately as we head into the throng of partygoers, and I feel abandoned. I'm out of my element – no, that isn't right. This *is* my element. Or at least, it used to be. I should feel comfortable and confident here. But I don't. I feel like a tiny flower, ready to meld with the walls. I make eye contact with Eileen, relieved to see a familiar face. I wave, but she either doesn't see me or ignores me. Is she mad at me? I wonder before mentally chiding myself. Since when do I care what others think of me?

Trying to fake confidence I don't feel, I make my way through the crowd, trying to figure out what to do. There's a dance party around the speakers, bodies gyrating against each other to the beat of the music. In another room, a round of Guitar Hero is going on. I catch sight of Adam O'Sullivan, looking much unlike himself as he duels with another teenager, the guitar his weapon. For a minute, I think he even smiles.

In the kitchen, people refill their red Solo cups, which then quickly fill a large rubber trashcan set at the end of the counter. There's a second large trashcan filled to the brim with a red liquid and floating fruit. I can smell the vodka wafting from it and feel no desire to join *that* party. I've seen Mother and her friends with enough hangovers to know I can have a perfectly good time without imbibing.

I push through the growing crowd and try to pick up shreds of conversation, bits of gossip, or at least something that sounds familiar, but it's a lost cause. If those around me aren't lowering their voices as I get close, their conversations are so thick with the slack-jawed Mainah accent that I can't understand them.

In an effort to find somewhere I don't feel out of place, I head to the staircase leading to the loft. Maybe this smaller area with less people is something I can use to work my way up to mingling with the rowdy crowd downstairs. Alas, the loft appears to be make-out central. The lights are dimmed and there are comfortable sofas and chairs everywhere, all full of kissing, cuddling couples. There are no other rooms off of this space, only the sliding glass doors leading to the deck where I saw Beckan. Looking through the glass now, I see him again, still talking to the same girl. She's about his height with long blond hair. She wears a stylish jacket, and stands close to him in a group of about ten people. She's an artist with her makeup. She's pretty without overdoing all of the face paint like a lot of girls. Like cheerleaders. Her elbow is almost touching Beckan's. He pulls out a cigarette and his monogrammed lighter to light it, then passes it to her and lights one for himself. Is this is the girl who gave him the lighter? Why haven't I seen her around before?

I don't realize I'm staring until the sliding glass door opens and several people come flooding in, hugging themselves and rubbing their hands together. They laugh at a punch line I can't hear, and I catch the stench of smoke wafting in on the cold air as my eyes meet Beckan's. He smiles and waves. Should I wave back?

"Rose!" A hand on my elbow turns me around before I make up my mind.

It's Ronan. Like all the other guys at the party, his usually bed-head hair is tamed with the perfect amount of gel. His cologne isn't as sweet as Shane's, but I like the muskier scent. He's wearing a thin Polo sweater and tight, distressed jeans. He looks *good*.

"I'm glad you made it! Wow," he says as he looks me up and down. "You look great!"

"Um, yeah, thanks," I reply, searching for something to say. "You guys sure know how to throw a party. Whose place is this anyway?"

"It technically belongs to the park," he says, "but the historical society uses it a lot for meetins and other thins. I snagged the keys from Dad." His smile is wide, full of perfectly straightened pearly whites, and I wonder how much money it cost.

At the mention of the historical society and his dad, I remember what Letta said about Ronan and Beckan's fistfight. Didn't it have something to do with the historical society and Wolfhowl? The historical society has been taking care of the house and employing the O'Dwyre family for years. What could Beckan and Ronan have been arguing about? As far as I know, historical societies are pretty boring.

"It's really nice," I say because I've paused so long that Ronan is staring uncertainly at me.

"Yeah, my mom decorated it. She loves to design interiors and such. Dad likes her hobby because it keeps her out of his hair." He chuckles and I'm surprised to feel myself smile back.

"So how was last night?"

"Last night?"

"Whatevah plans you had," Ronan says. "With Letta?"

"Oh, right." I feel stupid and blush. "Fine. Nothing special. Just girl stuff."

"That's not what I heard," Ronan says, but his voice is so low I barely hear him over the music.

"What?"

"Heeah," he says without answering me and takes my hand in his, leading me toward the stairs. "Let's go somewhere quieter where we can talk. In fact, I think I know the perfect place."

As I follow Ronan, I'm worried he's leading me into the room where people are throwing coats on the making-out couple. Instead, he yanks his expensive leather jacket out from under them and hands it to me.

"You'll need this," he says and throws the jacket over my shoulders. It's large on my thin frame. He grabs my hand again, weaving me back through the crowd, and leads me through a back door, back into the wintry chill of the night.

"Where are we going?"

"You'll see. You'll like it, I promise." He winks and keeps hold of my hand.

We walk down a path made of the same colorful rocks lining the beach. The moon, nearly full and peeking through a break in the clouds, lights our way through the trees. We walk without talking. The hoot of night owls and the song of crickets follows us. After a few minutes, I also hear the sound of rushing water. There must be a river nearby, and just as I have that thought, Ronan begins leading me away from the path. We come to the edge of the tree line and are faced with a large rock formation. Water rushes over the edge of the rocks, creating a waterfall just a bit taller than us.

I can't help myself and gasp as the light of the full moon twinkles endlessly in the moving water. "It's beautiful."

"We're not there yet. A mite bit more to go," Ronan says with a sly smile. "Heeah, let me help you." He takes both of my hands and leads me to the riverbank, helping me work my way down the slope and to the edge of the waterfall. "Careful. Don't slip on the rocks. Ready?"

"For what?"

"For this." He keeps hold of my hands and leads me behind the blanket of water, revealing a small pocket of rock where two people can sit comfortably, or closely, and stay hidden from view without getting wet. It's colder back here, especially as Ronan helps me sit on the freezing rock floor, but he pulls me close and puts an arm around me.

"Keep me warm," he laughs.

I smile back. Flirting comes easily to me and reminds me of fun times back in Texas, but I'm wary at the same time. Ronan is flirting with me, but *why?* He has the beautiful, if bitchy, Mary Donovan on his arm. What does he want with social outcast Rose Delaney?

"Where's Mary?"

He shrugs. "Back at the party somewhere with her gals. I lost track of her." His tone is nonchalant, uncaring. Why do the two of them bother to carry on this facade of a couple?

"Yeah, I lost track of my group immediately. I still don't know very many people. I was fixin' to melt into the wall when you found me." I smile again and Ronan laughs. It's a warm sound that echoes in the small space around us. I lean into him. For warmth.

"How did you find this place?"

"Unfortunately, it's not a secret," he says. "Couples have been comin' back heeah to make out for ages." He laughs again, but this time it's a little awkward. I again take notice of his Maine accent that he tries so hard to hide when Mary's around. I wonder why that is and decide to tease him a little.

"To make out, huh?"

"Well," Ronan says, quite charmingly pretending to be awkward, "you can do other stuff back here too."

"Is that so?" This time the sly smile is mine. "Like what?"

"Well, off the top of my head…fish, for example. Or…sleep? Camp, I guess? Or just hide…" From his tone, I think Ronan has been back here a few times for just that reason. I had him pegged as the popular kid, shallow and spoiled, and always following Mommy and Daddy's orders. Have I been wrong? Or is he just a good actor and working hard to charm me? But what advantage would hanging around me really get him? He'd lose more friends than he'd gain.

"So what brings us to this special place then?" I ask, staring pointedly at Ronan, wondering if he'll give me a straight answer. "Still trying to bring me over to your side, are you?"

"Is it that obvious?" He laughs. "No, I'm kidding. Look, I'm not responsible for the popularity divide. I can't help it if kids in this town look to me and my family for leadership. It's mostly because my dad's so important."

"Your dad?"

"Don't play dumb, Rose," Ronan says, a little unkindly. "It's not cute on you. You're smart and I like that. You know my dad is the head of the historical society, has been for years. He and the other society members are the sole reason that shack you live in still exists. That may not make us exactly popular with everyone, but even if the townspeople don't agree with Dad's decisions, they respect his power and position." With each word, his chest seems to puff up with importance.

So Ronan *is* a little full of himself. That's okay; I like a guy with confidence.

"The way everyone 'round heeah looks at it is you're either on one side of the fence or the other," Ronan continues. "You're on the side that believes in the curse, or you're on the side that thinks it's all horseshit."

I laugh. "Which side are you on?"

"I'm supposed to be on the side that thinks it's crap," he says hesitantly.

"But you aren't?"

"I dunno. I know what Dad believes, which is that it's just a big coincidence. That house isn't responsible for anythin' that's happened to this town or the people in it. It's their own poor decisions that put them on the wrong path." I have a feeling Ronan has heard this speech from his father many times. "So, I guess I'm on that side. But it's hard to really decide for myself. You're constantly hearin' rumahs about this or that 'round town."

I feign surprise.

"Oh, it's a taboo subject, but that doesn't mean the gossips don't find a way to talk about it."

"What side are the O'Dwyres on?" I immediately regret the question. Ronan's face falls and I almost apologize, but then he starts talking.

"They're supposed to be on our side, the side of the people who don't believe in the ghost stories. The O'Dwyres haven't been well liked for a long time because they support the land and the house. Their family has been taking care of it for generations, when no one else would, almost like it was a responsibility. But then…"

"Beckan's mom died."

"Yeah," Ronan says. "I was young when it happened, but I still remember. Everyone liked her even though she lived on the hill. A lot of people were upset when she died."

"Then why do you talk like you and Beckan aren't on the same side of the fence?"

"Last year, when the house had been vacant for a long time, and there didn't seem to be anyone who would take it off our hands, Derry came to one of the town meetins and asked for the house to be torn down for, like, the thousandth time. No one wants it, the townspeople think it's evil, so why keep it 'round? It created quite the stir, let me tell you," he laughs to himself. "It pit one group of townspeople against the other, and it eventually came to a vote. It was close, but the historical society won. The house is part of our town's history and kind of an architectural anomaly, so it deserves to stay standin'. Derry wasn't too happy 'bout that and he stahted yellin' at my dad. I told him where he could stuff it. That didn't sit too well with him – or Beckan. The next time I saw him, he decked me, for no reason other than tellin' his old man the way it is! Ever since then…" he shrugs.

I nod. The silence grows between us. The cold is getting to me and I start shivering.

"Are you cold?" Ronan asks, pulling me closer.

"A little." I pause, considering how to proceed. I decide being blunt is the only way to make my point. "Look, Ronan, you can stop being coy. I know you didn't bring me up here to chat about history class."

"Oh?" He raises his eyebrows. "Why'd I bring you heeah then?"

"To kiss me."

He laughs again, that nice throaty laughter echoing behind the watery curtain.

For a moment, we look at each other without saying a word. Then, Ronan leans his face toward mine. His lips are cool, like spearmint. I can taste the gum he's chewing to hide the aftertaste of beer. He's a little pushy, taking the lead over me, but clumsily. He puts his other arm around me and pulls me closer to him. I know Ronan has nice arms molded at the gym, but they feel thin and brittle around my body, like a pair of icicles. I wonder if Beckan's arms would feel this insubstantial around me.

"Really?" A voice interrupts us. "Him? Everyone in this town and you pick *him?*"

We break apart to face the shadow standing before the watery blind enclosing us. It's dark, but I can just make out Adam's features in the thin veil of moonlight.

"What are you doin' heeah?" Ronan's voice is hostile.

"You don't own this spot," Adam says venomously. "I don't have to tell you why I'm here."

"Well it obviously isn't to be with a girl," Ronan retorts acidly.

"That makes you better than me?" Adam laughs cruelly. "You're such a hypocrite. You ramble on all day about 'that weird girl' who lives in the house on the mountain and how she's going to be 'the end of us all,' and here you are kissing her." He rolls his eyes. "Mary will just *love* this."

"You keep your mouth shut 'bout Mary," Ronan snaps as he hops up, hunching slightly in the curve of the rocky roof above us. Feeling the situation quickly escalating, I stand too.

"Let's just calm down here," I say. "You can come in and hang out, Adam. There's plenty of room."

He looks at me with the same disdain he showed Ronan, and his hatred is so strong I have to step back. *"You?* Please! Your friendship isn't going to win me any favors in this town."

I'm taken aback by his anger. What does Adam have against me? I'd somehow seen him as different. Like me, he's an outsider, something that should bring us together. We're two bits of coal in a pit full of diamonds. We're supposed to be on the same side.

"You apologize to her," Ronan says, pointing an angry finger at Adam.

"I don't have tah listen to you," Adam shouts back. "Look at you, thinking how big and important you are around here, puffing up your chest like a little bird." Adam laughs his mean laugh again. "It's pathetic."

Without even taking the time to think about it, Ronan pulls back his fist and swings hard, clocking Adam in the jaw. Adam flies backward through the icy curtain and disappears.

*   *   *

After Ronan punched Adam, I made it back to the cabin. I'm ready to go home. Adam's sure to have a black eye – something else we'll have in common. He'd emerged from the water like an icicle, but otherwise unharmed. He glared at us, his eyes lingering on me as if I'd been the one who decked him, before he stalked off into the darkness. He didn't even turn around when I called after him to see if he was okay. I feel terrible, mostly about myself. The revulsion in Adam's eyes hurt the most, which just reminds me how much this place sucks. Rejection was completely unknown to me before Port Braseham.

Oh, how I hate this godforsaken place.

"Where've you been?" Letta pounces on me as soon as I return to the warmth of the cabin. "And whose jacket is that?"

"Huh? Oh." I shed the jacket and toss it back into the designated coatroom, which now has two couples making out on the mountain of coats. Ronan let me enter first and walked around to the back door. He doesn't want Mary to see us together, to be sure. "What's going on?"

"Is your lipstick smeared?" Letta demands with slits for eyes. "Nevermind. We'll get to who you've been up to in a minute. I've got some information for you."

"About what?"

"About Alva," Letta says excitedly. "After that last diary entry, she hanged herself."

"Hanged?" I remember the article from the travel magazine, which stated essentially the same thing, but I'm still shocked to hear it out loud, to have it confirmed.

Letta nods. "Eamonn found her when he came home from a fishing trip, hanging in that room on the second floor."

"The fire room?" I gasp. Is that why I feel so strange in that room? Because someone died in there?

"Yeah, and when Eamonn found her, he was so distraught he hung himself right next to her!"

"Oh my God! That's terrible! But wait, what about the baby? Emily Lenore?" I look around the room, trying to block out the noise. My eyes seek out the loft and I catch sight of Beckan, leaning over the railing. For a moment, our eyes lock.

Letta shrugs. "No one knows. And I know what you're thinking."

"You do?" How could Letta possibly know that my mind has shifted so suddenly from Emily Lenore's fate to Beckan's lips?

"Yeah. We need to figure out what happened to that baby."

Over the din of voices and music comes an explosion of thunder and lightning. A lull falls over the crowd, only the dance music breaking the silence. Over the deep bass, we begin to hear the sound of the heavy rain and hail assaulting the cabin.

The crowd gives a deafening cry. The party resumes.

Chapter Twenty-Six
The Noose

I'm ready to leave but Shane and Patty are nowhere to be found. When we can't find them, Letta drags me into an empty bathroom, where the tub is full of someone's stomach contents, and makes me tell her exactly what happened between me and Ronan, and between Ronan and Adam. Letta's eyes narrow when I tell her about the kiss. She probably wants to know why Ronan's showing so much interest in me. Well, join the club. His fist in Adam's face made it clear he didn't want Mary knowing he was off with me, but then why go off with me at all? Surely others noticed us walking away from the party together. It won't take long for word to get back to Mary. What's he gaining from this little flirtation? But when I tell Letta about the punch, she only shrugs.

"That Adam's an oddball," she says, but I have the feeling Letta's holding something back. Before I can ask her about it, Letta turns on her heels and leads the way back into the throng of drunken teenagers. I lose her again as she leads a renewed search for Shane and Patty.

I wait alone in the hall off of the kitchen. I catch another brief sighting of Eileen, this time with her lips wrapped around a bottle of Jack. I wonder if this is how Eileen always behaves at a party, or if she has another reason to drink so much – like what happened to her in my basement.

This time when I feel a hand on my elbow I yank it back and whirl around angrily, but freeze when I see Beckan's cool green eyes. He flinches, bracing for a punch.

"Sorry," I say, flustered. "I guess I'm a little jumpy."

"You? Never." He smiles and winks.

"Enjoying the party?" I ask, feeling stupid. Of course he's enjoying the party; he has a beautiful date.

He shrugs. "It's okay. Parties aren't really my thin', but this one's a tradition that must be honored," he says with mock importance. "Plus, my cousin swore she'd kill me if I didn't come."

"Cousin?"

"Yeah. You know, the girl with the long jacket?"

"Oh," I nod, trying to hide my spreading glee, and without taking the time to consider why I even care about Beckan's romantic attachments. "I just assumed she was your…"

"Nah, nah… nothin' like that." A nervous hand finds the back of his neck and rubs it absentmindedly.

"I figured she was the one who gave you the lighter," I say as I eye it in his other hand. He's fiddling with it anxiously, twisting it around and around between his thumb and forefinger.

"This? Oh, this used tah be Pop's." He holds it out to me, and for the first time I notice the letters D and O, not B and O. "Mom gave it tah him for their tenth anniversary, but he can't look at it anymore, so…" he shrugs. "It reminds me of her." His eyes move up from the lighter slowly, and then lock on mine.

There's a bubble of silence around us that momentarily blocks out the chaos of the party, the loud music fading to a muffled thudding. As we look into each other's eyes, I feel Beckan's stare like a tangible presence, as if he's trying to search my soul, trying to figure out what's going on in my head. I feel self-conscious but find myself unable to look away. What *am* I thinking? Why does his stare make me feel *naked?* Beckan's lips begin to part, drawing my eyes back to them. I feel my own lips parting, feel the heat rising to my cheeks. A nervous laughter bubbles up and I fight to keep it inside.

"I found Shane and Patty." Letta's voice bursts our silent bubble, the music and loud voices flooding back into our ears. Letta continues, oblivious to the current between me and Beckan. "They're waiting for us outside. Patty partied a little hard and she's sick."

"I guess we're riding home with the windows down," I say sarcastically, pinching my nose.

"I can give you guys a lift if you want," Beckan offers. "That way Shane's the only one who might get puked on."

Letta laughs, but it sounds forced. "Well, why don't you take Rose? I think I'll sit in the back and take care of Patty while Shane drives. I don't want her ruining the *plush* upholstery. It's the only thing that old jalopy still has going for it."

"Okay, sure," I say uncertainly. "You sure you don't need me?"

"Nah," Letta replies coolly. "I'll see you on Monday."

Without another word, Letta turns around and is once again swallowed up by the crowd. Now I'm *certain* she's keeping something from me, but for the life of me, I can't figure out what. She even seems a little mad at me, and I start playing the last few days over in my head, trying to think of anything I might've done to upset her.

"Is she mad at you?" Beckan asks.

"I dunno," I lie. If a clueless guy has noticed Letta's odd behavior, then yes, Letta is most certainly upset with me. "Come on. Let's go."

Beckan leads me back through the now drenched woods, holding me close to help me walk, and to shield me as best he can from the rain slipping through the tree canopy. As I walk alongside him, thinking about Letta, my only distraction is the sensation of how warm and strong Beckan's arms feel compared to Ronan's. I eye him a few times, noticing his striking profile in the bright flashes of lightning, my eyes darting away each time he turns toward me. I think I see him smile once or twice.

Beckan lets me off at the front door in the driving rain. He says a simple goodnight, but I feel his eyes watching me until I'm safely inside. I do my best not to think about it and check on Liam before going to bed. He's sleeping soundly and looks so peaceful. I touch his head lightly and think about how much I miss him – the *real* him, not this caricature of a rebellious five-year-old he's become. Then, for the sake of being thorough, I check on Mother too. She's also sleeping, but not peacefully. Her eyebrows are knitted, and her lips are taut with worry. I wonder what she's dreaming about as I find my way to my own bed.

*   *   *

Alva coos to the infant Emily Lenore, who is screaming and writhing in her twig-like arms. "Shh, sweet child. Shh." Emily Lenore does not listen. Of course she doesn't. She knows what Alva knows. Emily Lenore, tiny and only a few weeks old, knows and understands Alva is not her real mother. She may have carried her, birthed her, but Alva is not her true mother. She is merely a vessel.

"She's close," Alva whispers to Emily Lenore as she gently sets her in the bassinet at her feet. "I can feel her. She's near, and she is waiting for you. She's going to be so happy when she comes for you!"

Emily Lenore's cries from the bassinet grow quieter but do not cease. Alva disappears from the master bedroom for only a moment and returns with her bible and a length of rope. She looks tired, haggard. The weight of the bible and rope in one hand, and her tiny newborn in the other, is enough to make her grunt with effort. She walks slowly down the frosty hallway and opens the door to the room on the other end.

A frigid wind smacks Alva in the face as she stares through the unfinished wall toward the sea and into the darkening sky. Lightning skips across thunderheads in the distance. The storm is brewing. It will be upon them before dark. She must hurry.

Alva looks up to the exposed beams in the ceiling. The one at the center seems sturdiest, though it needn't be. Carefully, she sets down the bassinet and stands over it, staring into the eyes of her sweet child. No, not her child.

Very quietly, she opens her bible and reads a prayer to the child. Her voice is quiet and melodic, as if she is merely singing a lullaby. When she is finished, she hugs her bible close, whispers her own silent prayer, and then places the bible in the bassinet next to Emily Lenore. Then, she sets to work on the rope.

Alva is the wife of a sailor and she knows how to tie many knots. When Eamonn had been courting her all that time ago, he spent much of their time together teaching her different knots. Slip knots, sheet knots, bowlines, and yes, for a little bit of forbidden fun, the noose. Alva always knew it was only an excuse for his fingers to brush by her own during their innocent, supervised courting. Now, she uses that knowledge to weave the right knot into her noose. She must be certain it will not come undone under her slight weight. The rope is thick and coarse, scratching her delicate fingers as she works. It takes her longer than she thought it would. The rope comes undone a several times under her unskilled handiwork, but eventually, it is complete.

Alva turns back toward Emily Lenore with a knowing smile. "Soon, my dear," she whispers. "Soon." Emily Lenore coos back at her with a perceptive patience exceptional for a child of her age. Alva bends down to kiss her daughter one last time.

Alva retrieves Eamonn's ladder from the corner where he had left it and sets it up in the middle of the room next to the bassinet. She is still a little short for the tall ceilings, even with the rickety ladder swaying under her weight on the uneven floorboards. She tosses one end of the rope over the thick beam and does her best to tie a sturdy knot. She tugs on the noose a few times, putting a little more of her weight on it to be sure it will hold her small body. It will.

Then, without pause, without a look back at her daughter, without any thought behind her empty eyes, she slips the noose over her head and tightens it. A second later, she steps off the ladder and —

*   *   *

I wake with a start, confused and unsettled. Where am I? I nearly stumble several feet to the floor before I realize I'm standing on the top step of a ladder set in the center of the fire room. It's dark, but enough light filters in from the uncurtained windows for me to get my bearings. Looking down, I see a length of rope in one hand. Even in the semi-darkness, there's no mistaking the shape of the noose. My fingers are red and sore, as if I tied the knot myself, rubbing my skin against the coarse fibers.

I drop the rope and clamor down the ladder, breathing hard from the shock. Feeling a familiar warmth spread from my stomach and through my chest, I dash out of the fire room and into the bathroom, where I'm violently relieved of my stomach contents. My knees give way and hot tears roll down my cheeks. I fall away from the toilet and begin to sob.

Chapter Twenty-Seven
View from the Top

I fall asleep on the cool tiles of the bathroom floor. Liam wakes me around seven when he comes in to use the bathroom.

"Rosie, why are you on the floor?" He looks at me, his head tilted to one side like a curious dog.

I push myself into a sitting position, glad the room isn't spinning, though the way the rest of my body feels, it should be. I feel like I drank like a fish last night even though I didn't touch a drop of alcohol. I put a hand on my head and close my eyes for a minute, trying not to fall off the edge of the earth.

"Rosie?"

I open my eyes and slowly get to my feet. "Yeah, sorry kiddo. I don't feel good. I'm gonna go lay down. In a bed. It's all yours."

I stumble down the hall and fall into bed. When I next open my eyes, it's after eleven and I have the house to myself. And although the early morning events frightened me, I'm glad no one else is around. I don't have the energy to interact with anything more substantial than a muted television. I force some soggy cereal down and take a long, hot shower. Eventually I wash myself, but I spend most of my time sitting on the bottom of the tub letting the hot-as-I-can-stand-it water cascade over me, engulfing me the way the icy waterfall had engulfed Adam.

What's wrong with me? I feel so gloomy, like a troll hiding under the darkness of a fairytale bridge. *But why?* Sure, the last year's been tough on me, on my family, but I'd finally felt like I was adjusting to life here. It's been three months now. I have friends. Yet I feel this overwhelming sense of depression. I find myself thinking about Dad more and more, when previously I'd done all I could to *avoid* thinking about him.

Andrew Delaney was a quiet man. I've always wondered how he and Mother ended up together. Opposites must really attract because that's what my parents were. Mother is boisterous and loud; she laughs freely and openly. She's always been quick to any emotion, be it anger or happiness. But Dad was reserved. When he spoke, it was because he had something important to say. His voice was deep and melodic. People listened, *really listened*, when he spoke. He only laughed when something was truly funny, but even his laughter was more of a silent smile than a laugh. His face was sometimes like a stone, still and unreadable. Total opposites.

Dad was smart too, not to say Mother isn't. But he was smart in a different way. What did people always say about people like him? They're book smart. He may have been an accountant, but I always thought of him as a mathematical historian. He loved math and he loved history. "You'd be surprised how often the two go together," he used to tell me. He spent his days whiling the time away in a cubical over numbers that mattered to no one, but he enjoyed it because it was math. Then he'd spend his evening telling me some of the most exciting historical accounts he knew, mostly about World War II, his favorite topic. I remember all those evenings sitting around the family room with the television turned off, listening with rapt attention as he wove his tales of deceit and intrigue. It's those nights I miss the most.

And it's those nights I thought of when my parents told me I was going to be a big sister six years ago. At first, I was happy, but then angry and jealous. Why should I have to share Dad with this tiny little *thing?* I was here first. I can admit I was a difficult and selfish child, stubborn too, and for the first six months of Liam's life, I pretended he didn't even exist. He was my parents' imaginary child. It wasn't until Liam was walking and talking, and after a lengthy conversation with Dad, that I began to understand my responsibility to him as his big sister. It was Dad who helped me realize I loved Liam *so much,* in some innate way I still don't understand. But now…

Now the protective bubble of my family is broken. Mother is returning to her alcoholism, Dad is six feet under dry Texas earth, and Liam is fast becoming someone I don't even recognize… I feel a hollowness deep within.

I dress warmly when I finally emerge from the steam-filled bathroom. The house has grown cold since the rain started and I know it'll be colder on the upper floors. Since I'm sitting around by myself, I figure it's the perfect time to check out the attic and widow's walk without having to explain myself to anyone, if for no other reason than to provide me with a distraction from my depressing internal monologue.

I stand before the short hall Letta and I discovered on the third floor, staring down it apprehensively. It's a cloudy day, but the rain has paused and it's not only frosty on the third floor, but dark. I don't need the flashlight in my hand to see my breath fogging in front of me, but I take it anyway. In my other hand I wield a broom like a weapon. Who knows how long it's been since someone's been up there. What if there are bats or spiders or…whatever?

Just as I'm convincing myself this adventure can wait, I square my shoulders and muster up some courage. "C'mon," I say to myself. "You're Rose Delaney. You don't back down from anything."

I start down the hall, taking my time as a cool draft wafts toward me from the open door at the other end. I look at the portraits again, taking in every detail. I stare long and hard at Alva and Eamonn. There's no doubt now; it was Alva in my dream last night. I wonder if I'd dreamed so vividly of the young mother because I remember looking at the painting before, or if it was even a dream at all. Could it have been some kind of vision? Could my dream have been…reality?

I almost laugh out loud at the absurdity of it. I'm not clairvoyant. It's just a combination of this picture and reading Alva's diary. *It's just your imagination, Rose.*

I peer into Alva's dead eyes. I've read the woman's own words, yet I can't fathom what came over her. Staring at this dreary dead-eyed couple, I feel sorry for them. Even though I know their fate, I still find myself rooting for them, hoping for a happy ending.

I move to the next portrait, with the smiling woman and the man with the thick eyebrows. I know now that I'm staring into the faces of Robert and Barbara Olenev, the owners of Wolfhowl Manor after the Callaghans. I remember the brief article from the realtor's file detailing the discovery of Robert's body not long after Barbara's death. The man who died of a broken heart after his wife's untimely passing. I shake my head. I know what Barbara's secret smile means. She was pregnant.

I skip over the portrait of the flapper and her husband. Their tight, angry smiles remind me too much of my parents, too much of loud voices and angry insults. Staring into those smug faces will earn me nothing but sadness and resentment now – and I have more than enough of that, thank you very much.

I take the time to gaze at the portraits on the opposite wall that Letta and I skipped, transfixed and terrified as we were by the attic door.

The first is of a handsome single man wearing the style typical of the early sixties. Unlike the portraits opposite his, his smile is warm and genuine. I have no idea who this man could be. He wasn't anywhere in the file I'd taken from Mother. Could he be the owner of one of the diaries? E. L. perhaps? He's the first person I've seen in the portraits who looks genuinely happy. He looks comfortable in a pair of bell-bottoms and a loud t-shirt. He has a jean jacket slung over one shoulder and a hammer in his other hand. Even in the portrait, I can tell his hands are rough and calloused like Beckan's. Here's a man who's good with his hands, who truly worked to earn his living. Was he the one who restored some of the previous beauty to Wolfhowl Manor alongside the O'Dwyres? I make a mental note to ask Beckan about him.

The final portrait is another young married couple who had to be living in the eighties based on her mountain of hair-sprayed bangs and bright pink and green eye shadow. Instead of woman in front of man with a hand on a shoulder, this couple holds a loving stance. He holds her in his arms with a tight bear hug and she has her own arms swung around his waist. Both wear genuine toothy smiles. This is what two people in love should look like.

I think about the people who fill these portraits. How odd that all of the owners had chosen to have their portraits made and hung here. Such a deserted place, far away from where you'd entertain any company. And they'd all had their portraits made in the same location – in front of the intricate fireplace in the drawing room. Is it a coincidence?

I'm certain these are the women who wrote the diaries we found. What made them all decide to write down their thoughts? To document the rise and fall of their lives here on Wolfhowl Mountain? Was this another coincidence? And why are all the diaries *exactly* the same? Where did they *come* from?

I make up my mind then and there: there's a presence here, on Wolfhowl Mountain. I'd idly entertained the idea of a ghost before. Perhaps Alva's still hanging around, turning my family into strangers, reenacting what happened to her own family. Is it some kind of payback for her unhappy ending? But now, I'm not so sure it's Alva. I've read nothing that speaks to the malice I feel when I'm alone in the house. I've seen nothing to indicate why the fire room is full of despair so strong it's like a living entity. Did all of this strangeness and anger start with Alva? Or was she the victim of a presence that was here long before her time? Is there a true proverbial Indian burial ground pulsating deep below Wolfhowl Mountain? All of these thoughts give me the willies and I want to go back downstairs, but I came up here for a reason.

As I approach the attic door , I see an empty portrait. The background is there, the detailed fireplace and floorboards, but there're no people in it. That's strange. Who would hang an empty portrait? And why? More questions to add to my already long list of questions about this place.

Finally, I'm at the attic door. It's old and cracked. Spider webs billow in the corners of the doorway from an invisible draft, and I watch one of the residents scuttle away. It's been a long time since this door has been used. It has a lock, but the door lays open, a skeleton key poking out of the keyhole.

I start, thinking back to the other night, as Letta and I huddled close together staring at the *door*. Hadn't the door been *closed* on Friday night? But now it's open, as if someone – or some *thing* – has recently passed through this portal to the unknown.

Feeling my nerve weakening, I take a deep breath and force myself through the door.

I'm immediately faced with a short set of rickety steps leading up into a dark gloomy mist. Thin shafts of weak light peak through cracks in the walls and roof. I make my way up the steps, careful to leave the door open, just in case I chicken out and need to make a quick getaway; it's fairly likely at this point.

My steps kick dust into the air and I cough. The small shafts of light aren't enough to see by, and it's too dark for my eyes to adjust. I set the broom against the railing and flip on the flashlight. Disappointingly, but somehow expectedly, there's not much to see. Boxes are scattered throughout the large space, and everything is caked in eons of dust, but there's nothing else of interest.

I paw at some of the boxes half-heartedly and nudge a few with the toe of my shoe. Nothing's labeled, and none of the boxes stand out as any older or younger than the others. There's only one way to figure out what they contain, so I get down on my knees, pull a box toward me at random and open the flaps.

This box surely belonged to the flapper couple. The items inside are soot-covered and layered with grime, but I recognize the long cigarette holder from their portrait. I also find an old-fashioned hand mirror with an intricately carved handle and a matching brush, a few strands of hair still clinging to the bristles. Both are made of silver and I wonder if the set is worth anything. I also find a few dirty scarves, several bowties of varying tacky patterns, a box of bobby pins, and at the very bottom, under a swath of dusty ivory fabric, a revolver. I'm stunned. Which one of them had carried it? And who – or what – were they protecting themselves from on their isolated mountain?

Going through the other boxes leads to nothing of any real interest. I find some clothing that probably belonged to the eighties couple, and a few things that probably belonged to Alva and Eamonn. There's a box of heavy tools, and lastly, one lone box made of sturdy pine with a label: Emily Lenore. This box, I know immediately, is *special*. It's been hidden beneath all of the others, a diamond in the rough.

I pounce on the box, expecting to find some infant clothes circa the 1850s, maybe a handmade doll from Eamonn's skilled hands, or baby blankets knitted with love by women at their church, or perhaps an ancient photograph of the child.

But these things are not inside this box.

What I *do* find doesn't make any sense. Emily Lenore was an infant in 1851. What happened to her after the death of Alva and Eamonn, I've no idea, but the items inside this box couldn't belong to that Emily Lenore. What I've found are much more modern clothes and toys, probably from the 1930s or 1940s. There's a copy of *The Great Gatsby*, which I not only love, but thanks to my tenth grade English class, also know wasn't published until 1922. I also see *Brave New World*, which thanks to my eleventh grade English class, I know wasn't published until 1932. It actually has a scrap of paper tucked into the pages like a bookmark. There are a few non-fiction titles related to aviation, which seems out of place until I find a set of bed sheets with little cartoon airplanes on them.

Beneath all of these things, I also find one of the oldest Barbie-like dolls I've ever seen. There are some model airplanes that look like they were made from a kit, crochet hooks, and a few balls of colorful yarn. There are several other toys at the bottom of the box that, although older, definitely didn't exist in 1851 or the fifty years that followed.

"It doesn't make sense," I mutter to myself. It must be mislabeled.

I contemplate this box for a long time before finally removing *The Great Gatsby* and the airplane sheets, and replacing the lid. I put these items by my broom at the top of the stairs, and then turn back for my next mission.

At the center of the attic is a set of wrought iron stairs, black paint peeling, metal spiraling several times upon itself before reaching a latched trapdoor in the ceiling. These I climb carefully, for they wobble slightly under me. I have to push all of my weight against the trap door before it flies up and flaps backward against the roof with a loud *bang!* The cold wind rushes in and squeezes me like a vise, throwing my hair around my face, making it difficult to see. Fighting the cold snap, I go up the remaining stairs and find myself on the roof of Wolfhowl Manor.

The view from here is astounding in the most beautiful and terrifying way. I'm not afraid of heights, but I've never been staring down from the top of a mountain before. I find myself holding onto the chipped white railing boxing the widow's walk in with bloodless knuckles.

I follow my driveway with my eyes until it disappears into the tall pines of the forest surrounding the hill. The houses, the little stores, the school, the church; all is visible from this vantage point, but they are also very, *very* small. I fight off a surge of tunnel vision and faintness.

I turn around and find the other railing. Staring off the cliff behind the house and into the sea, I can see the small rocky beach below the cliff and the whitecaps on the waves as they assault the shore with their salty forces. Dark clouds hang low over the ocean and there's only one boat out, way off in the distance. They must be crazy. Today is not a day to be on a tiny ping-pong ball bouncing along in the stormy current.

I stay on the widow's walk for a while, thinking about Alva, and how she must've watched for Seamus and Eamonn's boat from this very spot over a hundred years before. I try picturing this part of the coast crowded with fishing boats and trawlers, now dwindled, to only one in a hopeless quest to make a living. To the north, way down the beach, I see the waterfront where I sat on the beach that first week. I can barely make out the roof of the Wharf Rat and its surroundings. I try imaging the area alive and full of ant-like people, buying and selling their wares. But even from here, the boardwalk looks derelict. With a frown, I wonder what kind of town this would be, what it would be like to live here, if none of the tragedies had occurred. What would be different if I'd found a town full of happy, small-town folk rather than these beaten down, curse-fearing wolves, scavenging for fish, for something to live off of, for a reason to *be?*

I notice a thin trail of smoke coming from the O'Dwyre's chimney. Would Beckan's mother still be alive? I would've liked her, I think, the happy, humming ballerina. Maybe Mrs. O'Dwyre could've even helped me with my ballet.

A noise from below calls my attention away from the cabin. Our station wagon makes its way up the long drive, like an ant climbing its hill.

I don't know why, but I don't want anyone to know I've been slinking around the attic. I head back down the spiral stairs, careful to latch the trap door behind me. I run down the attic stairs, close the door, and after a second's thought, twist the key and stick it in my pocket.

I'm coming out of the servant's stairway into the kitchen when the front door opens. I skip across to the table and pull my backpack off the floor, using it to hide the sheets and the book.

Liam runs into the room first, heading straight for the fridge, barely noticing me. He pulls out the makings of a turkey and cheese sandwich, turning from the fridge, arms laden with ingredients. "Oh, hi Rosie."

"Liam!" Mother admonishes him as she enters the room. "We *just* ate!"

"So," he says, irritated. "I'm still hungry."

I look at the two of them. Liam looks healthy as ever. His cheeks are pink and his form is rotund. He looks like he's gained a little weight since we moved. The next time he goes for a checkup, the doctor is sure to tell us he needs to curb his snack intake.

Mother, on the other hand, looks terrible. Although she seemed to gain vitality and life after the separation, something's changed since we came to Maine, to Wolfhowl Manor. Mother, who only a couple of months ago was so optimistic about a house that was "just a house" and about her new job where the head nurse was nice and understanding, now looks wan and depressed. Her face is drawn and gaunt. Her dress hangs on her body as it would on the hanger. She's lost a few pounds just in the last week. The woman, who'd been so happy and full of energy just the other night, is exhausted. She has dark circles under her eyes. Her hair frays away from her head and out of the bun at the nape of her neck. She sits down in the chair across from me, putting her head in her hands.

"Mom?"

"I'm fine, sweetie," she says with a pat on my hand. "I'm just tired."

"Did you get up early? Where were you guys?"

"Church."

I shouldn't be surprised. Mother is in her special church dress after all, but I am. "Church? Why?" We haven't been to church as a family since Dad died. Mother's gone once or twice for confession, and once that first Sunday after we moved, but that's it.

"I just felt it was time we go."

"Why didn't you wake me?" I have no burning desire to go lean on my knees at church, but I feel left out.

Mother looks surprised. "I tried, honey. You told me to leave you alone."

"I did?" I have no recollection, but I suppose it's possible. "I'm sorry."

"It's okay." She pats my hand again and tries to smile, but it looks strange on her sad face.

"Where did you eat?"

"Some old woman chatted us up after the service." Mother speaks as if each word takes supreme effort. "Name of…" her eyebrows knit as she tries to remember.

I take a shot. "O'Sullivan?"

"Yes, that's it," she says. "Mrs. O'Sullivan, her daughter Laura, and her grandson Adam – he's got a heck of a shiner. Must be a classmate of yours?"

I nod slowly, reliving Adam's fall into the water last night.

"Anyway, she invited us over for lunch afterward and I didn't feel much like cooking, so…"

"She's weird," Liam says from behind the fridge door. "I didn't like her at all!"

"Liam!" I scold him. "That isn't very nice." He doesn't reply.

"Well, what'd she say?" I ask, trying to hide my rabid need to know. "I mean, what's she like?" Is she normal? Or a crazy old witch?

"We can talk about it later." Mother sighs loudly and then stifles a yawn. "I'm going to lay down for a while."

I watch her leave the room.

I make an attempt at some homework before I begin to feel tired again myself. I try calling Letta to see if she's interested in hearing about the attic, but no one answers, so I shuffle upstairs and take a long nap.

Chapter Twenty-Eight
The Song of the Damned

I sleep a long time without even being aware I'm asleep. In a blink, the faded sun disappears into a wintry evening. Dark clouds hang low over the sleepy town, and the rain is *rat-a-tatting* against the silent house.

I haven't slept this hard or this long since Dad died. A few days worth of wrenching sobs has a way of siphoning your energy away from you until you feel like Hitchcock's chocolate syrup circling the drain. It's strange he only died in May and yet, it being late October, I still remember every minute detail. It isn't dreamlike, as many memories are. It's crisp, clear, like the glass of a lake or my reflection in the mirror. It might've been yesterday I looked down into the bloody water, that I heard my own scream as if from far away.

"He doesn't have his glasses on. He needs his glasses." I remember saying that many times to the paramedics. To the police. To Mother. To my shrink. "He's blind without them. How will he see anything without them? Where are his glasses?"

People who commit suicide are thoughtful, I've learned. Dad had neatly folded his pants and shirt, setting them on the toilet lid. On top of his clothes, he had carefully creased his underwear and socks together. And on top of his socks were his glasses, neatly folded, lenses up. They were shiny and recently cleaned. He'd folded and piled all of these things nearby, as if he'd planned on needing them soon. He might've just been taking a bath. He was just taking a bath and he'd need his things, his glasses, after he toweled off.

It's after eleven when the frigid air in my room wakes me. I get a blanket and wrap it around me. I consider checking in on Mother and Liam, but it's dark and the front door is *out there*. I'm not going into the hall, not at night. Not in the dark.

Instead, I shuffle over to the balcony doors. It's raining heavily, but not as wildly as the previous nights. I eye the town, trying to see its lights through the fizzy rain, then look where I know the edge of the forest to be, now a line of shadowy giants in the darkness.

Movement in the shadows catches my eye. Even in the blackness, I recognize the silhouette of a wolf. It sits on its haunches and stares up at my balcony. It stares at me. It stares into my eyes.

And then it howls, long and loud. There's no doubt in my mind; it's a warning.

I retreat from the window and return to bed. I sit under my mountain of covers and stare at the clock for a long time, watching each minute pass. My nerves are frayed, on edge, making sleep difficult. And even when my eyelids begin to feel heavy and my eyes begin to burn, I fight sleep, afraid of what'll happen. Of what I might see. Of what I might do. Each blink becomes longer and longer. Until, finally, all is black.

He's in the porcelain tub with the cheap curtain open, pushed aside as if he's ready to get out. His khakis and dark blue t-shirt are folded on the toilet seat. The stark white of his socks looks even whiter against the tiles and paint of the hotel bathroom, yellowed by years of visitors. White toilet, white walls, white tiles, white curtain, white sink. Everything white, except for the water. Even my father's skin is a bleach white compared to the blood red of the water.

Everything is clean. Not a thing is out of place or smudged or wet. It's just the water that needs cleansing.

I stare at my father's lifeless form lying back in the water. The crook of his neck cradles the edge of the tub and his submerged forearms float freely under the surface. His eyes are closed. He could simply have fallen asleep in the bath. Even with the red water, that was my first thought. I should wake him up before he drowns.

I sit on the edge of the tub, looking at my father's face. Peaceful. I reach a hand down into the water and splash it up onto his face to see if he'll wake up. It's all a joke; an awful, awful joke.

But, no. This is no joke.

"Daddy?" My voice is whiny, like a little girl's. "Daddy, are you okay?"

Suddenly his eyes open. His body shoots up out of the water and his hands grip my shirt, leaking the blood red water onto me. He yanks me toward him, so close our noses are almost touching, and I'm nauseous with the irony scent of his blood.

"I'm so lonely, Rose!" He shouts. "I'm so terribly lonely!"

He holds up a razor from beneath the red water, its edge still dripping with his own warm blood.

This time his voice is a desperate whisper. "I'm so lonely, Rose."

Suddenly I'm screaming in Mother's face. I grab her wrists, which are in the process of shaking me awake, and shove them violently away.

"Rose!" Mother says, confused.

It takes me a few seconds to get my bearings. My room. My mother. Bright sun coming in the windows. No bathtub. No bloody water. No ghosts.

"Sorry, Mother," I manage, my heart still hammering in my chest. "I'm sorry. I-I was having a bad dream."

Mother nods with a hand over her own heart. Clearly, I've frightened her.

"It's alright, honey," she says and then takes a deep breath. "I wanted to wake you because I'm getting ready to leave for work. I didn't want you to oversleep again."

I check the time. "Crap!" I hop out of bed and run to my closet, searching for an outfit before hopping into the shower.

Mother follows me and leans against the doorjamb as I throw garments all over the place, looking for something that isn't wrinkled or dirty. "Are you alright?"

I recognize Mother's tone of concern. I pause and look at her. She wears her nurse's uniform and her arms are folded across her chest. She looks better than yesterday, ready to face the coming day, not ready to climb back into bed and hide.

"Yes, Mother," I say slowly. "I'm fine. I promise. Just a bad dream."

Mother stares into my eyes for what feels like a long time, and then abruptly stands straight and nods. "Alright. Hurry up and don't be late. Liam's up and dressed. He's getting breakfast. Don't forget he'll be with the Bauers instead of the O'Dwyres this afternoon. I'll see you tonight." With a smile, she all but skips out of the house.

I hurry myself along and manage to get out the door only five minutes late. It's still raining, and when Beckan pulls up in his pickup, I'm glad to see him.

"Mornin'," he says with a bright smile. "Thought you'd like a lift."

I climb into the middle and Liam pops in after me. He has a pair of headphones and an old portable cassette player I've never seen before. Hearing a gush of obnoxious children's tunes coming from the headphones, I turn to Beckan.

"Hi." As Beckan puts the truck in gear, I keep my eyes on him. I feel differently seeing him today, relieved somehow. I've spent most of the weekend freezing, wrapped up in my bedcovers, but a warmth emanates from Beckan's body like an aura. It rolls down his arms toward me like a wave, seeping into my own body. As the house shrinks in the rearview mirror, my dreary mood begins to shrink too. It's as if a heavy weight I wasn't even aware of is being lifted off of me. I can finally relax.

"Hey," I say, trying to think of something to say, "what happened to you the other night?"

"Hm?" He tilts his ear toward me without looking away from the road.

"When Letta and I woke up, you were gone."

"Oh," he says, still staring ahead. "I didn't want tah bring it up at the party, but do you remember what I told you before, about my muthah?"

I think back to our conversation on the balcony, ages ago now. "Sometimes you hear her voice?" Beckan nods.

"Oh my God, did you hear her voice? What did she say?" I'm so eager to hear his explanation that I'm immediately apologetic, ashamed of my enthusiasm. "I'm sorry, that's rude."

"No, it's okay," he says. "I *did* hear her. She wasn't talkin' exactly. She was hummin'."

"Humming?"

Beckan nods. "She liked tah hum when she was workin' 'round the house. Hymns mostly. 'Just As I Am,' 'How Great Thou Art', 'Holy, Holy, Holy.' You know, the usual. But there's this one song she used tah hum all the time. It wasn't a church song. It was somethin' I only evah heard when I was 'round her." He pauses for a minute as he thinks. He starts humming the song, haltingly at first, but then with confidence as the tune comes back to him. It's sweet and cool, full of love and possibilities, but it makes me shiver, and the cold that dissipated only moments ago seeps back into my body. It starts at the nape of my neck, traveling slowly at first, then gains momentum. It raises every hair on my arms as it crawls down my spine and invades my stomach. The song Beckan hums so beautifully is the same song Mother has been humming. *It's the song I hear in my dreams.*

Mrs. O'Dwyre and Mother hummed the same song. And though I don't know the two are connected exactly, I start wondering... I know what happened to Mrs. O'Dwyre. What will happen to Mother? And where the hell did that damn song come from?

"Anyway," Beckan says as I try to control my thoughts and bring them back to reality, "I heard her voice hummin' that song. Clear as you're hearin' it from me, I heard it from her. That's what woke me up. I didn't mean to abandon you, but I just couldn't…" I hear him choking back the emotion in his voice, and we're both glad when we spot Letta at the bottom of the hill.

Letta smiles at me as she climbs in, pressing Liam, who barely notices her, between us. "Hey guys. What's shaking?" The aloofness of the other night is gone.

"Nothin'," Beckan says quickly. "How was the rest of your weekend? How's Patty?"

"Remind me to get your canopy for you later," Letta says to me. "Dad fixed it yesterday. And Patty's fine. She had a good doctor." She winks at us. "How about you guys? What'd you do yesterday?"

"A whole lot of nothing," I say. "Something about this weather. The Delaneys spent all day under the covers. We really know how to do it up."

"Yeah," Letta says, "this time of year has a way of doing that to you around here." Letta's voice carries a certain tone, as if she's relating something confidential without telling you anything at all, and I realize Letta *is* hiding something. And I'm certain whatever it is, is important.

*   *   *

I'm glad to be at school for once. I go through my day with ease and a smile, my weekend depression only a memory. Adam's absent, and I hope he hasn't caught pneumonia or something from the icy water. We've started *Macbeth* in English, which I actually read on my own last year and loved. Chemistry turns out to be fun with Bunsen burners and an experiment. Since I'm still a leper and the class has an odd number of students, I have to partner up with Mr. McLoughlin, but I don't mind. He's handsome to look at and has a dorky sense of humor.

I go to the usual lunch spot, but find a head missing when taking mental attendance. Shane, Patty, Letta… I search the cafeteria and I'm surprised to see Eileen sitting with Mary and Ronan.

"What's up with Eileen?" I ask, watching as Eileen laughs loudly at something Mary said.

The others follow my gaze. Shane shrugs, but Patty and Letta exchange knowing glances.

"She's defected tah the enemy," Patty says sadly. "Permanently."

"She's just returning to her natural habitat," Letta says bitterly as she pushes her peas around her lunch tray. "She's always belonged over there."

"Really?" I know Eileen occasionally sits elsewhere for lunch, but I'd assumed she's one of those people who's popular with everyone. She exudes a rare confidence, sometimes seeming mature beyond her years.

"She's got a nasty side," Patty says. "Last yeeah she couldn't decide who she wanted tah be, so she tried out everyone. When she stahted hangin' out with us this yeeah, I thought she'd finally figured it out and made the right choice."

"She's just a spy," Letta says, her voice dripping in venom, "getting reconnaissance for the other side so they can barbeque you."

Letta's comment is followed by an uncomfortable silence. For a moment it seems like Patty, Shane, and Letta are sharing an unspoken secret with each other.

"Alright," I say, "out with it."

"I'm sure I don't know what you mean," Shane says innocently.

"Come on, I'm not stupid. What is it?"

Patty sighs. "Eileen's spreadin' rumahs about what happened at your house on Friday."

"Patty!" Shane admonishes her.

"Rumors?" A familiar iciness takes hold in my stomach. Well hello, Monday. What took you so long to get here? "Great. What's she saying?" Is she telling people what happened to her in the basement bathroom? Is she telling them about the diaries? Is she telling them I fainted like a baby when the 'wind' blew the doors open?

"Does it matter?" Letta snaps. "The whole school's going to believe it whether it's true or not. Everyone's chomping at the bit to hear something bad about Ghost Girl. They can't wait to hear you've gone crazy, killed your family, been shoved in a straight jacket, or whatever."

"It matters to me," I snap, surprised by Letta's sudden negativity. "I want to know what's being said and I want to know *now*." My anger flares up and I struggle to keep it under control.

"She's tellin' people you're possessed by the house," Patty says. "Sayin' that you tried tah burn the house down with us inside."

"*Patty!*" Shane hisses.

I hold up a hand to silence Shane. "Oh? And why was my murderous plot unsuccessful?"

"Too much rain," Patty says.

"Seriously? That's ridiculous. She could at least use her imagination. What, I'm supposed to burn the house down because of what happened to the Boyle's? Because crazy ol' Enit tried to do the same thing?" I roll my eyes. "Anyone who believes that is stupid. Did she create some fantastical account about what happened to her in the basement too, or was that all a charade?"

"She's still not comin' clean on that one." Shane shakes his head and sighs. He uses a fake British accent to say, "'Tis a mystery."

There's another long silence. Shane and Patty look at each other while Letta stares at Eileen like she's going to burn a hole right through her. Eileen, meanwhile, is laughing and talking loudly. She and Mary sit close together, sharing a private joke. Ronan leans in to add his two cents to riotous laughter. Letta looks like she's going to puke.

"Well," Patty says finally, "did you find out anythin' else ovah the weekend? What'd you do yesterday?"

"Actually, I went up to the attic and I *did* find some curious things." I tell them about the owners' portraits, the empty portrait, and the boxes I found. I tell them about the gun in the Boyle's box and the clothes that might've belonged to the Callaghans or Olenevs. I save Emily Lenore's box for last.

"There has tah be some mistake," Patty says. "No one was there 'round that time except the Boyles, and they didn't have children. The historical society tried several tactics, but they couldn't unload it on anyone after they died."

"Well, that's not true," Shane says. "There was a guy in the sixties. I think people forget 'bout him because he kept tah himself and it was only him, no family."

I think back to the portrait of the single man. "What happened to him?"

"He was a handyman," Shane says. "Pop said he was independently wealthy or whatevah. The only place anyone ever saw him was the hardware store or church. He spent all of his time up on the hill, fixin' this or that while all the women fawned ovah him. He restored a lot of it on his own. But, like everyone else, he died up there."

Like everyone else.

"Do you remember his name?" Letta asks.

"Jonathan? Justin? Jason?" Shane shrugs. "Somethin' with a J."

"So he didn't use any of the diaries," I say. "I think I figured out that the diaries we found each belonged to one of the women. I read Alva's, the one with the letters A. C. on the front. I know from the file the realtor gave my mom that B. O. is Barbara Olenev and A. B. is Alison Boyle. But who's this E. L.? None of the owners had those initials."

"There's only one possibility," Letta says. "Emily Lenore."

"The infant?" Patty says incredulously. "Hardly."

"Well, we don't know what happened to her," Letta says. "Maybe she was raised here in town by Eamonn's cousin, just not in the house."

"Then why doesn't anyone ever talk 'bout her? Or her descendents? And how did her diary make it tah the house?" Patty lists one question after another. "Why does the box in the attic with her name on it have thins from the nineteen fifties and not the *eighteen* fifties?"

Letta shrugs and gives Shane a wry smile. "'Tis a mystery."

"Have you read any of the other diaries?" Shane asks.

"No. Only Alva's."

"Well there're three more right?" Shane says. "Barbara, Alison, and this E. L., whoever he or she is."

I nod.

"Let's take a look at them tomorrow night," Shane suggests. "We'll each read one. It'll be a diary party!" He laughs.

"That's a good idea," Letta says. "Maybe that'll get us some answers."

Yes, I need answers. Before it's too late.

*   *   *

I don't see any of my friends after school. I catch a glimpse of Eileen, still surrounded by the popular crowd. For once, *I* avoid *them* like the plague, and leave through a back door. As I begin the cold walk home, gloomy and alone, I wonder where my friends are. Are they doing something without me? Did they intentionally leave me out? Maybe it has something to do with why Letta's acting so weird. The isolation and depression of the day before begins to weigh me down again as I trudge down the sidewalk toward the dismal mountain.

Nearing the forest that leads me home, I hear music. At first, it's indistinct and intermittent, arriving and disappearing with the direction of the wind. I find myself at a street corner and turn, compelled to follow the strange music. As I near the source, I realize not only is the music coming from the grand organ of Port Braseham's only church, Saint Perpetua Our Lady Martyr, but the song being played is a familiar one – it's the song from my dreams. The song of Mrs. O'Dwyre. The song Mother hums to herself.

I follow the music, in a trance, across the parking lot, and through the heavy doors of the church. The door slams behind me, but I barely hear it over the song emanating from the large copper pipes. Somehow, the sound of the music coming from the organ, echoing around the great dome of the church, makes it sound distinctly more ominous than ever before, and my knees turn to jelly.

I pass through the entry hall into the nave, my tunnel vision focused on the organ at the end of the aisle, set off to the right of the apse between the altar and confessionals. The huge organ dwarfs the church around it. The pipes sail straight up to the edges of the dome. The light of an overcast sky barely makes its way through the tall stained glass windows lining the nave. Hundreds of candles have been lit, throwing the organ into a sinister, shadowy glow.

On the bench of the organ is a diminutive woman, sitting like a doll, zealously working the keys. Her gray hair is plaited down the back of her plain black dress, swaying with each attack at the keys. Although the organist is most certainly playing the song from my dream, I'm used to hearing it as a slow, low and cloying hum. But here it's a feverish, urgent hymn belonging at the height of action in *The Omen*. It certainly doesn't belong in the House of God.

All this time, I've been drawn down the aisle, toward the organ. The sound *commands* me, *demands* I come closer and listen.

A second woman mists out of nowhere. She's sitting in the front pew, quietly listening to the song. I can only see the back of her head, resting above the back of the pew. Her long white hair is in a tight bun at the base of her neck, but some unruly strands resolutely resist and stick straight out. I know when she turns around, I'll see familiar milky blue eyes, unseeing yet seeing at the same time.

The last note of the song resounds throughout the church, assaulting the far reaches of the dome before dissipating. The organist slouches away from the keys and stretches her gnarled fingers. When the octogenarian turns around, she's surprised to find a new audience member.

"Well, hello deah," she says with a warm smile. "And who might you be?"

"Oh, don't be so numb, Dottie," says Enit in a raspy whisper of a voice. "You know it's Rose Delaney."

"Well, yes of course," Dottie says, turning to Enit, "but I was tryin' tah be polite."

Enit waves a dismissive hand at Dottie and then pats the bench right next to her. "Have a seat, Rose."

I find myself doing as I'm told. I stare at the woman up close for the first time. The wrinkles in her face are deep canyons with tiny spidery ravines splitting off all over the place. Her skin is slack, hanging from her jowl and covered in age spots. Her own hands are twisted with arthritis and covered in shiny burn scars. I look into those milky blue eyes again, and I know this woman has lived a hard life.

Dottie gets up from the organ bench and stands for a moment before coming to other side of me. She rubs her old knees slowly and smiles. "My ol' prayer-handles get pretty sore if I sit too long."

I nod, putting on a fake smile. I'm immensely uncomfortable yet rooted to the pew at the same time. My muscles are in a strange fight; should we stay or should we run? Unable to make up my mind, I start bobbing one knee up and down like a yoyo.

"So, what brings you tah church this afternoon," Dottie asks. "Not much happens 'round heeah on Mondays."

"It was the music."

"The music, Rose," Enit asks, *"or the song?"*

I turn to Enit, my pulse quickening. The old woman says my name with familiarity, like my own grandmother would. "How do you know who I am," I ask. "I'm not trying to be rude, but aren't you blind?"

Enit smiles, revealing surprisingly few yellowed teeth. "You smell like *it.*"

"Like what?"

"Like the house, Rose," Enit sneers. "You smell like it, like *Her*... So. Rose. What brought you here? Was it the *music* or the *song?*"

I don't understand what difference it makes, but I admit, "The song."

"Mm-hmm," Dottie nods knowingly, like when the preacher gives the congregation a little bit of God truth, like "You should have faith in God because *He* has faith in *you,*" and everyone nods deeply, saying "Mm-*hmm.*"

"Can I ask you," I say, "what song *is* it? I've never heard it before.""Never?" Enit's shrewd tone chills me to the bone.

"It's a very old song, deah," Dottie answers politely. "It used tah be quite popular, actually. But not anymore." She sighs heavily. "No... not anymore."

"Why not?" I ask before I'm sure I want to know.

"It's the Song of The Damned," says Enit.

"Oh, Enit," Dottie sighs. "Don't be so cruel. You're goin' tah scare the poor girl."

"She *should* be scared," Enit says stubbornly, turning away from us with a frown.

"Rose," says Dottie, "the song has a very long history in this town. You see, it was written by Alva Callaghan more than a hundred yeeahs ago." She waited for my patient nod to show I know the name – of course I *know* the name. "She was a wonderful piano teacher. She wrote it for her husband, Eamonn. It was meant tah be a tribute tah their new life heeah in America. They emigrated from Ireland, you know. Such a sweet song for a sweet couple. Of course, I'm not allowed tah play it durin' services. Wouldn't be appreciated, not these days. But, once in a while, ol' Enit and I sit heeah and hum it together while I play."

The question is burning in my throat even though I think I know the answer. "Why aren't you allowed to play it anymore?"

Dottie is silent this time, so I wait for Enit to turn back to us, to explain what I so urgently need to hear.

"Because of the deaths," Enit says finally. "When Eamonn and Alva first died, the song was kept alive by the townspeople. It was a tribute to them at first, to play it during the services. They were important to this town. But, then the curse... Do you know the story of Bobby Flannagan, Rose?" I shake my head. "Well, poor Bobby Flannagan was around back in the early nineteen hundreds. History says he was a good boy, but he liked to get into a bit of trouble from time to time.

"In nineteen-oh-five the house hadn't been tended to for a while. The O'Dwyre's were there of course, but they weren't doing much because no one was living there. Bobby was actually good friends with the O'Dwyre boy at the time. They were about the same age. So Bobby, O'Dwyre, and a couple of other boys from town were being rowdy one night, and they dared Bobby to go into the house. He was the weak one, you know, and the other boys wanted to show they were stronger by teasing him. He wanted to be strong too, so he went through with the dare and went on into the house."

I can't stifle my gasp.

"Don't worry, Rose. Nothing happened to him while he was inside," Enit says, "except that he came out of it with Alva's song stuck in his head. Now, that isn't so unusual for a church-going boy, because the song was still being played during services back then. But Bobby told his friends he heard a woman humming the song when he was in the house. They thought he was making it up, trying to scare them. But he swore up and down that he'd heard it. Told the story over and over, told everyone he knew. Every time he told the story, he'd hum the song, but it sounded different than anyone had ever heard it before. It sounded threatening."

"What happened to him?"

"Well he died obviously," Enit says. "It was a slow death. He got sick a few days after he was in the house and no one could figure out what was wrong with him. He lost weight, became pale and lazy. Wouldn't get out of bed for no one. He'd just lay there and hum that song. Eventually he stopped talking altogether. He just stared out of his second story bedroom window and hummed that song."

"And then?"

"And then he jumped out of the window."

"So," I say, a rising sense of panic welling up inside me. "That doesn't mean anything. One boy humming a song and dying. That's nothing."

"Sure," Enit says. "One boy means nothing. But then Bobby's cousin Florence started humming the song. She got tired. She got sick. Then she jumped into a well and drowned. A few years later, and a few more dead children… That was the end of that. Alva's song became taboo."

"Why are you even playing it then," I say, "if it's so deadly?"

"It's still a pretty song," Dottie says innocently. "The pastor and his wife are out of town. It's the only time I get tah play it. Mondays are quiet 'round heeah, so most don't hear it."

"You shouldn't play it at all!" I shout.

"It's safe heeah," Dottie says, "in God's House."

"So you believe in its power then," Enit says to me. "You believe it's the Song of The Damned?"

"Of course not," I lie. "I don't believe in crap like that. It's just silly superstition." I'm desperate to believe Enit's crazy, that she's made it all up.   "Are you humming the song yet?" Enit asks quietly.

"No!"

"You know what happened to ol' Derry's wife, don't you?" Enit says his name like it's a curse.

I nod.

"Then you know that she, too, knew the song," Enit says. "That she hummed it."

"This is ridiculous!" I try to stand, but Enit lurches out and grabs my wrist, the arthritic grasp surprisingly strong.

"Are you having the dreams yet?"

"Let go of me!" I wrench my arm free of Enit's gnarled fingers and grab my bag. My anger replaces my fear and I lash out at her. "And what about you? Are *you* immune, Mrs. O'Sullivan? You hum it! You hummed it sitting right here! You ain't dead! What makes you so special?"

Enit's blind eyes grow cruel and she sneers. "No, Rose, I'm not *special*. I'm not *immune*." She puts one burned and shriveled finger on her face, pointing to a milky blind eye. "That house has taken from me everything it can. But let this be a warning to you, girl. *You* are not immune. *Your family* is not immune. And if you don't do something about it very soon, you're going to join the rest in the cemetery out back. Your death is certain."

Chapter Twenty-Nine
Reading Diaries

Y*our death is certain.*

Enit's words scare me so much I nearly faint on the spot. I barely manage to fight off the tunnel vision and flee the church, literally running away from two octogenarians. I try not to let Enit's words bother me, to let them seep into my brain and wrap their smoky tendrils around my thoughts, but I can't help it. The old git's in my head. Enit's words assault my brain as the downpour assault my body on the walk home.

I don't know how Enit knows about my dreams, or why they'd be so important to her. After all, they're only dreams... Right?

And so what if Mother hums some old song! It doesn't mean she's going to die like Beckan's mother. Like those children. It couldn't mean Mother's death is certain...could it?

Unless you do something about it very soon, your death is certain.

What exactly am I supposed to *do*? Enit was so cryptic, as if the mystery of it all makes sense to me, *should* make sense to me. She thinks I know exactly what my family is up against. Instead, I'm more confused than ever, and I can feel the old woman's disappointment in me. I'm even a little disappointed in myself for letting her down.

As I near the bottom of the hill, still saturated with my heavy thoughts, I'm surprised to find Letta standing under a large black umbrella.

"Hey," she says timidly.

"Hey." A moment of uncomfortable silence passes between us.

"Sorry I missed you after school," Letta finally says. "I stayed after to see if I could talk to Eileen, figure out what her deal is."

"And?" I decide not to tell Letta about what happened at the church. The act of omission makes us feel even again.

"No luck. She basically ran away from me. Anyway, I just got home and saw Mom and Liam were gone. I was on my way

229

up the hill to see if they're up there when I saw you. Wanna get under my umbrella?"

I shrug, still a little angry. "Sure." As Letta holds up the umbrella to include my much taller frame, the rain starts coming in at a slant so that she gets pelted from the knees down.

We walk up the hill in silence, and are surprised to find Liam sitting on one of the porch swings with Mrs. Bauer standing behind him, lazily pushing him back and forth. Both are red-cheeked and warmly bundled.

"Mom, what are you doing up here?" Letta asks.

Seeing me, Liam slips off the swing and runs toward the front doors with his backpack bobbing along behind him. He stands anxiously by the knob, hopping up and down on his heels as he waits for me to unlock them and let him in.

Mrs. Bauer shrugs. "Liam got a little homesick."

"From half a mile?" Letta says incredulously.

"He wanted to be home," Mrs. Bauer says apologetically, which makes me feel terrible. I should be the one apologizing for Liam's rude behavior. After all, I'm his role model, his example. Or at least, I used to be.

"He couldn't really get settled," Mrs. Bauer explains. "I brought him up here and was planning to watch him inside. We were already here before I realized he didn't have his own key. I figured we'd just wait a bit. A little fresh air never hurt anyone."

"Oh my gosh!" Mrs. Bauer is being a good bit kinder than the situation warrants. "I'm so sorry, Mrs. Bauer! I hope you weren't outside long."

"Oh, it was only an hour or so, but it's no problem," Mrs. Bauer adds quickly. "Don't you worry about a thing. I'll head back down the hill now, but before I forget, your canopy is over there, Rose." She indicates a bag by the front door. "Are you coming with me, dear?" She asks Letta.

"I'll be down in a few minutes."

Mrs. Bauer nods and gives Letta a kiss on the cheek. "I'll see you in a bit then." As she heads down the steps, she pops open her umbrella like a cheerful Mary Poppins and is on her way.

"Rosie!" Liam shouts, hopping up and down impatiently at the door. "Let me in!"

"Liam!" I scold him. "Liam, you look at me right now!" I kneel and grab his squirming shoulders, squeezing them until he glares into my eyes. "Liam, you made poor Mrs. Bauer sit out here for an hour in the cold. Why?"

"Because I wanted to be home!" He reaches for the doorknob and I shake him again.

"Why? No one's here! The house is empty! You can't behave like this," I say sternly. "It isn't fair to Mrs. Bauer and it's very rude! She's in charge of you, and you have to listen to her. Do you hear me?"

"Why can't I just come home after school?"

"And be by yourself in this house? I don't think so!"

"I'm not alone," he mumbles, staring at his feet.

"Excuse me?"

"Nothing."

I'm suddenly cold to the bone, and it has nothing to do with the weather. I shake Liam's shoulders one more time. "Now you look at me – look at me! – and promise me you won't do this again. You will stay with Mrs. Bauer until Mom or I come to get you. You will not come up here alone. You will not make Mrs. Bauer wait around up here with you. She is to be respected and obeyed. I don't care how bad you want to come home. Am I clear?" When he only glares at the wall with angry eyes, I turn his chin roughly toward me. "Am I clear, Liam?"

He nods, but refuses to look at me.

"Fine. And tomorrow you're going to apologize to Mrs. Bauer, do you hear me?"

Another silent, angry nod.

I take the skeleton key out of my pocket and Liam's eyes glow intensely in the gloomy atmosphere.

"I'll do it!" He grabs the key from my hand without waiting for an answer, and twists it into the lock. He flings himself through the door with the kind of eagerness deserving of Disney World.

"What's his deal?" Letta asks. "What's he so excited about?"

"Search me," I say, trying to hide how worried I am. I hear his tiny voice in my head again: *I'm not alone.*

"Listen," Letta says, her tone suddenly soft and confidential, "I know I've been weird and I want to apologize." I look at her warily. When I don't reply, she continues. "I can't really explain right now what my problem is –"

"It's about Ronan," I interrupt, "right?" I'm not sure how I know, but I've had this feeling there's something between the two of them. It seems unlikely – the most popular kid in school and tiny, plain Letta, but the tension between them is palpable.

Letta barely nods. "I'm just not prepared to explain it to you yet. I'm sorry. I know it's weird and whatever, but allow me this one secret, at least for a while. It's something I've never talked about – with anyone – and I'm just not ready yet."

I nod, relieved. "Sure. But you can trust me, you know, if you ever do want to talk about it. I mean it." Letta doesn't seem like the kind of person to hold anything back; she's always been blunt and honest. If she wants to keep this secret, it must be pretty bad.

"I know," Letta says through a trembling lip. "Thanks… I'll see you tomorrow okay?"

"Sure."

"Later." Letta turns and heads down the hill, disappearing into the rainy mist.

Liam is in the kitchen. I watch him from the doorway as he makes his own grilled cheese sandwich. He knows exactly where the pan is and sets it on the gas stove, lighting the burner, as if he's been doing it since he learned to walk. He scoots a stool out of a corner so he can see into the pan as he slabs it with butter and tosses in two slices of bread and some cheese.

I don't interrupt as Liam expertly works the stovetop. I just watch, wondering who showed him how to use the stove. Certainly, it wasn't Mother, who barely lets me use the microwave. I wonder why Liam's so desperate to be home, in this hollow house, rather than anywhere else. I wonder whom it is he talks to when he's alone. Who's he playing with? Who, exactly, is keeping him company when he's *alone?*

*   *   *

I go through the next day in a daze, unable to get Enit's words or Liam's sudden disobedience out of my head. I hear the taunts from my classmates, various insults coupled with the moniker Ghost Girl, but worry fills every available crevice of my brain so that I don't even process them. I zone out altogether in history, missing a lecture on gender roles of the Penobscot Indians, and study hall is wasted on analyzing everything I've noticed about my house since we arrived.

"Hey," Shane bursts my thought bubble at lunch. "You okay?"

"Huh?" I reply, foggy-brained. "Oh. Yeah. I'm just thinking."

"Quite seriously from the looks of it," Patty says.

Letta stays quiet, her eyes burning a hole into Eileen's backside as she once again sits with the popular kids. I remember what Letta said yesterday, about needing to keep her secret about Ronan. The drama queen inside me says it's a juicy piece of gossip, and I'm torn between my desire to know and respecting my friend's privacy. A girl like Letta is practically invisible to a guy like Ronan. How bad could it possibly be?

"Well, stop bein' so serious," Shane says. "It's stahtin' tah bring me down. So let's see... There's this joke about a horse, a priest, and a policeman – no wait, that's not right."

I find myself laughing anyway.

"So what's the plan tonight?" Patty asks while Shane digs up his punch line.

I shrug. "Do you want to come over after dinner?"

"What about your mom?" Letta finally joins the conversation, but her eyes remain dark and turbulent.

"She said something this morning about having plans, so she won't be around."

"Cool beans," says Patty.

*   *   *

"You coming, Rose?" Letta calls over the stair railing. My friends arrived around seven and I sent them ahead to my room while I make sure Liam's set for the evening – not that I need to.

"Yeah," I reply, watching Liam sit at the kitchen table with his sandwich – another grilled cheese of his own making – and a tall glass of milk. He pulls a notebook from his backpack and begins reading as he chews, doing his homework without having to be told.

I head upstairs where my friends are already paging through the diaries. Shane and Patty share the window seat and Barbara Olenev's diary. Letta, determined to get to the bottom of things, has picked up E. L., leaving me with Alison Boyle. I pick up the diary and plop onto my bed.

"Don't forget to take notes," Letta says without moving her eyes from the diary. "We're going to figure this out. I can feel it!"

Alison Boyle's diary reads like an F. Scott Fitzgerald novel in the first person. The young couple was bitter, their own apathy for each other, and for life, leading their descent into hell. And alcohol, there was plenty of that too. Based on Alison's account, I'm certain both were alcoholics, but Hagan was of the functioning variety whilst Alison soaked at the bottom of a

bottle of vodka, only pouring herself out to swim into another
bottle.

The couple moved into the house in the summer of 1933,
and Alison began the diary that September.

*This diary is the only thing that can compete with my endless boredom
in this comically dark place. Well, this and that bulldog of a caretaker,
O'Dwyre. At first, I found his accent absolutely appalling, insulting even –
though it does go quite well with his backwoods rag-a-muffin attire and third
grade education. Later, I came to find it a little amusing, and a few weeks
ago, I decided I liked it – and him – alright. He, at least, pays me some
attention.*

*Not to worry. Hagan has no idea, not that he'd care if he did. He is
constantly busy with meetings despite being in our 'summer home.' He was
the one who said we were coming here for relaxation, to get away from the
bright city lights. This was an adventure we were supposed to take together.
But often he leaves me here all alone while he takes meetings back in New
York. Or at least, that's what he says he's doing. I'm certain he goes into
town to play some young thing's Daddy, acting like some young lollygagger.
He goes dancing with some flour-loving smarty. Some vamp who makes me
seem like a smothering wet blanket. Oh Alison dear, why must you be such
a drag?*

*I used to have a pulse, you know. I used to care. I used to love life like
all those other pretty young things ankling around New York City, living
the fast life.*

*I should have divorced Hagan back then, when I still cared, back when
I believed one had a chance at being happy in this life. What a Dumb Dora
idea.*

It's sad from day one. Maybe they'd loved each other once,
but it seems like the only thing keeping Alison and Hagan
together is a shared laziness to actually file the divorce papers –
and perhaps Hagan's wealthy stake in Alison's family business.

*Hagan is quite handsome you know. A real looker. The first time I
saw him he was mopping the factory floor. He had a smudge of grease on his
cheek and I boldly wiped it away for him when no one was looking. Very
quickly, it felt as if we were one. I think, besides that cute little smudge on
his face, what really drew me to him was that he was different. Daddy's
opposite, or so I thought.*

*Hagan, you see, was poor. His parents had him later in life. After an
accident, his father was unable to work and his mother had to quit her job
to take care of him. Hagan went out into the workforce at fifteen to support*

his parents. I met him two years later, after Father hired him as a custodian. He was a hard worker, and very smart. Hagan figured things out quickly and was good with his hands. His work was physical, but he could have done the cerebral with Father just as well. That's why I liked him.

This was, unfortunately, why Father liked him too. Of course when Hagan and I married six months after that first adorable little smudge – a whirlwind romance my mother called it – it was only natural for Father to take him under his wing and train him in the family business. I was okay with it at first, because it meant I could spend more time with him (I worked as a secretary in Father's office after school). He may have been working hard over numbers instead of mops, but he was still working hard. He still came home to me, still took me in his arms and loved me...

But then he changed. He turned into Father, which despite what Freud says, I did not find appealing in the least. He became less and less passionate toward me, instead filling his mind with numbers, with jack.

Perhaps we just grew apart... Here we are six years in (or is it seven?) and what are we? Strangers under the same roof, barely even passing in the night, sometimes spending those nights in the beds of other strangers.

Perhaps you think me mad.

I notice in Alison's diary, like Alva's, there's a conversational tone, as if the diary is part of a conversation between Alison and someone else. It's like reading a series of letters, only the pen pal's words are missing. But unlike Alva, Alison arrived at Wolfhowl Mountain already depressed. Her descent into madness was faster than Alva's because Alison had a healthy head start.

We talked about children, you know. Before we fell out of love, we talked about children. We even tried for a while, and I quit my job at the factory, anticipating beginning my life as a mother with love and joy...

Richard III, after Father, or Gracie Linda... Those were the names we talked about. It's funny, now that Hagan and I have completely abandoned even the idea of a child, that I've realized how much I hate those names. So stiff and old-fashioned. If God chose to grace us with a child now, I should hope for a girl. What should I call her? Perhaps Emily. Yes, that is a nice name isn't it?

A chill races down my spine. Had the Boyle's actually conceived a child? Is this the Emily Lenore of the box upstairs? Is it possible they'd chosen the same name as Eamonn and Alva so many years before?

I skip a few months ahead, to December.

It was lovely for our friends to come see us again. Despite the chilly drafts, the rats in the basement, and the general disrepair of this cave, they find it to be the "bee's knees!" – At least O'Dwyre has fixed the hot water. Cold showers are not good for my skin. – Of course, they miss us in the city, but we have The Life out here! Social parties with the townies. Afternoons on the sea. Romantic walks on the shore… Yes, that's certainly what they think.

But now, our city guests have left, returning to New York to spend Christmas with their growing families, leaving Hagan and I alone. And that's what we are now – alone. I can't believe how much has changed. It wasn't so many years ago that we spent Christmas and New Years with each other, feeling young and gorgeous, families be damned! Would our lives be so different if we had stayed in the city? Would we still be eggs – out late dancing, drinking brown-plaid and getting the bum's rush come the witching hour? A girl can dream…

Gertrude and John have a little child now, a girl. They left her at home for the week of course, with John's parents, but they talked of her almost endlessly. She sounds precious. Strange how it feels like only yesterday we were making our martinis together and now they are parents. To think how much a mere child can change someone. Why Gertrude didn't have a single drink the week they were here, and the child wasn't even with them! Then, Judy and Simon just revealed to us they are expecting a child this summer. You should have seen their faces when they told us. They were the picture of joy. How I envy them that they can feel actual joy.

We have nothing in common now, not even with our closest friends, whom I feel we weren't actually very close to at all. It's strange how a life lived on the juice can make it seem like the world is full of your friends.

Speaking of which, thank you for the refill. It's quite strong, but then you did that on purpose didn't you, you little minx?

The 1933 winter holidays were miserable. They managed to keep it together, though barely, in front of their guests, but as soon as they were gone, both Alison and Hagan found their way back to arguments over things petty and medicating their tempers with martinis and scotch.

I feel bad for them. I wonder… Was it their stale marriage that made them miserable? Or was it because they found their unfortunate way to Wolfhowl Mountain?

Alison's diary becomes repetitive. No wonder the woman was miserable. She did nothing but drink and walk down to the caretaker's – Beckan's grandfather's – cabin. When she wasn't there, she was in the house fighting with Hagan. Though they were already strangers to each other, Alison did her best to alienate him even further. She practically dared him to leave, documenting all of these attempts in her diary.

Their friends from the city continued to visit on and off, mostly in the summer months or for holidays. But the summer of 1934, one year after they moved into Wolfhowl Manor, they'd given up trying to be nice to each other even in front of their friends, and the visits were clipped short. There was always an excuse to return to the city when Hagan and Alison became unbearable – a meeting Monday, the children missed them or had a slight cough. Alison wrote about her former friends with bitterness.

They think they're better than us, those dolled up high hats! Oh, they pretend alright, but I can see through their facades. And Hagan, he is on their side. "Alison, perhaps you shouldn't refill your glass," he says. "I think you've had quite enough already. Maybe you should have a lie down." In front of all of our guests, he says this! How embarrassing. Yes, dear Alison, you hoary-eyed sot, go to bed and stop embarrassing your husband.

He only stays with me for the business you know. Father would never let him keep his stake if I left him, and he knows it. It's my family's business after all.

Oh, he's made me feel so dreadful. And he will pay. We will make him pay.

Alison's torment took a different form than Alva's. Where Alva was deeply sad, Alison was angry and bitter, and she blamed Hagan and his greed for her misfortune rather than herself. She poisoned herself against him. He didn't care for her. He cared only for her family's business and the life of comfort it provided him. The children they had once talked about with love were only pawns he'd use to ensure inheritance when her parents died. He'd kill Alison in her sleep so he could have it all for himself. Eventually, she convinced herself money was all Hagan had ever been after, and he had never really loved her. This was the reason he allowed her to go down to the caretaker's, and why he enjoyed transgressions of his own. I have a feeling this wasn't the reality of their relationship at all, but simply how it looked through Alison's angry, green-colored glasses.

By late August of 1934, Alison's bitter depression permeated the atmosphere of the house, finally breaking any will Hagan had left. The couple became hermits, using Beckan's grandfather as a personal errand runner. They avoided town and sent any visitors away. The couple, really no longer a couple, spent each day wandering throughout the house like ghosts, avoiding each other and refilling their glasses. There was no hope left for them.

Hagan has made a fool out of me, and the life we lead. He has stolen my life from me, my what-might-have-been. If only Father had hated him when I loved him. If only I had left him before we came to this godforsaken little town. If only… but no. It is too late for ifs. It's too late for us.

It's too late. He will be sorry for what he has stolen from me. It's time we make him PAY.

This is the last entry in Alison's diary. When I look at the date, I see it was written on December 29, 1934, two days before the fire that took both Alison and Hagan's lives. On the next page of the diary is not an entry, but rather a drawing. It's a crude depiction of Wolfhowl Manor engulfed in black ink flames. In the front yard lie two stick figures with x's for eyes. One holds a gun in its dead hand…

I wonder about that fire… and about the gun in the attic.

Chapter Thirty
Barbara's Diary

I close Alison's diary and look up. Letta, Shane, and Patty are still bent over the other diaries. While we were reading, the sun sank below the horizon, and it's grown dark. As the moon rises, so does my depression.

"So, find anything interesting?"

"Maybe," Shane says.

"Definitely," Letta says, and our eyes flick to her. She shakes her head with a wide smile. "Uh-uh. You first."

"Alright," Shane says. "Shall we go in chronological order then?"

"I think that puts you first," I say, "but let's refresh what we already know." I reach into the drawer of my bedside table and take out Mrs. Carroll's file, to which I've added the travel magazine article. I flip through until I find the news article dealing with the deaths of the Olenevs.

"It's not much," I explain. "The Olenevs moved here in May of 1900. Barbara died in childbirth the summer of 1903, and Robert was found dead the following Thanksgiving Day, due to starvation or a broken heart, depending on who you talk to."

"Well, I think we can enlighten you on that a little bit," Patty says, "but we're also goin' tah have tah tell you that Barbara didn't die in childbirth."

"You're kidding."

Patty shakes her head, "Nope. Not only did the birth of their son, *Shane,*" she stifles a giggle and elbows Shane, "go just fine, but she was writin' in this diary *aftah* his birth."

"And then?" I ask.

Patty shrugs, "Your guess is as good as ours."

"So, we have a news article with *incorrect* information," Letta muses to herself. She hurriedly scribbles something in her copious notes. "Alright, let's hear it. What happened to the Olenevs?"

"Well the diary doesn't staht until 1901," Shane says. "The first entry is from July. It's mostly 'bout the reason they ended up heeah tah begin with."

"It's so romantic," Patty clasps her hands over her heart with a dippy smile.

"Right," Shane clears his throat. "Anyway, he was a poor Russian immigrant whose parents died aftah they moved tah New York. Barbara met him on the street with a bunch of her girlfriends –"

"Listen tah what she wrote!" Patty snatches the diary from Shane and begins to read in a wistful tone of voice.

He was just walking along in his little pit of despair, taking notice of no one – that is until he bumped into me and sent me sprawling into the street. I landed in a pile of horse manure! Can you imagine? The girls gasped at first, but of course, they then began to laugh. And how could they not? I even began to giggle myself.

Robert was quite mortified himself. He helped me to my feet and did the best he could to apologize, but it was very difficult to understand his Russian accent. Fortunately for him, I found his boorish attempt at an apology cute. I knew right then that I wanted to know more about him.

"It was love at first sight," Patty declares, looking up from the diary with misty eyes.

"Yes, well there was no happily evah aftah for them, was there?" Shane retorts, taking the diary back. "They were engaged two months aftah they met, but her family was against it. They told Barbara they'd disown and disinherit her if she ran off with Robert, so of course, that's exactly what she did."

"They eloped and ended up heeah," Patty explains. "Robert grew up on a farm, and thought they'd have a happy life in the country, raisin' crops and animals."

"Barbara wrote she would've followed Robert anywhere," Shane says. "She's the one who found the newspaper ad." He flips through the pages and then hands the diary back to Patty to read.

"Grand Victorian home for sale," Patty says, resuming her reading tone.

'Extremely affordable. Lots of land. Needs minimal work. Perfect for families! Inquires should be sent to etc., and etc.' I told Robert it was fate when I first found the ad in the back of the newspaper – some strange chronicle that found its way to us in the mail by mistake. It was in tiny

print and hidden among other ads that looked more important, almost as if whoever printed the ad didn't actually want anyone to see it! This is what made me tell Robert it was meant to be. I told him this was what God wanted for us, and He had left it up to us to make it happen!

"If she only knew," says Letta sadly.

"It didn't take her long tah realize her mistake," Shane continues. "I suspect the spell broke right 'round the time she stahted the diary. She has these few good memories at the front, like she was tryin' tah remember how happy they used tah be."

"It stahted slowly," Patty explains. "At first she stahts complainin' 'bout all the work the house needed; the deaths of Alva and Eamonn left it incomplete. Robert took on some of the work himself, but he also spent a lot of time workin' the land. They had some fields of corn and some apple trees, some cattle and chickens."

"The first harvest was fine," Shane adds. "They were actually able tah sell their produce and meat 'round town. Barbara thought the people in town were a little odd, a little private for her tastes, but she didn't think anythin' more of it. She chalked it up tah the *'charm'* of our little town."

"But," Patty says excitedly, "the followin' yeeah, in the summer of 1902, everythin' changed when Barbara realized she was pregnant. Listen." She clears her throat and begins reading again.

I feel them staring at us constantly, their eyes following every step we take when we are in town. Have they always been staring at us with such hateful eyes?

Robert thinks I am paranoid, or at least, he did. Yes, he thought I was quite paranoid until we took a stroll around the churchyard a few days ago. The cemetery was filled with gravestones belonging to children! There were nearly more infants resting their sweet heads there than adults. And many of their mothers lay in rest there as well, and the dates of death… They were the same.

Now I know what it is they are thinking. I know why they hate us. It is like you said – they are jealous… and that makes me very afraid. Jealous and desperate parents are a very dangerous thing… And you know something about that, don't you?

"So," Shane says, "Barb and Rob take a stroll through the graveyard and realize what everyone in this town knew then and knows now: life heeah isn't very lucky for women or children."

"And then she becomes supah paranoid," says Patty. "She stahts worryin' she and her unborn child will end up in the same graveyard. She worries somethin' will happen during the birth, and both she and her son will end up dead. Tah make matters worse, as she got farthah along in her pregnancy, things stahted tah go wrong with the farm. Listen."

Robert says the animals have caught something, some sickness, but I don't know of anything that would cause all of the animals to stop eating, stop drinking. They aren't dying of an illness. They are losing the will to live. They have given up. Imagine! An animal, just giving up... I wouldn't have believed such a thing possible if I had not witnessed it myself.

And the crops! Robert can think of nothing to explain the crops. The corn stalks grow, but there is no corn. The apple trees blossom with rotten apples. Have you ever heard of such a thing? What will we do now? How can we raise a child if we cannot even raise a chick or a plant?

Shane sighs. "Barbara became obsessed. She stahted doing her own research; talkin' tah anyone who would talk tah her, lookin' through old newspapers at the library. She read 'bout failed harvests going back several yeeahs, all the way back tah 1851. She realized there hadn't been a healthy child born in Port Braseham since Emily Lenore Callaghan; each died at birth or at a young age. Those who survived were plagued with illness. She couldn't figure out what happened to Emily though." He leans back against the cool glass of the window behind him and crosses his arms. "She became convinced the town had done somethin' wrong in the eyes of God. Why else would He be punishin' all the townspeople like this? She begged Robert tah sell the property, to take her away 'from all this death,' but he refused. All of their money was sunk intah this place. They had tah stay."

"And on top of all of that, she continued to worry 'bout her baby," says Patty. "She made Robert call the town doctor up heeah several times before the baby was born. The doctor eventually told them he wasn't going tah continue tah 'entertain the whims of a young, hysterical woman.' She called him a quack because she knew somethin' was wrong with her child. There had tah be, because of what she saw in the graveyard, and what she found in her research."

"But," Shane interrupts, "of course, there was nothin' wrong. Little Shane was born and everythin' was fine until —"

"Until 'bout two weeks aftah he was born." Patty snatches the diary back up and flips through the pages. "This is her last entry, in mid-August of 1903." She clears her throat.

Robert refuses to call the doctor up the mountain again. Shane is fine, he keeps saying. The baby is fine, and I need to stop worrying and learn to enjoy him… our child. But I can hardly enjoy him when I am certain something is wrong. Perhaps not today, not tomorrow, not next month… but before long, he will be dead, like all those other poor children. Robert will wish he had listened to us then.

I felt compelled to go down into the basement last night. I cannot explain it, but I could not ignore The Calling. It pulled me out of bed in the middle of the night, and I went down into that dark space with only a candle to light my way. As I descended each step, my mood descended also. I became angry. It was an overwhelming sensation of bitter hopelessness.

I sat in the middle of the basement on the damp floor, dirtying my nightgown because I was commanded to. I sat. I listened. I thought. I cannot explain it. This is when I had the Epiphany.

What Shane, my dear sweet boy, needs is a real mother. He needs someone who can ensure he will grow, and live, and become a handsome, hardworking young man like his father. Yes, that's what he needs… And I know exactly who it shall be.

And she is close… Yes, you are very close, aren't you?

Patty closes the diary and looks up. I'm staring with my mouth open, thinking how similar Barbara's last entry is to Alva's. Letta's smiling.

"What are you smilin' 'bout?" Shane asks in an accusatory tone.

"Me?" Letta says. "Sorry. I didn't mean to. Certainly very tragic."

"What happened to her if she didn't die in childbirth?" I ask.

"I think you know," Letta says.

I remember the noose in my hands and begin rubbing them absentmindedly. Yes, I think I know what happened to Barbara Olenev.

"I don't understand why the article says she died in childbirth," Patty says.

"I think a certain amount of doctoring of the articles in that file occurred," Letta explains, "if only to keep the outside world from knowing the tragic history of the house. The town couldn't deny Barbara died, surely her body is lying up there in the churchyard. But they can cover up the means of death, perhaps the date also. Not many people back then would buy a house where two women killed themselves."

"What happened to Shane?" Shane asks with a funny look. "It sounds weird tah say that." He chuckles, changes his mind halfway through, and coughs instead.

"Don't know," Letta shrugs and makes a note. "I think there're a lot of things we'll need to research after tonight."

"You're still smiling," I say. "Why?"

"Because I've got something that's going to make your hair stand on end." She holds up the diary of E. L. "The diary of Emily Lenore *the second.*"

"What, like Henry the Eighth?" Shane asks.

"Sort of," Letta says. "This Emily Lenore is not actually related to Emily Lenore Callaghan, or at least, I don't think she is. In fact, she doesn't even have a last name. She was adopted by the house."

There's a prolonged silence, as if we aren't sure we heard Letta correctly, and are waiting for her to repeat it or provide an explanation.

But I don't need Letta to explain what she means, because I suddenly know. Everything, I think, is about to make a whole lot of sense.

Chapter Thirty-One
Emily Lenore II

There's a commotion as Shane and Patty bombard Letta with questions.

"What does *that* mean?"

"What are you sayin'?"

"What, like this house is alive or somethin'? Come on! That's crazier than ol' Enit!"

"Who is she? Where did she *come* from?"

I sit silently, listening but not listening, thinking, analyzing.

"Just relax a minute!" Letta shouts.

"Relax? Woman, you better staht answerin' some questions," Shane shouts back.

"I will, I promise," Letta says. "But right now, shut your traps and *listen.*" She waits for Patty and Shane to collect themselves.

"Alright," Letta says when all is finally quiet. "Emily Lenore *the second* started her diary in 1927 when she was ten. She didn't write in it often, but her entries increased with her age and with her frustration at being trapped in this house."

"Trapped?" Patty interrupts. "How?"

Letta looks at her with the measured patience of a teacher. "Look, I don't know how to explain it in a way that's going to make any sense. Let me read some of the diary entries first. I think that'll answer your questions." Letta opens the diary and begins reading, slowly at first, but then with interest, emotion, and the measured rhythm of an author indulgently reading a few pages aloud.

My name is Emily Lenore, and I am ten years old. I am starting this journal because She says I am to practice my writing skills. Today my prompt is to tell you about myself, but that is hard to do because I don't really know a lot about myself.

I grew up here. Here is inside of my mother, this house. She loves me and takes care of me. I remember nothing before Her, and I knew nothing before Her. My birth mother did not love me and did not want to care for me. She brought me here to my True Mother, because she knew I would be safe and cared for her. That's what I'm told anyway.

I guess I believe Her. Why would She lie?

Who is She? She is a voice inside my head, kind of. She tells me She loves me. She makes me food, and clothes me, and plays with me. I can't see Her because She is not an actual person in front of me (not that I've seen many of those either), but I see Her when I look at all the little pieces that make up this house. I see Her in the carved wooden furniture. I see Her in the tears along the wallpaper on the stairs. I see Her in the light the stained glass throws on the foyer floor. Sometimes, when I think about how I would explain Her to a stranger, to an outsider from that town that I sometimes see from the windows, I think of Her as a spirit. I can't see Her, but I can hear Her and I can feel Her, and I know that Her presence is all around me and inside of me.

I know and understand that this is not a normal situation. I'm not stupid. I may never have been allowed into the outside world, but She believes it is important to know about it, and has explained many things to me. It helps that I like to ask a lot of questions! I know that most people have a mother and a father. I know that most children go to a school to learn. But I am special and fortunate (that's what She always says). She loves me and She protects me by keeping me inside of Her, which I guess I understand. The outside world is a dangerous place filled with criminals and violence, after all.

I spend a lot of my time reading and learning about the world. She has a great library on the third floor, full of hundreds, maybe thousands, of books. History, mystery, plays, crime… lots and lots of books on crime…

When I grow up, I want to be an explorer! I want to see the ruins of the Maya. I want to drink coffee in Paris. I want to go on a walkabout in Australia. But She cautions me against such silly, dangerous dreams.

I can't go far away. I can't leave Her here by Herself. If I love Her, She says, then I must stay. And I do love Her. She is my mother. So I guess I have to stay. But that doesn't mean that I can't dream. She cannot tell me not to dream.

"That's her first entry," Letta says, and then when she sees Shane's mouth open, she adds, "Just wait, don't ask me anything yet. It gets better."

"Does bettah mean creepier?" asks Patty.

Letta doesn't answer. Instead, she picks up the diary and continues reading.

Today is my birthday! I am eleven. She says that She is so proud of me today because I am growing into a lovely young woman who cares about Her and who makes Her happy. To Her, I am the most wonderful gift. I am glad because I try very hard to make Her happy and proud.

As a present, She has presented me with a dollhouse! It's wonderful! It was sitting on the floor of the playroom when I woke up this morning. I know that She worked very hard on it. It looks exactly like Her, down to even the tiniest detail.

I remember the dollhouse in the attic, the replica of Wolfhowl. It had to be the same dollhouse Emily played with almost a hundred years ago. I'd just assumed Liam had found it himself, but maybe... Could it have been a *gift?*

She even made me cake! – No candles to blow out though. There have never been any candles. Fire is too dangerous.

It was a wonderful day outside today – I think. I could see the great blue sky and white cotton ball clouds through the windows. Normally, I'm not allowed too close to the windows for too long. Someone might see me and come up the hill to investigate, which means that She and I would be separated, and I don't want that. Once, I lingered in the window too long and saw the caretaker and his boy as they took care of Her lawns. For just a moment, the boy looked up and caught sight of me. I ran away instantly, but I was not fast enough. Before I knew it, they were inside the house!

I felt all mixed up. I was filled with the fear of being discovered and separated from Her, but at the same time, I was very curious. I've never talked with another person before, or even been in the same room as one. Would the caretaker and his boy be friendly? Would the boy play with me? Or would they think I was some intruder and haul me out?

I didn't have the chance to find out. She immediately herded me into my room and into the little door in the turret. She told me to stay very quiet and I had to stay in there for quite a long time while the caretaker and the boy searched Her. Eventually they left, and I was released.

But today, I did ask if I could go outside on one of the upper balconies. I only wanted to feel the warm air and a breeze. I swore I'd only go out for a minute and only on the back of the house where no one could see me, but She said no. We can't take chances like that, She said.

But perhaps next year. Maybe when I am twelve She will let me. Maybe then, She will see that I am careful and can be trusted.

Maybe.

Letta turns the pages and finds the next dog-eared entry. As she reads the words on the page, I picture Emily Lenore, as if from an old black and white movie. She'd sit at the long, empty table and work through the pages of a handwriting book. She'd huddle in a corner of the drawing room reading and writing in her diary. She'd spend hours in the huge playroom with her dollhouse and one lonely doll. She'd sit in front of the bathroom mirror, brushing her hair a hundred strokes and dreaming of exploring the Amazon or the Pyramids of Giza.

She'd sit alone at the dinner table, wishing there was someone to talk to. She'd crouch near a candle and play a game of solitaire by herself, wishing for a friend to play Old Maid with. She'd wish for something more than a musty old house holding her hostage, and telling her the world was much too dangerous for her to go out into.

And somewhere deep down, her rebellion took seed.

Today I won a small battle. I feel guilty because I know that She is angry with me, but She will forgive me. It was so exciting! It was worth it.

I spend a lot of time investigating the house, though I know it like the back of my own hand. Sometimes She will hide gifts for me, and we'll have a little scavenger hunt, but that isn't what we did today. That isn't what I did today. Today, I broke the rules. Today, I went outside!

It was just before sunrise. I could feel the heavy, regular rhythm of a house asleep and I snuck upstairs. I snuck into the attic in stockinged feet. I moved slowly and carefully, and I found myself inside the attic, crawling up the spiral staircase to the door in the ceiling. So many times, I have dreamed of sneaking outside to see what the rest of the world is like – and today I did!

I slipped through the door in the attic before She noticed, and found myself on a curious little platform with railings around it. From up there it was like being on top of the world! It was windy and my hair was in knots by the time I came inside. I looked down on the town below and stared hard at each of the buildings and trees, trying to memorize them all because I know that I will never be allowed up there again.

And the most glorious sight of all was watching the sun slip up on the horizon, waking the trees and the birds – and what beautiful songs they sing! The colors were beautiful and speckled, like a kaleidoscope. Even though it was chilly, and I was freezing (of course I don't have a coat because I don't need one since I'm never outside), I waited until the sun was all the way up and starting to warm my skin before I came inside.

But, before I left, I saw the most wonderful thing. Despite Her assurances that She is teaching me all I need to know of the outside world, I saw something I did not understand. It was shiny and small, but also very far above me so I know it must have been huge. It was some kind of tube soaring through the sky...like a bird made of metal. I was fascinated! What must it be like to be inside of such a contraption, and to imagine how much of the world you could see from up there... For the first time, I felt a real jealousy of those who could live in the outside world. To be like them, to be free to do as you please... How thrilling!

Of course, She was very angry and I was punished. She has locked me in my room and says I must stay locked up here for a few days, until I've learned my lesson. She was so worried, so afraid. What if I had fallen? What if I had been seen and taken away? How would I feel about my little accomplishment then?

She said so many ugly things to me, and I began to feel ugly myself for what I had done. I didn't mean to worry Her. I didn't mean to make Her angry. But I am starting to feel like a fly in a jar, suffocating and begging for air. I love Her, but how long can She keep me here like this? How long must I be Her prisoner? If I love Her, then I must stay. That is what she says. But if She loves me, shouldn't she let me go? Shouldn't She want the best for me? For me to be happy and fulfilled?

And there it is, that seed of rebellion. The house had planted it despite all Her efforts not to. This is the moment Emily Lenore II was lost to the house, the moment both the house and Emily knew they would eventually be separated.

Deep beneath the floorboards of my bedroom, I feel a small tremble.

"What was that?" Patty asks, alarmed.

"Shh!" Shane hisses, oblivious.

"I'm going to skip ahead some," Letta says. "After she turned thirteen she really started to get hateful."

She thinks She can keep me here. She thinks reading about the outside world, reading about the science of aviation will placate me. She thinks it will handle my curiosity about the outside world. But She is wrong. It only makes me want to see it more.

She senses this in me. I know it because She has become stricter in Her rules. I can't go near any of the windows anymore — she has forbidden it. She has boarded all of them up, save for one in my room. And this I am only allowed to peek out of at night, and only if all the lights are out and there isn't a full moon.

Every once in a while, someone will come to see the house. A prospective buyer here and there, and always I am hidden in one of the turrets. In fact, that's where I've written many of these entries. It's where I'm writing this one right now. No one ever seems very interested in Her though.

She's slowly falling into disrepair. She's starting to look ugly. I doubt very much anyone would really want Her now.

She keeps me busy and distracted with lessons, and homework, and books, and hobbies. She tries to tempt me with that ridiculous dollhouse, as if I am only a girl and not becoming a woman. She doesn't understand me. She doesn't understand me at all. And how can She? After all, She's just a house.

There's another rumble, and this time Patty and I aren't the only ones who feel it.

"Hey," Shane says, "what *was* that?"

I think I know what it is, but I don't say anything as Letta continues reading. I need to know what happened to Emily Lenore. Did she escape? Did she make it to all those wonderful places in her dreams? If she did, why's her diary *still here?*

Letta's so involved in the reading she doesn't notice the growing unease in the room.

I come here, to these pages, because they are my only friends. This is the only place where I can truly be myself. I come here because She cannot see my words. I'm allowed so few secrets from Her, but She cannot know my thoughts when they are in here, because they are mine. The thoughts in here, they are truly MINE.

And my thoughts burn with dreams of the real world that I cannot keep quiet forever. I have to leave this place, and I have to leave Her behind. I am not Her child. She does not love me. She loves only herself, and I am her plaything, her doll.

I feel Her growing sadness growing alongside my dreams of travel. But I refuse to feel sorry for Her. Pity will not stop me from leaving as soon as I can figure out how to get out of Her. She can't keep the doors locked forever. I will find a way out. It's only a matter of time.

"What if it's an earthquake?" Patty cries.

"It's not an earthquake." Letta says dismissively, wide eyes fixed on the pages of Emily Lenore's diary.

"All the same," Patty says, "I think I've had enough for tonight."

"Cool it a few more minutes," Shane says. "I want tah know what happens."

"And you will," Letta says with a wink. "Let me read the last entry, and then we'll adjourn."

I should stop Letta, but I'm on the edge of my proverbial seat, prepared to hear the end of Emily Lenore II's diary.

The deep rumbling is definitely *not* an earthquake.

Someone came to the house today! I could hardly believe it when I saw them coming up the driveway. I felt my pulse quicken, and I felt my chest grow warm. This was my chance! This was my chance to flee, to get out! I will run down the stairs and rush the doors as they open! That was my quick and fleeting thought as I heard their voices grow near, but I was not as quick in my actions.

She saw my rising excitement and locked me away. She all but threw me into the attic and locked the door. I pounded, and kicked, and screamed, but they could not hear me. I don't know what the visitors' purpose was. They were inside for only a few minutes, and I think must have stayed down on the first floor or they would surely have heard me.

I watched them leave from a crack in one of the attic windows. Their fading taillights growing as faint as my chances at escape. And then I sobbed like a little girl, like the little girl She wants me to be. Forever.

I hate Her. It isn't pity. It isn't love. It isn't nostalgia over what once was. It is true and honest hate. I hate being Her prisoner. I hate being Her precious little gift. Her plaything. Her daughter. Ha!

I cannot keep pretending or hiding or being obedient to Her. I can't. I won't. I'm going to get out of this house, or I am going to die trying because if I have to stay here, I truly will die. And if I escape, I won't look back, not for one second.

Do you hear me? I'm never coming back. Never.

Letta closes the diary.

"That's *it?*" Shane shouts.

Letta shrugs. "There're other entries of course, but I only read the ones I thought would give you the whole picture."

"I'm not sure I understand the whole picture," Patty says, forgetting her fear for a moment. "Was this girl crazy? Was she kept company by Alva's ghost? How could she have been adopted by *a house?*"

"I think we can all agree that this isn't *just* a house," Letta says, gesturing at the ceiling with a diary.

"Can we?" Shane asks skeptically. "What evidence actually exists? Sure, the owners died under tragic circumstances, but there aren't any witnesses. We only have the diaries of a few women who descended into some kind of madness. For all we know, livin' up heeah on the hill, and bein' hated by everyone in town, was enough tah send them down the rabbit hole. We have no real evidence that a house or a ghost or whatevah made these women kill themselves."

"You're sayin' this is just any *regular* house?" Patty argues, crossing her arms.

"I've seen no evidence otherwise," Shane says. "I mean, like anyone else, I've heard the rumahs. I know what people around heeah think, that there's some ghost or curse or evil presence heeah, but all they're basin' that on is some old creepy stories told 'round the campfire. And this Emily Lenore II," he continues, "what of her? How do we know she's not just some crazy person who lived heeah, a squattah? If she lived heeah at all. It could be a stupid prank for all we know."

"And the stuff Rose found in the attic?" Patty glares Shane down.

Shane shrugs. "It's not like this place is a fortress. Anyone who can jimmy a door can get inside and mess 'round, plant thins, whatevah."

"So suddenly you don't believe in ghosts?" Patty asks combatively, standing akimbo before him. "You think this Emily Lenore is made up? You don't think she was *real*? You don't think her hatred for this house was *real?*"

Stop, I think. *Stop talking about it.* We're in real trouble here. I notice Letta is sitting on the floor with both of her palms flat against the floorboards.

"We need to get out of here," Letta says suddenly. "I wasn't thinking. I shouldn't have read Emily Lenore's words in the house."

I get up, but it's too late.

The house begins to shake. The loudest creaks and moans I've ever heard emanate from somewhere deep below, growing louder each second. It's an enormous roaring, a growling howl. The foundation wobbles and twists. Dust from the upper floors sifts through cracks in the ceiling. Pictures come off of the walls, and my alarm clock dances across the bedside table until it topples to the floor.

"What's happenin'?" Patty screams as she stumbles and Shane catches her.

"It really *is* an earthquake!" Shane shouts.

We make for the bedroom door as fast as we can. I know this is no earthquake. I know, in reading Emily Lenore II's private words, we've opened a fresh wound inside the house. And now I feel, for the first time, that our lives are in very real danger.

Chapter Thirty-Two
Certainties

We race out onto the front lawn just as Beckan and Derry come running up the hill. There's chaos as questions fly around, and tears fall – Liam and Patty are both crying. Shane has a protective arm around both Letta and Patty, who huddle close together, shaking like leaves. I hold a clinging Liam in my arms, staring up at the looming dark shadow of the house in the night. Derry halts on the edge of our little gathering, squinting up at the house as if merely curious. Beckan makes a beeline for me and Liam. As he puts a hand on each of our shoulders, the ground suddenly settles.

All grows very, very quiet.

"Are you okay?" Beckan asks, his green eyes searching mine. I nod slowly, feeling dazed.

I look at my friends. "You guys okay?"

"Yeah," Shane replies shakily. "Just stahtled." He tries to chuckle, but Patty's iron grip on his rib cage tightens, and he winces.

"What was that?" Patty demands, looking wildly from one of us to the other. "An earthquake?"

My eyes meet Letta's.

"Maybe," says Letta evasively. "Wouldn't be the first time right?"

"Ayuh," says Derry, keeping a steady gaze on the house, as if trying to bore through the walls with his eyes. He gives a nod and then turns around and shuffles back down the hill like an aging bulldog, satisfied he isn't needed.

I almost call out to him – *Wait!* – but Mother's car arrives at the top of the hill, the Volvo's headlights illuminating our small party on the lawn. She leaps out of the car, leaving the door open, and throws her arms around us.

"Oh my God! Are you okay? Are you? Look at me!" She grabs a chin in each hand and turns our faces toward her. Her eyes search us for any signs of injury, pulling our arms away from our bodies, the nurse looking for wounds that might need her attention.

"We're fine, Mother." I swat her hands away. "Really, we're okay."

"I was so worried," Mother says. "An earthquake in Maine! Who'd have thought, right?"

Uncomfortable silence stretches between us as we stare up at the house uncertainly.

"Well," Letta says awkwardly, "I guess we're gonna get going."

"I'm sorry guys. Thanks for hanging out tonight. Sorry about... I'm glad you're okay."

"Sure," Shane says with a sarcastic smile. "We had a *great* time."

Beckan gives my shoulder a quick squeeze. "You sure you're okay?" I nod and he turns to my friends. "I'll give you a lift home," he says walking toward them. "I'm sure thins will be a little crazy in town tonight."

"Thanks," Shane says as he, Patty, and Letta follow Beckan to his truck, moving like one entity.

After they disappear over the side of the hill, Mother turns back to me and Liam, who's still sniveling. "Let's get inside and assess the damage okay?"

I watch Mother's back as she walks toward the house, completely unaware of the truth. As I'm about to follow, Liam raises his head off my shoulder.

"Rosie?"

"Squiggle worm?"

"You made Her really angry."

I sigh. "I know."

*   *   *

We spend about an hour gauging damage and righting crooked pictures, replacing items on shelves in the kitchen, and looking for anything that'll need attention from the O'Dwyres. Fortunately, damage is minimal. It might be an old house, but it's sturdy.

Mother remarks how strange it is to have an earthquake so far up the coast and wonders when the last time such a thing occurred. I nod politely, but am too busy making observations to really pay attention – attention to Mother's words anyway. I'm paying attention to Mother – her mannerisms, her body

language, her tone of voice. Compared to the depressive state
she was in over the weekend, and her bubbly state as she left for
work this morning, she's tending more toward the depressive. I
can tell Mother's trying to fight it off, trying to keep her voice
light and airy, but I'm not fooled. I know that, like me, and like
Liam, Mother's falling under the spell of the house.

I'm now certain of three things. One, this house is alive. It's
a living, breathing thing. The strange voices in the night. The
front doors opening on their own. The constant sensation of
being watched. How had I missed it for so long?

Two, the house wants Liam for itself. It wants to love him
and to care for him the way it had Emily Lenore II. I go back
over the strange occurrences I haven't really thought about
before. The glass of water at Liam's bedside that first night.
Liam's "mystery" sandwich. The television coming on at Liam's
command. His sudden independence… Is the house already
controlling him? Taking *care* of him?

And three, in order for the house to succeed, both Mother
and I must die. I think back to the diaries, to the women and
their words, writing as if they were in conversation with
someone, with some *thing*. I think back to what they did – had
they really killed themselves or…?

I feel a fierce determination to protect my family. The odds
are against us, I'm sure of that much. I can't leave because I
know Mother, who'd never believe me, won't leave. As if we
could anyway – all of our money was sunk into this house from
hell. I also know if I'm going to protect my family, I'm going to
have to do it from the inside. I don't know how I'm going to do
it, but I'll just have to do my best to be strong and to keep the
house at bay until I find a solution – if one exists. My sudden
determination begins to falter, to give way to defeat and fear.
Enit's cold words ring out in my head.

Your death is certain.

*   *   *

"I know you don't *need* me to tuck you in," I tell Liam as I'm
doing just that, despite his loud complaining, "but you're my
brother, and we had a scary evening, and I want to make sure
you're alright with my own eyes. Your protests are useless," I say
with a smile.

"Fine." Liam, bathed and in his pajamas, settles down in
bed grumpily, and I pull the sheets over him – airplane sheets –

and feel a pang in my stomach. Ignoring it, I pull the heavy blanket over him and kiss him on the cheek.

"Goodnight squiggle worm. I love you." I wait for a reply that doesn't come. "Liam, I said – "

"I love you too," he says, vaguely annoyed, and rolls away from me. "Goodnight."

There's a tug on my heartstrings as I leave Liam's room, closing the door behind me. He's lost to me already.

*   *   *

Alison sits before the vanity in the master bedroom. She stares through her reflection with dark, unseeing eyes. Her long brown hair has been stroked a hundred, two hundred times already, but she doesn't stop. She slowly pulls the brush through her shiny hair again and again, as if in a trance.

Hagan is downstairs in the drawing room, she knows. He is sitting by the fire and listening to the sad Christmas music still emanating from the speakers despite Christmas being a week past, a vodka tonic in his hand. Alison hears the music seeping through the floorboards of their bedroom, sweet and low… A perfect soundtrack for tonight.

She looks at her empty glass on the vanity, sighs deeply, heavily, as if she is very, very tired and barely able to keep her eyes open, but she does not blink. She just keeps staring. Staring and thinking.

It's Hagan's fault, she tells herself. It was his blasted idea to bring her here, to separate her from the city and the life she loved. It was him who kept her imprisoned in this fortress, this dank, miserable eyesore. Maybe he thought it would save them. Maybe if they came up here they would remember who they were when they first fell in love.

Idiot. There is no saving them now. There is no saving him *now. Now is the time, she tells herself. Now is the time because it is already too late.*

Alison sets her brush down and rises, catching sight of her silken dressing gown in the mirror, the one Hagan had given to her on their first anniversary. It is a miracle it still fits, she thinks. Of course, that is the benefit of a mostly liquid diet; she only eats when she isn't drunk, which isn't often.

Next to the brush is the revolver, shiny and new. This she picks up with her delicate fingers, feeling its comforting heaviness in her hand. It is Hagan's of course, not that he knows how to use it. Like many of their possessions, it was bought to impress. This is some kind of special edition kept in pristine condition, but beyond that, Alison knows nothing of it. It is a gun like any other gun, made for an explicit purpose.

She slips into a pair of heeled slippers and slurs her way out of the room and into the hall. She pauses briefly and leans drunkenly over the banister.

"Hagan," she calls in a breathy voice he would barely hear over the music. She is a ghost already… "Hagan, darling…" She hears the music grow lower, followed by his impatient sigh.

"What is it Alison?" His voice is contemptuous, impatient. Am I so hard to love? she wonders.

"Would you come up here darling?" She coos. With any luck, he will think she is feeling surprisingly amorous and follow her sultry voice up the stairs.

"Come up?" he says, annoyed. "What ever for?"

"Please, Hagan," she says pleadingly, as if she needs him right now, in this moment. "Come up the stairs and meet me in this room at the end of the hall."

"At the end of the hall?" Hagan's voice grows louder and his form appears in the foyer below. He looks up at her with hands on his hips, a cigar hanging out of his mouth. "What the devil are you on about?"

Alison makes sure the hand with the revolver is behind her. She watches him do a double take when he sees her lithe figure beneath the gown.

"Darling, please," she says. "You ask too many questions. I have something to show you. In the room at the end of the hall." She doesn't wait for his response. She pulls away from the banister and walks into the room at the end of the hall. She goes around the corner once inside and waits, melting into the shadowy darkness.

"I'm waiting, Hagan," she calls seductively.

She hears him make his way up the stairs with those heavy steps she'd grown so used to; he stalks around like Frankenstein's monster. She hears his breaths as he pauses at the cracked door. He nudges it open with a shoe and speaks over the long groan of the hinges. "Alison?" He calls uncertainly.

"Over here," she says from the blackness of the corner.

"Why is it so dark?"

"So it'll be easier to see the light."

"What li—"

Alison doesn't wait for Hagan to finish his question. She pulls the trigger and watches his shadowed form fall to the floor, dead instantly. It was easier to pull the trigger than she expected – like plucking an eyebrow – and she stands startled, a deer in the headlights, as a thin trail of smoke lifts out of the barrel.

Coming to, she drops the revolver to the floor and bends down. She drags her husband's body to the center of the room. As she drops his limp, heavy body, his forehead, with a neat little bullet hole in the center, comes to rest in the rectangle of light coming from the hall. He always was such a handsome man, she thinks, looking into his frozen, dead eyes. Pity she had to muss it up.

Alison retrieves the gun and then lays down next to her husband, placing herself comfortably in the crook of his arm. She sighs, feeling content for the first time in ages, and lays her head back. "I told you, you would be sorry, darling."

Slowly, she pulls the revolver up and places it against the side of her head, staring straight up at the ceiling.

To no one in particular she says, "We're so lonely, Rose."

Then she pulls the trigger.

I shoot up and fall off the side of my bed. My ears are ringing, as if I've really heard the sound of the gun, like it originated from my very room and not from the confines of a dream. I bring my hands up to my head, but something chillingly cold and heavy is in my right hand. Slowly, I lower my hand to a shaft of moonlight on the floor.

Gleaming in my fingers is the revolver I'd seen in the Boyles' attic box.

I fling it away from me, horrified. It lands with a threatening *clunk* near the closet.

I sit on the floor for a long time, my hands on my chest. I try to slow my heartbeat and regulate my breathing. My chest is expanding desperately as I gulp for air, and I think my rib cage might burst.

It takes an hour for me to calm down. When I'm finally able to think, I think hard, trying to remember the dream. What did Alison say?

We're so lonely, Rose.

And what did my father say?

I'm so lonely, Rose.

What does it mean? What can it *possibly* mean?

Chapter Thirty-Three
Earthquakes

Beckan wakes up around three thirty in the morning. It's been his habit lately. He hasn't been able to make it through a full night's sleep since Delaneys on arrived on Wolfhowl Mountain. He's worried about Rose and her family. He can't be sure if they've noticed the changes in their personalities themselves, but he and his father surely have. It turns out you don't have to know someone well to see them beginning the spiral into depression, or to watch them fall under the hazy spell of the house.

Rubbing what little sleep there is from his eyes, Beckan makes his way to the kitchen for some tea and sees the kettle is already on the stove, a hot brew steaming within. He pours himself a cup and finds his father in the living room, a snoring Lady at his feet.

Derry stares into the flames of a dying fire, rocking slowly in his chair, a comically small teacup in his large mitts.

"You bettah find out what that *girl* is up tah," he says in his gravelly voice without turning away from the fire.

Beckan takes the other rocking chair by the hearth, remembers his mother rocking in this very spot, and looks at his father. The light throws dark shadows over the rugged crags of his worn face. Beckan wonders how much different his father might look if his mother had lived. "What do you mean?"

"You *know* what I mean, son," Derry says, turning his glare on Beckan. "That *girl* and her friends are up tah somethin'. They-uh meddlin' in somethin' they-uh don't understand. She's gonna get them all killed."

Beckan doesn't reply. He blows on his tea and takes a test sip, hisses away from his cup quickly; still too hot.

"Don't you fah-get," Derry adds quietly, "that it's *our job* tah protect 'em."

Beckan nods instead of pointing out their family's failure to do exactly that is the reason why so many people hate them.

259

"And don't you get tah attached tah her neither," Derry says. "One broken man in this family is enough."

Beckan nods slowly, knowing his father's warning is much too late.

*　　　　　*　　　　　*

Is it only Tuesday? This week feels eternal already. Mother skipped out of the house again this morning, glad to head to work, an environment she can control. Much like his fit yesterday afternoon, Liam desperately wants to stay home. He has no interest in going to school, in seeing his new friends, in getting out of the house at all. And, seeing another wet and cold day ahead, I understand.

But I'm strong, right? I'm the one who's going to protect this family. Step one is getting everyone out of the house as much as possible. So when Liam sinks to the floor, lifeless and heavy, I drag him onto the porch by an elbow and lock the door behind us.

Beckan pulls up as I'm tucking the key into my bookbag. He looks happy to see me when we climb into the truck, and I feel his eyes linger on both of us before putting the truck in gear and heading down the hill.

"How are you doin' aftah last night?" Beckan asks. "Everyone alright?"

Liam sulks between the two of us, crossing his arms and remaining silent. I roll my eyes at Beckan.

"We're fine," I say. "The rest of the night was…uneventful. Damage was minimal." I stifle a yawn. I wasn't able to fall back asleep after the nightmare, especially with the gun sitting on my bedroom floor. When the sun finally came up, I returned it to the box in the attic, where I hope no one will find it. I decide not to tell anyone about the dream – to talk about it would only make it too real.

"Good," Beckan says. "I was plannin' tah spend some time up there today. Check and repair the damage and take care of some other thins that've been needin' attention."

"You can't," I blurt without thinking, and Beckan looks at me questioningly. "I mean… not by yourself. You should wait until we get home. I could help, you know, hold your hammer for you or something." My recovery attempt is transparent, but after what happened last night, I don't want anyone in the house alone. There's no question in my mind the house is fully alert now. Who knows what it's capable of? Who knows what it's thinking? What it's *planning*.

"Don't worry," Beckan says with a smile and a wink, unconcerned. "I'll be careful. I'll only take care of the necessary thins. I don't want either of you gettin' hurt."

Beckan meets my eyes. We both know the other is holding something back. Beckan's afraid to tell me anything that might fuel whatever futile effort I'm making with my friends. I don't want him to know about my dream or the gun.

"I feel like a crazy person." The words are out of my mouth before I can stop them. Thank God, they're only a whisper.

"What?" asks Beckan with a peaked eyebrow.

I shake my head. "Nothing."

When the truck reaches the bottom of the hill, we're both surprised Letta isn't waiting for us.

"No Letta?" Beckan asks.

"Maybe she decided to walk?" Yet another pang of anxiety takes hold of me. Is Letta okay? Is she running late? Or is she mad at me because of last night? Could the house have somehow hurt Letta, even in the safety of her own home?

"Maybe," Beckan says, and we trundle down the road in silence.

There's a lot of activity on the school lawn when we arrive, everyone's anxious to talk about the "earthquake." With the rumble of the diesel engine, most of the eyes turn in our direction as Liam and I hop out of the truck.

"Listen," Beckan says before I close the door, "I'm gonna pick you up aftah school today. Okay?"

"Um, sure," I say, wondering what he's thinking. "Meet you here?"

Beckan nods. I close the squeaky door and bend down to Liam, who's still pouting. I remind him of his promise last night to stay with Mrs. Bauer and to behave. "There will be consequences if you aren't a perfect angel for her. Understand?"

Liam nods sullenly before walking very slowly toward the kindergarten doors, dragging his feet with each step.

I search the lawn for familiar faces, but find only one. Adam O'Sullivan leans against the building, far enough away from the main doors to ensure he'll be ignored by the other students, who've finally decided to head inside as the wind picks up.

"Hey." I'm not sure if Adam notices me approaching or not, but if he does, he ignores me. "How are you?"

Adam stares at his feet and the hood of his jacket hides most of his face. When he finally looks up, his black eye is obvious, and I wince. "I'm really sorry about what happened."

Adam shakes his head and pushes his body away from the building with a foot. He lifts his bookbag and throws it over his shoulder, brushing by me.

I don't know why, but Adam's stubborn refusal to speak to me makes my blood boil. "Hey!" I grab his shoulder and spin him around. "I'm talkin' to you!"

Adam rolls his eyes and stares at me. When I don't start talking, he leans forward with a hand to his ear, as if saying "Well?" His audacity fuels the fire and I curl my hands into fists.

"Why do you hate me so much?" I demand. "I've been nothing but nice to you. Even at the party. *You're* the one who earned you that black eye, not me."

Adam stares hard at me, his face the perfect picture of contempt. "Why does it even matter? Why's it so important to you that I take your notice? Why do I *have* to like you?"

I don't have an answer.

"I'm supposed to be grateful because you, the Great Rose Delaney, deigned to notice lowly peasant Adam O'Sullivan, pathetic descendent of crazy Ol' Enit? You're just like everyone else in this whole dumbass town," Adam says, his voice full of venom. "You *want* to be noticed. You *need* to be important for no other reason than to *be* important. Another sheep on the farm." His voice grows more irate with each syllable. He glares at me as if just the sight of me is offensive. "I don't owe you anything." He spits at the ground and turns away from me.

The old Rose, Texas Rose, would have followed Adam and popped him another black eye. Texas Rose might've knocked him down and kicked him in the ribs while shouting obscenities. But the new Rose, Maine Rose, just stares at his back as he walks away, feeling very small. Only when it starts to drizzle do I head inside with the last of the students.

I wonder when the sun will come back to Port Braseham. There's a strong desire from within to feel the warmth of the sun, and see its yellow haze overhead instead of these ugly rain-swollen clouds. An unnervingly strong swelling of nostalgia for Texas wells up inside me, and I think about poor Margot, locked in a closet while all the other children play in the sun.

*   *   *

Usually I like to sit up front in history so I can give my full attention to Mr. Lindsay. He's a good storyteller; sometimes I forget I'm in class, and his enthusiasm reminds me of Dad, but I'm not in the mood today. I sit in a back corner, retreating into myself.

I'm so lonely, Rose.

Mr. Lindsay notices the seat change with an arched eyebrow, but says nothing. Of course — *of course!* — he's going to talk about the earthquake history of Maine. What *else* would we talk about the day after such a strange and important event?

"You know, the earthquake history of Maine, though short, is really quite interesting," Mr. Lindsay says, pulling down an ancient map of the state from a roll screwed to the top of the chalkboard.

Mary, sitting in the middle of the room with her friends, mutters something I can't hear, and they erupt with laughter, glancing openly at me over their shoulders.

"Mostly," Mr. Lindsay continues, undeterred by our total lack of interest, "we feel earthquakes from other places, like Canada or Massachusetts, but we do have our own history." He picks up an old pool cue he likes using to point at his maps and jabs happily away as he orates. "The first earthquake reported with an epicenter in Maine happened in May of 1817. Historians think the epicenter was probably here in the center region of the state since reports of the earthquake came from all over.

"The next recorded earthquake was almost a century later, in 1904. This stronger one was felt by the whole of New England and would be nothing particularly special to Maine were it not for damage to three popular churches; one in Eastport, one in New Brunswick, and of course, our own Saint Perpetua." Mr. Lindsay jabs at another dot on the map.

Mr. Lindsay's enthusiasm starts to pull me out of my stupor, and I begin listening despite myself. The earthquake closest to Port Braseham came in 1912 when an earthquake hit the Bangor coast, the mainland closest to Mt. Desert Island. There was a 7.2 in 1929 triggered by a submarine. January 1943 in Delaware. Damage in Portland from an offshore earthquake in April 1957.

"And that would be it," Mr. Lindsay says importantly, tugging on the map and allowing it to shoot back up with a loud *snap*, waking a couple of students who've nodded off. *"Except for,"* he says in the plot-twisting tone I recognize, "an earthquake that happened in the summer of 1932. And why, you might ask, is this earthquake so special?"

Mr. Lindsay's question is rhetorical and I know the answer.

"Because," he continues eagerly, "the epicenter was *right here* in Port Braseham. It's the only earthquake to ever hit our town directly until –"

"Last night." I didn't mean to say it out loud, much less loud enough for the rest of the room to hear me. The room is filled with a heavy silence broken only by the creaks of desks as my classmates turn to look at me.

"That's right, Rose," Mr. Lindsay says evenly. "The earthquake in 1932 was not particularly strong by comparison, registering as a 4.3. Nothing much was damaged. In fact, most of the damage was limited to Wolfhowl Manor because it's a rather old piece of construction that hasn't been updated like the rest of our older buildings, Saint Perpetua for example."

I wish Mr. Lindsay would stop talking now. Some of my classmates are trying not to be so obvious, but Mary is looking straight at me in the most unfriendly way yet. Did Ronan confess what happened at the party? Did Adam follow through on his threat and tell her?

"And last night's?" Adam asks from his usual perch against the window, in his usual melancholy tone, and with his usual glum expression. "What did last night's earthquake register? I think it must have been stronger because there's been a lot of talk about damage around town."

Jackass.

"Well you're partly right, Adam," Mr. Lindsay says, leaning his short backside against his desk and pushing his thin framed glasses higher up on his nose. "There's been talk of damage, but it's a little early to be certain of how much. I missed the news this morning, so I'm not sure of the Richter reading –"

"5.9," Mary offers helpfully, winking at me.

"Yes, thank you Ms. Donovan. So it *was* stronger then. 5.9 is pretty remarkable, much stronger than the one in 1932 of course. It's likely there'll be damage to some of the older buildings around town, but a 5.9 isn't strong enough to swallow up Port Braseham. It was just a healthy jiggle to make sure we're paying attention." Mr. Lindsay smiles.

"Too bad that blight on the mountain's still standing," Mary says, looking at me. "I thought for sure we'd finally be rid of it… *And you,"* she adds, too low for Mr. Lindsay to hear.

Mr. Lindsay ignores the girl drama playing out in front of him and turns back to the board. "Well, that was a wonderful extra little lesson for us today! Now, let's move on to today's *real* lesson: the Abenaki Indians!" At the sound of his melodious voice, most of the eyes in the room finally turn away from me. All sets of eyes except for one.

Adam glares at me, as if he thinks his eyes can open me up, read my insides like a book. And then a venomous smile slides across his thin lips. It's so creepy it makes me shiver.

I tune Mr. Lindsay out and try to think about what he said. When was the earthquake in Port Braseham? Summer of 1932. I close my eyes to concentrate and picture the words in Emily Lenore II's diary in my head. I'm certain her last entry was in 1932, but when? Was it in the summer?

I'm obsessed all through study hall, blocking out all the sneers and jeers from the other students. It certainly doesn't take anyone of marked intelligence to make the connection between the earthquake and Wolfhowl Mountain. But my classmates are prejudiced. They want to believe the earthquake has something to do with my house because they want to believe I'm some sort of ghoul who'll play her part in the superstition about the damn mountain, like everyone else who's lived there. They just want another ghost to talk about at parties.

I make the connection between my house and the earthquake because I know the truth. No one else in town knows a child was hidden away up on Wolfhowl Mountain for fifteen years; it certainly would be part of the lore of the place otherwise. I think the 1932 earthquake probably occurred the very day Emily Lenore II managed her escape – if she'd managed it.

I scour the halls for Letta between bells and in the cafeteria at lunch, but I can't find her anywhere. Shane and Patty are sitting at our usual lunch table, but they're hunched close together with their heads bent, deep in conversation. I feel awkward intruding, so I don't. Instead, I stare around the cafeteria looking for somewhere else to sit, but every other seat seems to be taken. Eileen sits at Ronan and Mary's table again, and a crazy idea pops into my head, and I almost walk over to join them – but then I remember how Mary looked at me in history class and come to my senses.

I take my lunch out of the cafeteria, through the hall, and into the bathroom. Then I do the one thing Texas Rose never did; I eat my lunch by myself, sitting on a porcelain throne and fighting back tears.

Chapter Thirty-Four
The Fight

I suffer through art and creative writing, doing my best to be invisible. At least Adam and Mary aren't in either class, which leads to minimal enjoyment. I just don't feel like myself anymore. Moving across the country from a big city to a small town, and into the most cursed house since *Amityville Horror,* has a way of changing you.

I alternate between worrying about Letta, Liam's increasingly strange behavior, and how I'm going to save my family. By the time the last bell rings, I'm so distracted I forget Beckan is picking me up.

I'm putzing around at my locker, delaying my return to Wolfhowl Manor a little longer. I hate to admit that I'm terrified of what'll happen when I get home.

Suddenly, my locker slams shut, barely missing my hand as I snap it back. For a split second, I think the house's dark magic followed me to school, but then I see Mary Donovan standing there, radiating the kind of heat that can only be produced by unadulterated fury.

For the first time since I've met her, Mary looks ugly. Her perfectly plucked eyebrows press down over her wide, dark eyes, which are ringed like a raccoon's by her smudged mascara. She presses her dainty lips together so tightly the edges are white. The faint remains of tear tracks are visible as she glares at me. For once she's alone, but that doesn't comfort me; without her cronies to keep her grounded, Mary is only more dangerous.

"You." Her voice is menacingly quiet.

She's caught me off guard and my mind whirrs with possibilities. Mary's dislike for me has always been clear and followed a predetermined path – one queen bee will always be the rival of the other queen bee. But this passionate hatred etched on her face is a new dynamic between us, and I can only think of one explanation: Ronan.

"Me?" I finally manage to say, aware our classmates are slowing their exits out of the building to eavesdrop. I almost expect someone to start chanting "Fight! Fight! Fight!"

"You –" Mary snarls again. "You *slut!*"

The surge of anger is immediate, uncontrollable. My hands become tight fists as the heat of rage bubbles under my skin. I fight the urge to smack Mary across her perfect cheeks as hard as I can. "Excuse me?"

"Everything was fine until *you* and your idiot family moved here," Mary shouts. "I hate you!"

"Yes, well, no shit," I say, measuring my tone. "I don't like you either. Thanks for the relationship status reminder." I try to walk past Mary, try to take the high road, and hear the disappointed sighs around me. I'm not backing down from the fight I tell myself; I'm walking away.

Mary blocks me. "You've stolen everything from me!"

"What the hell are you talking about?" I snap.

"Ronan is *mine,*" Mary says, baring her teeth. "He's always *been* mine, he will always *be* mine."

"Yeah, well you'll have to have that conversation with him, won't you?"

"He dumped me at lunch," Mary says, "for you. Cheap, redneck, trashy *you.*"

"What?" I'm shell-shocked. Is Mary telling the truth or is this some kind of trick, a game? "You don't know me," I say, "and because you don't know me, I'll warn you that you had better watch what you say before I knock out those perfect teeth and add them to my ass-kicking collection. I didn't steal Ronan from you. I don't even want him. He dumped you, so what? You make up and break up all the time from what I hear. What's that got to do with me?"

Mary doesn't reply. Her face is red and she's sweating. Her manicured nails dig into her palms as she curls them into fists.

"Whatever." I shake my head. "Let me know when you think of a comeback." I push by Mary, knocking her with a shoulder as I do. I make it about ten steps before Mary shouts again.

"It wasn't enough for your *slut* mother to steal my father from my family," she screams, growing more irrational with each word. "Now you have to have *my* boyfriend too? When is it enough, Rose? Destroying families, relationships, this town? When's it going to be enough for you and your spooky slut of a mother?"

The hallway echoes with the low *ooohs* of the gathered crowd.

I turn around slowly and look at Mary, trying to gauge her. *"What?"* I've had enough surprises in the last twenty-four hours for a lifetime.

"Oh, didn't know that did you?" Mary says angrily. "Didn't know *Doctor* Donovan and *Nurse* Delaney were spending so much time together? What'd your mother tell you? Working late? Busy night at the hospital? *Happy hour?"*

I have no response. My brain is overloaded. I think about how happy Mother's been each morning as she skips along to work. I'd assumed she was just glad to get out of the house. Is this the real reason?

"Guess I shouldn't be surprised," Mary says, seeming to gain control of herself again. "Like *slut* mother like *slut* daughter."

I hear the *snap* in my head, the switch being flipped. My vision goes white for a second, the anger overpowering. My body moves forward and the hard smack of my hand hitting Mary's pretty little face that reverberates through me is satisfying. Mary is stunned and I take advantage of it, punching her, square in the eye, knocking her to the ground.

The chants I envisioned before are suddenly real, and Mary and I are rolling around on the ground in a tangle of hair and girl fight.

*   *   *

An hour later, I'm sitting in Principal Flynn's office with Mother, who sits prim and stern in the stiff wooden chair next to me. I slouch in my own chair, hair ripped violently from my bun and sprayed around my face like I've been electrocuted. I have a welt on my left cheek from the one swipe Mary managed to get in, and I'm holding a wad of paper towels up to my nose, stemming the blood flow caused by an errant elbow.

"As you know, Mrs. Delaney," Principal Flynn says in a clipped tone, her hands clasped in front of her on the giant mahogany desk she reigns from, "we take fighting very seriously. Rose's records from Texas show this is a pattern of hers." A finger taps the manila folder under her hands. "Given this record, I'm not sure this school is the proper placement for your daughter."

My stomach cramps with anxiety. The last thing I need is to be expelled from school my senior year. I can kiss all hope for a future away – not that it matters because Mother will kill me the second we get home anyway. Principal Flynn remains quiet, her plain face unreadable.

"I certainly understand your concern," Mother begins softly, more softly than I've heard in a long time, "but I don't believe expelling Rose is the right solution. Please try to understand that our family has been through a lot this past year, and we aren't quite out of the woods yet. I brought my family here for change, for a chance at healing. What Rose did was wrong, but she needs the strong routine and morals you provide here. Please give her the opportunity to change. I know she's trying, even if it doesn't seem that way right now. It's only been a few months. We need more time to adjust." Mother's practically begging Principal Flynn to give me another chance. It makes me sick. I glare at her, feeling a churning sea of mixed emotions. Here's my angry Irish mother being softer and gentler than I've ever seen her, trying to save my educational career. But all I can think about is Mary's angry allegation. I picture Mother wrapped in the embrace of some remarkably handsome doctor with Mary's perfect teeth, and her perfect tiny nose, and her long, delicate fingers. I'm nauseous.

Principal Flynn turns her carefully impassive stare on me. "Rose," she says, "have you anything to say for yourself? Letting your mother speak for you isn't doing you any favors."

I look at Principal Flynn. She's in her fifties. Her dark brown hair is slowly turning salt and pepper, and she's embracing it. Her hair is styled and soft, but not dyed. She wears a navy pantsuit and a perfectly ironed white collar pokes out at the top. Her nails are painted pale pink, but her lips and face are blank slates. She exudes the kind of natural beauty a lot of women her age would be jealous of. I don't know much about her, haven't even seen her, until today. I have no idea if she rules with an iron fist or if she's pliable under the right apologetic words.

I sit up straight and pull the paper towel away from my nose, which has finally stopped bleeding. I have no idea what to say and quickly search for something that'll save me.

"I tried to walk away," I say. "Mary confronted me, and I tried to walk away, but she wouldn't let me. She was spewing ugly things about my family and I couldn't let it go. I'm not going to say fighting with her was a good idea, but I'm not going to apologize for defending my family either."

"Rose!" Mother's horrified, but Principal Flynn holds up a hand.

"What exactly was this fight about?" she asks.

"Yes, what is it you and this Mary argued about that was so serious?" Mother says, eyeing me as if I couldn't possibly provide a valid reason for fighting.

"Mary *Donovan* and I," I say, watching Mother stiffen out of the corner of my eye, "have never gotten along. She accused me of stealing her boyfriend, which isn't true, and then she said some very nasty things about my family. When I tried to walk away, she blocked me and baited me with words I'd rather not repeat, if that's alright."

"Yes," Mother says tightly, "I don't see how airing dirty laundry in here will solve anything."

"Very well," Principal Flynn says after examining me for a long time. "Rose, I'm going to suspend you for two days starting tomorrow. Consider this me cutting you some slack – and know it won't happen again."

A protest rises inside me, but I stifle it, reminding myself I'm catching a break. Principal Flynn says nothing more, and we understand we're being dismissed. I follow Mother to the parking lot. Although I should be relieved, I'm filled with dread. How am I going to survive *two days* inside Wolfhowl Manor alone?

The silence in the car is deafening. It's filled with my own raging thoughts. Isn't Mother going to say anything? Doesn't she understand that I *know?* It's clear by her reaction to Mary's last name that Mary's allegations are true. I have to say something. I *have* to acknowledge what she's done or I'm going to start screaming.

Mother sighs as we near the mountain. "Rose, I –"

"Like to destroy families," I spit. "You're getting so good at it."

For a moment Mother's mouth is frozen in an O of shock. She stutters, "Rose – you – I – how *dare –*"

"How dare *I?*" My fury sparks into an inferno inside my chest. "How dare *you,* Mother! After everything that happened back home, you went to bed with another married man! You *lied* to me about it! And now *everyone* in Port Braseham knows! Did you even stop to think about what would happen if the truth came out? This isn't big city Texas! We're in podunk gossip central where everyone knows everything about *everyone!* And you had to hook up with the father of the girl who has made it her mission to make me miserable here. No Mother, not how dare *I*. How dare *you.*"

Mother turns the car into Letta's driveway, gritting her teeth so loud I can hear them grinding against each other. We park outside Letta's house, but don't get out. We glare at each other, both angry and stubborn. There's some kind of role reversal going on. By all rights, Mother should be lecturing me from here to eternity for getting into yet another fight at school and then mouthing off. Instead, I'm lecturing my own mother on her moral failures. Instead of leading us out of the darkness created by Dad's death, she's lead us straight into the heart of it. Somewhere deep down, I know I should cut her a little slack. After all, she lost someone too. But I can't find it in me to forgive Mother, to play the role of understanding daughter. Not this time. S*he's* the one who brought us here, who moved us into a real life Hell House. Our family is falling apart and it's all *her* fault.

I finally break the stare-off and get out of the car. Liam must have spied us through a window because he's waving goodbye to the Bauers and flinging himself off the porch before I make it past the car. I force myself to smile as I help him into the back seat.

As I'm swinging the door closed, the crunching gravel and rumbling diesel of Beckan's truck behind us surprises me. I'm more surprised when I see Beckan isn't alone. Sitting next to him in the cab of the truck is Letta.

I realize I'm clenching my jaw so tightly my muscles actually hurt. Beckan and Letta hop out of the truck and approach cautiously. Another emotion is fighting its way to the surface, competing with my anger at Mother.

"Hey," Letta says, looking concerned. "Are you okay? I heard about what happened with Mary."

"I'm fine," I reply curtly. "Where've you been?"

"I played hooky," she says, indicating a notebook she's holding. With a wink, she says, "We need to talk."

"Not right now," I say coolly. What does that mean anyway, playing hooky? Was she *playing hooky* with Beckan all day?

Letta's shoulders slump. "Okay. Tomorrow then."

"Maybe."

Beckan stands next to Letta, eyeing me carefully. "Are you sure you're alright?"

"Yes, dammit," I snap. "Why wouldn't I be?"

"Gee, I dunno," Letta says sarcastically, "because Mary baited you into a fight because she's pissed that Ronan dumped her so he can ask you to be his date for the Fall Dance, and then the principal suspended you for two days, basically confining you to Wolfhowl Mountain. That might put someone in a bad mood."

"Wait, wait." My brain is stuck. "Go back. What did you say about a dance?"

"The Fall Dance?" Letta says. "It's Friday."

"So?"

"Ronan wants you to be his date."

"What are you talking about?"

Letta rolls her eyes. "How can you be so oblivious, Rose? It's been around school for weeks. It's on the announcements every morning!"

"I guess I haven't really been paying attention," I say bitterly. "Been a little *preoccupied.*"

"Well you better get your head out of the sand," Letta says. "Suspension or not, Ronan's going to find a way to ask you to the dance. What are you going to tell him?"

"I don't know," I shrug, stealing a glance at Beckan, but his face is unreadable.

"You can't seriously tell me you're considering going with him?" Letta is incredulous.

I shrug again, frustrated. "I don't know, Letta. I've had a heck of a day and I can't think any more."

The tension is broken with a sharp beep. Liam is leaning on the horn, and mouthing "Let's go!"

"I gotta go," I say. "Enjoy playing *hooky.*"

"Later…" Letta says, watching me carefully as I climb back into the station wagon.

I barely have the door closed before Mother starts backing up, forcing Beckan to run to his truck before we run over it.

Chapter Thirty-Five
The Diary and the Note

I stomp up to my room the second we get home. I don't go down for dinner and don't say goodnight to anyone. I'm too angry and confused.

Mother's been gallivanting around town with a married man. How can she break up *another* family? How can pious Mrs. Delaney be such a hypocrite? As if the town needs another reason to hate the family on the mountain.

Where *was* Letta all day? Why was Beckan bringing her home? I don't know why I even care; I have no claim to either of them. If they want to spend time together, so what? It doesn't mean anything to me...does it?

And what kind of game is Ronan playing, dumping Mary like that, making a spectacle for the whole school to see?

And the dance! I have no idea what to do about the dance. It's only two days away. I'm filled with conflicting emotions. I desperately want to go to the dance, to dress up and be seen by everyone. The Texas Rose in me wants everyone to see how beautiful I can be. I want to be who I was once, when things were easy and simple. I want all the boys to crave me and I want all the girls to drown in envy, choke on it, especially that bitch Mary Donovan.

On the other hand, I dread and fear what might happen. Mary could make a scene, attack me again, maybe this time backed up by her girlfriends. If she does, I'll have to fight back and then I'll be expelled for sure. The principal put me on a short leash this afternoon and won't tolerate any more disruptions from me, no matter who the instigator is.

And I'm not sure if I want to be Ronan's arm candy either. Thinking about slow dancing with him reminds me of his bony embrace and his thin frosty lips when we kissed. He's great looking, and his personality exudes the kind of flare people want to be around, but his touch is a dead fish compared to Beckan's strong, warm arms and friendly smile...

Beckan. I'm suddenly angry all over again. I don't even know why I'm thinking about him, or why I'm so angry. I'm seventeen and he's twenty. He's a tough, brawny social outcast, some hick from nowhereville, and I'm his total opposite – or at least I *was*. Nothing will ever happen with those train tracks between us. Let Letta have him if she wants. They can be social outcasts together.

I lay awake for a long time before falling into a restless sleep. I dream about Dad again, his pale lifeless body floating in the murky, ruby red water. His eyes wide open, his hands reaching for me with desperate urgency.

I'm so lonely, Rose!

*   *   *

The house is quiet and deserted when I wake, but it doesn't *feel* empty. I'm groggy and disoriented, like I haven't slept at all. The late morning sun filters through the front windows and looking at my clock, I realize it's nearly noon.

Yesterday's events flood back, clawing their way to the surface, begging for my attention. The fight, the suspension, Mother bedding Mary's father, Beckan and Letta together, laughing and smiling…

I stomp downstairs, still wearing my pajamas, my hair a wild bird's nest. I mope on the couch for an hour, trying to pay attention to *Days of Our Lives* and a is-she-or-isn't-she-a-she *Maury*. My mind wanders back to school and the drama surrounding Ronan and Mary. I wonder what Letta, Shane, and Patty are doing, and if they're worried about me. Do they even miss me? Why would they? The other students are probably jeering at them for being so friendly with Ghost Slut and her slut mother. Maybe they'll join in, smearing my name with everyone else.

I wonder where Beckan is. I thought for sure he'd stop by to check on me by now. Didn't he say something about wanting to talk to me yesterday? But then, so did Letta. Maybe they want to talk to me about the same thing.

By one-thirty, I'm angry and jealous. Again. I turn off the television and try to figure out what I can do the rest of the day. I need a distraction from my depression, from the helpless sense of my world spinning out of control, from the feeling of being watched. I feel my feet moving without any real direction.

I find myself at Mother's door.

Without thinking, as if some spectral force guides my hand, I twist the knob and push the door open with a loud, echoing *creeaaaaak.*

The bedroom is dark and damp. As soon as I enter, I feel the chilly darkness creeping in on me. The curtains are drawn across the windows and balcony door, creating a dusty glow. Usually fastidiously neat, Mother's left her room in contradicting disarray. A trashcan near the bed overflows with crumpled tissues. Dresser drawers are crunched closed on top of unfolded and rumpled clothing. The walk-in closet is a tornado of un-hung dresses and nurse uniforms, mismatching shoes littering the floor.

I stare at the disarray in shocked silence. Mother used to yell at Liam if he left a single sock on the floor or neglected to tuck in a corner of his sheets. Her bedroom is usually a pristine example of the kind of order and cleanliness she expects in the rest of the house. Maybe she just hasn't been able to get settled since the move, between work and her new *friend.* I want to believe this is the truth, but having been in the house more than three months now, I know it's not.

My immediate instinct is to take advantage of the disorder and ransack Mother's room – and that's exactly what I do. I have no idea what I expect to find, but I'll know it when I see it. I spend half an hour pulling open drawers and tossing around their contents, throwing shoe boxes around in the closet and rifling through the medicine cabinet in the master bath. It's only when I give up on plundering that I see it– a small leather bound book, tangled in the sheets of Mother's unmade bed. I nearly faint when I realize what it is – *a diary.*

I snatch it up with trembling fingers, turning it over in my hands. It's exactly like the diaries from the basement. Mother's neat cursive initials are on the front and a bookmark sticks out of the top, nearly a third of the way through the pages. Mother must've been very busy with the diary. Where did she get it?

I pause. Do I have the right to paw through Mother's personal thoughts? Do I even *want* to? Maybe she's written detailed descriptions of her romps with Mary's father. Or about her frustration with her hateful daughter. Do I really *need* to read Mother's innermost thoughts? I think about our move to this unbearable hell, about Mother's callous behavior after splitting from Dad and her apathy after he died. Most of all, I think about what Mother would do if she found my diary.

I open the diary.

The first entry was written mere weeks after the move, before I even knew the other diaries existed.

Where did you come from, Dear Diary? I found this neat little book sitting on my pillow when I came to bed this evening. I want to believe it is a lovely gesture from Rose, a peace offering after the months of hate and anger she's been spewing at me, but something tells me that's not the case.

I have no one to talk to, here or anywhere else. I haven't had a confidant in years. Andrew used to be my one and only, the only person who knew me better than I knew myself. He used to ask me about my day and listen. He was the type of man every woman wants. He didn't try to solve my problems. He just listened. But it's been years since we shared that. The unhappier we became, the less and less we talked or listened to each other. We both retreated into ourselves and began to really hate each other for no real reason at all. I think we just fell out of love. Isn't that sad? I'm not even sure how it happened. It just did.

I pause. This is the first real glance into my parents' split I've ever had. Neither of them had ever spoken of it in specific terms to me or Liam. I digest this new information, trying to figure out how it makes me feel. Undecided, I keep reading.

Looking back on it now, I think I had a foot out the door about five years before we separated. Andrew had become withdrawn. He spent most of his time with Rose, and when I told him I was pregnant with Liam, I don't think he was happy, though he pretended as best he could. Ironically, after Liam arrived, I lost my husband completely to my children. It was almost like I no longer existed, like I was an outsider looking in on another family through their picture window. And I began to resent my own children for having the relationship with my husband that I used to have, that I so desperately wanted. So I began looking for attention somewhere else, and eventually found it, in the arms of one of the doctors at the hospital.

It was just harmless flirtation at first. A smile here, a wink there. But then Doctor Robert Jackson asked me to dinner under the guise of complaining about our respective bosses away from prying ears. But it was romantic from the start, our own little Grey's Anatomy. *He took me to The Melting Pot, an expensive and romantic fondue place. We did talk about work at first, but somewhere between dipping apples in cheese and strawberries in chocolate, it turned to other things. Then, before I knew it, he was feeding me chocolate covered cherries and then pawing at me in his car in the parking lot. It felt so wonderful to be wanted again.*

Robert was a passionate man. He sent me flowers and left me presents. He took me out to lunch. We "worked late" at a local hotel and talked for hours (among other things). And then, we became careless and the rumors started at work. Andrew began to notice the late nights, the odd charges on the credit card bill. It was then that I realized two things. One, I no longer loved my husband. Two, I didn't love Robert either. That was when I decided to break it off with the both of them and really take time to find myself.

Time for herself?! All Mother's ever seemed to want is time to herself. That's part of the reason Liam and I spent so much time with Dad. Mommy Dearest needed a quiet moment, or a bath, or time to sit and think. And all that time it was because she'd overextended herself by having a family *and* a lover? In a sudden burst of fury, I throw the diary across the room as hard as I can. It smacks into an open dresser drawer and then flops onto the floor, a piece of folded paper fluttering along beside it.

I take deep, calming breath before picking up the diary so I can tuck it back into the bed covers to hide my snooping. I pick the loose paper up, assuming it's a bookmark. It's only when I hold it in my hand I realize it isn't a bookmark at all. It's a note, folded over, printed with slanted block lettering I immediately recognize as Dad's.

Mother's name is printed neatly over the top fold, just like Dad used to do. He'd leave us notes, all three of us, littered around the house; some historical factoid, some brief little moment in time, to make our days a little more special.

Salt is the most common seasoning mentioned in the Bible. Eat your vegetables!

The average bullying incident lasts only thirty-seven seconds. Be nice today!

China is contained within one time zone. Don't miss the bus!

The first rhinoplasty was performed in the late 1700s. I love you just the way you are!

One in ten students drops out of school because they're being bullied. Seriously – be nice today!

They weren't daily notes, but they were frequent and always ended with an exclamation point. I have all of mine saved in a shoebox in my closet. Liam's too young to understand how important these notes will be to him one day, so I saved his too. And I know, despite everything, Mother has her notes saved in a scrapbook somewhere. They go all the way back to when my parents first started dating. The first note Dad ever gave Mother read: *It usually takes six to eight dates before couples enter into exclusive relationships. Let's get ahead of the curve!* I used to think it was really romantic.

And now, here's one of Dad's notes, but it's larger than usual, written on a regular piece of computer paper instead of one of his monogrammed note cards. The fold is well worn, having been worked open and closed many times. A corner is wrinkled by a drop of rosy pink water.

It hits me like a bullet to the gut. It's his note. *The* Note.

I hold the smooth paper in my hands for a long time, staring at the careful lettering of "Moira" from each side. I study the fold, flipping it halfway up and back down again. What does it say? Do I want to read it? *Can* I read it?

I flip the note open.

Moira,

> *How does one begin such a note? If you are reading this – no, too cliché…*
>
> *My darling Moira… I used to think we'd do such beautiful, wonderful things together. Where did we go wrong?*

I snap the note shut. I can't do it. Not yet. It's still too soon, too fresh, and my dreams have only washed the sadness back up onto the beach of my emotions, eroding my carefully constructed barriers. I'm not ready to read his words, to forgive or understand his sin.

I flip back through Mother's diary to slide the note back in. I have the diary half-closed when Mother's most recent entry catches my eye. It's from last night.

> *Rose knows about Alec.* Of course *she knows. What an idiotic little town this is. And what an idiot* I *am.*
>
> *Honestly, I wasn't being very careful, not around Rose and Liam. I figured they'd recognize the old pattern, or Rose would anyway. I had even talked myself into thinking that they* did *know, and we'd just determined not to speak of it.*
>
> *Alec, apparently, was just as careless – although I'm not wholly surprised. He has a string of affairs behind him, but mostly out-of-towners. If the rumors around the hospital are true, his wife knows about them. But his daughter… He is very protective of her. I didn't even know her name until I heard it in the principal's office this afternoon. But his daughter found out somehow and confronted Rose at school. As is typical of my daughter, Rose punched her and dragged her to the ground. As annoyed as I was to get that call from the school (yet again), after I heard what the girl*

had said to her... I silently cheered Rose for standing up for her family. Even if she wasn't doing it for me.

Poor Rose. She's so angry and withdrawn from me. Soon, she'll be lost to me forever. Every time I look at her, I see myself. I see the mistakes I've made, the mistakes that I have taught her to repeat. I desperately want to make things right, but I barely have the energy to keep myself together, much less worry about how she's adjusting her ego to this little town.

I honestly don't know what I'm doing anymore. I thought coming here was the right decision, but everything has been going so totally wrong since we arrived. I bought this house in this tiny little town because it felt like a quaint little project. Liam, Rose, and I — we could make this house a home together. Paint a few walls, replace a few boards. We could turn this place around and learn to enjoy each other again. I thought with time and hard work, Rose might forgive me. And now it's too late. She'll never forgive me. I can see it in her eyes. The second she turns eighteen, she'll be out of here. And my little Liam will be all alone...

I feel guilty as I read Mother's words. If I'd paused for one minute to think about how she's adjusting to all the change, I might understand why she's so sad and withdrawn. But I've been so busy blaming Mother that I haven't stopped to think how I've contributed to the problem. Even alone in Mother's room, my cheeks grow hot with shame.

The longer we're here, the more blatant my mistake is. Coming here, leaving Texas, leaving my family... That was a terrible mistake. I was failing as a mother in Texas; why should it be any different in Maine? Work keeps me distracted well enough, but here in this house... I'm just sad. So terribly sad all the time.

This house is cold and dark, always. I've felt my mood sink with it. I dread the commute home. The last few weeks I've caught my knuckles turning white the closer I get to home because I'm so tense. I can't continue to watch Rose spit hate at me. I can't continue to watch Liam turn into some insolent little stranger. He used to be so sweet, so loving. I can't continue on in this house. I can't...

Andrew would have known what to do. He was our guide, showing us the light through the tough times. I never gave him enough credit for that. He was so good with Rose and Liam. He was the one who brought control back to our home in the wake of Rose's adolescent tantrums. He was the one who brought us back to earth. I'm more reminded of that here than anywhere.

Of course, that keeps me wondering something I've been pondering ever since it happened — did the wrong parent die?

Chapter Thirty-Six
The Descendants

I close Mother's bedroom door behind me, having spent the last twenty minutes putting the room back together, erasing all traces of my presence, my brain whirring almost audibly the entire time. Mother's diary, her personal thoughts, Dad's note…the future of my family.

Suddenly the weight of all the things I've been trying to ignore is pressing in on me from all sides. The late afternoon sun disappears behind a cloud, and the dull *rat-a-tat* of rain begins. Darkness envelopes me, curls around my body, tightening like a vise.

I turn toward the door to the fire room. It's shut tight, but I feel the energy pulsating from within. The warmth of the room reaches out for me like tiny tendrils, vines curling around my ankles, my thighs, my waist. They tug at me. I remember waking up and finding myself on the other side of that door, standing at the top of a ladder with a noose in my hands, as vividly as if it had only happened this morning. I still feel the rope burn on my fingers though the marks have faded. I know it's still in there, the rope, on the other side of the fire-eaten door where I dropped it. Waiting.

Rose…

My feet pad silently down the hall. They move automatically, like a robot following a command, and for the first time I don't fight it, see no point in resisting.

Rose… I'm so lonely.

The door looms closer…closer…I remember the dreams about Alva, about Alison, about Dad. The gun.

What's the point in resisting? It's so tiring. Aren't you tired, Rose? Don't you want to rest?

The warmth coming from behind the door feels like the Texas sun. Familiar. My skin tingles with the heat, blocking out the cold winter day outside, and eating up the coldness in my bones. It's so nice to finally feel warm.

Won't you keep me company, Rose?

With each step toward the door, my depression fades. The weight on my shoulders lifts, becoming lighter and lighter. There's no reason to be depressed, not inside the fire room. There are friends in there, people who understand. They're waiting for me. Alva. Alison. Dad.

It's nice in here, Rose. It's warm and cozy. Your friends are here. We're your friends.

I'm in front of the door now. It throbs, beating in time with my heart. Soft voices call out to me.

Rose... We're so lonely, Rose. Come. Keep us company.

My fingers are reaching for the knob, pulling its hot metal into my hand.

Join us, Rose. It's easy. It's so very easy.

Everything will be easy in there. There will be no more worry, no more sadness.

I twist the knob.

"Rose?"

I snap out of my trance. The radiating heat disappears and I'm suddenly shivering with cold. Blinking rapidly, I realize how close I'd been to entering that awful room. I yank my hand back as if I've been stung. The cold dark, the heavy despair, falls back onto my shoulders like an anvil and I visibly slump.

"Rose? Are you okay?"

Beckan stands in the foyer, his hand still on the crystal knob as he pushes the door closed behind him. The sun's out, streaming through the stained glass windows. The rain is gone. Was I sleepwalking again? What's the last thing I remember clearly, without the fuzzy gauze at the edges of my vision? Having spent the last several hours in my own little depressive cloud, I can't be sure.

"Rose?" Beckan says again, worried now.

"I'm fine." My voice is hoarse. I clear my throat and reassure him, "I'm okay."

"What're you doin'?" His eyes are intense, his voice serious, like he knows exactly what I'd been about to do. "I've been knockin'."

"Nothing, um..." I look at the fire room's door one last time, and turn away, trying to shake off the hold it has on me. Beckan meets me at the bottom of the stairs. "Just wandering around I guess."

"Bored, eh?"

"Yeah, pretty much," I sigh, grateful for an excuse. "What's up?"

"Well, I've got some work tah do up heeah," he says, twirling a baseball cap around in his hands. "Figured I'd check up on you while I was at it."

"Making sure I'm not going crazy up here, huh?"

He smiles. "Somethin' like that."

There's a moment of silence and I notice Beckan's smile doesn't reach his eyes. I can't quite read him and I'm self-conscious. I realize I haven't showered or changed out of my pajamas and probably look terrible.

We both start talking at once.

"Let me grab a shower and get dressed –"

"Do you want tah get out of the house and – "

We laugh.

"Look, I have a couplah thins I need tah do up heeah," Beckan says. "Why don't you take a shower while I do that? Aftah, we can get out of the house for a bit. Okay?"   I smile back. "Okay, yeah. That'd be nice."

*   *   *

A little over an hour later, I follow Beckan out of the house and into his truck. He spent some time piddling around, fixing nail pops and creaky floorboards while I showered and changed. It's still pretty cold out, so I'm dressed in a warm thigh-length red sweater, paired with my skinny jeans and boots. Beckan's in his usual grass-stained jeans and a long-sleeved flannel shirt and a jacket.

"How was your day?" he asks as he puts the truck in gear.

I shrug and decide on a half-truth. "It wasn't the worst day of my life."

"But it was close," he says sympathetically.

My false smile falls. "How was your day?"

"Not bad," he says and those green marbles of his fall on my dark eyes, and we lapse into silence.

We drive for about twenty minutes, listening to the local blues station as Beckan taps his fingers on the steering wheel. We wind our way out of town, down skinny two lane roads wending between the colossal pine trees. Beckan finally pulls into a small parking lot next to a grassy trail and turns the engine off. He winks at me before hopping out.

I slide out of the passenger side. Beckan grabs a blanket out of the truck bed before coming around and taking my hand. I flash back to the first day we arrived, remembering his strong rough hands nearly breaking my fingers when he saved my life on the cliff.

I almost ask Beckan what that wink or that smile was about, but then quash the notion. The mystery of it is kind of romantic, and it's beginning to have an effect on me. I feel my body growing warm despite the cold air and energy replaces the depressive blanket that's been smothering me all day. I grip his hand a little tighter as he leads me down the narrow path.

"Here we are," Beckan says as we emerge into a clearing and nearly on top of a still, glassy lake. The water is surrounded by small mountains much like Wolfhowl, but these are far more beautiful. The trees have begun to change, and their flaming oranges, reds, and burgundies are reflected in the stillness of the water like a perfect mirror.

"Where are we?"

"It's called Beavah Dam Pond," Beckan says and points down the shoreline to a contour of muddied branches barely visible in the high water. "That's the work of the beavahs down there."

I take a few steps closer to the water and drink in the beauty of this scene, a cool breeze biting at my ears and nose, turning them red. "It's wonderful." I turn around. Beckan has spread out the tartan-patterned blanket over the damp grass and produced a thermos from the inside of his jacket.

"Heeah," he says, gesturing toward the blanket, "have a seat with me." I plop down Indian style, and Beckan stretches out his legs.

"Spiced apple cider?" he offers, indicating the thermos.

"Please," I reply with a curious smile, still wondering what all this is about. I take the tin cup Beckan offers and sip cautiously. It's hot, but delicious. "This is really good!"

"Thanks," he says, the smile returning. "I made it myself."

"You did?" I'm so surprised I almost start laughing.

"Yeah," he says defensively. "Don't be so surprised."

"You just don't seem the domestic type," I say, taking another sip.

"Oh, I'm not," he says with a chuckle. "This is 'bout the only thing I can make without stahting a fire. This and a cup of tea. It's my muthah's recipe."

There's the traditional moment of silence that follows whenever we talk about our missing parents.

"Well, it's beautiful here," I say finally, "and the cider is really good, but…"

"Why are we heeah?" he finishes for me.

"Yeah."

Beckan pauses and looks away before turning back and looking me dead in the eyes. "I have tah talk to you 'bout somethin'." His voice is serious, and I can feel the smothering blanket pressing down on me again, as if the house has followed us here. "I wanted tah talk tah you in private, away from…everythin'."

"It's about the damn house, isn't it," I say quietly, staring down into my cider.

He nods. "I want tah be a bit more honest with you 'bout a few thins. You and I, we've talked some…but there are some other thins I could've told you soonah, maybe should've."

"Why now then?" I ask, trying not to get angry. "What's the point?" We're all doomed anyway.

"I care about you, Rose," he says, and I hear the sincerity in his voice.

"You do?" I look at his face again and blush when I realize he's staring at me.

"And your family."

"Oh." I'm disappointed somehow, and look away, hoping Beckan doesn't notice.

"And I know what you're doin'," he says, the tone of his voice forcing my eyes back up. "You're meddlin', and you're diggin', and you don't understand that it's puttin' you, your family, and your friends at a terrible risk." His gaze is intense, like a parent lecturing a child. "But I also know you're stubborn." I stiffen defensively. "I know you love your family, and you're not goin' tah stop until you understand the whole story."

"The whole story?"

"You need tah stop diggin'," he says, frustrated. "Stop stirrin' thins up."

"I can't."

"I know. What you really need tah do is leave."

"I can't do that either."

"I know that too," he says. "So heeah's what we're goin' tah do, because I like you alive more than dead." He finishes the rest of his cider in one gulp, grimacing as the hot liquid singes his throat. "First, you're gonna tell me exactly what it is you and your friends have been doin' that's got the foundation of that place all stirred up. Then," he sighs. "Well then, I'm going to confess a few things tah you that'll probably answer a lot of questions."

I look at him expectantly, but he shakes his head. "You first."

"Well that's not fair," I say, rolling my eyes, but Beckan only shrugs.

"Fine." I look at Beckan with all the concentration I can muster and tell him exactly what I've been up to. I tell him everything that happened before he arrived the night we searched the house. The reading of the diaries. The story of Emily Lenore II – which he didn't even balk at, proving that he's been keeping a lot more from me than I thought. I'm also honest with him that it's my desperate hope that, by understanding the past to the house, I'll find some clue that'll help me save my family from what seems a certain fate.

Beckan listens patiently. He nods in the right places and mutters the occasional "Mmm-hmm," but says nothing more. Nothing about what I tell him surprises him. Nothing, that is, until I start talking about my dreams. That's when he sits up straighter, when he looks in my eyes, and when he really begins paying attention.

"She's movin' faster than I've ever heard of," he says when I'm finally finished. "That first day on the cliff, I knew then she was stahtin' early, but I never expected..." His voice trails off with his thoughts. "It's too soon."

"Beckan?" I say, and he turns toward me. "I haven't told anyone about those last couple of dreams. I mean, Letta knows about the first one, but not these, not the ones about the women. Please don't tell anyone."

He shakes his head. "No, of course not. I'm glad you told me though."

The mood of our afternoon has taken a nosedive into the chilly water beside us, and both of us feel the gloom rolling in on the fog as the sun dips behind the mountains.

"Well I guess it's my turn," Beckan says. "Look, I haven't told anyone what I'm 'bout tah tell you either. What I'm going tah tell you is not common knowledge outside of my own house, and if Pop ever finds out I told you, he'll kill me."

I nod and scoot so close to him that my knees brush his thigh, determined to hear every word.

"Let's talk about the daughter of Eamonn and Alva first," he says, "Emily Lenore Callaghan. You of course know what happened tah her parents, but not a lot of people know what happened tah Emily."

"You *do?*"

"I do," he says matter-of-factly. "Aftah the funeral for the Callaghans, Seamus moved his family out of Maine and down into Massachusetts somewhere. He took Emily with them because they were her only family on this side of the Atlantic."

"Why'd they move?"

Beckan shrugs. "It could have been for a fresh staht or tah find a better place tah fish. Or it could be tah hide from the embarrassment of two suicides in a Catholic family. It's hard tah know for sure. But I *do* know they changed their last name from Callaghan tah Murphy."

"Maybe it *was* embarrassment then."

Beckan shrugs and continues. "So, they moved out of Maine, changed their name and stahted a new life. Emily grew up believin' Seamus and his wife were her parents. It wasn't until she was fifteen that one of the boys let the truth slip. When she confronted the only parents she'd evah known, only tah have her worst fears confirmed, it was tah much for her tah handle and she fled. Ran away."

"Where'd she go?"

"Don't know. What I *do* know is she pops back up in the historical records in 1881. That yeeah, on Christmas Eve, she gave birth tah a son out of wedlock."

"Bet that didn't help her any," I say dryly.

"It didn't do her any favors, no. It didn't help stabilize her life any either. Aftah she realized no one was goin' tah take her and her illegitimate son in, and havin' no desire tah return tah the lie she led with the Callaghans, she dropped her son off at a church and disappeared into the mist. She was nevah heard from again."

"Okay…" I squint at him. "Beckan, I get the feeling what you're telling me here has a point, and that I'm meant to understand something about what happened to this family, but I'm going to need more help than this."

"I know," he nods. "Be patient. So, Emily Lenore abandoned her son at a church, which then sent him tah an orphanage. Unfortunately, he was never adopted. He was released when he turned eighteen."

"Alright…"

"So," Beckan continues as the sun finally disappears over the fiery tree line, "Emily Lenore's son went tah the only othah

place he knew – the church where his muthah abandoned him."
He stops and stares pointedly at me, as if he's trying to send me
a telepathic message.

"So," I say, "are you trying to tell me that I should know
what church you're talking about?" His nod is almost
imperceptible. "You can't be talking about Saint Perpetua!"

"Oh but I am."

"Okay... So, Emily Lenore abandons her son here in Port
Braseham, where he's unlucky enough to stay in the orphanage,
and he returns to Port Braseham at eighteen. Then what?"

"He gets a job. The only job available in this town in 1899.
The only job no one else wants."

"Caretaker," I shout. "Caretaker at Woflhowl Manor!"

"Right," Beckan says, almost pleased. "He stahted the yeeah
before the Olenevs took ownership."

"Wow." I lean back to absorb this new information, truly
shocked. "Did he know the significance of where he was?"

"No."

"Well, wait a minute." The cogs in my brain are still turning.
"If he didn't know, then how do you?"

"My great grandfather loved a good puzzle. He's the one
who stahted the research and worked it all out. The story's been
passed down in my family for ages."

The click in my brain is almost audible. "Beckan...what was
his name? What did Emily Lenore name her son?"

Beckan's smile finally returns, but it isn't joyful. "His name
was Patrick," he says, "and she gave him his father's last name.
She named her son Patrick Ethan O'Dwyre."

I gasp. "You can't be serious!"

His laugh is mirthless. "I wish it was a joke."

"You're telling me," I say, rising to my knees, "that you,
Beckan O'Dwyre, are a direct descendant of Emily Lenore?
You're telling me you're a *direct descendant of that house?*"

His face is grave. "Yes, Rose, I am."

Chapter Thirty-Seven
What Letta Has Been Up To

We sit in silence for a while before Beckan finally stands, helping me to my feet.

"It's gettin' late." Keeping my hands in his and pulling them to his chest, he pulls me close. I'm drawn into the green seas of his eyes as electricity sizzles between us.

Beckan suddenly drops my hands and steps back. "I bettah get you back home. But listen, before I do, everythin' I've told you, I told you in confidence, you know?"

"I know."

"I don't know if it'll help you any," he says with a shrug, "but given everythin' that's goin' on, it seemed like the right thin' to do. What happened the other night was a warnin', Rose. Pop and I will do everythin' we can tah protect you, but if you go diggin' 'round and stirrin' things up, it's goin' tah make things more difficult than they already are. As it is, I don't know what's gonna happen."

I nod again, knowing what he's afraid to say; it might be too late to save my family.

I help Beckan fold the damp blanket and he slips the thermos into an inside pocket in his coat. He holds out his hand and I take it, keeping my smile hidden as he leads us back down the path to his truck. The evening is loud with the noises of nature. The music of crickets falls into a rhythm with the hooting of the owls, out early in the darkness of the forest surrounding the trail.

Beckan holds the driver's side door open and I hop in, sliding to the middle instead of the passenger side. Beckan doesn't comment as he climbs in beside me, but he smiles as he turns the ignition.

We head back into town, which is already beginning to fall under the blanket of night. It's a few minutes past five by the time Beckan pulls into the Bauer's driveway so I can pick up Liam.

"Do you want me tah wait and drive you back up the hill?" Beckan asks.

"Actually, I was going to walk Liam home."

"You sure?" He looks through the windshield at the sky. "It's goin' tah storm somethin' fierce tonight."

"I know," I say, "but Liam's been so weird lately. He acts like Mother and I don't even exist when we're at home. I just want to enjoy a little extra time with him before he starts ignoring me again."

"Okay," Beckan says. "Be careful. And you call me if anythin' weird happens, alright?"

"I will. Promise."

"One more thin'," Beckan says as he reaches inside his jacket and produces a small black leather book. A diary. He hands it to me with great care and holds onto it for an extra second when I take it. "This was my muthah's diary," he explains. "I think you should read it. It might help you make sense of…thins. But for the love of God, Rose, don't read it out loud."

I laugh and slip it into a jacket pocket. "Lesson learned… Thank you."

"I'll see you tomorrow."

I nod. "Goodnight, Beckan." I zip up my jacket and hop out of his truck, swinging the heavy door closed, and he drives away.

The Bauer's house is nice, more traditional than the Victorians I've seen in town, and small. The porch light flips on and the front door swings open, revealing a small silhouette in the yellowy light.

"Are you going to stand out there all night or what?"

"Letta!" A sudden relief rises up inside me and I run up the steps, throwing my arms around my small friend.

"Well, geez," Letta says, hugging me back, "no need to get all sentimental."

"Sorry." I release her. "Look, I feel bad about yesterday. Do you still want to tell me where you were?" My chest tightens; will she say she spent the day playing hooky with Beckan?

"Yes! I played hooky the last two days to check out the library and the historical archives," Letta explains as she moves to let me in. "Didn't Shane or Patty tell you?"

I shrug off my jacket and Letta hangs it on an old-fashioned coat rack in the foyer.

"I didn't talk to them yesterday," I say. "I didn't see them before school and they seemed like they were in some kind of serious conversation at lunch. I didn't want to interrupt."

"Oh really?" Letta says, interested. "Hmm…"

"Hmm what?"

"Oh, nothing," Letta replies with a shake of her head. "Well, I'm sorry. I would've texted you but…"

I roll my eyes. "Yeah, yeah. Anyway, where's Liam?"

"You won't believe this, but Mom was actually able to spark his interest in a game of Chinese Checkers. I can't believe he's never played before!"

"We aren't much of a board game family."

"No kidding. Anyway, he was all pouty after Mom picked him up, just like the other day. I've only been here about an hour, but Mom said she finally told him he needed to 'buck up and be a big boy and big boys don't pout!' She tried a few distractions, but Chinese Checkers is what finally won him over. They're down in the basement."

I feel a small weight lift off my shoulders; I'm glad to hear Liam is behaving himself and actually having a little fun. "Thank goodness for that."

Letta leads me up a set of dark wooden stairs. "Listen, I found out a ton of stuff, and it *has* to be important because I had a heck of a time getting into those records, even at the *public* library."

"Really?"

"Apparently, the town leaders and the historical society aren't keen on letting anyone in on all the secrets of Wolfhowl Manor. Probably afraid it'll affect tourism," Letta says sarcastically.

Letta's bedroom is small, much smaller than mine, but cozy. She has a double bed in the center, a comfy chair for reading in a corner, a small closet off to one side, and a desk on the other. The walls are covered in floral print wallpaper with a dark green border trailing the top. One large window lined with dark green curtains looks out over the tree covered front yard. The only light comes from a small desk lamp illuminating some math homework.

"I was trying to distract myself when I heard Beckan's truck pull up," Letta says, indicating the math work. "I'd actually expected you to beat me here. What were you two off doing anyway?" She asks with a smirk.

"We'll get to that," I reply evasively. "You first."

"Alright." Letta takes her desk chair and wheels it around to face her bed, so I sit on the edge of the mattress, the forest green comforter matching the curtains perfectly. "First, I found out there's one more set of owners that weren't in Mrs. Carroll's file. The Hollisters, Clark and Deborah, bought the house in February of 1980. They were one of those what do you call it... flippers? You know, they bought it to renovate and resell."

"Oh, yeah," I say, thinking of *Flip This House*, a home renovation show Mother made me sit through a few times before we moved. Remembering what Mother wrote in her diary about renovating Wolfhowl Manor being a family project, I feel guilty again. "How'd you know all that?"

"I found the original deed with the date of sale," Letta says. "I also found a ton of permits they filed between February and June for work they were doing. They also placed a couple of ads in the paper looking for a contractor to help them with the work, because I'm sure no one around here wanted to help."

"What happened to them?" I scoot further back on the mattress and, running my hands over the cover, I realize it's a hand embroidered quilt. It's beautiful and I wonder if Letta's mother, or maybe grandmother, made it for her. "Why haven't I heard of the Hollisters before?"

"Probably because they aren't dead," Letta says frankly, "which may also explain why there isn't a diary for Deborah either. They abandoned the house in September. I found the bankruptcy paperwork to prove it, with a forwarding address in California. They seem to have picked up and left abruptly, and then got as far away from Maine as they could. By December, the house was back in the ownership of the historical society."

I stare at my hands for a minute.

"What is it?"

"It just really nags at me," I say. "Why's the historical society so determined to keep this house around? I mean, even someone who *doesn't* believe in ghosts or curses would have a hard time keeping a house with such a tragic history hanging over it. Why not just demolish it and move on?"

Letta shrugs. "Revenue probably. Every few years someone writes an article about the house and its history, which makes all sorts of ghost hunters and nut jobs flock here to get a look at the place."

"Anything else on the Hollisters? Any reason for their sudden abandonment?"

"No, not without something more personal, like a diary," Letta says, "which we don't have. No newspaper articles about them either, again because they aren't dead. All I could find was legal paperwork. But," she turns around and picks up a pile of papers from underneath her math textbook, "I *did* find some interesting things about the other owners. Here, these are the legal papers on the Hollisters." Letta shoves a handful of paperwork at me. I look it over. They're crooked copies Letta made on what was probably a very old copier at the library, but there's nothing much of interest in them.

"Now, about Barbara Olenev and Alison Boyle. Their deaths," Letta says importantly, "were *not* exactly as reported in those articles from the file."

"What do you mean?"

"Well, according to a couple of coroner's reports I found, Barbara didn't die in childbirth like the article said – which agrees with the diary – and Alison and Hagan didn't die of smoke inhalation. Also, the fire was arson, not accidental." She shoves more papers at me, and I diligently look them over for the clues Letta mentioned.

"Barbara actually died a few weeks *after* Shane was born," Letta says. She reaches across and points to the date on a coroner's report; July 15, 1903. Letta shoves another paper under my nose, Shane Olenev's birth certificate. The date is listed as June 30, 1903. "See the dates? She died two weeks *after.*"

"How'd she die if not in childbirth?"

Letta points to another box on the coroner's report and the familiar pit returns to my stomach. The typed script in the box labeled Cause of Death reads *asphyxia by hanging.*

"She hung herself?" I say in disbelief, my mouth going dry.

Letta nods. "And it was common knowledge at the time. The cover up didn't come until Robert was found dead almost five months later. The article you have is the first one that exists saying she died in childbirth. Every article dealing with the deaths in the house since then repeat that lie. In fact, getting that coroner's report, and *this* one," she hands me Alison Boyle's death certificate, "was the most difficult thing I did all day."

"Why?"

"They were locked in a filing cabinet in Mr. Quinn's office at the historical society offices." Letta avoids my eyes.

"Mr. Quinn? Ronan's father?"

"Yeah," Letta says, "but don't worry, he wasn't there. It's not a full time job after all, and based on the sheer amount of dust on his desk, he hasn't been there in a while."

"How'd you know where to look?"

"I could only find so much at the library," she says. "Mrs. Foley, the librarian, who's about as old as ol' Enit, helped me find what I was looking for. She showed me the newspaper databases and stuff, but I could only be so honest about what I was looking for since she's on the Quinn's side of this...whatever it is. She stood over me the whole time, staring at the screen. What I found was pretty limited anyway, which didn't really surprise me. The only other logical place to look was in the historical society archives."

"And they were happy to help," I say skeptically.

"Hell no," Letta laughs. "The only person there every day is Ms. Talbot. Her husband died a few years ago and she picked up the part-time job with the historical society to kill time. She sits around, knits from nine to noon, and answers the phone, not that it ever rings. Anyway, I made up some lie about an extra credit assignment for history – same thing I told Mrs. Foley – and she wasted no time telling me all the files were under lock and key and I'd have to fill out a request to get access to anything that might be *pertinent.*"

"And?"

"No dice. They'd never give me access to what I really needed anyway, which I realized after I spent an hour buttering up Ms. Talbot and listening to her incessant talk about her nine cats, and agreeing to buy one of her baby blankets for a pregnant cousin I made up – at a rather inflated price if you ask me."

"So how'd you get all this?"

"I stayed until Mrs. Talbot left, which wasn't until after one since she was really on a roll with all the cat talk. I walked her to her car and then left the parking lot, pretending to go home. Then I went back and broke in."

"Letta!" I say and then lower my voice. "You *broke in?* What if you got caught?"

Letta waves a hand. "Trust me; there aren't many people who spend their time staking out the historical society. Anyway, it wasn't really breaking in. One of the windows was unlocked. Everything in that building was unlocked except for the front door and the filing cabinet in Quinn's office."

"How'd you get into *that?*"

"I have my ways," Letta winks. "Anyway, we're doing all this talking and you aren't learning anything." She points at the coroner's report for Alison Boyle.

I read the cause of death, but I already know what it says – self-inflicted gunshot wound, not smoke inhalation as the news article had said. Letta hands me another sheet of paper – Hagan's death report. He'd also been shot, and it was listed as murder. It's just like my dream.

"So another cover up," I say. "I wonder why. And how."

"I think we know the why," Letta says. "As for the how, Alison had a rich daddy in New York City. He probably paid the town off to keep the scandal out of the papers. Your daughter committing murder-suicide doesn't exactly make for good business."

"What about the fire?" I ask. "That part isn't a lie. There *was* a fire."

"I found an arson report. It's here somewhere," Letta shuffles through the pile of papers in her lap.

"But, Letta, if Alison shot Hagan and then herself, *who set the fire?*"

Letta shrugs, and for a moment, we're both silent. I'm in information overload. Between what Beckan told me and what Letta found, my head's ready to roll right off my shoulders. I'm taking in all these puzzle pieces, but I can't fit any of them together. What does it all mean? And how will it help me save my family?

Letta breaks into my swirling thoughts. "Do you want to hear about the children?"

"Children?"

"Shane Olenev and Emily Lenore Callaghan."

"Oh." I'd nearly forgotten about them. "Yeah, let's hear it."

"Let's start with Shane, because he almost didn't even exist based on the records," Letta says. "I found his birth certificate *and* death certificate, but that's it. There's no mention of what happened to him after his parents died."

"What happened to him?"

"I don't have details," Letta says. "All I have is the date he died – Christmas Eve 1903."

"Oh god, Christmas is so depressing around here! How'd he die?"

Letta shrugs again. "It's a question mark." I think she's being funny, but when I look at the death certificate, I realize she's just being honest. The cause of death is literally listed as "?".

"Okay, now to the good stuff," Letta says excitedly, as if she's talking about going to Disney World and not a string mysterious deaths. "Emily Lenore – the first one. There's not a file, an article, even one word about Emily Lenore II anywhere. Although, under the circumstances, that's not surprising."

I proceed with caution. I already know plenty about Emily Lenore thanks to Beckan, but he told me in confidence. I'm not going to lie to Letta; I have to tell her what Beckan told me, but I'm going to wait and see what she already knows. Then I can just fill in the blanks and feel a little less guilty about betraying Beckan's confidence. It's the kind of white lie that makes me feel better when I know I'm doing something wrong.

"So what did you find out about Emily Lenore Callaghan?"

"Well," Letta's eyes light up as she makes a mess of the papers in her lap and shoves several at me. "She was adopted by Eamonn's brother and his wife after the deaths. They left Maine and moved to Fall River, Massachusetts and changed their last name to Murphy. Clearly, they didn't want anyone knowing where they came from and what they left behind. Anyway, they raised Emilly until she was fifteen, when she ran away." She hands me a missing poster with a detailed drawing of a young girl's face on it. It's probably a pretty good likeness of Emily. It looks a lot like Alva, but she has Eamonn's bushy eyebrows. The poster also shows Emily Lenore went missing Christmas Eve of 1865, in line with what Beckan said.

"Then?" I ask hopefully. I'm silently praying Letta found the connection between Emily Lenore and Beckan, that she found the birth and adoption records for Emily's son.

"That's it," Letta says disappointedly. "The trail goes cold after that. I prefer to think she lived a long and happy life somewhere, but I doubt it."

"Me too," I say, knowing she didn't.

"Oh, and here's one more juicy tidbit I was saving for last," Letta says. She hands me another birth certificate.

I read the name on the certificate and then look back at Letta, confused. "This is Adam O'Sullivan's birth certificate."

Letta nods, but says nothing more, so I look back at the certificate. His birth date jumps out – Christmas. Laura O'Suillivan, presumably Enit's daughter, is listed as his mother. It's the name of his father that nearly makes my heart stop: Derry O'Dwyre. I look back at Letta.

"I know, right?" Letta exclaims. "I found it by accident. I'm not even sure why Mr. Quinn had it in his office and I don't think it even means much for our purposes, but it's interesting right? I mean, there've been rumors here and there that the O'Dwyre's weren't so happily married, but to have it confirmed…" Letta pauses when she sees my grave expression and her smile fades. "Anyway, I'm sure it means nothing, but I had to show you."

"I'm not so sure about that," I say breathlessly.

"What?" Letta says, sitting up straighter. "What do you mean? Which part?"

"Remember when you asked me what Beckan and I had been doing?"

"Yeah, what about it?"

"Well, it turns out he knows quite a bit more about the history of the house than we thought."

"*How* much?"

"A lot. And I think it's going to change your view about Adam's birth certificate." I then spill everything Beckan told me about his family. When I'm finished I add, "But he told me in total confidence and swore me to secrecy, so you can't tell anyone what I told you. Not even Shane and Patty. Okay?"

"Yeah, sure," Letta replies dismissively, her eyes unfocused, like she's daydreaming. "Wow. I don't know what it all means, but wow."

"I know."

"Alright…" Letta says, shaking her head as she shuffles all of her papers together and hands them to me. "Put these with that file of yours until we can figure out what it all means. I've been thinking all day about how this could help us – help you, but I'm drawing a blank."

"That's it?" I ask. I'd expected more of a reaction.

"For now," Letta says. "It's getting late and we both have homework. I'm going to spend the rest of the evening letting all this information marinate and trying to finish that math work. I suggest you do the same. Maybe if we're lucky, one of us will have an epiphany by morning."

I snort as the faint sound of a telephone ringing floats up from downstairs. As I get up, tucking the papers under an arm, I say, "You won't tell anyone what I said right?"

"Of course not," Letta says. "We're friends aren't we?"

"Yeah," I smile, relieved. "We're friends."

"I won't tell anyone what you said," Letta promises as she makes for the hallway, adding quietly, "and you won't tell anyone I stole those papers from the historical society."

"Right," I say, and then, "Wait, what?"

"Nothing." Letta leaves her room and I have no choice but to follow.

Chapter Thirty-Eight
Strangers in the Same House

When we get downstairs, Mr. Bauer is coming down the hall from a cozy kitchen, a cordless phone in his hand.

"Hi Rose," he says with a smile and a crinkling of his crow's-feet. "Nice to see you again." He's short like Letta, and his hair is the same sleek black, but that's where the similarities end. His eyes are blue and too close together, perched atop his beak-like nose. He would've looked like a seedy little homeless man were it not for his warm smile and genuine nature.

"Hi, Mr. Bauer," I say, and then remembering my manners add, "Thanks again for fixing my canopy."

"I was happy to do it," he replies, glad to be complimented on his work, and hands me the phone. "Your mother wishes to speak with you."

"Oh, thanks," I say, accepting the phone cheerfully, the exact opposite of how I'm actually feeling. I don't know what time it is, but it's dark out. If Mother's calling, it's because she's home and Liam and I are not.

"Hi, Mom," I say lightly, taking a few steps into a room opposite the stairs. It's a nice formal living room at the front of the house, the kind no one ever uses unless there's a baby shower or something. More floral print wallpaper abounds, but it's busier and more colorful than Letta's wallpaper. The room is full of mismatched patterned chairs and an old fashioned up-against-the-wall piano. Cozy. The piano looks as though it's weathered many years and many moves, and I wonder who tickles the ivories in Letta's family. Or maybe this piano is like the baby grand we left behind in Texas: decoration, conversational piece, a heavy as heck waste of money and space.

"Rose!" Mother snaps in a tinny voice. "Where are you? Is Liam with you? I just got home and the house was totally dark! I was so worried!"

"Really?" I'm taken off guard. Usually when I'm not where I'm supposed to be, Mother's go-to emotion is anger at being defied, not worry about what might've happened. "I'm sorry, Mom. I came over to get Liam and Letta and I got to talking. I didn't realize what time it was."

"Well you two get your buts home right now, do you hear me?" Mother's voice is strained, agitated. Now that she knows we're safe, she's switched over to the anger I'd expected.

"Yes, Mother, of course," I say obediently, which is starting to become more comfortable than I like. "I'll get Liam together, and we'll be on our way up the hill in a few minutes."

"You're going to *walk,*" Mother says incredulously. "Rose, it's pitch dark out there and there're no street lights. Not to mention the storm!"

"What storm?"

"Oh, it's coming," Mother says quietly, her voice a menacing whisper. "The storm is coming alright... Well stop wasting your time talking to me! Get my son and bring him home right now!"

Click.

I stand motionless for a few seconds, staring at the phone in my hand as dread seeps back into my bones.

"Is everything alright?" Letta asks, still standing at the bottom of the stairs.

"Yeah, I guess... maybe." Mr. Bauer has disappeared and I hope he didn't stay to hear my end of the conversation. "Anyway, Mother wants us home right away."

"I wouldn't waste any time myself," Letta says. "The storm clouds are gathering. It's going to be a good one tonight."

Fortunately, Liam's voice is suddenly filling the air as he comes down the hall, Mrs. Bauer following him with his backpack.

"Hello, Rose, dear," she says. "I heard that was your mother calling. Sorry to keep Liam so late, but we were having such fun, weren't we?"

Liam smiles at Mrs. Bauer as she hands him a chocolate chip cookie.

"Hi, Rosie," he mumbles, mouth already filled with cookie crumbs. Innocent and cherub-like, chewing something sugary, just the way he's supposed to be, and it makes my heart ache.

"Liam," I say in a sisterly tone.

Liam turns to Mrs. Bauer. "Thank you, Mrs. Bauer. I had fun!"

"I'm glad." She grabs both of our jackets from the coat rack and hands them to me, trading them for the cordless phone. I put on my coat on and then help Liam into his.

"Thanks so much for watching Liam," I say.

"Of course!" Mrs. Bauer replies. "Anytime. But you two need to get on up the hill before the rain comes. It's going to be a strong one tonight. I can feel it in my bones." All the time she's speaking, she's herding us toward the door. "Now you get home safe and we'll see you tomorrow." I barely have enough time to say goodbye before we're on the porch with the door closing in our faces.

"Well, come on kiddo," I say, taking Liam's hand and leading him down the stairs of Letta's porch. "We need to hurry up or we're going to get wet!"

Together, we brace ourselves against the increasing wind and make our way down Letta's long driveway. By the time we reach the bottom of the hill, both of our faces are red and our lips are chapped. Looking down to check on him, I notice Liam's frowning. I'd hoped to enjoy this walk with him, but it's too difficult to hear each other over the wind, especially with our chins pressed down into the tops of our zippers, and huffing heavily as we try to beat the rain.

I keep my eyes on the menacing sky as we hurry up the hill, my thighs burning before we're even halfway up. The moon is already high in the sky, and the storm clouds are gathering, curiously, directly above my house. The deep plum colored clouds are riddled with white caps, as if I'm seeing the reflection of a rough sea in the sky. Bursts of silent lightning begin illuminating our way as the clouds block the moon. It's so strange – the storm clouds are not only gathering above my house, but also seem to be *circling* it, thick galaxy-like spirals flowing out over town.

When the house finally comes into view, Liam's practically running, yanking on my arm.

"Come on, Rosie!" He shouts. "Hurry!"

I start to trot with Liam as the first raindrops fall. They're large and heavy, exploding on the driveway like overfilled water balloons. They fall closer together and with more force. In a sudden gust of wind, we're thrown through the front door, into the golden light of the foyer.

I turn and latch the doors closed, double and triple checking the deadbolt's engaged – there'll be no open doors tonight – listening to the sound of lashing wind and rain beating against them, begging to be let in. When I turn around, I'm met with Mother's angry jade eyes.

"Liam," she says sharply, "did you have dinner at the Bauer's?"

"Yeah," Liam replies.

"Yes," Mother hisses through tight lips.

"Yes," Liam corrects himself, his eyes sinking to his shoes.

"Then I want you upstairs and in the bath right away," she snaps.

"But, Mom –"

"Don't argue with me, Liam," Mother says, hands on her hips. "Upstairs. *Now.*"

Liam shrugs off his coat and leaves it on the floor next to his backpack before he stomps toward the stairs on the right. "I don't have to listen to you!" He shouts, though it's clear he's going to.

I'm startled by Liam's response to Mother. Only moments ago at the Bauer's he'd been a perfect angel, my normal little brother, and now his little devil horns are popping out. He's lipped me plenty in his short five years, but Mother? That's crusin' for a bruisin'.

But something else startles me even more – Mother doesn't even turn around to look at Liam, doesn't scold him or demand an apology. Instead, she aims her anger directly at me.

"Where the hell have you been all afternoon, Rose," Mother snaps. "Chatting to Letta since school got out? I don't believe your lies for one second young lady! You know, I called you a few times from the hospital, to check up on you, but you didn't answer. Just like old times, isn't it? Need I remind you, that you are *suspended?* You shouldn't be out gallivanting around town! You're being punished! Now, where the hell have you been?"

I take my time responding, in part because I'm shocked I'm the one in trouble here, but also because I don't want my own temper to get me into more trouble. I stoop over and pick up Liam's jacket and backpack, placing them on the coat rack. I hang my own jacket next to Liam's before turning around to look at Mother.

She stands akimbo, still dressed in her nurse's outfit, a pale pink pant set with dark brown Dansko clogs. Her hair's pulled into a bun of fire at the base of her neck, but several long strands have come loose, making her look crazed and tired. Her anger has her huffing like an angry bull, and I can smell the alcohol on her breath.

"Answer me right now, Rose," Mother says, practically spitting my name.

"Mom, I'm really sorry we were late getting home," I say as calmly as I can. If Mother's been drinking, it won't take much to push her over the edge. "Beckan came over to do some work around the house. When he was finished, we went up to a nearby park."

"For what?" Mother sneers.

"Just to talk, Mom," I keep my tone even while swatting away a surge of anger. "We talked for maybe an hour. Then he dropped me at Letta's. What I told you on the phone was the truth. Letta and I got to talking and I lost track of time. And Liam was having a nice time with Mrs. Bauer. The move's been tough on him, and I wanted to let him enjoy himself for once. It isn't like he's made any friends here."

"What are you trying to say, Rose," Mother shouts. "Are you telling me I'm a bad mother? Are you saying She's a better mother than me? Are you saying Liam doesn't enjoy his time with me? Is that it?" With each word, she advances on me, coming closer and closer, until I'm practically in the coats and my eyes burn from the alcohol on her breath.

"What? No! Mom, I –" I stutter as I see a familiar flash of ire behind Mother's bright green eyes, something I haven't seen since Texas, something hateful. I lower my voice even further, cowering away from her pointing finger, returning to memories of my childhood, memories of the pain from when Mother was this angry. "Of course that's not what I'm saying, Mom! Liam loves you. You're his mother. We all know you're doing the best you can."

"And what exactly were you and Letta talking about that was so *important?*"

I carefully reach out and take hold of Mother's jabbing finger, pushing it out of my face. I put my other hand on her shoulder and gently push her back so I can escape the plush arms of our winter coats.

"Mom, please," I say, stepping away from the coat rack, my arms up and palms open in a gesture of surrender. "Please don't yell. I wasn't at school today, so Letta and I didn't get a chance to talk until I went to get Liam. I swear I'm telling you the truth." Mostly. I'm not about to rat out Letta for skipping school. "I hung out with Beckan, I went to Letta's, and then I came home. I swear."

"Ugh!" Mother rolls her eyes. "You and that Beckan are spending too much time together. His bad manners are starting to rub off on you."

Bad manners? Until today Mother's practically thrown herself at him. Why the change? "Mom, I —"

"And I don't like not knowing where you are," Mother says. "You have all this *free* time now that you aren't in cheerleading or dance, and you're just *painting the town red,* aren't you? I had no idea what was going on when I got home tonight! Honestly, Rose, what's happened to you? Where's your sense of responsibility? Where's your sense of family?"

My hands tighten into fists as my calm determination unravels. I've been more responsible than ever since arriving in Port Braseham. It's Mother who's losing sight of her duty to our family, falling back into familiar patterns of alcohol abuse and chasing married men.

"You're just like your *father,*" Mother continues acidly, flailing her arms as she talks. "Off going wherever you want and doing whatever you want, never mind letting anyone else know what's going on, least of all your family. Selfish, both of you."

I hear the snap, the last straw in my brain finally giving. And then I say something I shouldn't, desperately trying to keep it inside while simultaneously spitting it out.

"Well maybe, just maybe, *Mother,* I could keep you privy to all my movements, all my whims of fancy, if I had a proper cell phone from which to call you and keep you up to date on all my idle time wasting while I'm busy ignoring just how much you've had to drink!"

The release of anger accompanying my ugly words doesn't dull the immediate regret. But Mother has shoved me over the edge of my carefully built wall, so I've turned around and yanked her right over the brink with me.

Mother lunges at me, gathering the collar of my shirt in her talons and screaming. "You rotten, rotten brat! You ungrateful, disrespectful little bitch!" She smacks me so hard I fall against the coat rack again, knocking it over.

Mother throws me to the floor, falling on top of me and swiping my clothes and face with her nails, doing everything she can to rip my shirt or tear out tufts of my hair, all the while screaming shrilly.

I'm surprised by the strength Mother's rage gives her; I'm barely fighting her off. She uses my hair as a vise, lifting my head off of the floor and then slamming it against the wood. I throw a hand up, pushing Mother's chin away from me, hoping she'll let go. Struggling for an advantage, I manage to get on top of her, and pry her fingers from my hair. I shove myself backward, my feet finding the floor again. I catch my breath, backing away from Mother.

Mother stays on the floor, glaring at me, huffing through strands of hair that have fallen into her eyes in the melee. Staring into her eyes, I soften. I tell myself this isn't really my mother looking up at me. This isn't the woman I know. This is a broken woman being controlled by the presence in this house.

"Mom –" I begin, but she interrupts me.

"You should have died with him," she whispers menacingly. "He should have taken you too."

"Mom," My heart breaks and the tears come. "How… how can you *say* that?"

Mother responds by spitting at my feet.

Keeping a careful eye on Mother, I back away and go upstairs, never turning my back on this crazy puppet, terrified she'll leap at me again, and tear out my throat. Mother stays on the floor, but her enraged eyes follow me until I'm out of sight.

I lock myself in my room. Touching my cheek, my hand comes away wet; one of Mother's nails struck home. I cry, uncontrollable and ugly, like so much rain.

I don't understand what's happened to my family, how Mother could say those things. Who *is* that down there, wearing my mother's skin like clothes? Mother and Liam are becoming strangers, sharing only a past, under this dilapidated, rotting roof. And they're rotting away too. Will they become feed for the worms, like the rest of the families that've passed through the doors of Wolfhowl Manor?

I leave my lights off. I walk over to the balcony and push the curtains aside, watching the lightning and the rain through a curtain of my own tears, waiting for the anguished moans of thunder to follow.

Chapter Thirty-Nine
The Invitation

I sit in front of the balcony doors for a few hours, watching the storm rage. Within minutes the power is out. I watch the lights in town disappear all at once, as if Port Braseham itself was swept out to sea. Mother calls out to Liam when the lights go out, but he insists he's fine, still splashing around in the tub by himself. She doesn't check on me.

The thunder crashes against the eaves of Wolfhowl with unbridled fury. It's the loudest thunder I've ever heard, like Zeus and Athena are bowling in the attic. The wind spins the weather vane on top of the O'Dwyre's like a top, and the trees bow under its power, worshipping the weather gods. Pine needles and twigs fly against the windows and siding. I decide it's time to move when rainwater starts trickling through the seams of the balcony doors.

I'd put a few candles and a box of matches in my bedside table after the first storm. I'm not afraid of the dark, but I certainly don't enjoy it, so I pull out the candles and light them. Curiously, it takes several matches; the first few don't light or immediately burn out. Old matches I guess... I set one candle each on my bedside table, a dresser, and the window seat. They light up the room about as well as my bedside lamp.

Without my electric alarm clock, I'm not sure what time it is. The house is quiet aside from the storm. I heard Liam go to bed about an hour ago, and Mother's door closed shortly thereafter, so it's probably close to eleven. I should probably be in bed, but what for? It's not like I have to go to school tomorrow. One more day of suspension. One more day of hell in this house. And then the weekend. It's enough to make me cry again.

My thoughts drift to Texas. I think about my supposed friends, and how they've abandoned me; out of sight, out of mind. I think about the cute pink tutus of my former ballet students. About Liam and how much he looks like Dad. About

Dad. I feel the empty space in my soul created by his absence, and my eyes well up. I close my eyes and see his handsome face, sinking beneath red water.

I start at a loud crack of thunder and blink away my tears. I don't want to dwell on Dad, not right now, especially not after the dream.

I pull out the pages Letta gave me, the crooked copies on thin library paper and the thicker sheets of official smelling textured paper she'd stolen. I shake my head, still surprised Letta could be so devious, and hoping Mr. Quinn won't notice the missing documents.

Grabbing Mrs. Carroll's original file from between my mattress and box spring, where I'd hidden it after stealing it back from Mother, I add the new information to the old. As a distraction, I organize the information by date, from oldest to newest, carefully setting Adam's birth certificate on top.

I let out a loud sigh of disbelief when I see Adam and Derry's names together again. I can't believe it. I wonder if Beckan knows Adam is his half brother. If he does, why didn't he tell me at the lake? Not that he has to tell me, I guess. Adam doesn't really have anything to do with the lore of the house, so it isn't any of my business. And it's entirely possible Beckan doesn't know; he told me his parents' marriage was happy, "peaches and sunshine." An affair doesn't jive with that. I wonder if Adam knows. Maybe he does and that's why he's so awful to me, because I'm friends with Beckan, the half brother who gets their father all to himself while he walks around like the bastard child with the scarlet letter on his chest.

I put the growing file back under my mattress and retrieve Mrs. O'Dwyre's diary. I feel a little guilty for not telling Letta about it, but that would be too much of a breach of Beckan's confidence. Maybe I'll tell her about it if I find anything important. I settle down on the window seat, in the flickering candlelight.

Mrs. O'Dwyre's diary isn't the same as the others. It's slightly larger, and it's cover is black instead of red. Her initials aren't embossed on the front. Instead, her full name is written in her own neat print on the inside cover. *Cynthia Patton O'Dwyre.* It's clean and dusted, the binding well worn. I wonder who's been holding onto it for so long, Beckan or Derry? Do they use it to remember the woman they lost, to hold onto her? Or did they use it to discover who their wife and mother really was after she was gone?

I flip idly through the diary. Mrs. O'Dwyre started it around the time Beckan was born, but it's clear by her writing style that she'd been keeping diaries for a long time. I wonder if this is one volume in a collection that sits on a shelf somewhere in the O'Dwyre cottage.

Beckan was right; his mother was obsessed with the house. It's clear her fixation started long before this diary. She wrote about it as if she and the house were old friends.

Every time I look down at sweet Beckan, I'm filled with equal parts happiness and sadness. He is my dream, of course, but sometimes I feel haunted by the Hollisters. Debbie wanted so badly to have children. I wonder if they ever succeeded, if they ever came to know the joy that Derry and I know. I understand what they went through, just as many of the families in Port Braseham do. Infertility has created a great hole in each of our hearts that should be filled with the joyful laughter of children. Every year we watch our population dwindle and suffer, we watch the earth of the graveyard get turned again and again. So many children...

I know it's Her. Her sadness and misery creates misery for all of us here. Derry tells me not to believe in fables, that I'm smarter than the rest of "the idiots in this town." But Derry, God love him, is the idiot in this case. I say that with love, because I love him with all my heart, but it's foolish of him to deny what the rest of us know. He's putting himself and our family in danger. By the time his stubbornness gives in to the truth, it might be too late.

I worry for Beckan. He's only a few months old, but does that mean he's safe from Her? It's hard to say. Children older than a year have been stolen from their parents by Her before. Her whims choose which child will survive and which will die. And Beckan is so close to Her. How can I know that he is safe? She takes our children to punish us for a crime our ancestors committed against her, though none of us knows what that crime was.

But I have one very good theory of my own. It's the only thing that makes sense in a town where nothing makes sense.

The house was built by the Callaghans, who themselves wanted a family so badly, especially Alva – or so the fable goes. It's my belief that, as Alva's wish for children grew stronger, the house grew stronger under Eamonn's careful hands. It's some kind of dark magic, truly. Alva's strongest desire was somehow imparted into that house, and the house itself came alive with that desire. I think we stole Her child from Her, so She steals our children from us. Seamus and his wife stole Emily Lenore from the house, and She has not forgotten.

I have nothing to support my theory. How could there be any evidence to support something so fantastical? Naturally, I have not spoken a word of this to Derry. He's a practical man, a good Catholic man, and he wouldn't approve of me spending my idle time dreaming up motives for a killer house who steals children. He'll tell me, "It's just terrible bad luck, terrible coincidences, and we all ought to move on and forget all about that house." I want to believe him, but then I realize he must not even believe that himself. If he did, why would we still be here? Why would he continue taking money from the historical society? Why would he continue to take care of Her if we "all ought to move on?" I tried talking to him about it once, and only once, but he became angry so quickly that I was frightened into obedience. I vowed never to bring Her up again… to him.

Here the entry ends, leaving me confused. Who did Cynthia tell her theory to? I think it's a very good theory, maybe *more* than theory. Cynthia knew Emily Lenore was spirited away from Wolfhowl Manor by Eamonn's cousin, and that's around the time when all the trouble started. She knew Shane Olenev, son to Robert and Barbara, died a few months after his parents' own deaths. Surely, he'd been taken from the house when Robert's body was found, so that could be considered another stolen child. And then there's Emily Lenore II, who wasn't stolen, but who ran away. If the house really is alive, wouldn't it feel the same sense of abandonment?

I keep thinking as I page through the diary, trying to find out who Cynthia talked to. My mind races and Mr. Lindsay's face pops up. What would it look like if I compare a weather history to the events of Port Braseham? What would it look like if I compare it to the birth rate over the years? Would there be a correlation in the data?

There! It's the entry where Cynthia relates her theory again, and who she told. It was written in the summer of 1990.

Derry told me to forget about it. He knows me so well that I don't even have to tell him my mind still wanders to Her, trying to discover the secrets that will save our town, our children. Beckan is three and he's healthy, happy, a perfect little boy. Why must I dwell on Her? That's what Derry can't to understand. It's because he isn't a mother…and because he doesn't have those awful dreams about what She's done.

I nearly crawl out of my skin. Dreams? *Dreams about what She's done.* Did Beckan's mother and I have the *same* dreams?

She consumes me so deeply lately. My eyes are always drawn to Her through the windows. My feet take me to Her boundaries when I take my afternoon walk. Yesterday morning, when Derry went into town to help Ms. O'Sullivan with some home repairs, I stole his keys and went inside for the first time on my own. I've been inside with Derry every now and then to help him or to bring him his lunch as he worked, but it's been years…certainly not since Beckan was born.

Stepping inside, that's when I knew that I had to do something, that I had to find someone who'd talk to me about Her. It was the overwhelming sense of dread that overtook me. It started at the top of my head and trickled down through my nerves until I felt that my whole body had been encased by this depressing alarm, this icy feeling that something awful was waiting. I was only in the house a moment, my two feet just over the threshold when the feeling came over me, and I had to leave. There's only one person in this whole town who might listen to me, who might understand me. So I waited several hours for Derry to come home. It was nearly dinnertime when he arrived. I created some story about a women's meeting at church and left him a hearty dinner in the oven. I kissed his cheek and then drove directly to Enit O'Sullivan's.

Enit! Of course, *of course* it's Enit. She'd tried to burn Wolfhowl down in the sixties. Certainly she'd had a reason, though the only thing she's ever said publicly about the fire makes her sound like a crackpot. Even though Enit might provide Cynthia with some answers, it sure was taking a chance. Adam's mother had to be pregnant by then, based on his birthday. She must not have known about the affair, or else she wouldn't have gone there. It was probably a very good thing Cynthia hadn't been honest with Derry about where she was going.

Enit was certainly surprised to see me. At first she thought I was looking for Derry; she could think of no other reason for my showing up on her doorstep at eight at night. I haven't talked much to Enit ever. I see her and her daughter at church, and I've exchanged pleasantries with them now and again, but that's about it.

Laura, Enit's daughter, lives with her. She was there when I arrived, but left almost immediately. Being pregnant, she's understandably tense. I desperately hope her child survives.

Enit was pretty welcoming, especially considering why I'd come. When I confessed my true reason for visiting, she smiled and led me into her parlor where she does psychic readings. Honest! The whole idea makes me chuckle, but I can hardly criticize her when I believe in haunted houses. I'm surprised she makes any money at all, but she must do alright. Most of her business

*must come from tourists who pass through and think what a thrill it will be
to get a Tarot reading or gaze into a crystal ball.*

*Sorry, I keep getting off the point. Even now, as I write this, I'm so
distracted by Her presence. I can't see Her, but I feel Her, looming there on
the hill. Like She's* watching me *as much as I'm watching her.*

*Enit listened to me without interruption as I explained my theory.
Although Enit didn't say much, I could tell she believed me, that she had
maybe even had the same ideas about the house herself. Perhaps that's why
she tried to burn it down all those years ago. I tried asking her this of course,
but she didn't want to talk about the fire. I guess I can't blame her. But I
also asked her why she stayed. Why does she stay in Port Braseham, where
she has become the butt of jokes? Where people whisper about her behind her
back, and outright insult her when she's right in front of them? Why stay?
Her reply scared me to death.*

She said, "Someone has to keep Her in check."

I tell you, her words, her tone… It chilled me to the bone.

I feel a chill reading the words too. *Someone has to keep Her in
check.* Enit O'Sullivan. Why haven't I given the woman much
thought before now? I've actually been pushing the woman out
of my mind entirely after that day at the church.

I flip through the diary some more and finally find an entry
explaining the dreams Cynthia mentioned before. I read
hungrily, but I don't feel any better afterward. I didn't think it
was possible, but I feel even *worse*.

*I might be able to hold onto my sanity if it weren't for the dreams. The
same ones, over and over. They are always exactly the same, not a single
detail ever changes. And with each dream, my terror rises so that I can
hardly contain it. Derry says nothing, but he knows me well enough to know
something's wrong. And sweet Beckan, even he knows there's something
wrong with Mommy. He constantly asks me what's wrong, and I'm forced to
lie to him, my only child. He's too young to understand and he deserves to
hold onto that childish innocence as long as possible. I won't be a party to
destroying it.*

*The first dream was about Alva. I've had several dreams about her
and her life with Eamonn, but only one continues playing out when I sleep.
It's the one where she dies. To hang yourself… I can't even imagine. And in
front of your child! She abandoned life so completely. I can't pretend to
understand why she did it, but it would take a strong person to go on with
life while experiencing the kind of despair and depression she was going
through. (Post partum they term it now, but I doubt that was the true cause
of her depression.) Every time I dream of her, I wake up in a cold sweat and*

I swear it's days before I feel right again, as if I've absorbed Alva's feelings and emotions just by dreaming of her.

And how can I dream about her? How can I know exactly what she was thinking and watch the last minutes of her life play out in front of me like a movie? I used to laugh at the idea of psychics like Enit, but…is that what I am? Am I a psychic? Or am I just another crazy person who believes her dreams are visions? I swear I don't know anymore.

Between dreams about Alva, I dream about the Olenevs and the Boyles. The dreams of Barbara are so similar Alva's, their lives and their emotions were so similar. Barbara gave up just as Alva gave up, abandoning her husband and her child. And poor Robert, just giving up after Barbara died. Even his love for his son couldn't keep him on this earth. How awful.

But the dream about Alison is the one I truly dread. She was so volatile, so hateful, so violent even before she moved into the house. I feel like a bad person even writing this, but I don't know if there was ever anything about her to like! Spoiled and rotten from the beginning, but that doesn't make what happened to her right. It doesn't justify what she did, either. I can't even write about the dream, but every time I close my eyes, I feel the blood burned onto the underside of my eyelids.

The next few lines of Cynthia's neat print is obscured; the paper is bubbled and wrinkled as if she'd cried while writing. I feel for her. The dream about Alison and Hagan *is* awful. The continuing thunder reminds me of the loud *crack* of the gunshot Hagan never saw coming, and I remember how he'd slumped to the floor, slowly, his last moment of surprise and confusion frozen on his face for eternity.

They keep telling me they're lonely.

That gets my attention.

They keep telling me, right before they die, how lonely they are. At first, I couldn't make sense of it, but I think I'm beginning to understand. I think I know what it really means, and in these pages is the only place that I would even dream of admitting it. Those women, Alva, Barbara, and Alison, they didn't actually utter those words before they died. Those parts of my dreams are false. It's Her, the house. She's toying with me, doctoring these dreams.

"I'm so lonely."

I'm meant to believe that these women, these ghostly women, are lonely. They want company. My company. It's an invitation.

"I'm so lonely." It's an invitation to die.

I almost throw the diary across the room I'm so afraid. I see my father again, in the tub full of crimson water, staring at me. Begging me. *I'm so lonely, Rose.*

I keep reading, hoping to find in Cynthia's words the answer I so desperately need.

That's why, when I had the dream about Debbie Hollister, I had to tell her. She and I had become friends, you see. Both of our husbands were busy working on the house. I'm a stay at home mother for Beckan and Debbie was still unemployed, looking for a job nearby. It was nice to have a woman to talk to about womanly things. Derry is such a caveman sometimes and the women in town are so tightlipped and uptight. I'd come to enjoy talking with Debbie so much that I felt an obligation to tell her what I saw, what I dreamt.

Dreaming about Debbie was the first time I dreamt about something that hadn't happened. Yet. It felt like I was seeing her awful future.

Debbie was in the basement, pacing back and forth. She muttered to herself as if trying to convince herself to do something or not to do something. Her words were so unintelligible in the dream that I couldn't be certain what she was talking about, but the wildness of her hair and the craze in her eyes pointed to nothing good.

Suddenly, she made a decision, and she flew up the stairs from the basement, sailed into the kitchen and up the servants' stairs to the third floor where Clark was working on the library. He had his back to her, working in the alcove at the back. It's a cozy little reading corner with a red wingback chair resting in it. Clark had covered it with plastic to protect it as he worked.

Debbie stalked quickly across the room, silent as a cat, grabbing the claw hammer from Clark's toolbox as she went. He was so busy working and humming so loudly that he didn't hear her. He didn't even turn around when she slipped into the alcove right behind him and dug the hammer into his skull, painting the plastic with red on red.

It was awful, what she did to him, the man I know she loves with every fiber of her being. As if to prove it, she sat on the floor and pulled his head into her bloodied lap. She cried loud and wretched sobs. Then, without even stopping to think, she picked up a shard of mosaic tile that he'd been using to create a sign that read "Debbie's Reading Corner," and used it to slit her throat.

That's when I woke up. Right after she told me how very lonely she was.

I spent an entire day thinking on it. Tell her? Don't tell her? What would happen if I did tell her? More importantly, what would happen if I didn't?

I started to tell her about the dream like I was telling a joke, or as if something funny had happened to me on the way up the hill. We sat in the swing on the gazebo as we often did, Beckan playing on the floor. As soon as I spoke the word "dream," I felt her entire body stiffen next to me. Right then I knew I'd made the right decision in telling her. I tried to spare her the details, but she insisted on knowing everything. I did what I could, but regardless of the lightest vocabulary chosen, she was horrified by the time I finished.

She tried to laugh it off, just as I had. "Oh, Cynthia, it's only a dream!" But her smile was too tight and I knew she was shaken. Something had been happening to her inside the house, that much I knew, but she refused to tell me anything about it, even when I insisted that I wouldn't criticize her for even the most ridiculous of things.

She and Clark disappeared the next day like ghosts in the night. I felt a certain loss when we realized they had gone, but I was also relieved. If she was not here upon the hill, then certainly, she and Clark were safe.

Chapter Forty
Mine.

I don't finish reading Cynthia O'Dwyre's diary. I can't –
it's too terrifying. I can reconcile all the hard facts in the file, the
pages of emotionless data. But it's the diaries that give these
women faces. All these women, these families, destroyed simply
because they'd tried to make a home out of this cursed jumble of
rotting wood. In the end, their only successes had been
insulating themselves from the outside world, losing sight of
reality and humanity. Disillusionment, depression, desperation;
these were their prizes – closely followed by death, of course.
And that fills me with a fear so thick it's clouding up the
atmosphere.

The power is still out and the storm's still raging. I gather
the lives of Alva, Barbara, Alison, Emily Lenore II, and Cynthia
in my hands. I hold them away from my body, as if by holding
them any closer I'll absorb their miseries through my skin. I
carry my balancing act across the room to my open closet door
and stack the diaries in a back corner. Then I methodically bury
them behind shoe boxes, piles of clothes, sheets, towels, and
other detritus. Then I close the closet door, tugging tightly to be
sure no mystery draft pushes it back open. I'd lock it if I could.

When I turn around, I'm met with a most unwelcome sight
in the dim candlelight: the blank diary. I thought I'd gathered it
up with the others. It sits innocently next to the candle on my
nightstand, glowing in the flickering flame, as if to say *Look at me*.

I'm unnerved by that lone blank diary. What's it doing
there? What does it want? I have a sudden desire to leave my
room, to turn my back on the diary, afraid of what might happen
if I open it.

I open my door cautiously. The cavernous hall and foyer
echo with the rumblings of the storm, lighting up like a strobe
light in the powerful lightning. I step into the hall, carefully
balancing a candle so as not to drip the burning wax onto my
skin or extinguish the flame. Willing myself not to look down

into the foyer and at those red doors, I scoot along the wall and make my way to Liam's room.

Liam's asleep, snoring faintly, blissfully unaware of the storm. He's lying on his side, cuddling a wad of the airplane sheets against his cheek, mouth open.

Setting the candle on the bedside table, I gently lower myself onto the edge of his bed. I watch him breathe, try to hold onto the moment, commit it to memory so I can pull it back up the next time he acts like a stranger, my sweet little brother whom I vowed to take care of.

Sitting there and watching him sleep so peacefully helps me start feeling sleepy. I stifle first one yawn, then another, and decide it's time to lie down and hope for sleep. Before getting up, I bend down and press my lips lightly to Liam's forehead.

Mine.

I leap back with a jolt, my lips burning. It feels like I've been electrocuted. Liam still snores quietly, as if nothing happened.

I heard the word as sure as I hear Liam snoring. It hangs in the air, right there with us, in the very same room. It's loud and sharp, as if someone stands right next to me. I recognize the voice because it's the exact same voice I hear in my dreams. I know it's *Her*.

I'm terrified. My eyes dart around. I study the walls, the ceiling, every nook and cranny, looking for a presence. Willing myself to remain calm, I retrieve my candle and leave Liam's room, closing the door softly behind me.

I feel my way back to my room, sticking close to the wall. I'm even more determined not to look down into the foyer now, my nerves shot and my hair standing on end. I move as quickly as I can without spilling candle wax or stubbing my toe. As I pass Mother's bedroom door, I hear muffled sobs from within. I consider consoling her, trying to understand the woman's crazy mood swing only hours earlier, but when I remember the anger behind Mother's eyes, I think better of it. Who's to say she won't throw me over the banister just for opening the door?

Back in my room, the door closed and locked, I sit on my bed, hugging my knees. I stare at the door.

Watching.

Waiting.

Vigilant.

*   *   *

315

The rain has stopped and the pastel glow of morning lights up my room. I look at my bedside clock, but the power is still out. When I glance out the balcony windows, I see Mother's car in the driveway. Why isn't she at work?

I find the hall much as I'd left it early this morning, quiet and full of closed doors. I lean an ear against Mother's, but hear nothing. I consider going in, but my thoughts quickly switch to Liam.

He's in the playroom, already dressed in a warm blue sweater, jeans, and matching socks.

"Hi, squiggle worm," I say after watching him play with that odd soldier set again. He's pitted them against an army of Lego men and – I freeze.

Liam has laid out his battle in front of the dollhouse from the attic, the miniature Wolfhowl Manor. How did it get to the playroom?

"What's going on," I ask, just to test my voice, to see if it trembles. "Do you know what time it is?"

"Morning, Rosie," he replies without looking up from his army men. "Beckan says there's no school. The storm was real bad. He said to tell you he's out around town helping people with stuff. If you wanted to know where he is."

I'm only half listening. The battery run SpongeBob clock hanging on the wall has both of Patrick's arms between ten and eleven. I can't believe I slept so late.

"Wow, no school!" I try to get excited, to think of something we can do together, out of the house, but the thick haze of depression hangs over me again. "What are we gonna do today? We could go exploring around town. We could take a bike ride down to the beach and see what washed up in the storm… Ooh, or maybe we could go down to the Bauers and see about playing another game of Chinese Checkers. What do you think?" I'm desperate to find that brother-sister normalcy again, but Liam isn't interested.

"No, thanks," he says, knocking over a couple of Lego men with a soldier. "I'd rather stay here and play."

"By yourself?"

Liam turns around finally, looking up at me impatiently. "I'm not by myself."

I suck in a cold breath, a wave of fear washing over me. "What's wrong, Rosie?"

I don't reply. I can't. He's sitting here as if he's playing a game with an imaginary friend, but he has no idea he's playing war with an evil, calculating presence.

I back out of the room carefully, last night's threat still fresh in my mind. I take a long, hot shower and change into fresh clothes, hoping to clear my mind.

Although I'm suspended, with Liam and Mother at home, it's like a snow day. Snow days were fun back in Texas because they almost never happened. When the rare one came around, it was a wonderful free-for-all kind of day. I'd get together with my friends and we'd pelt snow at each other before it melted away and the sweltering heat returned. If we were lucky enough to know about the cancellation the night before, one of the boys whose parents were out of town would throw a party.

Days like this are supposed to be fun, but I don't feel any sense of adventure. I feel soggy, like the weather outside. I was serious when I suggested getting out of the house to Liam, but I'm also relieved he said no. I don't feel like going anywhere now. I consider calling Letta, but we'll just end up talking about *Her*, and for the first time that fills me with a healthy dose of fear – just putting my worst nightmares into words, saying them out loud… What if they come true? Like Cynthia O'Dywre's dream about Deborah Hollister. Would it have come true if Cynthia had kept quiet?

I need a distraction. I haven't seen or spoken to Mother since last night's argument. Remembering, I raise a hand to my cheek, feeling the raised scratch, proof I wasn't dreaming. I can't believe my own mother attacked me. The kind of anger in her last night was unreal. Mother's always had a temper, and we've always had arguments, but mostly we yelled, cussing and hurling insults, practically spitting at each other. But Mother'd never been violent toward me – not since I was little anyway. I'm the one whose temper tends toward throwing anything within reach. For Pete's sake, *I'm* the one who stomped on another person's head! And while anger is still a daily struggle for me, Mother's been so much better at controlling her temper since the divorce.

I'm sure Mother's mood swings have everything to do with *Her*. She gleefully skips out of the house on the way to work every day. And every evening she comes home irritable and looking for a fight. Sometimes she smells like alcohol, a silent battle she's been struggling with for years. She's given in to Her, has allowed Her to slowly siphon away her will to live. How much time does Mother have left?

Feeling a sense of urgency, I knock on Mother's door and hear a weak "Come in." She's curled up in bed, her blankets wrapped around her body like a mummy. The longer the power is off, the colder it gets in our huge, cavernous house. I'm wearing a heavy sweater with a long-sleeved shirt underneath, and a warm pair of old cheerleading sweatpants. I wonder if I'll have to put on my winter coat before the power comes back on.

"Hi, sweetie," Mother whispers.

"Hi, Mom." I cautiously approach her bed. She smiles weakly and releases some of the covers. I crawl beneath them and we lay facing each other silently for a few minutes. I know we're thinking the same things as we evaluate each other. *My, how tired you look my dear. My, how thin you are my dear. The easier to swallow you up* my dear.

"Mom, is everything okay?" I ask, testing the waters. "Last night was pretty scary."

"Last night?"

"The fight we had. I don't know if I've ever seen you so angry. I swear I feel terrible that you didn't know where we were, but you've got to believe me when I tell you it was a total accident."

"Rose, honey," she stifles a yawn, "what on earth are you talking about?"

"The fight we had last night."

Mother laughs, but it's not a cheerful sound. It's closer to a cougar's cough, a creepy sound that sends shivers through me. "Sweetie, I don't know what you're talking about. You must've had another bad dream."

"You don't remember?" I can't believe it. Did Mother actually black out? Can she really have forgotten what she said? What she *did?* Flustered and confused, I change the subject. "Shouldn't you be at work, or is the power out at the hospital too?"

"The power's out?"

"Mom! The power's been out since last night because of the storm. They cancelled school. It's almost noon!"

"Oh?" She yawns. "Well, that's nice. You and Liam can have a nice little break from school then."

"Why aren't you at work?" I ask more insistently.

She shrugs. "I just couldn't make myself get up today."

"Did you call in sick? Did you tell your boss you aren't coming in?"

"What? Oh, no," she says, unconcerned. "I forgot."

"Mom!" I shout and she winces. "You have to call in! You'll get fired!" I'm panicked. If Mother loses her job, we'll never have the money to get out of this hellhole. We'll be doomed.

"It'll be fine," Mother says, stifling another yawn. "Now go find something to keep yourself occupied. I'm gonna take a nap."

I'm stunned for moment, but then get up. "Maybe if the power comes back on we can watch a movie together, as a family," I suggest. *"Toy Story* or *Monsters, Inc.* or something."

"Sure, maybe." She says as she rolls over and closes her eyes.

As I turn to leave, I spy Mother's diary on the nightstand, open to a new entry.

I rush downstairs and grab the phone, thanking God it still has a dial tone. I pull out the Port Braseham phonebook, which is about ten pages, but realize the hospital in Bar Harbor won't be listed there. Without power and the Internet, I can't look up the number. I end up calling the number for the police department, which is also outside of Port Braseham because it's such a tiny crap little town, but it's the closest emergency station, so it's in the book.

When a Mainah accented woman answers, I ask for the number to the hospital in Bar Harbor.

"Is this an emergency?" She asks.

"No," I reply quickly. "No, I'm…just trying to reach a relative who's in the hospital." I lie, because what am I supposed to say? *My crazy mother's too depressed to get out of bed, and I'm calling to make sure she doesn't get fired, because if she does, we'll all die, hanging in one of the upper bedrooms of our new house. Now, what did you say the number was?*

The woman gives me the number and offers to connect my call. I'm on hold forever after a flustered woman answers, saying *"Can you hold please?"*and puts me on hold before I can reply. I guess it's busy today, maybe because of the power outage, which means it isn't just Port Braseham. That makes me feel better somehow.

Eventually I get through to a Nurse Wanda, who thankfully knows Mother. I make up a lie about food poisoning and say Mother's been throwing up all morning, or she'd have called herself. I make sure the lie is enough to keep Mother out of trouble, but not so serious her coworkers think she needs to be admitted to the hospital herself. Wanda thanks me, saying she and the other nurses had been worried since it isn't like Mother to be late. Apparently, they'd tried calling the house, but couldn't get through, and Mother's cell phone went straight to voicemail. Wanda tells me to take care and make sure Mother drinks plenty of water.

I spend a while putzing around the kitchen, rinsing some dishes and putting them in the dishwasher. I wipe the counter and the table and then sweep the floor and toy with the idea of mopping it too, but decide take out the trash instead because I can smell it from across the room.

I grab my coat and carry the bulging bag through the back door and put it in the larger trashcan on the back porch that Beckan will wheel down to the bottom of the hill on trash day.

Today's weather is the coldest so far. The tall pines survived the storm, but lost most of their needles to the wind. Derry mowed the other day, so the porch is covered in a wet pelt of grass clippings. It's grey and dreary, the sun a hazy orb behind the clouds.

I stare out toward the cliff, which I've avoided entirely since I nearly jumped to my death that first day. The distant sound of waves crashing on the rocks below floats on the wind.

I step off the porch into the soft bed of grassy mud, carefully picking my way to the cliff's edge. I tell myself I'm just curious to see if anything interesting washed up in the storm, but in the back of my mind this rings false. I plod toward the cliff's edge, propelled by some unseen force.

When I'm close to the edge, I get down on my hands and knees, and crawl through the wet grass, soaking the knees of my sweatpants. I crawl right up to the edge on the skinniest piece of land jutting out over the rocks even though my brain is screaming at my body to stop. Stop! *STOP!*

The sea surges over the rocks below and only the tallest, sharpest of them slice through the water like knives. The beach is invisible underneath the swollen green waters. The churning waves reflect my anger and desperation.

My small perch lurches forward unexpectedly, slanting toward the water. Gripping at the grass, I look behind me. Just behind my feet is a large crack in the ground. My heart pounds. My brain goes into overdrive. I have to get off this precipice, but I'm terrified the slightest movement will send me careening toward the roiling waves.

Mine.

Slowly and deliberately, I turn my body around, toward the crack. There's only a few feet between me and solid ground…

MINE!

The ground falls away from me with the loud snapping of tree roots. I'm weightless in the second before gravity takes hold. I lunge out to grab onto something, anything, and manage to get the fingers of my right hand around one large tree root as the ground crumbles away. I dangle a few feet below the cliff's edge, but there's nothing else to hold onto, no footholds. I dangle, helpless and terrified. I can think of nothing else to do, but scream.

So that's exactly what I do.

Chapter Forty-One
The Blank Diary

I scream as loud, as hard, and as long as I can. I scream until my throat is raw, exerting all of the power I can without letting go of the tree root that is now my only lifeline. But it's pointless. No one can hear me over the roaring wind and the crashing waves.

"What am I doing," I yell at myself, beginning to cry. "Why did I come out here!"

I frantically claw at the muddy side of the cliff with my free hand, trying to find a way to climb back up onto the cliff, a mere two feet away. I pray the slippery root I'm clinging to is strong and connected to one of the ancient pines rather than one of the drying up spruces. It feels like a dry twig in my hand and I'm terrified it'll give any moment. Think light, I tell myself. I'm as light as a feather. *I'mlightasafeather.I'mlightasafeather.I'mlightasafeather.*

Huge water droplets begin to pelt me as it starts raining again. The side of the cliff becomes wetter and weaker with each drop.

"Of course!" I scream. "Of course it starts to rain! *God dammit!*" I have a ridiculous moment of Catholic guilt but God understands, right? I mean, He is about to let me die.

A gust of wind rushes up and twists me around. The soft earth is at my back. I'm looking out over the ocean, and then… down. My vision narrows. All I see are the sharp rocks below, ready to pierce my comically small body…

My lifeline tears out of the dirt. I slip a foot closer to the churning surf. My wave battered body is there, bloody and shattered on the rocks.

Help isn't coming. I'm only postponing the inevitable.
Yes…

Eventually this root is going to break.
Yes…

Or my muscles will give. Or the root will cut into my fingers and the pain will force me to let go. This is how I die.
Yes…

My grip loosens. Death is easier…

Yes, so much easier…

Will it be quick, or will I have to drown? Will it hurt?

It's easy, Rose. It's so easy…

My grip loosens a little more. One more flinch and I'll plummet into the abyss. I let out a final, gut-wrenching sob, ready myself to let go, to give up on this life. *She* will take care of Liam. This is what She wants. It's what I want…

"Rose!"

I'm shocked back to my senses. "Hello? Help! Down here!" My relief breaks through the calmness that claimed me seconds ago.

"Rose! It's Letta!"

"Oh Letta, thank God! Help me!"

"Hold on!"

"Hold on? *Hold on?*" What the hell else am I going to do?

"Beckan's getting a rope!" Letta shouts to me. "Just hold on!"

"I am," I shout, grimacing against the pain in my hand, "but I don't know about this root! Hurry! Please!" Desperation burns in my throat.

A thick rope falls a few feet away from me.

"Grab the rope, Rose!" Beckan's voice is calm but demanding.

To grab it, I'll have to turn around to face the cliff and lunge with my free hand. I'm certain that alone will be enough to snap the root. I'll only have one shot. Grab the rope or die.

I take too long thinking it over, and the root gives again. I slide another foot closer to the water with a yelp.

"Rose!" Letta screams.

"Grab the rope, girl!" Beckan shouts urgently.

Taking a deep breath, I steady myself against the side of the cliff with my feet. I say a silent prayer for Liam and Mother, and then launch myself at the rope, twisting in the wind.

The root snaps. I'm falling fast and my hand isn't on the rope yet. At the last second, a gust of wind throws the rope into my hands and I latch on with only an inch of rope to spare.

Letta sighs from above, "Oy Gevalt!"

"Do you have a good hold?" Beckan shouts.

I inch my grip up a few inches before I shout that I do.

"Hold on tight!" Beckan says. "We're gonna pull you up!"

The rope starts moving upward very slowly. I try to lessen my weight and climb up the side of the cliff with my feet. When

I'm within reach of the cliff's edge, Beckan keeps his straining muscles on the rope and Letta reaches down and grabs onto my jacket. Finally, and with a relief so strong I feel the bile rising from my stomach, I'm back on solid ground.

For several minutes filled only with our panting, the three of us sit on the wet grass in the falling rain. Beckan and Letta stare at me, and I stare at my shaking, rope-burned hands.

I almost gave up. I *did* give up. Another second longer and…

"Do you know how close you came to being fish bait?" Letta finally says. "What the hell were you thinking?"

The giddy laughter builds deep in my belly before exploding into hysteria.

"Are you okay?" Letta asks dubiously.

"Oh, Letta," I say with my head in my hands. "It's so, so silly." I wipe the laughter tears from my eyes. "I just wanted to look down at the beach to see if anything good washed up in the storm." *Right?* "I just wanted to stick my head over the edge." *Right?* "I had no idea… It never occurred to me that part of the cliff might *actually* fall away." *Right…?* "I mean, how often does that happen?"

"It's a bit of bad luck, I guess," Letta replies.

"Yeah," Beckan says flatly. *"Bad luck."*

I try standing but my legs are jelly. Beckan hops up and takes an arm. "Thank you so much. Thank you, thank you, *thank you!* And also, I'm sorry." I'm looking at Beckan when I apologize. *"Really* sorry."

"How many times do I have tah save your life?" A smile tugs at the corner of his lips, but his eyes remain intense.

"Let's hope that's the last time." I try taking a step forward, but stumble again.

"Heeah," Beckan says, "let's get you inside." Letta grabs my other arm and the three of us go in through the back door like soggy dogs, shaking off the rain and leaving puddles at our feet.

I throw my coat over the back of a kitchen chair and collapse into it, leaning my head in one hand. I'm exhausted. Letta plops down across from me, equally adrenaline depleted.

Beckan stands near the door, leaning against the counter. He leans his head back and closes his eyes for a moment before seeming to re-energize. He looks around, catching sight of the digital clock on the stove, blinking and winking in the dull light from the windows.

"The power's back on," he says. "Hey, when was the last time you ate?"

"Um…" I haven't had anything to eat today and I skipped dinner last night. "Well…"

"If you have tah think that hard," Beckan says as he starts rooting through the cabinets, "it's been tah long." He finds a large pot and then pulls open the refrigerator to view the pickings, which are embarrassingly sparse. I'm not sure when Mother went to the store last.

"You don't have to cook," I say, making a weak attempt at politeness. "Really, you saved my life – again. *I* should be making something for *you.*"

"I insist," he says, bending over to look more closely at the contents, overflowing with condiments. I catch Letta staring at his butt.

"Letta!" I hiss, and she shrugs before squeezing some of the rain from her hair with a jacket sleeve.

"How'd you guys find me anyway?" I ask. "I'd –" *Given up.* "I wasn't sure how much longer I could hold on."

Letta explains while Beckan begins cooking. "I'd called a couple of times to see if you wanted to do something with our free day, but no one answered. Mom sent me up here to do the neighborly thing and check on you. I ran into Beckan on the hill, who was coming to do the same thing. Your front door was unlocked, but no one came down when I called out. Beckan saw the empty trashcan and figured you were taking out the trash, so we went outside. I said something to Beckan about how the cliff looked different, and from the look on his face, I knew he thought you'd…*fallen* off. So I ran over there and saw you clinging to the side."

"I'm *so* lucky," I whisper, and repeat it silently. *I'm so lucky. I'm so, so lucky.*

"Where is everyone anyway?" Letta asks. "Your mom's car is here, but no one's home."

"Oh, they're here," I say. "Liam's been up in his playroom all day."

"By himself?" Letta asks, now having to speak up over the noise Beckan makes as he clunks around.

"Sort of," I say evasively. "And Mom's been in bed all day."

"Oh?" Letta's eyebrows go up.

"Decided to take a sick day with us, I guess."

"But not to spend time *with* you?"

I shrug and change the subject. I ask if there's any other news to report, so Letta fills me in on the storm damage and Beckan jumps in every now and then, like the two of them have already been through the play-by-play. There's some flooding downtown, but it doesn't include the school. ("Unfortunately," adds Letta.) There's wind damage to most of the buildings on the wharf, and some of the fishing ships are sure to be total losses. (Beckan notes sarcastically, "One of the ships nearly went through the Quinn's front window, but missed and hit one of their BMWs instead. Shame.") The Wharf Rat will be shut down for a few weeks to make repairs. ("So naturally, there'll beeah decline in food poisonin'," Beckan says.) Letta's talked to Shane and Patty, who are fine, but Eileen's still playing hard to get. (Letta rolls her eyes, "I don't even know why I bothered.")

"And of course," Letta says finally, "Wolfhowl Mountain suffered a minor loss upon the cliff, which nearly resulted in loss of life."

"Har, har."

"Hey, I've got to laugh about it," she says, "or I'll start crying. That was some serious business, Rose, all kidding aside. Seeing you clinging to that tree root scared me enough for three lifetimes."

"Gee, only three," I say sarcastically.

"What's goin' on?" Liam appears in the doorway, following his nose, which zeroes in on Beckan busily working over the stove.

"Well hello, stranger," Letta says. "You hungry?"

"Yeah," Liam says eagerly, standing at Beckan's side. "What're you making?"

"It's a surprise." Beckan winks.

"Come over here squiggle worm," I say. "Come sit by me and keep me warm."

Liam leaves Beckan's side and surprises me by climbing into my lap instead of the chair next to me. I shift my weight until we're both comfortable, and Liam puts his arms around my neck. Tears well up in my eyes; it feels good to have my brother back, if only for a moment.

"Why are you all wet, Rosie? And what happened to your hands?"

For the first time I realize how wet and dirty I am, and how badly my hands hurt. They're red and swollen in the middle and I have a few blisters.

Letta grabs a few ice cubes from the freezer, wrapping them in a paper towel and handing the bundle to me.

"Thanks." I put my arms around Liam, joining them by wrapping them around the ice.

"Did you hurt yourself, Rosie?" Liam asks.

"Oh, we were just goofing around outside," I say nonchalantly. "It's not a big deal."

"In the rain?"

"Of course," I poke Liam's pudgy belly. "It's fun playing in the rain. It's a shame you wanted to stay inside." I play it up so Liam might feel like he's missed out on something fun because he was playing with Her instead. He doesn't need to know part of the *fun* had been his sister nearly falling to her death.

"Aww," Liam frowns, and I feel like I've achieved a small victory.

"Are we having a party down here or what?" Mother appears in the doorway, fresh faced and warm in a long cardigan and a pair of skinny jeans and wool socks. She's showered and put her wet hair in a bun. "Oh, Rose, are you making Beckan cook?" She's drawn to his side by the smell of something scrumptious, just as Liam was.

"She begged me not tah," Beckan lies. "It's no problem."

"It smells wonderful," Mother says. "Thank you so much!"

Beckan blushes all Opie Taylor and *aww shucks ma'am*.

Mother joins us at the table. "Singing in the rain, were you?" she says, pinching my wet sleeve in her fingers.

"Something like that," Letta says evasively and changes the subject, repeating her news about the storm damage. Mother nods in all the right places, making an effort to appear normal and conversational, but I can tell she's struggling. At least she's trying though.

"Tada!" Beckan finally announces with a bright smile, carrying a large pot over to the table and setting it on a hotplate. We peer over the edge of the pot into a murky looking, but delicious smelling stew. Clearly, our faces are not what Beckan expected and his smile falls. "What?"

"What *is* it?" Liam asks.

Beckan sets bowls down in front us and says, "Odds n' Ends."

"Odds and Ends?" Letta crinkles her nose distastefully.

"Yeah," Beckan pulls up a chair and ladles his creation into each of our dishes. "That's what my muthah used tah call it. Whenever she hadn't had a chance tah make it tah the store, she'd go through the fridge and the pantry, find whatevah she could, throw it all together and make somethin' wonderful. Trust me, I learned from the best."

I look at my bowl of muddy broth dubiously and pick around with my spoon. I think I see some potatoes, peppers, and tomatoes, maybe even some sausage.

Liam is the first to give it a try, his grumbling stomach giving in to the appetizing aroma. He spoons Beckan's mixture into his mouth, clumsily blowing on it first, and then rolls it around on his tongue like a professional food critic. He chews carefully while we await his expert opinion. After a large swallow, he smiles."It's good!"

"I told ya," Beckan says.

We laugh and eat without hesitation. I can't remember the last time we've enjoyed a meal at the kitchen table like a real family. For a while, I forget about the oppressive negativity pervading the entire house and enjoy this moment.

After lunch, I help Beckan with the dishes while Letta takes Liam and Mother into the family room to pick a movie.

The rest of the afternoon and evening is spent in the darkness of our family room, sitting too close to the television while watching *Monsters, Inc.* and then a few episodes of *SpongeBob Squarepants*. The party breaks up around seven when the Bauers call Letta home and Beckan offers her a ride down the hill. I quash my jealousy – Beckan spent the afternoon sitting so close to me our legs were almost touching. He spread his long arms around the back of the couch and I had to fight the urge to fold myself into him.

This afternoon is a small pinprick of light, a small ray of hope, that it's possible to beat Her. The how is still allusive. The moment Beckan and Letta leave, the depressive cloak falls back over the household. It's potent and immediate.

Mother stifles a huge yawn. "Liam – "

"I know, I know," he says, already slumping toward the stairs. "Bath time."

"Rose, can you help him tonight?" Mother asks. "I don't know what's wrong with me, but I just don't have the energy."

"I can do it by myself!" Liam shouts from the top of the stairs.

"As you wish," Mother throws up her arms. "I don't have the energy to argue either." She heads upstairs after Liam, splitting off toward her room and they each close a door at the same time, leaving me alone. I watch a little more TV before turning it off and going upstairs.

When I open my bedroom door, my eyes are immediately drawn to the blank diary on the nightstand, glowing under the lamp that was on when the power went out.

Without really thinking, I go to my backpack and take out my pencil case, which is full of colorful, girly, inky pens that are perfect for scrawling hot pink hearts and little blue curlicues. I sit on my bed with the diary in my lap and start drawing. I spend the next thirty minutes doodling over the cover.

When I finally stop doodling and look down, I'm shocked. What I see is not at all what I thought I was drawing. "What...?"

There's no colorful pen in my hand, nor on the diary. Instead, I'm holding a thick black Sharpie, and when I pull my hand away, what I see is not a collection of hearts and flowers, but something far simpler. Initials. *My* initials. R. D., in a prominent calligraphy I've never used before. It's exactly like the letters on the covers of the other diaries.

Diaries of dead women.

I open the cover of my new diary, turn to the first page and write today's date.

And then, I begin writing.

Chapter Forty-Two
Fitzwilliam Ronan Darcy

Nﾠovember

If Her goal is to destroy my family from within, then She's winning. We are officially three strangers sharing one roof.

Mother becomes more distant and moody each day. It's a lot like how she was before the split, only worse. She was miserable at work, miserable at home. For a while I only saw her at dinnertime, and then not at all. Even when she was around she was fuming mad about something stupid or depressed and soggy with tears. If it weren't for her total black out about our fight the other night, I might shrug this all off as same ol' same ol'. Dad's reaction before the split ﾠﾠand after – was the same. He was moody and depressed, and basically absent. His body was there, but he wasn't. It really forced Liam and me to rely on each other not just for support, but for the daily necessities. Food. Rides to school. A hug.

Oh, Liam. My sweet brother. He becomes more independent each day. He acts like a teenager instead of a five-year-old. He makes his own meals. He takes baths by himself. He tucks himself into bed. He doesn't want a bedtime story. He doesn't talk to me about Dad… It's like he doesn't need me anymore – at exactly the time when I need him the most. If he doesn't rely on me, if Liam doesn't need me – then who really cares about me anymore?

What if I disappeared? Would anyone notice?
I wonder how long it would take.
A few hours?
A day?
A week?
Eternity?

Logic tells me that even if Mother and Liam didn't notice, certainly Letta or Beckan would. That should tell you how disillusioned I am, just what kind of hold She can have on you. I know there are people out there who care about me, but I'm able to ignore the fact. It's like object permanence and babies. Isn't that what they call it? When the people who care about me leave the room, they cease to exist. They're gone forever. And if the people who care about me are gone forever, what's the point in me hanging around?

Not that I would ever… I couldn't.

I wonder if the women who died here thought the same thing. "I would never commit suicide!" …And then they did.

The air in the house is a thick haze that only we can see. I feel it every time I come through the door, this tangible, sticky thing. It starts at the top of my head and trickles slowly down. It coats my skin in ice, fogs up my brain, makes my lungs feel wet so that every breath I take is like inhaling water, and I become heavier and heavier.

How much longer can I hold Her off? Mother's barely hanging on, and we all know what'll happen when she finally gives in.

I'll be an orphan. I won't survive that. If I become an orphan, She wins. Everyone who can protect Liam will be gone, and then She will take him for herself. And we'll just be another family who disappeared on the hill. More ghostly fodder for the tourists. This diary my only legacy. The only proof that I ever existed…

*   *   *

When my alarm wakes me Friday morning, my whole body hurts and my palms are throbbing. My muscles are finally letting me know exactly how much trouble they'd gone to in keeping me alive yesterday. I fight the urge to stay curled up under the covers and manage to shower and dress, delicately buttoning my jeans to avoid irritating the blisters on my hands. Gingerly grabbing my backpack, I head downstairs, meeting Mother in the foyer as she rushes around.

"Mom, what are you still doing here?"

"Running late, obviously!" She snaps. I notice the puffy purple circles under her eyes as she throws her purse over her shoulder and grabs her umbrella. Realizing she's forgotten to put on her coat, Mother drops everything, hurriedly throws on her coat again and then puts her purse back over her shoulder, picks up the umbrella, and starts frantically searching the pockets for her keys.

"Do you need help?" I offer, hoping to calm her burgeoning anger; an angry nurse is no good to anyone.

"Rose!" Mother spits my name like it's a curse. Her purse falls back to the floor and she rubs her eyes, smearing her mascara. When she pulls her fingers away, I can see the glassy tears trying to get out.

"Mom," I say softly, putting my hands on Mother's shoulders. "Mom, relax. What's wrong?"

She stifles a sob and meets my eyes. "I don't know, Rose. I'm sorry. I feel like I'm falling apart. I thought coming up here was such a *good* idea. I thought if we came here and started over we could move on and we could all try to forget about... about..."

I nod and give her shoulders a squeeze.

"I don't know what it is about this place," she says. "It's so big and far away... It's isolating. I'm glad you kids are doing okay. Beckan and Letta are good friends. And Liam seems happy. It's just, for me, I guess... I'm *so* lonely."

I'm so lonely. It's as if Mother's words are in someone else's voice. She doesn't sound like herself. She sounds like Alva. Like Barbara. Like my father.

Mother is staring at me, so I try to recover, try to comfort her. "I know, Mom. The adults in this town are kind of stuffy. But you've met...*people* at work. You should ask some of them to hang out. Have dinner. Go to a movie... a *girls'* night or something."

"I know, I know." She nods, seeming to gather herself. "It sounds so simple doesn't it?"

"It *is*, Mom," I say. "I promise."

"Thanks, sweetie." She gives me a quick hug and then rushes out the door before she changes her mind and goes back to bed.

It's weird how our roles have reversed. When did I turn into the rational, responsible one? Mother is becoming obsolete; I can see that now. And I'm one step closer to becoming an orphan.

*   *   *

Liam and I meet Beckan at his truck. We pick up Letta on the way as usual. The cab is quiet today, the rumble of the diesel engine all that breaks the cocoon of silence. Liam plays with one of his soldiers he snuck out of the house in his pocket. I stare through the windshield unseeing, preoccupied.

"Look, there's Shane and Patty," Letta says, waving at the two of them through the window.

"Ooh," Beckan smiles, "holdin' hands now?"

I look up, see the two of them strolling slowly along the road, hand in hand. They smile at each other as if there's no one else in the world.

"About time," Letta says. "They've been playing footsie since summer." She laughs and smiles at Beckan. Beckan smiles back.

What is that? Is that just a smile? Why is it such a *big* smile? And why is Letta looking at him *like that?* I try to push the negativity away, but like a dense mist, it diffuses only a moment before oozing back over me, and my mood sours.

Beckan drops us off with another warm smile and a cheerful "Have a good day!" Liam darts toward the kindergarten doors without saying goodbye, and Letta and I are left standing on the curb in silence.

"You're quiet today," Letta says. "Are you alright? I mean, you *did* almost die yesterday, but ...why so glum?"

"Do you know what my mother said to me this morning?" Letta shakes her head. "She said she was lonely."

"Yeah? So?" Letta doesn't get it; I haven't told her about the other dreams, the ones where everyone's so lonely, where the dead want company. Mother's company. My company. I'm not in the mood to explain right now.

"It means," I say, turning toward the school, "that I'm running out of time."

"That sounds ominous," Letta says, falling into step beside me. "I've gotta say, Rose, I'm stumped. I've been thinking about it all nonstop since...well, since we met. And the more we find out, the more confused I am. I don't understand any of it – or maybe I don't want to. I'm starting to feel like the rest of the dopes in this town, like there's nothing we can do."

"That's encouraging," I snap sarcastically.

"Sorry. What I mean is, maybe it's time we start thinking about getting your family out of there. We can try to convince your mom to sell it back to the historical society."

"Letta! That would be a huge financial loss. It's impossible. We have nowhere to go. Without that house, we've got nothing!"

"Nothing?" Letta says with a disbelieving eyebrow.

I sigh wearily. "Letta, that house is all we have to our name. Mother sunk every dime we had into that hell hole. My parents were spenders, not savers. My dad was especially good at it. Before he died, he made sure he spent every dime he had out of spite, and Mother spent most of her money on the divorce.

Whatever she had left went into the house. I know she won't say it, but between the mortgage and the utility bills on that drafty piece of crap, we're living paycheck to paycheck. And," I take a deep breath, "even if we could convince her to sell, it won't matter."

"What do you mean?"

I've been giving this next part a lot of thought. "I've been thinking about the children of Wolfhowl."

"Children? You mean Emily Lenore and Shane?"

"Emily Lenore escaped the house, but her life didn't get any better. She suffered, like the curse followed her, you know? And Shane… Shane just wasted away and died after he was taken from the house."

"Yeah…"

"I think," I say, speaking slowly and carefully, considering my words, "I think if we just pick up and leave, it'll follow us. *She'll* follow us and to punish us, she'll take Liam just like she took Shane. He'll stay in that house or he'll die."

"Rose, you can't seriously think that –"

"Letta, I gave up rational thought a long time ago. It doesn't apply anymore, not to that house and not to my family. Maybe I'm wrong," I say, knowing I'm not, "but I can't take that chance. I just can't. If I can't save Liam from Her, then what *can* I do? We have to stay so I can protect him."

"What about Emily Lenore II," Letta asks. "Maybe she survived and led a good life."

"I doubt it," I reply sourly. "But even if she did, how would we know? She's untraceable. We don't know where she came from, who she really was, or what happened to her."

"But, Rose," Letta says softly, "you know what will happen if you stay."

"I know. I'll die."

*   *   *

For once, as I sit in Mrs. Brennan's homeroom, I'm immune to the sneers and jeers of my classmates. It might be my first day back at school, but I may as well be at home with the cloud of depression that hangs over me. I can feel the pull of the house, of the fire room, on my mind. I sit in the back corner, massaging my raw, angry-looking palms. My eyes are pulled to the windows, looking out for a glance at the mountain, at the deadly cliff I can't see.

"And don't forget to get your ticket to the dance!" The crackling whine of the morning announcements pierces through the haze and my attention is drawn back to the classroom.

"We'll see you in the gym tonight at eight!"

The dance! How could I have allowed myself to forget about that damn dance? Am I relieved Ronan hasn't sought me out during my suspension to ask me to the dance, as Letta said he would? Or do I feel rejected because no one's asked me to be their date? I would've been at the top of every guy's list back in Texas. But I don't need to keep reminding myself this isn't Texas, and I'm not Texas Rose anymore.

I don't want to go to the stupid dance anyway. I've been trying to impress the local yokels since I got here and have been met with nothing but ridicule and hatred. They don't want me around, don't need me as their queen. They have Mary Donovan for that, even if Ronan dumped her. That doesn't unseat her…does it?

I feel Mary's murderous gaze on me and for a second, our eyes lock across the room. Suddenly, my heart is filled with an anger and hatred so hot I can feel the bile bubbling in my gut like lava. Mary's piercing stare says she feels the same. If the bell didn't ring at that precise moment, I'm sure Mary's head would've exploded under the heat of my own rage.

I go through my first two classes, drifting invisibly through the halls with my head aimed low like a dog, sticking to the back corners and stewing on thoughts of the house. I don't come up for air until lunch.

Patty and Shane sit close together across from me and Letta. They smile at each other like dopes, holding hands under the table and eating their lunches one-handed. Obviously, they're going to the dance together. I try to be happy for them, but the longer I look at them, the sicker I feel.

"What 'bout you guys," Patty asks. "You're comin' right?"

I don't reply and Letta shrugs, "Pass."

"Aww," Patty whines. "C'mon! We'll have fun!"

"Yeah," Letta snorts, "we'll look real cute, you, me, and Shane, slow dancing in a triangle. It'll be a regular ol' square dance." Her face sinks into her tray as she pushes some cold peas around with a bent fork.

"Rose?" Patty looks at me hopefully.

"I dunno… I don't have a date and Mary'll find a way to ruin it anyway."

Patty's smile shrinks away from her face. "Aww."

"Yeah," Shane says, oblivious to Patty's disappointment. "She's been gunnin' for you the last few days. Oof!" Patty kicks him hard under the table. "Uh, but who cares 'bout Mary anyway, am I right?"

"Don't worry," Letta says. "You'll have fun without us. It'll be more romantic that way." Patty's encouraged, but I detect the subtle sarcasm lurking in Letta's voice. "Rose and I'll find something to do with ourselves."

"I really thought Ronan was gonna ask you tah be his date," Patty says. "Everyone did."

"Why? So he can pour pig's blood all over me? No thanks. I'm relieved he didn't ask me, to tell the truth. One less thing to worry about."

Shane's eyebrows suddenly begin fleeing to his hairline as he looks over my shoulder. "I think you're speakin' a mite too soon…"

Patty follows his gaze, her mouth agape, and Letta guffaws in angry disbelief. When I finally turn around, I'm shocked into silence.

Ronan strides across the cafeteria with just a shade of red in his cheeks, a smile plastered ear to ear. His short hair is brushed back, glistening with gel. He wears a long navy blue waistcoat with large ivory buttons down the middle. A blood red cravat pokes out of his perfectly white shirt collar. Beneath the coat he wears a pair of tight tan slacks with a red stripe racing down the side, which end in a pair of shiny black boots. One hand holds onto his waistcoat collar, and the other grasps an ornate cane. He struts across the cafeteria like a peacock, like he isn't wearing clothes that belong in a Jane Austen novel while his classmates catcall and whoop with laughter.

Ronan smiles as he approaches, and I try to close my mouth. He takes my hand daintily in his own. "My lady," he bends stiffly at the waist and gently brushes the back of my hand with his lips.

"Ronan," Letta spits, *what the hell?*

Ronan ignores Letta, his smile faltering for only a second as he releases my hand. The cafeteria fills with a charged silence.

"My lady," he says in a terribly fake and loud British accent, performing for the whole cafeteria, "Colonel Fitzwilliam Ronan Darcy – that's me – would like Miss Elizabeth Rose Bennet – that's you – to join him at tonight's ball. He shant take no for an answer." He winks.

I'm too shocked to respond. I can't believe what he's wearing, that he's put this elaborate costume together for me, or that he's embarrassed himself in front of the entire student body *for me*. My feelings are confusing; I'm simultaneously flattered, distrusting, embarrassed, happy – all wound tightly together. But the student body demands an answer.

"Um," I try to think of how Jane Austen would write this scene. "Why, Miss Bennet would be delighted, Mr. Darcy."

"What?!" Letta yelps.

"Excellent," Ronan straightens and throws another wink my way. "A coach shall pick you up promptly at seven. We shall dine and then head to the ball. You will find your dress awaiting you when you arrive home this evening. Ta-ta." He tucks the cane under an arm and turns on his heels, strutting back across the cafeteria, bowing to the erupting applause and hoots of his classmates. As I look away, I glimpse Mary, sprinting from the cafeteria in tears. A smile slithers onto my lips.

When I turn back to my friends, Shane is confused and Patty's about to faint from the romanticism of it all. Letta is absolutely furious.

"You're actually going to go to the dance with *him*," Letta says indignantly.

I shrug. "How am I supposed to say no to a performance like that? Seriously?" It's a grand gesture, a sign that maybe I've misjudged Ronan. And it's a small pinprick of light in my life, something to be happy about for once. And most importantly, it gets me out of the house.

"I can't believe you're going to fall for that crap!" Letta's insults and jeers continue, uttered to no one in particular. "It's obviously some kind of ploy."

But I can't hear anything Letta's complaining about. I'm looking at Patty, who's as awestruck as I am. "What did he say about a dress?"

Chapter Forty-Three
The Fall Dance

Letta disappears after lunch without another word to anyone. I don't see her after school, but there's no room in my brain for Letta right now anyway. Shane appeared after the dismissal bell long enough to give Patty a quick kiss on the cheek before disappearing on some mysterious, but Patty fantasized romantic, errand. Patty walks halfway home with me, spouting off about how great the dance will be the entire way, barely stopping to breathe. She practically floats down her street when we part ways.

The Bauer's house is dark and empty. Puzzled, I wonder if they've taken Liam on some errand around town, but when I get home, Liam sits alone at the kitchen table with his snack. Mother apparently left work early with a headache and picked Liam up from school.

I sit next to Liam with a bright smile, bursting to tell someone about my day. "How was your day, squiggle worm?"

Liam shrugs. "Okay."

I deflate a little. "Just okay?"

"Kelly wasn't there," he says. "She's one of my friends."

"A *girl*-friend?" I ask with a wink.

He scrunches up his face, "No!"

"Oh, well, why's that got you down? Is she sick?"

Liam pauses, his blue eyes sinking away from mine. "I dunno. There's a box for you," he says, changing the subject. "It's on your bed."

Remembering what Ronan said about a dress, I leap from the room like a gazelle without another thought about Liam or his little girlfriend. A large gift-wrapped box tied with fancy red ribbon lies on my bed. I pounce on it and tear the wrapping away, gasping with glee when I see what's inside.

I stand in front of the mirror, holding the dress up to my shoulders and admiring my reflection. It's so perfect my eyes water. It isn't so old-fashioned that it needs layers of crinoline, nor is it so modern that it looks like a cheap costume. The long lacey sleeves will reveal the pale, alabaster skin of my arms. The plunging neckline is much too low for Elizabeth Bennet's taste, but it's perfect for me. The high waist is outlined with a blue ribbon that laces up the back. The smooth, off-white silk flows to the floor like the skirts of a Greek goddess. I'm so in love with this dress that the perma-smile on my lips hurts my cheeks.

As I twirl around the room with the dress, contemplating how I'll accent it and what I'll do with my hair, I pay no attention to the diary on my nightstand. I don't notice it's open, pen lying beside the once naked pages. I don't see the new entries, entries I don't remember writing.

An unseen breeze flips to a new blank, yellowed page. Scrawling black ink appears as if oozing from the diary itself like venom. First a word, then a sentence, a paragraph. More paragraphs. Another unseen breeze, another filled page, another entry…

*   *   *

Once I see the dress, everything else disappears. My eyes are doused with images of ruling over the dance, Queen Rose and King Ronan. I don't need to check with Mother about going out on short notice; that's not Texas Rose's style. I don't need to check in with Liam; he's being taken care of. With those two small weights off my mind, I'm free to be who I want, who I truly am. For the first time in months, the world is tilting back onto its normal axis and I finally feel like myself.

I finish primping right before the doorbell rings at seven sharp. I've accented my new dress with a string of pearls and matching earrings from my great-grandmother, and a dainty gold bracelet, a sweet sixteen present from my parents. My hair is swept into a dramatic up-do with a few soft curls framing my face. My face is made up in the perfect Texas Rose fashion with dark mysterious eyes and velvety red, kissable lips.

I slip into my low silver heels so I won't tower over Ronan, who's a shade shorter than me, on the dance floor, and try to slow my beating heart. I'm excited, thrilled even. I can't remember the last time I felt so alive. I'll show up to the dance with Ronan, the most sought after boy in school. I'll be radiant, beautiful. All of those small town bitches will be jealous of *me* for once, and I'll delight in their envy. It'll be perfect.

But I don't want Ronan to know how eager I am. He's the one who should be excited to attend the dance with me. He's the one who should feel lucky, like his prayers have been answered. So as I waltz slowly down the stairs, I take several deep breaths and master a look of calm, cool detachment.

Ronan presents me with a broad smile and a small carnation wrist corsage, which he places gently around my wrist. He's wearing the same outfit he wore for his grand invitation at lunch, but has accented the dark blue fabric of his suit jacket with a small red rose peeking out of the front pocket. He seems startled when he finally looks at me, like he's been expecting someone else. My beauty has stunned him, I realize with relish.

"Uh – erm, my lady," he says, bowing before me.

I giggle despite myself and curtsy in return. "Good sir."

"Our chariot awaits!" He stands tall and motions toward the familiar black BMW SUV.

I reach for my scarf and coat, which Ronan helps me slip into like a perfect gentleman, and then close the door behind us.

As Ronan helps me into the car, I'm not thinking about Mother, or Liam, or the house. I'm not wondering why there isn't a thin spire of smoke coming from the O'Dwyre chimney. I'm not thinking about Letta and her empty house. I'm thinking of nothing save for all of the green, envious eyes that will greet me at the dance.

*   *   *

True to his word, Ronan treats me to an elegant dinner. Between Port Braseham and Bar Harbor is one lone restaurant, Borachio's Cucina. It's a small shack on the outside, a place I wouldn't have looked at twice, but it's incredibly opulent inside and crowded with couples from all over the island, being well known for its authentic cuisine. The menus are entirely in Italian and with a discreet nod from the maître d as we arrived, I have the feeling Ronan is well known here. I wonder how many candlelit dinners he's enjoyed here with Mary. Was this *their* place? Well, even if it was, it doesn't matter. *I'm* the one who's here with him now.

We're seated at a small table in front of a large window overlooking the water. The sun has set and the water is a roiling black mass twinkling under the light of the full moon.

"So," Ronan says, somewhat awkwardly.

I look at him, refreshing my memory on how attractive he is. Glossy, dentist brochure smile, gym sculpted muscles, light chestnut hair… An Adonis. I smile, but let the silence grow between us as I think of how many times I've misjudged him. Initially I'd pegged him as an ally, a way to raise my own stature in the Port Braseham high school politico. Then I'd found him to be an egotistical manwhore. But at the storm party he'd revealed what I thought was a sensitive underbelly. And here he is, mixing up my thoughts all over again, being sweet and romantic – but I don't trust him. There's something slick and oily beneath his gentlemanly demeanor. So, let him sweat it out.

"Do you like the dress?" he finally asks, after the waiter bows obsequiously and slips away with our menus. Ronan ordered for both of us in flawless Italian, impressive, even if he's only flaunting it to impress me.

"It's beautiful," I say, trying not to gush as my hand absently runs over the smooth fabric in my lap, and then I ask him a question that's been bugging me all afternoon. "How'd you know I liked *Pride and Prejudice?*"

He laughs, but then leans toward me conspiratorially. He slides a lotioned hand across the table and lifts mine from the stem of my water glass, cradling it gently. "It's not a big secret is it? You only carry it with you everywhere. I've seen it mixed in with your books more than once, and a few times on the table at lunch." He shrugs. "I took a shot."

Took a shot. Pfft. As if the great Ronan Quinn ever just improvises. No, it was a calculated move. I wonder what exactly he's planning.

"Have you read it?" I ask hopefully, and a tinge of red flushes his cheeks.

"No, actually."

"Isn't it required reading for junior year?"

"Yeah," he admits with a sheepish smile. "Mary and I had the same teachah last yeah, and she read it, so…"

I stiffen at Mary's name. I wonder if this is all some kind of game to him, if I'm just some new conquest to add to his belt. My guard rises like hackles.

"Why do you like it so much?" he asks, and he sounds genuine. "A bunch of old Victorian stiffs vyin' for the hearts of silly little tarts? Sounds *awful.*"

"It's romantic," I reply defensively. "Two people who seem to hate each other, from opposite sides of the tracks, who fall victim to their own hypocritical beliefs and pride. In the end, they realize they're wrong, that they were really falling in love without even knowing it. I think it's beautiful."

"So is that the secret tah your heart, Rose Delaney?" Ronan's eyes are now piercing mine, one eyebrow raised ever so slightly. "Wistful, Victorian romance?"

I control the urge to laugh. He's trying so hard to woo me, but it's awkward for him. No doubt I'm his first real challenge in a town where most girls are dying to go on a date with him. And I'm certainly not going to throw him a bone. It's fun to be chased again, to see someone so confident struggle a little bit, to feel power over someone. "I'm afraid it's a lot more complicated than that. The secret to my heart is just that," I say coyly – two can play this game – and pull my hand away from his, "a secret."

"We'll see 'bout that," he murmurs as he lifts a goblet of ice water to his thin lips.

Before I can respond, the waiter returns with our appetizer, which he lays before us with a flourish of his wrists, as if presenting a great feast.

*   *   *

I eat quietly, listening to Ronan, who likes the sound of his own voice. He tells me more of the town's history, mostly related to his own family, especially his father as head of the historical society. I try to appear interested, but I don't want to talk about history. I want to enjoy this night away from the house, spend my night trying to remember who I used to be, the strong and powerful Texas Rose who didn't take no guff from nobody. Eventually Ronan asks me about myself, about Texas, my family, my hobbies; but it's a perfunctory effort. I'm careful with my responses. Let him work for it; if he's being genuine, he won't mind.

Ronan tries convincing me to split some tiramisu, but I decline. I wasn't really hungry to begin with and don't want to feel fat in my beautiful dress. Ronan snaps his fingers for the bill and leaves a very generous tip. He lets the billfold sit open an extra beat, pretending to check his math, to make sure I notice.

We arrive at the dance fashionably late. Judging by the cars in the parking lot, Ronan and I are the only ones still missing. No doubt everyone's anticipating our arrival, dying to know what I'm wearing, how I look. Ronan, playing the part of Perfect Gentleman, helps me out of the car, and walks me to the doors of the gym with care, making sure the hem of my dress doesn't drag through the mud puddles.

My heart flutters as we approach the doors. This is it. This is my moment. This is the moment when everyone will realize how wrong they were to judge me.

Ronan opens the squawking gym doors just as a song is ending. All heads turn in our direction as he hooks his arm through mine and we make our grand entrance. The collective gasps of the girls are audible as they see my perfect beauty. Immediately my eyes search out Mary, finding her on the dance floor with her usual cronies. Her jaw clenches in silent fury, her fists as tight as screws. I have to admit she looks pretty good, even if a little clichéd, in a short, black number. She's ordinary compared to me and her girlfriends know it. They pat her shoulders in consolation, as if to say *Better luck next time, Mare*. A devilish smirk slides onto my lips and I wink at her.

Drown, I think. *Drown* in your jealousy. *Drown* in your envious, green ocean.

Sound fills the room again as a slow song warbles from the D.J.'s speakers and couples head for the dance floor. With a huge smile, Ronan leads me to the center of the floor, holding our hands high, as if showing me off to everyone. We stop amid the other couples who are now slowly swaying to the music. Ronan twirls me toward him and pulls me close. His cool hand slips around my waist and rests on the small of my back while the other guides my hand to his shoulder. We dance, face-to-face, eye-to-eye. His russet doe eyes cry innocence, but his crooked smile says something else entirely. As his other hand slides lower, I conjure the image of a tightly coiled snake ready to spring.

"You're beautiful, Rose Delaney," he says, looking deeply into my eyes and then leans his head forward.

"I know." I look away and put my cheek on his shoulder, avoiding his impending kiss. His step falters only a moment before his muscles relax and he pulls me closer so our hips almost touch.

I survey the scene as we casually drift in a spiral. The gym looks basically the same as it always does despite a large disco ball hanging from a rafter, and a sprinkling of patio tables and chairs with little paper lanterns on top. Students have gathered together in their usual social circles around the dance floor, which is sparser, with perhaps ten couples daring to slow dance along with us. As we turn, I catch sight of Patty and Shane.

Patty wears a short canary yellow, A-line dress. With a yellow headband, a pair of opal earrings and a matching necklace, she's the perfect fifties beauty. Shane wears a tight fitting hipster suit with a red bowtie and a small carnation peeking from the lapel. Patty rests her head on Shane's chest as he rests his chin on her soft hair. They wear lazy, blissful smiles. It's an adorable sight and my heart trills for them.

Ronan and I continue shuffling our feet, and Patty and Shane disappear. A few groups are obviously gossiping about Ronan and me. A young couple paws each other next to the bleachers before being pulled apart by a chaperone. It's a typical high school dance: gossip, jealousy, and hormones. God, I've missed the normalcy that accompanies something as simple as a school dance. I'm reminded of my old girlfriends in Texas. Did they miss me at Homecoming? How's the cheerleading team doing without my leadership? Did I leave any real impact on them at all?

Screw them. They don't matter. They're nothings. I'm the star tonight. All I have to do is look at Mary's pretty face, made ugly by her envy; I'm finally beginning to leave my mark on Port Braseham. They'll remember Rose Delaney. As our eyes meet, I allow myself a slow wink at Mary. Her cheeks flush and she whirls away in a blur.

I'm facing entrance to the gym again and notice shadows moving beyond the doors a second before they open with a loud and ominous *squeeeeaaaakkk.*

My thudding heart comes to a cold stop, and my face drains of blood. I'm shocked, confused, angry; I can't even process what I'm seeing.

Beckan has stepped out of the darkness beyond the doors and into the dim light of the gym. He wears a buttoned up long-sleeved dress shirt, simple and plain, tucked into a pair of dark slacks that run a little long. The hems crumple on top of black dress shoes, dulled with age. He's clean-shaven for the first time since we met. His bottle green eyes dance with gold specks in the sparkling light of the disco ball. His reddish brown hair is trimmed and neat with a little gel to keep it out of his face. He's the most handsome I've ever seen him, and I suddenly remember how his strong arms pulled me away from the cliff, how his soft eyes comforted me when I told him about my father, and most vividly, how his warm hand felt leading mine through the park.

Beckan locks his eyes on mine immediately, as if he's been looking for me his whole life. I raise my head off of Ronan's shoulder, my heart suddenly beating again. He starts to smile, but falters when he sees I'm shaking with pure fury.

Because right there, clinging to Beckan's arm, is Letta.

Chapter Forty-Four
What Happened to Eileen

The music fades as the doors clatter closed. Letta is her usual, tiny, pixie self. Her dress is a short, simple baby pink number, and despite the height difference between them, she wears a pair of black ballet flats. She smiles awkwardly and, taking Beckan's huge lion mitt in her tiny kitten paw, walks toward me.

My head is filled with angry white noise and the edges of my vision blur.

"Rose?" Ronan's voice breaks through the haze. "You okay?"

"What? Yeah. Yes," I stutter. "But, um, would you excuse me a minute?"

"Um, sure," he says, a hint of displeasure in his voice.

"Be right back." I retreat from the dance floor and dart across the gym, fleeing Beckan and Letta as fast as my shoes will allow. I burst into a darkened hallway and slip into the girls' bathroom. I press my back against the closed door and take a deep breath, trying to ward off the sudden urge to cry. What's *wrong* with me?

"Hello? Is someone there?"

Startled, I gather myself and round the privacy wall. Eileen stands in front of a sink, several pieces of toilet paper crumpled up in the basin. Her classically beautiful face is red and her makeup is splotched, dark mascara circles under each eye.

"Um, hi," I say awkwardly. I haven't talked to Eileen since she ran screaming from my house. Now here she is, crying her eyes out.

Eileen smiles weakly. "Hi."

"So…" I lean against the furthest sink from Eileen. "Are you okay?" It's a ridiculous question; obviously she's not okay. But you can't walk away from a girl sobbing alone in a bathroom in the middle of a school dance. It's an unwritten code among women: You must ask the lonely crying girl in the bathroom if she's alright. Even if you don't want to help her, at least you'll get something to offer up to the gossip gods later.

"Gawd!" Eileen laughs and rolls her eyes. She rips several squares of toilet paper off of a strand she has bunched up in one of her hands and wipes her nose. "No. Can't stop cryin' tah save my life." She laughs again and then glances at me through her reflection. "I'm sorry. Why should you care 'bout my problems? You probably hate me."

A little, I think, but I say, "No. I'm confused though."

"Me too." She dips her head, holding onto the sink with both hands and her shoulders shake with sobs.

Cautiously, I step closer and put a hand on her shoulder. "Do you want to talk about it?"

Eileen sniffs loudly and looks at me for a long time before she replies. "Rose," she says with real regret in her eyes, "I'm sorry 'bout what I told everyone 'bout that night at your house. I don't know why..." She shrugs and looks down, frowning. "I was scared."

Well, hello old friend, I think as the hole in my stomach reappears. I've managed to keep it at bay since lunch, but now it crawls back down into my gut and I have the sensation of being pulled by my belly button, as if the house is calling to me, saying *Hey, Rose. Remember me?*

I think back to that night. Eileen's scream, seeing the whites of her frightened eyes, like a deer right before it jumps into the headlights of your car. My own fear as I watched the front doors bulge open. My own scream and the strange voice calling to me.

Let me in.

I grab Eileen's shoulders and turn her around, looking into her dark eyes, pleading. "Eileen...what *happened* that night?"

Eileen's eyes well up again and she chokes on a sob, looking away, but I force her to look me in the eyes again. "Tell me, Eileen. *Please.*"

Eileen takes a deep breath and steadies herself with a nod, preparing to relive the worst moment of her life. "Okay... Okay." Another deep breath. "I was in the basement," she begins, "with Shane and Patty. We went intah the room underneath the stairs, the one with the dirt floor, right? I saw this little door in the back corner. And, I dunno, I just *had* to go in there..." She turns away from me, putting her hands back on the sink, and I watch her knuckles turn white.

"As soon as I went in, the door closed behind me." Her voice is quiet, made sinister in the echoing bathroom acoustics.

"It was cold. Freezin'. It smelled coppery, like mud. And it was pitch dark. Couldn't see anythin'. Then all of a sudden, there was this *light* comin' from a mirror."

"The one with all the cracks?" I'm surprised to hear how hushed my own voice has become. I immediately remember my first and only encounter in the basement of Wolfhowl Manor; the strange dirt room, the broken kaleidoscope of a mirror, the strong, invisible hand on my shoulder... Dread cascades over me like an icy shroud.

Eileen nods. "Curious, right? So, I went ovah to it. Looked intah the mirror."

A long silence passes between us, the deep thud of the D.J.'s bass barely penetrating the thick walls. I finally ask, "W-what did you see?"

"Death." Eileen's voice is so low I barely hear her. "It was like watchin' an old home movie, dark and kind of blurry. I saw my parents layin' in their bed. But the covers weren't right, their bodies weren't... And that's when I saw the light again. Only it wasn't a light. It was a reflection. It was the glint off of my dad's gun in his hand. And then I saw Kelly—"

"Kelly?" I interrupt, the name ringing an urgent bell in my mind.

"My little sistah," Eileen smiles a little. "She just turned six... She's got class with your brothah, right? Liam?"

I swallow hard. My mouth runs dry. "Yeah."

"She's just a tiny scrid of a thin', you know? All of a sudden, there she was in front of me, in that cold little room, in the mirror. She was in her little princess bed, sleepin' I thought. But her head was layin' funny. Her neck was *twisted*. They were all dead. My whole family. *Dead...* And then this strange music began to fill my ears, quiet at first, but then loud. I thought maybe Shane and Patty had found an old music box or somethin'."

I think I know exactly what song Eileen heard, but I don't dare interrupt her.

"And then I was holdin' a shard of glass in my hand." Eileen holds up a hand, as if holding an invisible piece of glass between two delicate fingers. She brings it over to her other wrist, turns it up. "Must've been a piece of the mirror. I think... I must've pulled it loose with my nails, pried it off of the mirror. And I couldn't look away from it. I couldn't look away! My family was there, dead, splayed out before me like ragdolls and all I could do was gawk like some gawmy idiot..."

"And then I heard *the voice.*" Eileen turns toward me, her eyes unfocused, still far away, as tears fall silently down her cheeks. Her voice trembles with urgency. "It said *'It's so easy, Eileen. Easy.'* It said, *'Look at them. Look how* lonely *they are. Your family needs you, Eileen. They* need *you. Join them, Eileen. It's so easy.'"*

I watch, horrified, as Eileen moves the hand with the invisible shard of glass over her pale wrist, her sinuous veins fairly glowing beneath her skin. She makes a slashing motion, quick and angry. I can almost see the spurt of imaginary blood. It makes me nauseous.

"I felt it, Rose," Eileen says, looking at her hands for a long time, and then slowly lowering them back to the sink, holding onto the edges as if they're the only thing keeping her standing. "I felt that shard of glass slicin' into my skin as sure as I feel this porcelain." She looks at me hard. "I thought I'd done it. I thought I was dead... All I remember aftah that is screamin'."

My mind is overloaded with images and sounds. I search for something comforting to say, something to make Eileen feel better, but come up empty. Instead I ask, "Is Kelly okay?"

Eileen frowns. "I dunno. She hasn't been to school all week. Mom's been takin' her to doc aftah doc."

"Why?"

Eileen shrugs, a helpless gesture. "She stopped talkin' aftah..." Her voice trails off.

"After what?"

"Aftah I told her what happened on the mountain."

"You *told* her?"

"She was askin' a lot of questions," Eileen explains desperately. "She has a little thin' for your brothah, you know? A crush. So she was askin' me all these thins about you and your family and Liam... And I couldn't get away from what happened that night. I've thought about it *every* second of *every* day. Dreamed 'bout it at night. I couldn't talk 'bout it with anyone and heeah Kelly was, askin' me all these questions. I thought... I thought if I told someone, *maybe it would all go away...*"

I sigh. I want to tell Eileen she's crazy. You can't tell a six year old something like that. For a six year old to see her teenage sister's naked fear is to take away all safety and innocence from the world. But I don't say this. I can't; I know exactly how Eileen feels. Liam's cherub-like face pops into my mind and my heart grows heavy.

"I nevah thought 'bout suicide before. Never," Eileen says, shaking her head. "But evah since that night... I think 'bout it all

the time. *All* the time. I don't know why. I don't *want* to die…
but deep down, it feels like it's only a matter of time before I end
it. It's only a matter of time, and I can't stop it."

Eileen's words chill me to the bone.

"D'you think she'll be okay," Eileen asks. "Kelly? She'll be
okay won't she?" Eileen's dark brown eyes are begging. *C'mon,
Ghost Girl. Tell me my little sister will be okay.*

"Yeah," I lie. "She'll be okay. Of course she'll be okay."

Eileen smiles weakly. "Thanks, Rose. Thanks for list'nin'.
Bet you're glad you asked, right?" She laughs, but it's mirthless, a
dead echo against the porcelain and tile. She turns back to the
mirror with resolve, an emotionless mask sliding over her
features. She rips off another square of toilet paper and goes
about fixing her makeup. "Well, you bettah get back tah the
party," she says. "You don't want tah keep Ronan waitin' too
long."

"Yeah. I'll see you around, I guess."

"Yeah," Eileen replies without turning around. "See you
'round."

I back slowly out of the bathroom and return to the gym,
now thumping with nineties club music. Someone should let the
D.J. know it's okay to play songs from this decade.

"Rose!" Ronan calls me over to a table where he's talking
with some of the usuals from his lunch table. He stands as I
approach. "I was startin' tah worry," he says, irritated.

"Sorry," I reply, trying to sound normal, unflustered. "Ran
into some friends in the bathroom. You know, girl talk." I
manage a convincing smirk, hoping he'll think I've been talking
about him for the last fifteen minutes.

"Oh, well," he says with a smile, "I suppose I can forgive
you." He puts his hands on my waist and pulls me close. "Want
tah get back tah the dance floor?"

Ronan is really letting his accent come out around me, like
the night at the waterfall. Without Mary hovering around him
and demanding perfect diction, he's more relaxed. I look at the
dance floor. On the opposite side Letta and Beckan stand with
Patty and Shane. The four of them huddle close together, talking
animatedly. Shane says something funny and they all laugh. Letta
tilts her head back and puts her hand on Beckan's arm. He starts,
surprised by the familiar gesture. When he looks up, his eyes
catch mine. He raises a hand, as if to wave, and a surge of bitter
anger overtakes me.

I turn back to Ronan, laying my hands on his chest and letting them slide up toward his neck. I pop his collar and pull him close. For a second he's startled, but then he smirks, and leans his face in. We kiss.

Ronan's lips are cool, familiar. He's delicate with me, but I'm not in the mood to be delicate. I guide his lips apart with my own and bite his bottom lip.

Ronan pulls away with a pained, surprised smile. "Well aren't you friendly?"

I give him another light peck in response and his eyes reappraise me.

"Do you want tah get out of heeah?"

"Yeah," I say with another glance over his shoulder. "I do."

As Ronan takes my hand and leads me toward the exit, I catch sight of my friends across the dance floor. Letta and Patty share an O-shaped gape while Shane stares with a raised eyebrow, but Beckan... Beckan looks confused, and maybe a little hurt.

I smirk. *Good.*

Chapter Forty-Five
The Portrait

Beckan pulls his truck into the gravely patch serving as the O'Dwyre driveway a little after midnight. A steady drizzle falls, dampening his mood as much as his clothes. Although it's a frigid evening, he didn't wear his flannel coat over his dress shirt – it seemed wrong somehow to pull something so casual over his formal attire, and he was nervous enough attending the dance to begin with that a coat hadn't seemed important five hours ago.

When Letta came to his door earlier that evening, he'd steadfastly refused to go along with her scheme. He's a twenty-year-old high school dropout whose unpopularity followed him into adulthood. Attending the dance was a stupid, ridiculous, utterly *insane* idea… How had she ever convinced him that his opinion on the matter was *wrong?* I'm an idiot for listening, he thinks. It was a total disaster. Rose practically burst into flames the second she saw him, her anger flowing off in heat waves so hot he felt them across the gym. Why was she so angry? What had *he* done to invoke such bitterness? He'd thought he'd finally broken through that icy wall of hers, had himself convinced she cared for him, that she was finally realizing what a great person she could be beyond all of the superficial crap.

And then she'd left the dance with that haughty asshat.

As if he needed a reminder, Ronan's BMW speeds down the mountain's steep driveway as the sound of the closing red doors echo toward him. What did they do after they left the dance, he wonders. He'd stayed for Letta, who was determined to pretend to enjoy herself. True to her word, she'd tried desperately hard to have a good time – dancing to every song, singing along with Patty, laughing at everything a little too loudly. But even though Beckan hardly knew Letta, he could tell it was all a show. He saw the sadness through the smiling mask and found himself wondering if the rumors he'd heard about Letta and Ronan were true – that would certainly explain her odd behavior. But he didn't dare ask her. She deserves more respect than that.

After the dance, they'd gone for a late night snack at The Wharf Rat with the rest of the dance-goers. Shane and Patty were syrupy and languid across from his stiff form and Letta's twitchy energy. Others stared at Beckan and Letta – they made an awkward couple – and he'd felt his ears burning all night long, knowing people were talking about him. It's a feeling he's unfortunately familiar with.

But where did Ronan take Rose? They weren't among the rest of Port Braseham's teens flooding the only place in town still open. What had they been *doing* for the last few hours? Abruptly, the image of Ronan with his wiry arms around Rose as they kissed floats before his eyes.

With ugly, unpleasant thoughts, Beckan stalks to his own front door and enters the blackness of the cabin, slamming the door like a petulant child.

Derry waits for him in his rocking chair by the hearth, Lady at his feet. She lifts her head for a brief scritch between the ears before Beckan sits heavily across from his father, the wood of his own rocking chair letting out a protesting creak. Derry holds a steaming cup of tea in his mitts and his chin juts toward an identical mug on the coffee table. Beckan picks it up but doesn't drink, instead letting it warm his hands.

"Well," Derry says, his deep voice making Beckan's tea erupt in small ripples.

"I don't want tah talk 'bout it."

Derry sits silently, ever so slightly moving his chair back and forth. He stares at his son, his little pinhole eyes boring into Beckan, the only sound the groaning of the wood beneath their chairs and the hissing crackles of the dying fire in the hearth.

"She's so stubborn," Beckan finally says when he thinks the silence might kill him. "And angry."

Derry doesn't reply.

Futility wraps around Beckan like a blanket. He sags, his heart sitting slightly lower in his chest. Lady crawls over to him and lays her head in his lap with a whine and a thump of her tail. As he pets her soft head, the moisture brims up behind his eyes. The urge to cry becomes stronger and he fights it with all he has in him. He hasn't cried since his mother's funeral and he suddenly feels like a small boy again, watching the undertaker crank the shiny black coffin lower, lower, lower… until it disappeared into the shadowy abyss of the grave. Then, as suddenly as the image appeared, it's gone, and he steels himself with resolve. No. He won't cry over her.

"I'm losin' her, Pop," he says quietly.

"Ayuh." Derry sighs sadly, thickening the air of desperation in their little cabin.

In the distance, a wolf howls and Lady thumps her tail on the floor with a whimper.

*　　　　　*　　　　　*

As I approach the bloody doors of Wolfhowl Manor, I turn and wave to Ronan. He waves back, a little disappointedly, before speeding away.

Tonight was certainly interesting. It had started out with such promise, such potential… and then had gone so quickly and steadily downhill that I'm as angry and depressed as ever.

Beckan and Letta showed up at the dance *together.* Unshakeable shock and betrayal clamped down on me like a vise. How could Letta do that to me? I shake my head to rid it of my depressing thoughts, but they refuse to loosen their grip. How could I have been so wrong about Beckan? And Letta – who was supposedly my friend? They don't really care about me. They aren't my friends. I'm nothing to them. *Nothing.* Like ships passing in the night, we'd had our brief and fleeting moment, and now Rose Delaney will fade into the darkness, becoming another piece of Port Braseham folklore.

I pull out my keys as I remember kissing Ronan at the dance. It'd been an impulsive reaction to my anger, something Texas Rose would've done. He'd practically sailed out of the dance with me, smirking ear to ear. He drove me to some deserted spot. It was dark and lonely, thunder rolling in the background. He barely had the car in park before he was pawing at me. I played along for a while, but leading him on wasn't my intent. I'd just wanted Beckan and Letta to feel a shade of the anger I felt.

Ronan's hands were greedy. He was gentle at first, but then became more insistent, passionate even, and his strength in the lonely darkness unnerved me. I'd barely managed to fend him off. I know what Ronan was after of course, and I have zero intention of giving it to him – I didn't achieve popularity among the boys in Texas by giving them what they wanted. It was *not* giving them what they wanted that kept them interested, kept them coming back with puppy dog eyes, begging for more like little orphan Oliver. I'm a conquest, a challenge…and boys, especially those like Ronan Quinn, crave a challenge, want to add Rose Delaney to the notches on their belt.

Now, with Ronan hooked, I may as well use his influence to better my situation. I'm done playing the role of social outcast, done taking a back seat to Mary Donovan, done carving myself into the bottom of the totem pole. I *deserve* my rightful place, *deserve* to be wanted and adored by my classmates, and with Ronan on my arm, I'll finally usurp Mary's throne. After all the grief Ronan and his friends have caused me, he owes me that much.

So, I played coy. I'd cocked a sly eyebrow at him, adjusted my wrinkled dress, and gave him a smile. "It's getting late," I'd said quietly. "I'd better be getting home. Mom will start to worry soon." He has no way of knowing that's a total lie.

Ronan returned my smile with a crooked one of his own, something dark lurking behind his eyes. He leaned back and straightened his jacket, taking a deep breath. "Sure," he said with a great deal of control before reaching for the key and starting the engine.

Ronan begrudgingly offered to take me for some ice cream before going home. We'd talked for a while, sitting in a convenience store parking lot and eating ice cream sandwiches, but Ronan was moody and I just wanted to forget this whole night ever happened.

And now, here I am, back home. Bitter. Angry. Sad. With a long sigh, I open the door and go inside. I'm surprised to find the chandelier still on and it takes a moment for my eyes to adjust. When they do, I'm confused to see Mother at the top of the staircase, standing outside the fire room's door. She's as motionless as a statue, one hand resting lazily on the banister. Her long, fiery hair is pulled back into a loose ponytail, a few errant strands pasted to her cheeks by sweat. Her eyes are unusually dark and far away, like Eileen's when she told me what happened in the basement. She wears a long form-fitting nightgown. The ivory color glows in the yellowy light of the chandelier like a ghostly aura. Something about the thin straps of the shoulder, the low v of the neck with the pearl embroidery at the center is familiar. Where had I seen it –

And then I know. It's Alison Boyle's nightgown, the one from my dream. The one she wore when she killed poor Hagan. The one she lay next to his body in, right before putting the gun to her head.

"Mom?" I check to make sure the doors are locked and then head up the stairs, slowly at first, and then as fast as my feet will allow. "Mom?" She doesn't look at me until I grab her shoulders and turn them toward me. She blinks once, twice, as if coming out of a dream.

"Rose, honey," she says slowly, "what's wrong?"

"What's – I – you – um." I don't know what to say, can't put my thoughts into words. I take a deep breath, trying to slow my racing brain. "Mom, what are you doing? It's after midnight."

Mother looks at me, then around, finally realizing she's not in bed. "Oh, I got up to...well...I guess I forget what I got up for." She smiles sheepishly. "Well, say, don't you look fancy? What are you all dressed up for?"

"Mom! The dan –" I start impatiently, but then remember I'd never told her about the dance. "Nevermind. Let's get you back to bed." I put an arm around her shoulders and gently guide her back to her bedroom. I help Mother climb back into bed, throwing crumpled tissues out of the way and darting my eyes around the room, inspecting, looking for something, but I'm not sure what.

"Mom," I say as I pull the duvet up to her chin, "where did you get that nightgown? Is it new?"

She yawns. "Oh, I was wandering around earlier, cleaning up. Found my way into the attic. Did you know there are a bunch of boxes up there?"

"Oh?" I reply nonchalantly, my eyes still searching the room. What am I looking for?

"Yeah. Anyway," Mother continues, stifling another yawn, "I found this laying at the bottom of one of them. It was a little dingy, but in good condition. Had funny some stains on it, but they came out with a little elbow grease and detergent."

"Good condition," I repeat, my uneasiness growing.

"Yeah. Can you imagine, all those years in the attic, and no moths had gotten to it? It's pretty comfortable." She gently rubs the fabric between her fingers. Then she smiles at me and closes her eyes. "Goodnight sweetie."

"'Night, Mom." I say, my skin erupting in goose bumps. I back out of her room, my eyes searching the whole way, beginning to realize what I'm looking for.

Leaning against Mother's door, I close my eyes, trying to conjure up the memory. I picture the box Mother mentioned, try to see its contents. It's smaller than the other boxes and had been nearly full to the brim with bow ties, a cigarette holder, colorful scarves, bobby pins, a gold hand mirror, and underneath some glossy ivory fabric – Alison's nightgown – something dark and shiny...*Hagan's gun.*

My eyes burst open. I run to my room, flinging off my shoes as I attack my closet, digging like a dog through clothes and shoes, throwing everything behind me, as I search for the gun. What did I do with it after that awful dream? It has to be in here. *Has to be.* But it isn't.

Where is it? I have to know.

Panicking, I go to my nightstand and rip the drawer out, sending it clattering to the floor. I drop to my knees and snatch up the old skeleton key. My bare feet race down the main stairs as the skirt of my dress flutters around me like a ghost. I run through the kitchen, and up, up, up the servant stairs until I burst into the dark open air of the third floor. I reach out and flip on the dingy bulb at the center of the large space.

The third floor is as I'd left it; cold and echoing with the increasing patter of the rain, the footsteps Letta and I had left in the dust. The doors to the library and the two smaller rooms are closed. The door to the balcony at the top of the stairs rattles in its frame as it's assaulted by the wind. I close my eyes and listen, but hear nothing unusual over the roar of the storm outside.

Tentatively, I head for the portrait hall, my heart thudding in my chest and pounding in my ears, and stare hard into the darkness. I can barely make out the attic door at the end. It's open, a black pit yawning beyond. Why didn't I grab a flashlight? I'd rushed up here so quickly and completely forgotten how creepy this floor is, even in the daylight, and how terrifying it is in the dark.

Then I wonder how Mother got into the attic. I know I locked the door last time, and the only key is in my trembling hand. I did lock it...didn't I?

I work my way down the hall slowly, sliding a hand along the wall to guide me. A soft, icy draft flows from the open door. The wind whistles through the house. Somewhere the rain has penetrated and a slow *drip, drip, drip* echoes back toward me. As I approach the open attic door, it begins to swing closed from the draft – I hope – and I lurch out to catch it. I can barely see the bottom stair in the dim light of the bulb far behind me.

It's freezing. My dress provides no protection from the damp chill, and my bare feet feel like icicles on the old wood. Taking a deep breath, I push myself over the threshold and up the steps. I reach blindly for the string to the light.

I blink in the sudden light. The last time I was up here it'd been an overcast morning with blips of light sneaking in through cracks in the wooden slats. In the dark of a stormy moonless night, no light filters in. The walls lay beyond the darkness, invisible. I feel like a target in my small circle of light.

The boxes are here. It's a matter of seconds to locate the Boyles' belongings. I rip open the box, rifling through it. I paw my way to the bottom and see the old gun is here, laying innocently on the bottom. I let my hand caress the cold metal, proving to myself it's really there, that I'm not hallucinating, that my family is safe from this particular threat... but *who* put the gun back up here? The question fades in my relief that Mother hadn't grabbed the revolver on her sleepwalk. If she had...

I begin crying. My sobs are loud and uncontrolled, shaking my whole body. One emotion becomes another, and then another. I feel myself letting go of everything I've been holding back since we moved, since Dad died. The dam has finally been overwhelmed, and everything I am comes pouring out.

A loud boom of thunder finally brings me back to my senses, back to the mountain, to Wolfhowl Manor. Sniffing, wiping my face on one of the old scarves, I slowly close the Boyle's box and get to my feet. I retreat down the stairs, close the door to the attic and lock it, jiggling the knob hard just to be sure, and then take the key back into the open air of the third floor. Impulsively, I walk into the old bathroom in the corner. It's similar to the one downstairs, with a tank hanging on the wall above the toilet. I lift the lid, drop the key into the moldy bowl, and flush, watching as the key swishes around in the swirling water and then disappears.

I'm at the top of the stairs and reaching for the light switch when a tingling at the back of my neck stops me. Two realizations hit me at once; I forgot to turn the attic light off, and in that extra light at the bottom of the attic steps, right before I closed the door, I noticed something on the wall – one of the portraits is different.

I return to the hall, walking to the last portrait before the attic door. It's the oddly blank portrait, containing only the background of the fireplace in the drawing room.

Only it isn't blank anymore.

Standing in front of the fireplace is my family. Liam, cherub-like face beaming from ear to ear, waves one hand while holding a sandwich in the other. He wears his favorite SpongeBob Squarepants t-shirt and blue pants, his Spiderman backpack at his feet. Sticking out of the front pocket is one of his little army men. Mother stands behind him, arms hanging limply at her sides. Not reaching out for her son, not waving, just drooping. Her whole frame folds in on itself under an invisible weight. Her dark eyes are fixed and vacant, staring beyond the phantom photographer. She's wan and thin. It's an unfortunately accurate likeness of who she's become.

And that's it, just Liam and Mother.

I'm an orphan now. Daughter of no one. Sister to no one. Mother and Liam have been lost to the house.

Chapter Forty-Six
Letta and Ronan

Thanksgiving came quickly. The steady drizzle of rain continued throughout November, knocking the orange and red leaves off the trees before they could be admired. The soggy weather didn't stop the inhabitants of Port Braseham from celebrating the holiday appropriately, however. The main street was decked out in streamers of brown, red, and orange. Banners declared the time and location of the annual parade. At this precise moment, the town is gathered, viewing floats under a hoard of black umbrellas. The Bar Harbor Volunteer Fire Department leads the way with their brightly polished red engine, horn blaring. The townspeople allow themselves a day of friendly faces, good times, and light hearts.

But inside Wolfhowl Manor, all is dark, cold, quiet...

Liam sits on the couch, watching cartoons under a warm wool blanket with a PB&J in one hand and a hot chocolate in the other. He chews each bite thoroughly, washes it down with a gulp of liquefied chocolate, and carefully keeps the couch and floor clear of crumbs or dribbles – he doesn't want to upset Her by making a mess. He licks his lips, smacking at his chocolate moustache, then remembers his manners and uses a napkin.

Upstairs, two women sit alone, each shut up in her room, each feverishly scribbling in identical diaries. The real world outside Wolfhowl Manor has become increasingly fuzzy to one, and all but invisible to the other.

*　　　　　　*　　　　　　*

I'm huddled up under the comforter for warmth. I pause to look over my entries from the last few weeks. I pour over the mysterious words I'd found upon returning from the attic the night of the dance.

I feel so lost. So lost and so sad. What's the point in trying anymore?

I run a finger over the words, feeling their indentation in the soft paper.

Anyone who cares about me is gone. Why do I insist on staying? There's nothing here for me. Nothing. It would be so easy.

I don't remember writing these words, yet here they are, in my own curly handwriting. And, most disturbing of all, they're *true*.

I return to my current entry. I've started several times, but keep crossing out my words and starting over. It's getting more difficult to express my thoughts. I take a deep breath and try again.

What a strange trinket you are, Little Diary. So substantial in my hands, yet so mysterious. Magical. When I pick you up, I feel a compulsion, a need to spell it all out, all my anger and sadness and bitterness. I've never felt so strongly about anything in my life. Maybe this explains the mysterious entries that seem to ooze out of you every few days. Am I so depressed that I can't even remember writing in my own diary?

It's still raining. I thought the only place that rained like this was Seattle – or maybe Forks. It's cold enough to snow, to cover Port Braseham in a beautiful, heavy, pristine winter wonderland, but all it does is rain. I don't even know what silence is anymore. There's always the drip, drip, drip of the rain. Even when it isn't raining, I hear it. I hear it in my dreams. It's tangled up inside every thought. Rain. Rain. Rain. For some reason, it reminds me of a poem I heard once:

> Yesterday, upon the stair,
> I met a man who wasn't there
> He wasn't there again today
> I wish, I wish he'd go away…

But the man – the rain – never goes away.

I haven't seen Letta in forever. Sure, she pops up in the edges of the crowd every once in a while, but then dissolves like a ghost. She doesn't eat lunch with Shane and Patty anymore, which is probably good because they're still sappy and puppy-dog eyed. She's paler and darker than ever. Her jaw and her fists are always clenched, like she'd like to punch someone (maybe me). Obviously, when she does see me, I'm with Ronan. (We've been

spending a lot of time together, not that I need to remind you!) She's so
angry. I wish I knew –
    No. I wish nothing for her. Not even happiness. She betrayed YOU,
Rose. She broke YOUR heart. You owe her nothing but hatred.

Yes, exactly, I think, looking down at the diary. I wipe a tear
from my eye and keep writing.

I haven't so much as seen Beckan's back since the dance. At first I
thought he was avoiding me and coming into the house when I'm at school,
but now I don't think he comes up here at all. Nothing seems different.
Physically, the house remains the same – stagnant and falling apart. I
haven't even seen Derry's bulldog face checking in. Are they content to let
Her sit in disrepair, in the hopes that She'll just collapse and melt away?
Then I'd disappear too, and they can stop worrying about me. Not that they
actually worry about me. Have they given up on me?
    Whatever. Good. So much the better. I have no desire to see any of
them, the whole hateful lot of them. Derry, Beckan, Letta… they can all
kiss my Texas ass.
    I'm so cold. Are you cold? It's like I've fallen into an emptiness of the
soul.
    It would be so easy, Rose. Yes, it would be so easy…

    Ronan.
    The dim light in the dark. (Sort of.)
    He's growing on me, I'll admit. If it weren't for him, I'd spend all my
spare time shut up in here, waiting for my face to appear in the portrait hall.
As it is, he struggles to get me out. I have to give him credit for being so
persistent. He's been working hard to win me over. Is he truly done with
Mary? Does he actually care about me? It doesn't seem possible that he
could care about anything besides his own reflection. He's always looking in
every mirror, every window he passes, preening like a peacock. Is that for me
too?
    He invited me to the parade today, to hang out with him and the other
Populars, but I just don't feel like pretending today. Maybe if he comes over
later he can convince me to go to dinner. Not that I'm hungry. I haven't been
hungry in at least a week. I can't even remember the last time I ate…
Yesterday? The day before? A banana, I think?
    I see Ronan in the hall between every class for a chaste peck on the
cheek. He'd love to go for more – and he's tried – but I'm determined to
start over around here because my reputation is all I've got left. Although
removing "ghost" from my moniker and just calling me Slut Girl is a small
improvement, I won't settle for that. Ronan needs to struggle before he can

*conquer me — if he conquers me — because the whole school must see that it's
me who has power over him. Being Ronan's Girlfriend isn't the title I
want. It's Ronan who should feel lucky to carry the title of Rose's Boyfriend.
To conquer Ronan is to conquer the whole school.*

And how they will pay for the way they've treated you.

*I've been getting little morsels of Ronan a bit at a time. He's a hard
one to crack. No one really knows who he is on the inside, not even him. In
many ways, Ronan reminds me of myself.*

*Ronan's parents don't put much time in their schedule for him, and
maybe that's why being popular is so important to him. His father is always
busy, away on business, in meetings, working late (with his pretty secretary, I
hear). His mother does some interior design, but it's more like a hobby. She
spends more time at the bottom of a wine bottle and watching bad reality
TV than she does decorating. At the same time there's this pressure on
Ronan to be great at everything. His grades must be great. His friends must
be great. (I bet they just love me, the very un-great pariah. Perhaps that's
why I haven't been invited to Chateau d'Quinn yet.) He must be great at
basketball since he, disappointingly, didn't make the football team. (His
father says his football performance is "embarrassing," "dreadful even.") I
would feel bad for him, but…*

*I'm right about him being a ladies' man. Although he's been with
Mary since freshman year, he's been caught with other girls before, at parties
or parked somewhere in the dark. Apparently, Mary is just as guilty, or so
Eileen's told me. — She spends a lot of time with Ronan's group, but she
still seems sad.*

*Apparently, there was a significant break up last year, before
Christmas, in which they both dated other people. Mary dated someone
unimportant, but Ronan, he found someone important. He found a girl who
caused quite a stir — but no one will tell me who she was. They whisper
about her like she died or something. Every time her name is about to slip,
Ronan appears and someone changes the subject.*

*What happened? Did he actually have his cold little heart broken? Is
that even possible? I wonder if —*

The doorbell startles me. Checking the clock, I see it's
almost five. Maybe Ronan really has come up to pry me out of
my hermit shell.

I put the diary in my nightstand drawer. I stop by the mirror
on the back of my closet door. My hair is dull and my face is
pale, but my clothes are fresh and clean. I pop into the bathroom
and paint on my red lips before answering the door, doing my
very best to ignore how much every muscle aches, how much

my face hurts if I try to smile, and how very full my heart is of the miserable rain.

The doorbell rings a second time right before I open the door.

My forced smile falters, fades, disappears.

Letta.

I can't hide the flush of anger and betrayal rising on my cheeks, but I do manage to clamp my mouth shut before I burst into obscenities. Crossing my arms and glaring, I wait.

Letta looks just as furious and uncomfortable. It's still cold outside, still raining, and she hugs a heavy rain jacket around her small body. For the first time I notice how *haunted* Letta looks. Dark circles ring her eyes as if she hasn't slept in a month and her face is so pale she's almost transparent.

Letta sighs heavily before finally speaking in a clipped voice. "May I come in? *Please.*"

I hesitate, but curiosity beats out anger and I step aside.

Letta steps over the threshold, but doesn't take off her jacket. She turns toward the living room and sees Liam, eyes glued to the T.V., and looks back at me.

"Let's go to the kitchen." I lead Letta through the hall. I walk to the kitchen sink and peer out at the darkening winter sky beyond the cliff. I see Mother standing there, ready to jump. For a moment, my heart lurches, but a creak overhead reminds me she's still in her room. I relax. Mother's image flickers and disappears.

Letta sits at the kitchen table and picks at her hands. I hear her sigh, but she says nothing.

"What do you want?" I finally ask.

"I came to talk to you," Letta replies quietly.

"Obviously." I turn around, prepared to spit something nasty at her, but Letta's eyes are glassy as she looks up. Something tugs at me and I leave the sink and sit across from Letta, suddenly worried.

"What's wrong?"

Letta keeps her eyes down. "I need to talk to you about Ronan."

"What about him?"

"Remember a while ago, when I told you that something happened with him, but I couldn't tell you?" She sounds absolutely pitiful.

Of course, I realize. *Of course!* What an idiot I've been. "Vaguely…" I say, beginning to feel like a class A bitch.

"It isn't any easier," Letta says, carefully avoiding my eyes, "telling you about it now. But every time I see you with him – I," she sighs. "You've got to know."

"Know what?" I reach across the table and grab one of Letta's tiny, cold hands. "Know *what*, Letta?"

She finally looks at me. Her shoulders sag under the weight of the coming confession. "About what happened between me and Ronan last year."

I freeze as a violent urge to disbelieve everything Letta's about to say wells up within me. It *can't* be. It's not possible. Letta *can't* be the girl everyone's afraid to talk about, because if she is, then I'm the worst friend to ever live.

"Tell me," I whisper, swallowing with difficulty.

Letta stops and starts several times before her story finally comes tumbling out. "I'd only been here about a year, you know? I moved here right after winter break my sophomore year. Like you, I wasn't exactly popular at first. There wasn't anyone to hate up here on the hill, so most people directed their nastiness toward my family because we're the only Jewish people within, like, a hundred miles. And I didn't make friends with Patty until after all of this happened."

"What did they do?"

"They called me Anne Frank, made comments about my 'schnoz' and mocked Hanukkah and put a gas mask in my locker." When she sees my shocked face, she adds, "No, it's okay. That didn't even really bother me. It isn't even the first time I've been treated like that." Her nonchalance about such ugliness makes me feel sick.

"Anyway," Letta continues, "Mary and Ronan had some explosive fight over Eileen right after school started last year. Yeah, you didn't know about Eileen either, right? They had some fling at the storm party, and Mary went ballistic when she found out. I guess it's okay for Ronan to kiss other girls, but the rumor is he and Eileen did *a lot* more than kiss.

"Anyway, after all that blew up, Ronan started talking to me, but you know, nicely. I was so stunned I guess I didn't really stop to think about why. One time I was talking to him at my locker. When I opened it, there was that damn gas mask for, like, the twentieth time. Ronan reached in and pulled it out, shook it around and yelled for the whole hall to hear, 'It ain't funny, ya gawmy idiots!' and then threw it to the ground. It was a nice gesture." Letta smiles a little. "It was nice to have someone stand up for me for once…

"Then he started walking me to class every day. He'd give me rides to school. Then he asked me for help with some of his classes, so we spent a lot of time together at the library or wherever. Of course, I thought he was *so* hot, and he knew it. But I never had a shot with him. I figured, as nice as he was being, he just wanted to copy my homework without being an asshole about it. Maybe he just wanted to make Mary jealous."

"But you were wrong."

Letta sighs. "So wrong, and so *stupid.*"

"The Fall Dance?" I ask.

"Yeah," Letta answers quietly, and adds with a wry smile, "How'd you guess? ...He asked me to the dance about a week before. I was totally floored! I mean, why me? The drama with Eileen had died down. Mary had dumped whoever she was dating, so I'd assumed he'd be going with her. I'm not gonna lie. I felt a little like Cinderella." She flashes me a sheepish smile. "So, Mom made me a dress – don't make that face. It was actually very nice. – He picked me up at exactly seven and we went to some expensive Italian place for dinner." My cheeks grow hot as my complete idiocy becomes clear.

"After dinner, we went to the dance. It was an *okay* time. I'm not a very good dancer, but he was patient and he complimented me all night, told me how pretty I was... That fucking windbag!" She takes a deep breath to calm herself. "We left around ten and went for a drive..." Here Letta looks down at her lap. She takes a few deep breaths and I realize she's fighting back tears.

"Sorry," she says, sniffing. "It's still hard to talk about... We went for a drive near the park. There were some other cars around, all with steamed up windows. I knew right away he wanted to steam up his own windows. I'm ashamed to admit I was flattered. I'd never had a boyfriend before or really dated at all. I'd certainly never kissed anyone before."

No one? It seems impossible when I think about how many lips mine have met.

"So, we kissed. He's a good kisser." I nod when Letta looks up with a small smile – it's true. "And then it became clear that wasn't *all* he wanted. I told him I didn't want to. He told me I was just nervous or scared. He said it'd be fun. He'd be gentle. Everyone else was doing it and didn't I want to be like everyone else? Which, of course, I did."

I suddenly feel very sad for my friend. "Letta... did you...?" I let the question hang in the air; I've no right to even ask it.

366

"No," Letta shakes her head vehemently. *"No.* I thought I wanted to at the time, but I couldn't bring myself to do it. It just didn't feel right. When I pushed him away, he seemed hurt or confused. Maybe angry. I don't know, but his eyes got very dark. It scared me."

I silently cheer Letta for standing up for herself when so many other girls wouldn't have. I know how charming Ronan can be, and how persistent. "Then?"

Letta shrugs. "He took me home. Said he'd talk to me the next day, which he didn't. I didn't see him again until Monday. My bra, which he'd wanted to keep as some kind of *Sixteen Candles* souvenir, was stuck to my locker. Someone wrote 'Jewish Slut' across the front in red paint. Ronan was laughing with all of his friends, said 'Isn't that funny, Anne Frank?' I was crushed. I thought I mattered to him, that he cared about me. And, though it hurt, and it was so very, *very* embarrassing, it wasn't even the worst." I can't imagine how it could get any worse.

"Even though he didn't get past first base, the rumors spread pretty quickly about how I'd begged him to…*you know.* He said it was all my idea and he'd only given in because he felt sorry for me. He told everyone we did *it,* and that I was *awful* at it. Then he was so mean to me. He'd shout at me across the cafeteria and say the most disgusting things, or he'd make kissy faces at me in the hall and then pretend to vomit. Everyone laughed. It's the worst I've ever felt in my whole life. I wanted to die." The tears finally begin to roll down Letta's cheeks, and I wish I could do something to make her feel better. It's awful. *Ronan's* awful. And here I am, Letta's supposed friend, dating the guy who'd done something so terrible to her. I feel like the worst kind of idiot on planet Earth.

"Oh, Letta," I say, "I'm such an idiot! I'm *so* sorry."

"Me too," she smiles. "I'm sorry about the dance."

"You don't have anything to be sorry about," I say. "I should've known." Or worse, maybe I *had* known all along and just ignored it so I didn't have to feel guilty.

"I want you to know I didn't bring Beckan to hurt you," Letta says. "I only went to the dance to keep an eye on you and Ronan. I was afraid he'd do the same thing to you that he'd done to me. I made Beckan go in case I needed some muscle. I had a really hard time convincing him to go, if that makes you feel any better. In the end, he only went because he cared about you. I actually thought I could get you away from Ronan and get you dancing with Beckan. Then you wouldn't leave the dance with

Ronan. But when I saw your face, I realized I'd made a *huge* mistake… Beckan really cares about you, you know."

I snort.

"No, really," Letta says earnestly. "I think he might even love you."

I laugh; if only that could possibly be true. "No, Letta. He doesn't love me. I haven't even seen him in weeks."

"I know, and it's my fault! I should've been honest with you. Then all this could've been avoided… What'd you guys do after the dance anyway? Did you…"

"No," I shake my head. "He tried, but I've been playing that game a long time." I realize how condescending I sound, which makes me feel worse. "I'm sure that's the only reason he's still hanging around. He'd just as soon do me dirty the way he did you."

Letta stares at her lap. "I wish I was stronger, like you."

That cuts me deep, and I rush to make Letta feel better. "Oh Letta, you *are* strong. What happened isn't your fault. It's *Ronan's* fault. He's a convincing liar and you trusted him. He's the one who took advantage of you, and that can never be your fault. You *should* be able to trust people. It's just a shame in this world that you can't. The only reason you think I'm strong is because I've made a life out of not trusting people. I don't want that for you."

Letta squeezes my hand. "Thanks."

Letta's cell phone starts ringing from a jacket pocket just as the ominous echo of the doorbell sounds.

I hand Letta a napkin so she can dab her eyes and smile. "Answer your phone. I'll get the door."

Ronan's ears must've been burning because he's standing on the other side of the door, confident and cool as ever.

"Hey baby," he says with a toothy grin. "Miss me?"

"Hey," I reply icily. "How was the parade?" I stand just inside the threshold with crossed arms, the door just wide enough for me, which puts Ronan off.

"Oh, the usual," he says, sounding suspicious. "You know, turkeys, lots of orange and red. And rain of course." He holds up a folded black umbrella. "Get your shoes and let's get some dinnah. A bunch of us are headed for The Wharf Rat." Looking beyond him, I see his SUV idling in the driveway, the shadowy figures of friends waiting for his return.

I stay quiet, waging a silent war in my head. What am I supposed to do? My gut tells me I have to refuse him, have to break up with him on the spot, for the sake of my friend. He's an asshole, will always be an asshole. It's only a matter of time before he treats me the way he treated Letta, right? But the other side of me thinks about how different things have been since we started dating. How different it feels to be accepted and talked to and invited places. I picture Mary's angry face every time she sees us together. I enjoy that image, hold it up in my mind, salivating at the sensation of revenge. Is it really worth it? Is popularity worth the only real friend I've made here – or actually, ever?

"C'mon," Ronan says when I don't' reply. "Let's go. Shake a leg!"

Letta's footsteps come up behind me. When I turn, her face is dark, her phone still held up to an ear and her demeanor is urgent.

"What the hell's Anne Frank doin' heeah?" Ronan demands when the door falls open to reveal Letta.

The *snap* sounds in my head a second before I ball up my fist and knock Ronan square in the nose. The pain in my knuckles is immediate, but so is the sense of relief that comes with it. The anger vibrates out of my body with the jarring stop of my bones as they hit Ronan's face. His painful grunt brings me sheer joy. Somewhere, my anger management counselor is frowning.

Ronan stumbles backward cradling his nose as he half-falls, half-stumbles down the front steps, landing on his ass in the mud. Blood colors his fingers as he shouts. "What the hell, Rose! What was that for?!"

Letta rushes up next to me as I shake out my hand. "Oh my God, Rose!" She's positively gleeful.

"You broke my nose, bitch!" Ronan shouts as he gets up, still clutching at his face. "You broke my damn nose!"

"Good," I say, staring down at him.

"Good?" Ronan glares at Letta with pure hatred. *"You!* This is *your* fault!" He looks at me, sees my fury growing and starts backpedaling. "Rose, baby, I can explain," he pleads. "For God's sake, get me a towel!" His eyes tear up and he squints in pain.

I'm unmoved. "Get off my steps and don't come back." I slam the door.

"Bitch!" Ronan yells before finally retreating, more obscenities following him.

"I cannot believe you just *did* that!" Letta shouts, the phone call nearly forgotten. "How'd it feel?"

369

"So good," I say, almost laughing. "But my hand hurts something awful."

Letta bends over my hand and examines it like a professional. "It seems okay. Probably going to be sore for a few days."

"Yeah," I sigh, knowing from experience she's right. I look at her, tiny little Letta, my true friend, even though I'm completely unworthy. I feel a rush of terrible guilt. "Thank you, Letta. Thank you for telling me about Ronan. Thank you for trying to protect me. I'm sorry I was such a bitch. Really, *really* sorry. Can you forgive me?"

"Of course!" Letta shouts. "You just broke Ronan's nose! We're friends forever now! I can't wait to tell Patty —" She breaks off, looking down at the cell phone in her hand. "Oh. Right."

"What's wrong now?" I ask, wondering what else could possibly go wrong.

Letta frowns. "That was Patty on the phone."

"And?" I'm growing more anxious by the second.

"Eileen's sister is dead."

Chapter Forty-Seven
The Funeral

It's been three days since Patty's phone call. I still feel like wind has been knocked out of me. Mother Nature seems to understand the Pattons' loss; their grief is accompanied by a torrent of rain, hail, and thunder.

I try to picture Kelly, a miniature Eileen – classically beautiful and mini-fashionista. I bet she was a fiery little girl full of love and tantrums at the same time. I can't fathom how something like this could happen to a child.

Kelly's death spread through town like fire. Eileen's family gathered on Thanksgiving Day, intending to attend the parade together. Aunts, uncles, grandparents – all had arrived as usual. They were determined to carry on as they normally would, hoping it would help Kelly get better. As they prepared to set out for the parade, they noticed little Kelly was missing. Eileen went to get her, figuring she was taking a nap in her room, as she'd been doing so much lately. It was less than a minute before the family heard Eileen's scream.

There's nothing violent about Kelly's death. She looked peaceful, as Eileen described her in the vision. Her neck wasn't broken. Her wrists weren't slashed. She was simply dead, as if she'd died in her sleep. No foul play is suspected but, of course, everyone's pinned the blame squarely on Wolfhowl Mountain, and by association, on my family – we've awakened the beast within.

I want more than anything to tell everyone they're wrong, to prove the house has nothing to do with it. That *we* have nothing to do with it.

But that, I know, is a lie.

It's Monday, but school is canceled in remembrance, the flag at half-staff. Saddened as I am, I'm glad there's no school. I don't want to face Ronan or his friends. With his broken nose, on top of Kelly's death, I'm certain I'll be met with pitchforks and flaming torches. I wouldn't be surprised if they show up on the front lawn.

The sound of clicking heels breaks into my thoughts as Mother descends the staircase and enters the living room, where I'm moping with Liam. She's gaunt and dull looking in her long black garb. "Ready?"

Mother insists we attend the funeral, much to my horror. That's exactly the *last* place we should be. But my pleas fell on deaf ears, which is why, at this moment, I'm wearing a knee-length black skirt and an equally black sweater and black flats. Liam, on the other hand, hasn't bathed or dressed and refuses to go. After all, he'd insisted earlier, Kelly deserved to die.

I'd rebuked him immediately. *"Liam!* You shouldn't say such things! Why would you say something so terrible?"

"She wasn't nice," he'd whined. "She said mean things about Her, that She was haunted and She should burn down! Kelly said She was evil!"

I was taken aback, frightened even, but Mother didn't have the energy to argue with him. She'd said he could stay home and watch cartoons. She refused my protests that Liam shouldn't be left alone, reasoning, of course, that he *wouldn't be* alone.

I get up, trying to ignore the sense of foreboding squirming inside me.

"Should we bring something?" Mother asks, shrugging on her coat. "Flowers?"

Fuel for their torches?

"No." I put on my coat without looking at Mother.

The short drive to the church is silent. There are so many cars in the parking lot we have to park on the street and jog through the driving rain in our fancy clothes and footwear. My feet are soaked and frozen. We enter the nave like soggy dogs just as the funeral mass begins. The heavy door closes behind us, disrupting the reserved silence.

The church is beautiful. The altar is covered with the most flowers I've ever seen in one place. Roses, lilies, daffodils, shamrocks, pansies… It's amazing to see, and their fragrant scents flow all the way to the back of the church. The colorful walls of stained glass are darkened by the storm outside. Each attendee holds a small candle, sending the flowers into a gauzy glow before the little coffin. A priest stands beside the shiny mahogany box, Bible open in his hands. Enit sits in the front pew. Her friend sits at the organ, frowning as she plays a dirge. Most powerful of all are the sorrowful faces turning to us, moistened by their tears. I feel their anguish. My own eyes well up. *Is this what it'll be like if Liam dies? Will he lay in a beautiful church, surrounded by an entire town who loved him?* But I can only picture the church, huge and empty, Liam resting alone in his tiny coffin. No flowers. No tears. No mourners. I close my eyes, seeing Liam's dead body in the coffin, not Kelly's.

Mother reaches out and squeezes my hand just before a loud jeer echoes from the silence of the crowded pews.

"You! What do you think you're doin' heeah?" A woman at the front of the church stands and makes her way toward us at alarming speed. *"Just what do you think you're doin' heeah!"*

I recognize Eileen's features immediately – Mrs. Patton. Eileen follows her mother down the aisle.

Oh no. I start backing up, tugging on Mother's coat sleeve. I feel like a deer frozen in the headlights of a Mac truck, about to become meat in the road.

"I told you this was a bad idea," I whisper, trying to pull Mother toward the doors. "We should never have come."

"We've done nothing wrong, Rose," Mother says angrily. "Nothing!"

There's no mistaking it now; we're not welcome, here or anywhere else. Others are on their feet now, glaring at us, an angry mob. They flood the aisles, following Eileen and her mother. The nave echoes with their angry shouts. Ronan's at the front of the pack, sporting two black eyes and a bandaged nose. He's next to Mary, who's smiling cruelly. Shane and Patty are there too, watching the ugly scene unfolding before them with horror.

Mrs. Patton reaches us first, her teeth bared, practically snarling at us. Grief has turned her into a feral animal. She raises a claw and smacks Mother with all of her strength.

Mother stumbles backward, her mouth open in shock. "We only meant to express our sympathy," Mother says, her voice shaking and a hand on her reddening cheek.

Mrs. Patton raises her hand to smack Mother again, but Derry, materializing out of the shadows with Beckan right beside him, catches her wrist. She writhes in his strong grip, but he doesn't let go.

"You don't get tah be heeah!" she shouts, gesturing wildly with her free hand as the tears flow. "You don't get tah tell me how sorry you are when your children live! This is all your fault, witch! You and your dammed family! You took my Kelly from me! *You!* It should be your child who's dead, not mine!"

"Calm down, Marnie," Derry says soothingly. It's the most I've ever heard him say. Mrs. Patton turns on him, finally wrenching herself free.

"Don't you go comfortin' me, Derry O'Dwyre! If she's the witch, then you're the devil! All of you!" She falls back into another man, Mr. Patton, dissolving into wracking sobs.

"I'm so sorry," I say, pulling Mother away from the mob. "We're so sorry, Eileen."

Eileen keeps her wide eyes on her mother, her mouth sewn shut, and my heart sinks to my feet.

"Get out!" Eileen's father shouts. "The whole lot of you!" He points to Derry and Beckan, who look ready for a fight, fists and teeth clenched. "None of you belong heeah!"

"C'mon," Beckan says, pushing past Derry and taking my hand. "Let's go."

Derry follows, guiding Mother by her shoulders. Tears stream down her cheeks and she manages to choke out a very small sounding, "I'm sorry for your loss," before Derry finally turns her around and leads her out of the church.

As we descend the front steps, the doors swinging slowly closed, we hear the anguished cries of Mrs. Patton echoing after us. "It's you who should be dead! *You!*"

*   *   *

An hour later, I'm seated in one of the O'Dwyre's rocking chairs, staring at the fire. Derry took Mother home to rest. She was so distraught when we left the church that Derry had to drive our car, afraid she'd run it off the road. I'm delaying my return to Her as long as possible, so I ride with Beckan, joining him in the cabin while we wait for Derry. I sway in the rocking chair with a cup of cooling tea in my hands and Lady's warm head resting on my feet. Beckan stands at the window, gazing out in the direction of Wolfhowl Manor.

"They've been gone a long time," I say. When Beckan doesn't reply I ask, "Do you think everything's okay?"

Beckan turns away from the window with a forced smile. "Everythin's fine. He's probably makin' her a cup of tea."

"I didn't know Derry was so domestic," I say, trying to sound normal, as if Beckan and I had never stopped speaking.

Beckan sits across from me. "Oh, he's got a soft undahbelly when he chooses tah show it." His eyes find their way back to the window. He tries to hide it, but he's worried.

"Is this the first time Derry's been inside since…" I don't know how to finish the question and it dies in my throat.

"Not the first time," Beckan sighs, sitting back in his chair. "Just the first time in a long time." He closes his eyes.

I stare at him as he rocks slowly. He looks good in black slacks and the same shirt he'd worn to the dance. He's clean-shaven, which I don't like as much as his usual five o'clock shadow. I smile when I notice he's wearing his mud-caked boots instead of dress shoes.

He looks dead tired. The worry lines run through his handsome face like tiny dried up riverbeds. I could be staring at a map of the draught-ridden Australian outback instead of his face. The stress of the last few months has aged him and I suddenly realize how much he looks like his father. I wonder if this is what happened to ol' Derry. Would he still have quarter deep wrinkles and beady, suspicious eyes if his wife were alive? Somehow, I assumed he'd been born that way, all frowny and wary.

Lady hears Derry's footfalls first, lifting her head and looking at the door expectantly. Derry enters, moving like his feet are made of lead. Lady whines and approaches him, her head and tail hung low. He reaches out to scratch her behind the ears and then shrugs off his wet jacket, hanging it on the coat rack by the door.

I set my untouched tea on the hearth. "Is she okay?"

Derry nods. "Just needin' some rest. Made her some tea and put her tah bed."

"Thank you," I say, feeling small in front of his penetrating gaze.

Derry grunts and disappears into the bowels of the cabin, Lady's paws clicking on the wood behind him.

Beckan stands and stretches, trying to rid himself of a tiredness that never seems to leave him anymore. "I'll walk you home. Rest would do you some good too."

I grab my coat from the rack without replying and Beckan is suddenly behind me, holding my coat for me as I shrug it on. He grabs an umbrella and then we're out in the cold rain, trudging up the muddy hill in silence.

The looming shadow of Wolfhowl Manor rises on the hill. The sharp turrets emerge like knives piercing the storm clouds. Ivy leaves flip over and over in the wind, waving us away. The crooked attic windows glare down disapprovingly. I feel heavier and heavier with each step.

Beckan walks close to me, holding the umbrella over the both of us with one hand and propelling me forward with his other arm around my shoulders. The wind brings the rain in horizontally and we're both soaked from the waist down. It's not until we reach the porch that we're finally sheltered from the rain.

I turn to Beckan and mumble, "Thanks." A gust of wind rushes up the hillside, throwing strands of hair into my face.

Beckan reaches up and gently tucks my hair behind an ear. "For what?"

I shrug. "I dunno. Just...thanks."

He smiles weakly. "Take care of yourself, Rose," he says seriously. "I'll be 'round in the mornin' tah check on you." He pauses, as if debating something in his head, and then bends down and brushes my cheek with a kiss. Then he turns away and disappears into the driving rain.

I stare after him, a small spark of warmth, the most I've felt in months, blossoming inside me. Then the rain and wind drive it away.

The house is dark and quiet, as usual. Liam is nowhere to be seen, probably playing in his room. I hang my dripping coat and go upstairs. I'm ready to change into sweatpants and spend the rest of the day zoning out in bed, but decide to check on Mother first. I open her door, expecting to see her thinning form under the comforter, but her bed is empty.

"Mom?" I take a few steps into the room and look around. The bathroom door is open and the light is off. A small trashcan overflows with used tissues. A cup of tea sits on the bedside table. Perplexed, I search out Liam.

He's in the playroom, sitting in the corner by the back turret. His back is to me as he quietly hums a familiar tune and plays with the dollhouse replica of Wolfhowl Manor. He doesn't turn around.

Standing behind him, I examine the dollhouse in more detail. I'm staring at the house as it would appear if someone had cut off the front wall. I can see into every room, down every hall, and I'm shocked to see how identical it is to the house as I know it. My room has the same princess bed with the repaired canopy and, as I lean closer, I realize the nightstand holds a tiny replica of *Pride and Prejudice*. Mother's room is in disarray, the bed unmade and the trashcan full of tiny tissues. A small television in the living room has a picture of Spongebob Squarepants taped to the screen. It sits in front of our own miniature couch. The upstairs library has the fancy chandelier and the shelves are filled with hundreds of tiny books, many of them lying in a heap on the floor as I remember finding them. Unpacked boxes are stacked in the drawing room. Liam's room has all of his tiny furniture and there, in the playroom, is a tiny little Liam sitting in front of a tiny little dollhouse.

"What the…" I whisper, leaning forward.

Liam holds up a hand, cradling a small doll with my long dark hair. He sets it carefully behind his own doll in the dollhouse's playroom. My pulse speeds up. Searching the dollhouse with my eyes, I look into the fire room, with the same fire-eaten wood beams and soot covered walls. There, lying on the floor of dollhouse's fire room, is a third miniature figure.

I turn and stare in the direction of the fire room, as if I can see through the walls. My heart leaps into my throat as I feel the fire room calling to me, pulsing behind the wall.

*   *   *

Beckan pauses halfway down the hill and stares back up at the house, the rain pelting him in the dim light of a stormy winter afternoon. He can't shake the worried thoughts from his head. For the first time in his life, he's truly afraid of what will happen, not just to Rose and her family, but to his town. The cycle has come back around and all he can think about is Kelly in her tiny coffin; innocent, peaceful, lifeless.

Something terrible is coming.

The faces he'd observed at the church were distraught. People who'd never even met Kelly flooded the church with their grim frowns, holding their own children tightly. Everyone's angry, but also afraid. They're all wondering, just as he is, how many children are going to die. And they're all hoping the Delaneys will die first, as if their deaths will satisfy the dark magic of the mountain, will save their own children from sharing Kelly's fate. He can see it in their eyes. A little desperate himself, Beckan wonders, as his family's ancestors had, What can *I* do to end the curse? How can they be saved? *Can* they be saved?

Suddenly he's alert, listening intently, focusing past the pelt of rain on his umbrella. He'd heard something over the howl of the wind. What was it?

There it is again. An animalistic sound, strange yet familiar. At first, his eyes dart around the yard, expecting to see one of the roaming wolves leering at him from the trees, but it isn't the typical bay of a wolf. It's a heartrending, totally inhuman sound. As it dies on the wind, Beckan realizes what it is.

A scream.

Beckan drops his umbrella and runs back up the hill as fast as his adrenaline can carry him. His boots slip and slide in the mud. He throws himself onto the porch and bursts through the red doors. They fly open and slam against the front wall. Rose stands at the top of the staircase, staring through the open door of the fire room from her knees. Her mouth is open so wide he thinks a demon might come pouring out. He races up to her as the awful shriek vomits from her lungs a third time. He falls to his own knees and grabs her by the shoulders. Her eyes are empty, unseeing.

"Rose!" He shakes her. *"Rose!* What's wrong?" He shakes her again, violently this time, but the scream dies in her throat and she faints. Beckan cradles her and then looks into the fire room, wondering what could possibly be so disturbing.

And that's when he sees Mrs. Delaney, swinging from one of the beams, a noose around her neck.

PART THREE

Chapter Forty-Eight
Orphan

My eyes sear with pain from the bright light. I turn my head to the side, trying to avoid the luminous, stark white. *Everything white except for the water.*

I blink rapidly, shielding my eyes with a hand. My vision adjusts and I find myself staring up at taupe, even straight squares of bland taupe with thousands of tiny divots. Ceiling tiles. My ears register the soft murmuring of voices nearby as the sound of rushing blood in my ears fades. Rubber-soled shoes patter quickly along linoleum halls. Faint beeping, phones ringing beyond. These, all the sights and sounds of a busy hospital.

I sigh, my lungs heavy, like they're full of water.

I'm so lonely, Rose.

I jolt upright. I'm alone in a narrow, windowless room. Two empty beds lay to my left. I'm dressed in a hospital gown, white with pale green dots. A small port has been inserted into the top of my left hand, an IV snaking out of it, and it throbs painfully. I contemplate pulling it out, but the sound of approaching voices stops me.

Letta, Beckan, and a stern looking man in police blues enter the room. Where's Mother?

"Rose!" Letta runs to me and hugs me tightly. I lift my arms, robotically folding them around her, still trying to understand what happened, why I'm here, and where exactly, *here* is.

I turn to Beckan as Letta releases me. "Where am I?"

"Bar Harbor Hospital," Letta says with a wince, as if afraid of what I'll say or do in reply.

"When is it?" I ask. What happened? Why can't I remember?

Beckan smiles weakly. "Wednesday morning."

"Wednesday!" My brain whirrs. What's the last thing I remember? Was it Sunday? Monday? And then it all comes

flooding back. The funeral for Kelly Patton. Mrs. Patton's hard slap against Mother's cheek. Our ejection from the angry church. And, oh no…

"Mother?" I lift my face, stealing a look at the policeman, who has yet to speak. He stands stiffly, a pad of paper and a pen in hand, a silent observing sentinel.

Beckan lowers himself onto the edge of my bed and gently takes my hand. "She's alive."

My body sags with relief. I close my eyes. Mother's limp form appears on the underside of my eyelids, jerking and gagging like a dying animal, and my eyes pop back open. "Why am I here?"

"You fainted," Beckan replies. "You woke up when the ambulance arrived, but you were hysterical. They sedated you."

"For *two* days?"

"You were pretty upset," Letta says. "They were afraid…"

"Afraid of what?" I fix Letta with a hard stare.

"Well, uh," she stutters, "they thought you might, um, hurt yourself."

Of course they thought that. *Of course.*

"Where is she?" I ask the policeman. "Where's my mother? Can I see her?"

The policeman finally steps forward and Letta and Beckan instinctively pull away. "She's here," he says in a deep voice, a frequency that puts me at ease, softens my nerves. His eyes are dark and piercing, questioning me without speaking. He perches lightly at the end of the bed. "I'm Officer Reagan with the Hancock County Police Department. Do you feel up to answering some questions?"

I don't know how I feel, but I nod anyway. Maybe I'll get some answers out of it.

"Good. First, can you tell me your name?"

"Rose," I say weakly, momentarily put off by such a simple question. "Rose Delaney."

"And where do you live?"

"In Port Braseham. On Wolfhowl Mountain. I—" Saying it out loud makes me realize, absurdly, I have no idea what my house number is. "I'm sorry. I don't know the address."

"That's okay," he says, his head bent over the pad of paper. "You're relatively new to town, I understand."

"Yeah," I reply. "We moved here from Texas in August."

"That's an awfully long way," he says kindly. "Mind if I ask why?"

"Because my mother is cra—" I catch myself, but the damage is done. Officer Reagan's eyebrows arch. I take a deep breath. "My dad died. It was tough on us. Mom thought new scenery would help. And what's more different from Texas than here?"

Officer Reagan nods again. "So your mother was having a tough time."

"We all were."

"All?" His eyebrows arch again. "Does someone else live with you and your mother?" He sounds confused. I glance at Letta and Beckan before replying. The stiff shake of Beckan's head is almost imperceptible.

"Um, no," I say. "Not anymore." I think about Liam, trying to hide my rising panic. Why isn't he here? Is he okay? Why doesn't Beckan want Officer Reagan to know about him?

"Let's talk about the other day," Officer Reagan says, clearing his throat. "Can you tell me what happened?"

My heart's beating too fast. My palms are clammy and my neck is hot. "Don't you know what happened?" I want to close my eyes, but remember Mother's puffy face and bulging eyes, and I force them to stay open.

"I have the basics," Reagan says, "but I still need you to tell me. I need to hear what happened from a witness."

The warmth creeps down my spine, my muscles tensing. I nod.

"Start with the funeral, if you please."

"Sure, yeah," I say, trying to stop the shaking in my voice, "We went to the funeral – well, we tried. But we aren't exactly popular in town and we were essentially chased out."

"Chased?" Reagan asks dubiously.

"Kelly Patton's mother smacked mine across the face."

"Why?"

"She was upset. Her daughter just died. Something like that makes people crazy, doesn't it?" Officer Reagan's eyes meet mine at the c-word and I chastise myself for using it.

"Then?" Reagan prods.

"We went home. Well, Mom went home. Mr. O'Dwyre drove her because she was so upset. I went home with Beckan and we talked for a while. Mr. O'Dwyre came back, said he put Mom to bed. Then Beckan walked me home."

"What did you do when you got home?"

The taught rope looked new.

I hesitate as my memory begins to swirl away like fog. I fold my hands together to stop the shaking. "I went to check on my mother."

"What did you see?" Reagan's voice is falling away and I look at him intently, trying to hold onto him with my eyes. "Where was she?"

A few feet of un-frayed, straw-like material gave way to a near perfect noose. Where had she learned to tie such a knot?

"She was in the fire room."

"I'm sorry, fire room?"

One slipper on a twitching foot, one lying on the fire-eaten floor beneath her.

"It's damaged," I say, my voice far away. "It was damaged in a fire before we moved in."

"Okay. What was your mother doing in this room?"

My chest tightens and my breath flees my lungs. "Um, she was...she..."

Fingers jerking at her sides, not reaching up for the tight noose. Tongue lolling between purpling lips.

Officer Reagan shifts his weight, looks up from his pad of paper. "It's okay, Rose. Take your time. Take a deep breath." He reaches out and puts a comforting hand over my shaking hands. He gives them a squeeze before letting go.

I fix Officer Reagan with a hard stare, the image of Mother now complete in my mind, a sharp photograph at the moment it was lit by flash. When I try to continue, my jaw clamps shut. My lips are glued together. I take a deep breath in through my nose. After what feels like forever, I finally manage to speak through clenched teeth, "She was dying... I – I screamed..." My whole body begins to shake, on the verge of convulsions. The world begins to fade, to get dark. I'm going to pass out again.

But suddenly the light comes back into the room. Beckan is at my side, a strong arm around my shoulders as he holds me to the earth.

"I think that's enough, Officer," he says coolly. "I arrived right aftah that and then she fainted."

Officer Regan looks at Beckan, sizing him up, trying to figure out how hard he can push. "That's right," he says. "And it was just you that found her, correct?"

Beckan nods. "Yes. I – I found them both. It was Rose's screams that alerted me. Rose's muthah was still alive. I cut her down and called the ambulance. Now, if you don't mind," he says sternly, "I think Rose has been through enough."

Officer Reagan, realizing he isn't going to get anything more from me, nods and puts his notes away. "Thank you, Miss Delaney, for your patience." He smiles, but it's a sad smile. "When you're feeling better, you'll have to come down to the police station and sign a statement. Just a formality. Give me a call when you're ready." He drops a business card on a tray by my bed, tips his hat, and then he's gone.

*　　　　　　*　　　　　　*

An hour later I'm dressed in the same dark clothes I'd worn to Kelly's funeral. I haven't officially been discharged yet, but a nurse came by with the doctor to remove the port from my hand, which now itches furiously. The doctor explained I need to rest for a few days, drink plenty of fluids, and avoid stress. Yeah, sure. *Let me get right on that.*

Beckan leads me through the bright corridors of the hospital, a strong hand cradling mine, Letta trailing quietly behind us. I lean into Beckan, his presence reassuring and calming. I realize he's the only thing keeping me grounded in this moment. Without him, I might float away, drift like a leaf on the wind for eternity.

We approach a set of heavy double doors beyond a busy reception area. Nurses bustle around, answering phones, laughing together in a corner, as if everything's normal. As if my world hasn't fallen apart. Why can't they see that the world is fracturing and dissolving away? Soon, we'll all disappear, fall into the dark and roiling abyss. Don't they know that?

Above the doors, painted in black block letters, I read: Psychiatric Ward. No one gets through without a code.

"Can I help you?" asks a nurse clad in a stark white uniform behind the desk.

"Yes," Beckan says, gesturing to me, still clinging to his arm, "This is Rose Delaney. Her muthah, Moira, was brought in a few days ago. She'd like tah see her."

"Just a moment." The nurse turns to her computer and types several commands, her face growing darker with each keystroke. "Delaney, you said?" Her voice is flat, unreadable.

"Yes."

The nurse stands. "Wait here please."

Letta sidles up next to me. She takes my other hand and squeezes it tightly.

After several minutes a loud buzzing sounds. A doctor emerges from the doors, walking briskly toward us. He's in his late fifties, with close-cropped white hair and kind blue eyes. His thin lips are pressed together seriously, but I can tell he's a caring man. He's devoid of anything marking him as a doctor, except for the long white coat. He doesn't carry a stethoscope, a clipboard of charts, or a pen. He wears a turtleneck with no buttons or zippers. Looking down, I notice he's wearing worn penny loafers, a shoe without any laces.

"Rose Delaney?" He says, looking between Letta and me.

"Yes?" I step forward, finally releasing Letta and Beckan's hands.

He smiles gently and shakes my hand. His grip is warm and reassuring. "Hi, Rose. I'm Doctor Fleur. How are you feeling?"

"Um, I dunno," I say, suddenly feeling like a specimen under a microscope. Dr. Fleur looks at me intently, appraising me.

"It's okay," he says when I find myself unable to continue. "I understand. So. You'd like to see your mother?"

I nod.

"I'll walk you back to see her, but I must caution you," he says quietly. "Her condition is not good. Don't worry," Doctor Fleur assures me when he sees my anxious expression. "She's perfectly safe here. But she's been through quite a lot, as you know. She won't look or behave like herself. It might be quite a shock for you."

"What do you mean?"

"Well, for starters," Doctor Fleur says, "she told me her children were dead."

I walk through the psychiatric ward with Doctor Fleur, forced to leave Beckan and Letta behind – only family allowed here. We pass several doors along the corridor, each locked and sealed with a small, reinforced window at the top. With each step, my apprehension increases. Why did Mother tell the doctors Liam and I were dead? What else has she told them?

Doctor Fleur finally pauses before a door, identical to the rest. "Here we are," he says, as if Disneyland is on the other side instead of my mentally unstable mother.

My heart leaps into my throat. "What's her condition," I ask. "I mean, is there a diagnosis?" As if having a name for whatever's wrong with Mother will somehow make me feel better.

"She's in a dissociative fugue state," he explains, "which is a fancy way of saying she isn't aware of herself or her surroundings. She has a vague memory that she was once a mother, but that's where any sense of who she is ends. We've also had to medicate her to prevent violent outbursts. When she first arrived, she tried to strangle an orderly and then began ripping at her own throat, so she's restrained for her safety and the safety of my staff."

Well, I was wrong; I feel worse. "Will she recover?"

Doctor Fleur frowns. He looks me directly in the eye. His voice softens. "Rose, I feel you're the kind of girl who likes to hear the blunt truth, so I won't sugarcoat it. In my experience, it's about fifty-fifty. She might get better with treatment. She might not. And if she does recover, she may never be the same or may suffer memory loss. Based on my observations since your mother has been under my care, it's quite possible this could be a permanent state for her. However, it's hard to be sure."

I stay silent, feeling my own sense of self slipping away.

Doctor Fleur pulls a ring of jingling keys from his pocket and, finding the right one, slips it into the lock. He opens the door, motioning for me to proceed ahead of him.

The room is small and bare, painted a familiar, soothing taupe. There are no windows, no chairs, no watercolors of flowers, no equipment of any kind; only a small bed with a metal frame. A frail body is strapped to it, staring at the ceiling.

Doctor Fleur lets the heavy door close behind us. He gives me an encouraging look and I slowly creep toward Mother. I'm amazed to see a stranger lying before me.

Mother's long red hair is dull, almost transparent. It splays out on the pillow like a dying fire. Her arms are bony, held to the bed frame with a pair of soft but sturdy-looking restraints. Her small feet protrude from the end of the hospital-issue blanket, also restrained. She has bruises on her ankles and wrists where orderlies held her down while she fought being restrained. Her neck is raw from the noose. The only thing telling me this empty shell is, in fact, Moira Delaney, are her fiery eyes, still unfocused and staring at the ceiling.

"You can talk to her," Doctor Fleur says. "Be careful to keep your voice positive and calm."

I approach the side of the bed, Mother's head tilting toward the noise of my footsteps. Her eyes don't move, don't focus on me. I sink to my knees to be eye level with her. I lean forward, struggle to find something to say, and finally settle on a quiet, tentative, "Mom?"

Mother's reaction is instant and violent. She lurches from the bed as far as the restraints will allow and hisses at me, *"I am no mother! My children are dead!"*

I fall back onto my hands and into the wall behind me. Mother's still reeling toward me, spitting hate and rage as I stare at her, awed and frightened.

"She took them from me! My children are dead! I am dead!"

And then, as if reaching the eye of a storm, Mother calms. Her eyes glaze over and she lays back on the bed, comatose, as if nothing happened.

I stay frozen on the floor, staring at Mother's pale face, until Doctor Fleur retrieves me. He gently helps me to my feet and practically carries me from the room, pausing long enough to lock the door behind us.

*　　　　*　　　　*

Doctor Fleur deposits me back into the care of Letta and Beckan, apologizing for Mother's outburst. He bids me a sad farewell and promises to keep me informed on Mother's condition. Neither Beckan nor Letta ask about Mother and I don't explain. We make our way silently back to the reception desk near the room I'd occupied, so I can be formally discharged.

"Now, as a minor, Miss Delaney," the discharge nurse says, "I can't release you to your own devices."

"What 'bout me?" Beckan asks. "I'm twenty and I live on the same property with my dad. We can look aftah her."

"I appreciate that," the nurse replies, "but unfortunately the law is clear. I have to release Miss Delaney into the care of a relative."

"A relative?" I echo.

"Yes. Fortunately," the nurse continues, "your grandmother arrived a few minutes ago."

"Grandmother?" I repeat, feeling like a confused parrot as I hand the clipboard of paperwork back to the nurse.

The nurse gestures to a row of chairs along the far wall. Following her gaze, I see several people sitting in the waiting area, but my eyes are immediately drawn to the small figure in the center row. Calmly, blankly staring at me from behind milky blue eyes is Enit O'Sullivan.

Chapter Forty-Nine
Emily Lenore II

The ride back from the hospital is quiet. Letta rides with Beckan, following Laura as she chauffeurs Enit and me to their house. Apparently, Enit thought I'd be safest with her and knew I couldn't be released to her if we weren't family, hence the lie about being my grandmother. The hospital hadn't even asked for her I.D. Why Enit thinks I'm safer with her, I've no idea, but I can't go back to the mountain, so I don't argue.

I stand in the cramped bathroom of the O'Sullivan's house. I run the freezing, rust-tinged water over my face several times, trying to wake myself up from this unending nightmare. I gaze into the dingy mirror, trying to take everything in – the shock, the disbelief. My gaunt face stares back at me with its sharp, pale cheekbones, its deep purple circles under dull, listless eyes. I barely recognize myself. Is it possible I'm still Texas Rose? The cheerleader, the confident beauty, the popular girl, every boy's dream? Does that Rose still exist in there somewhere?

I'm doubtful.

"The house has him now."

That's what Beckan told me, his eyes dark and his voice low. He sounded like he was apologizing, as if it was his fault. He explained that after I fainted and the ambulances arrived, along with the police and fire departments, Liam was forgotten in the chaos. His bedroom door, like all the others on the hall save for the fire room, was closed. No one thought anything of it. By the time Beckan remembered him, several hours had gone by and the house had already sealed Herself up. As if She'd finally gotten what She wanted and now no one would be allowed in. The keys don't turn the locks. The unlocked windows can't be opened. No one will be allowed to take away what's Hers this time.

Liam has become part of Her now, but what does that mean? Is he lost forever? Will he absorb into the walls and become part of Her? Will I ever see my baby brother again?

Fresh tears pool in my eyes, and a gut wrenching sob crawls from my throat. *Liam...*

There's a soft knock on the door. "Rose?" It's Beckan. "Are you okay?"

I take a deep breath to steady my voice. "Yes. I'm – I'm fine. I'll be out in a minute." I wait for his heavy footsteps to retreat before crying again, wiping my tears on the sleeve of the oversized white sweater Laura lent me. We're hardly the same size, for Laura O'Sullivan is heavier and a little shorter, but I can't exactly reject the generosity. All of my clothes are still up on Wolfhowl Mountain. I'm just glad to be out of the uncomfortable funeral attire and finally in something warm and soft. Laura also managed to find a pair of old jeans that actually fit pretty well with a belt, aside from being a little short.

After rallying myself and drying my face, I emerge from the bathroom into a narrow hall lined with framed photos, haphazardly hung with zero respect to gravitational forces. Enit's house is one of the oldest in town, right down the road from Saint Perpetua. It was originally a tiny log cabin occupied by a priest, but was later made suitable for a small family by a mismatching whitewashed addition. Every angle is crooked, every ceiling concave, every floorboard creaky, and the wind barrels through it like a windsock. But it doesn't feel ominous or dreary. It doesn't feel like someone's always watching you, breathing down your neck, stalking you... I rather like Enit's dusty old shack. It's cozy in a grandmotherly way.

I take my time walking down the hall, gazing into the eyes of the portraits. Most of them are of Laura and Adam. Adam even looks happy in the older ones. There are several family shots. It looks like there's a photo for every year Adam's been around, which I think is actually kind of nice, except Adam appeared to get darker and sadder with each one. There are almost no family photos of the Delaneys, except for that one up at Wolfhowl...

I search for younger photos of Enit, curious to see what she'd looked like as a girl. My hopes are high for some old black and white in front of a schoolhouse, a pale frowning Enit with her once brown or green eyes peeking out of a small crowd of smiling classmates, dark hair accented with a white bow to keep it out of her eyes, little saddle shoes at the bottom of pigeon-toed feet. But I'm disappointed; there are no photos showing Enit any younger than about forty-five or fifty. I almost give up, but then I retreat to the very back of the hall, outside of a bedroom, and see a small frame containing a yellowed newspaper clipping from 1932.

"Mysterious child appears, sent to local orphanage," I read aloud. My eyes rove the paragraph below. It's short and succinct. The girl, thought to be around fourteen or fifteen, had appeared on a stretch of highway between Bar Harbor and Port Braseham, alone, shoeless, in worn and outdated clothes. She refused to speak, identify herself, or tell them where she came from or where her parents were. It was speculated she was a mentally impaired runaway. She was being placed in a local orphanage until such time as her parents could be located. Anyone with information was encouraged to contact the Hancock County Police Department.

I read the paragraph again, trying to understand why something so obscure is framed and hung with all the other family photos of the O'Sullivans. Is this a relative, perhaps some kind of genealogy mystery? I let my eyes fall to the small, blurry photo below the paragraph. It's of a young girl with dark hair. Her eyes are lighter, not quite brown, but perhaps green…

With a mental *click,* the puzzle finally snaps together. I'm suddenly incensed, feeling a wild loss of control. I run down the hall and back into the sitting room where Beckan and Letta sit with Enit and Laura. I fly at the old woman, and almost make it to her, but Beckan restrains me, pinning my arms from behind. Letta shoots to her feet, dumping a little china cup of hot tea onto a paisley rug. Laura is on her feet too, standing protectively in front of her mother as I fight against Beckan's iron grip, leaning forward and spitting like a rabid dog.

"You!" I scream at Enit as her milky eyes turn toward the commotion. *"It's you!"*

"Rose," Letta shouts, startled and a little frightened. "Get a hold of yourself!"

"What in Gawd's name, Rose," Beckan says, struggling with my arms like they're a couple of slippery eels.

"You," I hiss furiously as hot tears begin falling down my cheeks again. "You're… you're *Emily Lenore the second.* It's *you!"*

Enit peers around her daughter, her face livening up with a knowing smile. She puts a gnarled hand on Laura's and motions for her to sit. "Well," she says, sounding pleased, "I'm glad we've finally got that sorted out. Perhaps we can talk now, Rose. *Really* talk."

*   *   *

The front room of the O'Sullivan's is cramped. Several rugs of varying patterns overlap each other in their race from the center of the room to the termite-eaten baseboards. An old radiator sits in a corner, clicking along as it tries to set one of the frayed ends of a rug aflame. Crooked shelves line one wall, filled from edge to edge with tacky bric-a-brac. There's a pair of mismatching loveseats, a rocking chair, and two deep fabric chairs that swallow their occupants. Each seating piece is accompanied by a knitted throw hung over the back. A room full of old lady crap surrounded by more old lady crap.

I force myself to take in all these little details to keep my mind from giving in to the inviting darkness. Despite the heat of my anger, I'm now cold, so very, very cold. I sit on one of the loveseats, leaning back limply and staring at the ceiling, trying to imagine what warmth feels like because I can't remember anymore. Beckan sits next to me, an arm around my shoulders. Even as I want to lean into him for comfort, I lean away.

Enit sits in the rocking chair across from me, eyeing me silently with her blind eyes. I avoid her strange gaze, unnerved. She stares into my soul, picking it apart, trying to come to some sort of decision. She said she wanted to talk, to explain, but she had to have her tea first, and of course, I had to be subdued, which was no easy task. My nerves are still frayed, twitchy, but at least the murderous red haze has retreated from my vision. If only I could get warm.

Letta and Laura finally reappear from the kitchen with a teakettle and several china teacups on a tray. They're smiling tightly, having evidently made some attempt at awkward pleasantries while preparing the tea. A plate of small cucumber sandwiches is also produced and I feel like I've been transported to Savannah or some other genteel southern society.

Letta pours the tea and passes the cups around while Laura offers sugar cubes and cream. I try pushing my cup away, but Letta forces it into my hands with firm lips, nearly spilling it in my lap. Laura adds a couple of sugar cubes and a little cream for me. With the cup now full to the brim, I'm finally forced to sit up and confront Enit's milky gaze. Sometimes I swear the old woman isn't blind at all.

Beckan sits stiffly, on edge, as he cradles his own teacup. I'm certain he didn't know Enit's true identity; he's as shocked as I am. He takes a slow sip of his tea, eyes staring straight ahead, waiting just as anxiously as I am for the truth to be revealed.

Laura and Letta finally sit down. Letta takes one of the swallowing chairs, looking like Alice in Wonderland, while Laura perches on the loveseat near her mother, ready to protect her again if necessary. In the moment of silence that follows, Letta's stomach lets loose a loud, angry growl. Embarrassed, she reaches for one of the cucumber sandwiches, rethinks it and grabs three, then passes the plate around. I take one too, not because I'm hungry but because I can't remember the last time I ate. I take a small bite, but it lodges itself just past my throat and threatens to reappear. I set the rest of the tiny sandwich on my saucer and then set the teacup on the coffee table.

Resolved, I take a deep breath. "Well?"

"Impatient, I suppose?" Enit says, almost playfully.

My anger rises again, but it's quickly overwhelmed by something stronger: despair. My eyes water and I find myself begging the old woman. "Please," I plead. "Tell me how to save my family."

Enit's grim frown is seared into my memory for eternity.

"Had you guessed?" Enit nods toward Beckan.

Beckan lets out a deep breath and I feel his body relax. "Not initially," he replies, absently rubbing his neck with his free hand while his other cradles the delicate teacup. "But when Rose told me 'bout the diaries… I suspected. Can't say why. Just a feelin'."

"Truth be told," Enit says, "I was expecting you sooner. Or maybe I was just *hoping*. I've been carrying this secret for so long and I haven't told my story in a long, long time."

"Other people know?" Letta is incredulous.

"Well now, don't make me sound like a gab, dear," Enit says. "My daughter knows, of course." She reaches out her hand and Laura grasps it, gives it a squeeze.

"And Adam?" I ask. Laura and Enit exchange guilty glances.

"No," Laura says in a small, delicate voice. "Not Adam."

"Just Laura and…" Enit's voice falters and I'm surprised to see the old bat's confidence waver. "And Derry."

"Pop?" Beckan's shocked. "Pop *knows?*" His teacup starts to tremble on its saucer and he's forced to set it down.

"Well of course," Enit says matter-of-factly. "He had to be told. Without him, we wouldn't have Adam."

"Adam?" Beckan's voice grows higher each time he speaks.

"Of course," Enit replies, "Adam is your half-brother." Her unseeing eyes watch carefully, her ears pricked, waiting to see how Beckan will react.

I'd known Adam was Derry's son ever since Letta had availed herself of the files at the historical society's office. I'd assumed this would be news to Beckan and he'd be shocked or angry. But he doesn't jump up and tell Enit she's lying. He doesn't shout or get angry. Instead, his eyes go wide for the briefest of seconds before his shoulders sag and he leans back into the loveseat.

"You knew?" I ask quietly.

Beckan sighs and shakes his head. "Not for sure. I'd suspected, but I guess... I guess I always hoped Pop was more faithful than that."

"Oh, but he *was* faithful," Laura whispers earnestly, her eyes watering. Letta can't stifle her snort and then looks at her feet apologetically when Laura glares at her.

Beckan shakes his head, disbelieving. "I don't understand how that's possible."

"You will," Enit reassures him. "You will. As soon as you hear the whole story."

Chapter Fifty
The Story of Emily Lenore II

My earliest recollection is in Her playroom, playing with Her dollhouse. You've seen it, haven't you? Looks just like Her, down to the tiniest details. The wallpaper, the scuffs on the wood floors, the cracks in the windows even.

I loved playing with it, imagining there were other...people I guess you'd say. But I wasn't even aware what *people* were or that I was one of them until I was much older. I just remember being a little lonely, playing by myself. Oh, She was always there somewhere, this fuzzy entity in the corner of my eyes or a whisper behind my ears. But She couldn't hug me, couldn't warm me, couldn't brush my hair or tie my shoes. So I always had this powerful sense of *longing.*

For a long time I thought I was the only person, that we were the only *things* that existed. I didn't know there was such a thing as *Maine,* or the *United States,* or *Earth.* It was just the two of us, me... and *Her.*

It wasn't until She tried to educate me, teach me a little bit of the three R's, that I realized I was part of a whole *world,* that there were all these other people, creatures, the universe!

There was a book she used to read to me, *Adventures of the Wishing Chair.* Two children find a magical chair that takes them on all these exciting adventures in amazing plaices. Oh, it sounded so wonderful...but it also highlighted my growing sense of loneliness, this sense there was *more* and I was missing out on all of it.

I made a doll, a little Mollie like the girl from the book. She was a little playmate for the mini-me that I used in the dollhouse. I found a ball of string and some other odds and ends to fashion her from. At first, She was curious about what I was doing. And then She was pleased, proud even, that I had created something with my own hands. But once She realized what the doll represented – a friend – She became angry. Poor little Mollie burned up right in front of me, just disappeared in a puff of smoke. Nothing left but a scorch mark on the wood.

And that's what growing up in Her was like. She was jealous and vindictive. I spent my time walking on eggshells, afraid of upsetting Her, of being punished. Oh, She couldn't spank me. But she could lock me away in the turrets, or in the attic, which she often did. And it was so cold there, *so cold*. There never seemed to be any warmth about Her, not even in the summertime. She'd keep me away from the windows on the nicest weather days because that's when the others would come out, the other people. In the winter, I'd chatter away, shiver, cry... but She never gave me more than an old threadbare blanket left behind by one of the previous tenants. Once I learned about fire, from one of the old encyclopedias in the library, I *begged* Her to light a fire on the coldest nights so I could be warm, but She refused. Fire was too dangerous, *much* too dangerous.

Just as being near the window was dangerous. Going outside was dangerous. Yelling was dangerous. Reading anything other than the books She chose was dangerous... Oh the library! It was so wonderful! I wish you could've seen it when it was still gorgeous and gilded. I used to sneak down there when She locked me in the attic and page through all the books I could reach. Sometimes I'd pilfer a volume or two while She slept and hide them in the turrets for my next incarceration. That's when I first found the diaries, where She'd hidden them from me on a high shelf.

I confronted her about the diaries. That's when she told me about the *others*. She allowed me to read the diaries and to ask her questions. I was about ten... not that I was ever really sure how old I was – I'm still not sure. She warned me the diaries were a cautionary tale; Alva and Barbara were lessons. Bad things happen to people who disobey Her. And for a long time the fear kept me in line.

As I matured, as I became more woman than child, I began to doubt Her, to think there were things She didn't tell me or that She skewed. I found an old book about the Revolutionary War. That's how I came to understand freedom, freedom of thought and actions. And then of course, I became a teenager. Freedom was no longer something I longed for, but something I *deserved*.

I think it was the diary that really set everything in motion. She'd forced me to start it to practice my penmanship. And I found that, although She was able to force me to write even in my most rebellious of moods, She could not control *what* I wrote. It became an outlet, someone to talk to if you will. A confidant. In the diary, I could write my innermost thoughts, my disappointments, my wishes, my angry thoughts…and She would never know what I'd written unless I wanted Her to. It was wonderful. I retreated to the diary more and more. It was the diary that put the wedge between us, made the idea of leaving even a possibility for me. The world seemed such a scary place, as She had told me…but that didn't mean I didn't want to experience it.

And then I saw the plane… The beautiful, shiny, gravity-defying plane… And I knew I could leave Her. That I *would* leave Her.

It was a year or more before the opportunity arose. One of the O'Dwyre's, your granddaddy in fact, came up to the house to open Her up for a viewing. I'd seen him approaching from one of the cracks in the boarded up windows. I'd been hiding in the dining room for several days at that point, determined to find a way out. It was one of the only two rooms with no door She could use to lock me in, and it also afforded a good view of the hill where the O'Dwyres lived. They'd been showing Her off more regularly, looking for a buyer, so I figured waiting for them would be my only chance.

I crouched in the shadows behind the front doors. My heart pounded in my chest and I held my breath while I waited for him to open the door. She was yelling at me the whole time, trying to distract me, to get me to stay. She told me how dangerous the world was, that I'd be begging Her to let me come back, that I'd regret leaving. I *did* love Her – She was the only mother I'd ever known, but I *couldn't* stay. I didn't want to die there.

And then the moment came. O'Dwyre unlocked the door and stepped in. I bolted through the doors as fast as I could. They both yelled at me. O'Dwyre yelled something about homeless vagrants; She told me I'd never make it. But I didn't stop running for anything. I just kept running…

I stayed in the orphanage for three years, until I turned eighteen – or as near as they could guess to eighteen. I was hard to handle. I'd never been socialized. I didn't understand how the world worked. I just cried and screamed in a corner for the first few days. The human touch was so sensitive that it was painful, and I had to wear special glasses in the sunlight for a long time.

That didn't help me much. The other kids loved making fun of me. Casperetta the Four-Eyed Crazy Ghost they called me, on account of the glasses and how pale I was. It was in those lowest moments that I thought of Her, thought maybe She'd been right.

But then the fire happened. I read about it in the paper, but it wasn't very detailed. Two people died, who I later learned were the Boyles, and I thought She was dead too. One whole wing of the house had been damaged. I didn't think it'd be possible for Her to recover. So, when they released me from the orphanage, I left town. Didn't even say goodbye, just disappeared like the ghost they all thought I was.

I spent a long time traveling. I got as far away from Her as I could. I finally got on a plane. I spent explored the south. I went to Canada, Brazil, and finally, Paris. I saw all the great sights I'd read about in books. I did all the things I'd dreamed of doing, yet... I wasn't happy. I wasn't *full*. I still felt that sense of longing. I eventually understood that the longing I felt was really Her, calling me home. I ignored it for many years, even had Laura in the hopes of putting Her behind me, of filling the void. But it didn't work. So, eventually I came back to Port Braseham. I didn't know what my goal was, if I was going to return to Her. I just wanted to come back, be near Her, and see if I could sort it all out. That's when I came to understand the local 'curse.'

I looked into Her history, trying to understand what happened from a different perspective. I learned what really happened to the Boyles, about their terrible downward spiral. I came to a better understanding of the demise of the Olenevs and the Callaghans. Slowly, from the townspeople and from my own experience growing up inside Her, and my knowledge of the diaries, I came to realize the truth about Her, a truth no one else could understand – She's evil. A manifestation of evil that conquers all.

And then along came Jason McBride. He was a wonderful young man, so full of life. He brought such hope to us because he seemed untouchable. She was going to let him be, let him live. We were so desperate and held onto this hope like a bunch of idiots. Jason was being drawn into yet another of Her traps. I tried to warn him too, but he wasn't interested in my "old lady crazy talk." And so he died. Oh, they'll swear up and down it was a construction accident, but don't be fooled. She killed him as sure as She's killed all of them. Jason wasn't going to give her a family, wasn't going to give her children. So She killed him.

That's what She wants. *Children.* It took me a long time to understand how such a thing as Her could exist, could *be.* But I finally realized what She wants, what She *needs,* is children. I spent a lot of time thinking about what I'd read in the diaries, and what I'd learned from the townspeople. I spent many hours staring at the names of mothers and children in the graveyard. Here is what I finally realized:

Alva and Eamonn poured their souls, their very being, into Her as they built Her. Alva's eyes looked at the house and thought of filling it with their children. Her desperate need for children someway, *somehow* seeped into the eaves and floorboards of the house. It oozed into the walls and furniture. What Alva wanted became what the house wanted. The house came alive with Alva's dreams and desires. But then the baby was here and Alva couldn't take care of her, or wouldn't. Perhaps she suffered from postpartum depression. And then she died. And Eamonn died. And Emily Lenore was left up there all alone. Someone...some *thing* had to take care of her...so the house took over, and She was created.

But then Eamonn's family found Emily Lenore, took her away from the house, stole Her reason for existing. And She's been punishing the town for it ever since. Stealing their children because they stole Hers.

After Jason died, I was depressed. I felt responsible. I was the one who left Her. *I* was the one who'd unleashed Her upon the town once more. Shouldn't I do everything I could to stop Her?

I left a note for Laura. Said my goodbyes. And then I went to Her.

She knew I was coming. I could hear Her calling to me. It started raining. The moon was behind the storm clouds and it was dark. The town was blanketed in a silence that only happens around Christmastime.

When I got to the top of the hill, the doors were open. She was calling me in, welcoming me home. And in a way, She was right. I *was* home. I'd intended to stay there with Her, to die there. It was my hope She would accept me as her final victim and we could go into the dark beyond together, and no more would have to die.

I collected the diaries first. I buried them in the basement, buried the souls of those women beneath Her. Buried the women who had made Her...*Her.* Then I went to work on the fire.

I'd intended to take every last bit of Her down with me. I went to the library first, caressed the old spines I'd left behind. She began to coo in my ear, to lure me back in. I could read all the books I want, have all the time I want. All I had to do was stay. She almost convinced me, too. But I thought of Jason, of the women, the children. I knew in my heart She had to be destroyed or no one would ever be safe. When I resisted, She became angry, knocked a shelf over, pouring my precious books all over me.

I ran as fast as I could to the room at the top of the stairs, where the Boyles died. I figured this was the best place to start because it was already weak. I covered it in gasoline, soaked everything I could. Then I lit the match. The flash was instant. Took my vision almost immediately.

Before long, I heard the cries of the caretaker's boy, Derry. He raced in there like a mad man, paying no attention to the flames, and yanked me out, screaming and kicking up a storm.

Laura found my note, made a call to the O'Dwyres. While your father was saving me, your grandfather was calling the fire department. They were there much faster than I'd expected, unfortunately. Put the fire out quite efficiently, with me screaming at them the whole time. They couldn't understand what they were doing, had no idea the impact… In saving Her, they'd made it possible for Her to kill again, to grow stronger. I knew the next family that found Her, thinking she was some diamond in the rough… They'd never stand a chance.

Oh, how I wish it hadn't been you, Rose.

Chapter Fifty-One
Adam

W e sit in contemplative silence. Enit's lost herself in her reverie, her skin faintly glowing with sweat. I'm furiously trying to digest the facts of her story, to find some solution in them, a way to save my family. How does it all fit together?

"What 'bout Adam?" Beckan asks, finally breaking the silence. "You said I'd understand why Pop cheated on my muthah, but I don't." His face is tight. I feel bad for him, having to find out his father was unfaithful like this, no doubt stinging all the more because his mother isn't here.

"To understand, my dear boy," Enit replies cryptically, "you must first think of the Greater Good."

"The greater good?" Letta echoes. "What does that even mean?"

"Yes, dear," Enit says, "the Greater Good. You see, years after my attempt to destroy Her, I realized my mistake. It wasn't *me* she wanted. It isn't some random child She seeks. She wants Her child. She wants the child who *created* Her, made Her come alive. I was always a substitute, like Liam is now. A substitute for the child She lost so long ago."

"Emily Lenore?" I ask. "Alva's baby?"

Enit smiles.

"That's ridiculous," Letta says. "Regardless of what happened to Emily Lenore after she left that house, she's long dead now. We can't exactly return her to the house."

"Well, no, not exactly," Enit replies.

Beckan and Letta stare at the old woman expectantly, waiting for her to give them The Answer, but she won't. She wants us to figure it out for ourselves. She's gotten us this far, explained as much as she's going to. Now we have to prove to the crazy old bat we're paying attention.

My mind drifts back to the afternoon at Beaver Dam Pond with Beckan and the story he'd told me, about his family, his ancestry, and how he's related to the first Emily Lenore through the son she abandoned. The gears in my head turn, turn, turn...

"You're talking about a descendant," I say, my tone accusatory. "You think you can satisfy Her with a direct descendant." Beckan stiffens next to me.

"Very good, Rose," Enit's smile is cruel. "But I'm not talking about any descendant. After all, if I were, dear Beckan might have been swallowed up by Her long before now, or Derry, or any of the O'Dwyres. No, I'm talking about something much more powerful, a much stronger bloodline, if you will."

And suddenly I understand how Adam fits into the fold. I understand why he's so moody and angry. And why he hates me so much.

"You're crazy!" Letta says, appalled. "You're telling us you created Adam, *conceived* him, just so he could what? Die? Some crazy human sacrifice – for *you?*"

"Best watch your tone," Enit says menacingly, but Letta isn't cowed.

"That's the most awful thing I've ever heard! You're awful." Letta crosses her arms and looks away.

"Wait," Laura pleads, "please wait. I know it must sound terrible, but I –" She stops and stares at her feet, unsure what to say. When she looks up again, her tearful eyes are fixed on Beckan. "Don't be angry with your father, Beckan. He's a *good* man. And please don't think of him as some faithless cad. You're mother knew. As crazy as it sounds, she knew and she understood. She condoned what we did."

"She…she *knew?"* Beckan is crushed. His whole body sags into the furniture under the weight of this new information.

Laura nods. "I'm sure you know the house began calling to your mother the moment she realized she was pregnant. She felt compelled to go up the hill, to go into the house. She did everything she could to fight it. You of all people must understand.

"After you were born she became even more aware of the evil She spread. She wanted your mother, She wanted *you.* Your mother was so worried you would end up Her prisoner. It terrified her. And then the Hollisters came, and your mother became even more convinced something terrible would happen. Your mother came to mine for help.

"We talked a long time, the three of us. We tried to find some solution, some endgame to end the suffering of all of us, of the town. And that's when my mother suggested another child – a union of both bloodlines, that of Emily Lenore and Emily Lenore II. Surely this child would be too tempting for Her to resist. This would satisfy Her so our future children would be safe, *all* of the future children of Port Braseham. And for such a child to exist… Derry and I…" Laura's voice trails off.

"I've felt so guilty about it for years, you have to understand," she continues through her tears. "But your mother, she was so wonderful, so understanding. She truly was a remarkable woman of faith. After Adam was born, she accepted him immediately. The two of you used to play together when you were little. Do you remember?"

Beckan nods silently, swallowing a lump in his throat.

"Anyway, your mother and I decided, because of Adam's purpose, Derry shouldn't be involved. It would be too hard for him. It's hard for me too." Laura fights against her sobs. "That's why you were never told about Adam and his relation to you. We thought that would make it all easier …" Laura completely dissolves into tears. Enit pats her shoulder. It's oddly cold, like Enit's telling Laura to dry it up already.

"But it isn't easy, is it?" Letta says disapprovingly. "You can't send your own flesh and blood to the wolves, can you? That's why Adam's still here." Enit's lips press into a firm frown and Laura cries harder.

"Tell me, does he even know about his *purpose,*" Letta demands. Another slow shake of Laura's head. "This is ridiculous! It's insane! You created a person, a child, to die in some supernatural blight to save yourselves? It's heartless! It's wrong! And it isn't even working! For Pete's sake, a child just died!"

"It isn't your fault you can't understand," Enit's voice rises angrily. "You're too young. Don't you *dare* judge us! You're lucky you're even still alive. We all are. If She had Her way, we'd all be dead up there on that hill. All of us! And so Adam must die – my own grandchild, my own flesh and blood, yes. Adam must die so the rest of us can live." Enit sets her jaw and throws her chin forward, as if that's that. "It's an unfortunate, but necessary, sacrifice."

"But isn't Adam seventeen," I ask, "like me?"

Laura nods.

"So time is…running out?" I say tentatively. "When's his birthday?"

Laura chokes back more tears. "Christmas Eve."

"Oh," I reply, dazed.

"Oh what?" Letta asks.

"It's just…well…Christmas Eve…is my birthday too."

Chapter Fifty-Two
The Call

I lay awake in the darkness of Enit's living room, crumpled up on the loveseat. Laura offered me her room, but I declined. I want to be in a room that I can sneak out of – not that I have anywhere to go. But I don't know if I can stay here, in Enit's – Emily Lenore's – house. Listening to the regular *tick, tock, tick* of a grandfather clock on the far wall, I reflect on the last few days. It doesn't feel real. I've been away from Wolfhowl Mountain for three days, but it feels like an eternity. And yet, the pull is still there. I can feel Her calling out, feel her smoky tendrils reaching out for me.

Come back, Rose. Liam needs you. We *need you.*

I hear Her quietly menacing voice as if I'm already there, back inside the house. The sound of Her voice slithering around in my head makes my mood more despondent than ever. But I'm not fooled. I know what'll happen if I go back.

I sit up, frustrated. I'm so tired, but sleep isn't coming. And how could it? My father's dead, my mother's in the hospital convinced her children are dead, and Liam's being held hostage by a fucking *house*... My family has been completely decimated, scattered like leaves in the wind.

I get up and pace around the crowded room. The flannel pajama pants Laura lent me flap around my freezing ankles. I shake out my arms, feeling restless. I need to *do* something.

I stray to the edges of the room, looking at the shelves teeming with dust-covered knickknacks. I touch one or two, feeling the little neglected ornaments are somehow happier for it. I blow the dust off a few of them, sneezing in the darkness. Passing by the clock, I reach out and nudge it slightly off kilter to stop the infernal ticking.

I stand facing the hallway leading to the bedrooms. I stand there a long time, remembering it was only a few hours ago I discovered the strange news article that changed everything.

A cool breeze pulls a few strands of hair loose from my ponytail. It's much too cold to be the movement of air in a drafty old house. Somewhere, a window is open.

I tiptoe down the hall, past the creepy-sad family photos. A shaft of light slides along the floor outside Adam's room. Standing next to the doorway, I listen, hearing nothing but the loud silence of the night. I peer around the doorframe and find an empty room. The window is open, its long dark curtains flowing toward me in the breeze.

I pick my way over to the window, avoiding several piles of dirty clothes, crumpled papers, and smelly shoes. Leaning my head out into the night, I look right – nothing – and then left – Adam.

He's leaning against the side of the house, his head tipped up toward the full moon. He's wearing a dark green winter jacket that looks black as coal in the shadow of the eaves. He sighs heavily, leaking a thick cloud of cigarette smoke from his nostrils like a dragon.

"I didn't know you smoked."

"I didn't know you spied on people." Adam turns slowly toward me, his eyes black holes in the darkness. He flicks the cigarette into the grass and says, "I don't smoke. Not really."

I eye him skeptically. He shrugs. "It's just another piece of my character."

"Character?"

"Sure," he says. "The character Port Braseham's created for me. Quiet loner, pouty and friendless. Gets bad grades. Listens to metal music. Smokes cigarettes…cursed." He gives me an ironic smile.

I shake my head. "This isn't some bad teen movie, Adam. The only one holding you to any stereotypes around here is you."

Adam snorts. "That's rich coming from you." I feel a weak spark of anger but I don't have the energy to argue.

Silence.

"I didn't know how…" Adam begins, *"special* I was when I was little. Oh, I know all about the curse and Gram's be-all-end-all solution," he adds when I balk. "Figured that one out a while ago."

"What's a while ago?" I ask cautiously, worried my arrival in town somehow ruined his life, but he doesn't answer.

"I grew up knowing it was a *special* thing to be a child in Port Braseham," he continues. "I wasn't sure why, of course, but

I knew I was special and I knew the other children were special too. To be young in Port Braseham was so very *special*. And of course, none of us minded. We got everything we wanted. The children must be happy, must always be happy. And life was good for me early on. Sure, I didn't have a dad, but everything else was just peachy." It's impossible to miss the sardonic tone in his voice.

"I even had friends. Once," he says. "Ronan. Mary. Shane. Eileen. Surprised? Don't be. They were all nice when we were young. Isn't everyone? It wasn't until fourth grade things started changing. It started with Mary. She snubbed me at school. Didn't invite me to her birthday party. The others followed suit. To his credit, Shane resisted to the very last. That was about the time my classmates figured out who I was, who I was related to. Crazy Ol' Enit. And, unfortunately for me, that meant I was the black sheep around here.

"At first, I thought it was because they were afraid of me, afraid of the curse, like I had some kind of magical powers. We were children, after all, and influenced by the ghost stories the older kids told us. I figured they thought I was some *Carrie* sequel out to get them all. And maybe that's what it was at first. But then it began to feel like more, like hatred. That's when the bullying started. Ronan was the ringleader, and as always, the rest of the idiots around here followed suit. No surprise to *you*, I'm sure."

"No," I reply in a small voice. Adam doesn't continue, the rest of his story as predictable as the bad teen movies I ridiculed earlier. Only Adam's story doesn't have the feel-good warm fuzzies at the end.

"How did you know," I ask. "How did you find out about—"

"The truth of my conception?" he interrupts. "You think you're the only hotshot detective around here, Rose Delaney? I've been around this stupid town a lot longer than you. I've had a lot more time to visit the library, to stand around corners listening to secret conversations. And to break into historical society records."

I gasp. "How did you—"

He shrugs. "I guess I'm a better detective than you."

Clouds block the full moon and a gentle breeze rattles the naked tree branches nearby. The night is crisp and fresh, but I still smell the sour stink of Her in the air, like rotting flowers.

"Come on," Adam says.

"Come on what?"

"Get a jacket. I want to show you something."

"Where? What do you mean?"

"Do you always ask this many questions?" Adam's joking manor evaporates as he stares at me. "We're going to go answer The Call."

*   *   *

We walk slowly through the darkened, silent town. We stroll past the pastel palette of Victorian businesses, all bluish-white in the moon's light. We're each lost in our own thoughts of misery and what-ifs. We're just two lost souls who sought each other out for comfort, two balloons bumping together at the ceiling. It isn't until I realize we've strayed to a road walled in on each side by ancient pines that I break the silence.

"No!" I'm surprised by the volume of my voice echoing against the fortress of trees. My feet stop, glued to the pavement, but all the while feeling a tug forward.

Adam stops too, staring into the blackness.

"Why did you bring me here?"

"I didn't bring you here," he says, "You brought yourself here."

"What? That's ridiculous, I –"

"Think, Rose. I didn't grab your arm and wrestle you here against your will anymore than you forced me here. We're just walking. Did you think we were aimlessly strolling around town? A nice little early morning stroll? Think again. Think about your feet. Where did they go? They followed the path before you, the *only* path before you. No, Rose, I didn't bring you here. *She* did. She's calling you home, calling *both* of us home."

I desperately try to resist Adam's words, try to block out what he's saying so I can hold onto the last sense of any self-control I have left, but I know he's right. I hang my head, tears stinging my eyes.

"I don't want to go up there, Adam," I plead. "I don't want to go."

"Me either."

We start walking again.

Forward.

Onward.

Home.

Twenty minutes later, we're puffing heavily. We stand on the crest of the hill, staring at the blood red of Her doors under the glow of the porch light. I tell myself it's just the walk up the steep hill making my lungs burn and filling my chest with the familiar tight sensation so much like fear.

Adam stands next to me, staring intently at the house, at the doors. Suddenly he stiffens, still as a deer in the crosshairs. A long, low *crrreeeeaaaakkk* fills the silence.

Slowly, the doors begin opening, revealing the darkness beyond.

Welcome home, my children.

The voice is a low hiss in my ear and my body goes rigid. The pull becomes stronger, demanding I enter. I resist with every bit of strength I have left, my muscles shaking in exertion.

Come in my darlings.

Next to me, Adam takes a step forward, his eyes staring straight ahead, entranced. He takes another step and then another. I snatch his hand. "No, Adam!" He turns toward me with a look of surprise, as if he'd forgotten I was there. "Don't go, Adam. *Please.*" I start crying, terrified of going in and of staying away. "Please. Don't go in there."

Then suddenly, there's a very different noise. Footsteps, at first light and slow, but then fast and heavy.

"Rosie?"

I look at the house. A small shape emerges in the darkness beyond the doors and my blood runs cold. "Liam?"

Liam's cherub-like face appears in the porchlight, standing on the threshold. "Rosie! Rosie, help me!"

"Liam!" I start forward, but this time it's Adam holding me back, his grip firm, painful.

"It's a trap, Rose," he says firmly. "It's a trap. Don't fall for it."

"But it's Liam," I plead with him, trying to free my arm, but his grip is like steel.

"It isn't him," Adam says. "That isn't your brother. She's tricking you!"

"Rosie," Liam shouts, "help me! She's hurting me! She's going to kill me!"

"Liam!" I frantically try to pull away from Adam, but he will not relent. Hot tears stream down my cheeks as I stare at Liam's frightened face.

Abruptly, Liam is torn away from the doorway, thrown back into the darkness, screaming. *"Roooooosie!"*

"No!" I shriek as the blood red doors slam closed. *"Liam!"*
Time is running out, dear Rosie.

Chapter Fifty-Three
Yes

"You felt her calling you, didn't you?"

I nod slowly, hugging my knees and resting my forehead on them. I still can't sleep. Every time I close my eyes I see Liam's terrified face.

"When I first felt it," Adam says, "I didn't know what it was. For the longest time I just had this sense that I was forgetting something, but I didn't know what. You know the feeling?"

We're sitting next to each other on Adam's bed, leaning against a glossy Slayer poster on the wall, shoulders nearly touching. The walk back from Wolfhowl Mountain was silent and anxious. I lift my head, my eyes straying back to the window. The blackness beyond is graying. Dawn is on her way.

"One night it was so strong I couldn't sleep," Adam continues. "Laid awake a long time. It was this nagging feeling and I wasn't going to be able to sleep until I did something about it, so I got up and went for a walk."

"In the middle of the night?"

Adam shrugs. "Come on. This is *Port Braseham*. It's not like I'm going to get mugged or kidnapped. I just thought I was going to stroll around the block, maybe down to the wharf, clear my head… and then there She was." Adam's voice becomes a quiet, almost reverent whisper, and his eyes go far away. "I'd never been so close to Her before. She was always this mysterious presence on the mountain, but now here She was right in front of me, real and powerful… The red doors were so beautiful, so bright, even in the dark.

"An overwhelming sense of peace came over me as I stood there that first time. I can't even explain to you how wonderful, how *commanding* it was. All of my problems were gone, all of the bad memories vaporized just by standing in front of Her. And the closer I got, the better I felt. I wanted to go inside. I *needed* to go inside.

"And then the doors opened. Everything was shattered. The darkness closed back in on me. All the bad things washed over me like a wave and I felt myself drowning in the knowledge of how awful the world is, how frightening life is. But there was also this sense that the calm and peace I wanted was inside Her doors. All I had to do was go in... But I didn't."

"Why not?"

Adam turns to me, his face still dark in the light of dawn. "Because I looked into the darkness behind Her doors and I knew there was no peace waiting there. There was only the blackness of death. To go inside was to die. I looked into that darkness and I heard my own screams in my ears, as if I were really screaming, like I was dying right then. I looked into that darkness and I saw my death. And I wasn't ready to die."

"When was that?" I ask quietly. "When did you go up there for the first time?"

"I was ten."

It seems impossible that Adam's been dealing with this his whole life. How can he be so strong? What must it be like, to have that weight on you every day? I've only been here a few months and I'm almost ready to give up. I'm starting to think death would be a relief. I don't want Liam to die, and I don't want to die, but what choice is there? What's left for us? At least death would be peaceful.

It's easy, Rose. It's so very easy. Just come home...

"Why do you stay?"

"Huh?"

"You know your grandmother's plan." Adam nods. "Then why stay? Why don't you leave Port Braseham? Leave Her behind you and just run away?"

"She won't let me," he says simply. "I've tried to run before, but the farther away I get, the stronger Her call is. The same thing happened to Gram. That's why we're here to begin with. It's stay here and be miserable, or run and be driven crazy by that nagging sensation that I've left something behind. At least if I stay here, everything's familiar."

I almost laugh. "Do you –" I start, but find myself unable to continue.

"Do I what?" Adam urges me, "It's okay. You can ask."

"Do you... Do you think your grandmother's plan would work? Sacrificing yourself... Would it work?"

Adam looks down, suddenly very intent on picking at his cuticles. I don't think he's going to answer me, but then he sits up and looks into my eyes with a profound sadness.

"Yes," he says. "Yes, I think it would work."

And then, very clearly, I understand why Adam's so sullen and withdrawn.

A phone rings. Neither of us moves, or even seems to register the continued, persistent tinkling. Five rings. Ten. Fifteen —

"Rose?"

Laura stands in Adam's doorway. She has a floral print robe wrapped tightly around her. In her hand is a cordless phone. "It's for you," she says quietly, as if the early morning hour forbids the use of normal volume.

My limbs feel heavy as I crawl off the bed, Adam's eyes fixed on my back. I stumble over a shoe on my way, and when Laura thrusts the phone forward, I recoil, as if I know bad news awaits me. I slowly reach out and let my fingers curl around the smooth plastic casing. Laura retreats the second she lets go of the phone. I wonder if she's afraid too.

Bringing the phone to my ear, I hear a frantic voice on the other end.

"Rose? Rose! It's Letta."

"Hey, Letta."

Adam watches me as I listen to Letta. He watches my muscles stiffen, sees my grip on the phone tighten and my knuckles whiten. An icy dread creeps through his veins.

"Are you sure?" I ask. "Thanks." I hang up without saying goodbye. My face is carefully blank.

"Well?" Adam asks in a hoarse voice.

"Eileen's dead."

Adam nods in silent acceptance. "How?"

"She hung herself," I say in a daze, "in her sister's room."

Several moments go by, Adam sitting quietly on his bed, me standing motionless inside the doorway.

"Are you okay?" he finally asks.

"Yes," I say, my voice suddenly resolute as I look him in the eyes. "Because now I know what to do."

Chapter Fifty-Four
December 24

Weeks. It's taken *weeks* to get to this point. When Adam asked me about my plan, I was vague, trying to erase my certainty from that night in his room. I'm afraid if I tell him what I've planned, he'll stop me. But it's become increasingly difficult to put him off.

Letta and Beckan have tried to visit several times, but everything's become so difficult. As Christmas creeps closer, I find myself hiding, trying to live like I'm the last human on Earth while I plot Her end.

Adam and I still take our nightly walks. Since our first walk together, we've visited Her every night after Enit and Laura go to bed. The call gets stronger each night, and I obey it, hoping to see Liam again, but She won't allow it. Some nights I'm the one holding Adam back, dragging him away from Her, and other nights it's Adam who drags me back home. We take turns begging the other not to enter the beckoning darkness behind the doors. Her power is nearly all consuming now. And that's why I have to act tonight.

I'm standing in the cold, thirteenth straight day of sheeting rain. The ground is fully saturated and the icy rain slides down the hillside like a river, covering my sneakers and soaking my socks. I stare at Her red doors as the lightning illuminates them, beacons in the night. I wait almost an hour. Standing straight. Tall. Still.

I have to be sure.

I noticed a pattern in Her as Adam and I approached each night. Sometimes Her energy is so palpable I can feel it weighing down the air around me like humidity. Other nights it's fainter, almost as if Her energy has slid beneath Her surface. It's some kind of inert state, something akin to sleep. And I know the only way I even have a shot at success is to try when She's asleep.

Tonight, I knew. I knew as soon as the sun slunk beneath the horizon tonight would be the night. I've planned so carefully. I can't allow anyone to stop me. Not now. My plans even involved my first real crime – shoplifting some sleeping pills from the pharmacy.

I've played the good houseguest for the last few weeks. I act like I'm recovering, or at least managing. I've worked my way into the Sullivan family, become closer to Adam, to Laura. Only Enit keeps her distance, eyeing me suspiciously every chance she gets. Two weeks ago, I started helping Laura make dinner. It's all part of my plan – becoming the most polite version of myself I've ever been. I became a little more helpful each day, until Laura loosened up. That's how I was able to slip the crushed pills into their drinks. It took longer than I thought for them to kick in. My nerves were frayed. I wanted to scream out what I'd done, beg their forgiveness and run away from it all, but finally, *finally* they fell asleep, surely suspicious, but unable to do anything about it.

And now, here I am. In the dark. In the rain.

Listening.

Watching.

Waiting.

When I'm sure She's asleep, I head toward the O'Dwyre cabin, walking with purpose, the tools in my backpack weighing down my shoulders. I'm surprised to find a light on and smoke rolling out of the chimney this late. I hear the drone of a television inside as I sneak around the back in search of the utility lines. I've had to research many of the things in my plan tonight, including how to disconnect phone lines, which I do quickly with the aid of a small flashlight and a pocketknife I took from Adam's room. I can't have anyone calling nine-one-one when the fire starts. That'll spoil everything.

I feel a pang of sadness deep in my gut as I walk away from the cabin. I try to conjure up a picture of Beckan's soul-deep eyes, or the sound of his voice, but it's all so hazy. When was the last time I actually laid eyes on him? Two weeks? Three? I can't be sure. I've forgotten how it felt sitting next to him in the small cab of his pickup. I miss him.

No, Rose! I chastise myself when my feet hesitate in their march up the hill. Don't let him get in the way of The Plan. It's essential everything go right tonight, or it'll all be for nothing. *No more distractions.*

I approach the side of the house facing the O'Dwyre cabin. Lightning illuminates the damaged porch, half repaired before the awful night Mother –

A clap of thunder focuses me. I skirt the edge of the property, keeping in the line of trees leading up to cliff. I come close enough to hear the turbulent waves throwing themselves on the rocks. I see the roiling black mass in the distance, a soupy River Styx that makes my stomach flip. I hop like a gazelle across the gap in the trees where I'd seen Liam's tiny body fall over the edge so long ago.

I creep up to the far side of the house, where my bedroom window looks out on the wild forest. Staring into the darkness, I think I see the large, glowing orbs of wolf eyes, hear a small whine. A warning.

I approach a small rectangular window looking into Her basement, moving painfully slow. I retrieve a crowbar from my backpack and begin prying at the edges of the window, which as I'd hoped, is crumbling with decay and rot. It comes out of its socket easily and I toss it to the side.

Gently, I lift off my backpack and maneuver it through the tiny window. I hang it from my fingertips until it stops swaying and then let it fall to the floor. It lands with a dull thud. I wait, listening, before making my final, fateful decision.

Resolute, I make the sign of the cross and dip my feet into the black abyss of the basement. I work my body through the window slowly, trying not to drown in the torrential downpour or get myself stuck in the narrow opening. There's one full, heart-pounding minute where I think I'm stuck at the shoulders, drowning my face in mud while I struggle, before I finally slip loose and fall to the concrete floor.

I wait for my eyes to adjust to the darkness. I can barely perceive the bottom of the staircase. Sitting in the blackness, the heavy tattoo of rain and roars of thunder echoing in the cool dank of the basement gives me the unsettling sensation of being buried alive. I paw the floor for my backpack. Finding it, I pull out a homemade torch, which I put together after some Internet searches using some scrap wood from Beckan's porch repairs, and some old gasoline-soaked t-shirts from the O'Sullivan's garage.

Then, I pull out the matches.

I hold a match close to my face, nearly touching it to my nose. I stare at the telltale red bauble at the end. If people really do have their lives flash before their eyes at the moment just before death, this is when I should see the fleeting faces of my father, my mother, and Liam swimming before me. But I see nothing. No matter. It ends tonight.

Calmly, I strike the match against a slab of cinder block. It erupts into a bright blue flame. The flickering flame stables, turns reddish yellow, and I hold the yellowy dance of light to the torch in my other hand.

Fire.

Chapter Fifty-Five
Fire

I blink rapidly at the sudden burst of flame. It's several minutes before the phantom flashes fade and the darkness sets back in. Holding my torch high, I get my bearings and head straight for the little door under the stairs.

Again, I've carefully planned every move. The door, which likes to stick, is too much of a risk. I don't want to wake Her up prying the rotten wood apart. Instead, I kneel down before the door and pull a screwdriver from my backpack. Unscrewing the rusted hinges with one hand while holding the torch in the other is hard, slow work, but I can be patient. The end will come soon enough.

When the last screw finally loosens, I gently pull the door away from the frame and rest it against the wall. The interior of the dirt room is a black pit. I step over the threshold carefully – for She keeps special watch on Her room of trinkets. From my bag, I retrieve one of several water bottles I've filled with gasoline and sprinkle it around the room. The toys – rocking horse, alphabet blocks, rusty tricycle, teddy bears – all go up with a satisfying *foom.*

Ladybird, Ladybird, fly away home
Your house is on fire and your children are gone.

I smile. The old nursery rhyme's been stuck in my head ever since I first formed my plan. The catchy little rhyme describes my situation perfectly. By sunrise, She'll be swallowed by flames and Her children will be gone. For good.

I stand motionless in the doorway, watching the flames consume Her things. It's only when the rising smoke makes me cough that I head upstairs. As I ascend to the first floor, I pull another bottle of gasoline from my bag and let it dribble on the steps, like Gretel leaving breadcrumbs along her path.

The house feels different on the first floor. *I* feel different. There's no comfort here, no warmth, no love. A cold, oppressive hopelessness presses down from all sides. The air is thick with mold and dampness, as if no one has ever lived here. In fact, as I gaze around, I can see a terrible difference all around me.

Destruction.

The velvety wallpaper and carpet on the stairs is peeling and rotten. The chandelier has fallen and made a shattered kaleidoscope on the floor. The couch is in pieces on the living room floor. The TV splintered and crooked on its perch. Picture frames are broken. The dining room furniture Eamonn carved with his own hands is broken in the middle, as if someone sawed through it and went to the chairs, china cabinet, and mantle with an axe. The kitchen cabinets have exploded, their shiny contents strewn across the floor. In the drawing room, the few remaining unpacked Delaney boxes are scattered, their contents strewn across the floor. Only one thing from my old life is undisturbed, as if it's been placed specifically for me: my parents' wedding photo on the ornate mantle piece. I drift toward it like a magnet. I hold the cool pearl frame in my hands and stare into my father's eyes.

The growl erupts from deep within. My eyes burn with rage. I forget my careful, quiet plan and release the scream. I feel wild and uncontrolled. I throw my backpack to the ground, tear another bottle of gasoline from its depths and sling it around the room, covering the boxes and curtains liberally. Touching my torch to the floor, everything seems to blaze with fire at the same time. A flash of heat rolls over me, so hot it sears off some of my arm hair. I watch the rapidly spreading flames with satisfaction. I wait until the fire starts to eat at the shared wall of the living room before turning away.

Ladybird, Ladybird, fly away home
Your house is on fire and your children are gone.

The floorboards begin vibrating so slightly that, at first, I think it's the energy from the fire. But as it grows louder and stronger, I recognize the same headless growl that preceded the last "earthquake." *She's awake.*

I race up the closest staircase, screaming out to Liam as I sprint for his room. "Liam! Liam, it's Rose! Where are you?"

My only answer is the white noise roar of the flames. Sinews of smoke drift up through the cracks in the floorboards. Her growl becomes louder and louder, until the wolf-like cry erupts from every room, every wall, every beam of wood with ear-bursting volume.

NOOOOOOOOO!

I cover my ears, falling to my knees as the floor shakes with Her wrath. I close my eyes and crouch against the wall as a burst of flames seems to come from everywhere at once. The flash is scorching hot on my skin. When I open my eyes, they're filled with blue-orange flames on all sides. The fire has engulfed the entire first floor and crawled up both staircases.

"Liam!" I scream, panicking. I jerk my head, staring intently at his door through the smoke. Did I hear him? I turn an ear and wait.

"Rosie! I'm in here!"

I crawl on my hands and knees to Liam's bedroom, slipping in through the cracked door. Getting to my feet, I frantically search for him. His room hasn't been destroyed like the rest of the house and it's almost pristine. I throw everything out of order. I look under the bed, under the covers, in the closet.

"Liam! Where are you?"

"The playroom, Rosie! I'm in the playroom!"

I burst into the playroom. My hope deflates when I don't see Liam anywhere. "Liam!"

"Here, Rosie!" Liam's voice is followed by pounding coming from the little closet in the turret. I run to it.

"I'm here, Liam! I'm here!" I pull at the door with my fingers, tearing up my nails and the skin on my fingertips, but I don't feel the pain. "Kick, Liam!" I shout. "Kick as hard as you can!" I hear Liam's little feet on the other side of the door as he obeys me. It takes five kicks and all of my strength to break away the door. Liam floods into my lap. I hug him against my body so tight I feel his lungs trying to inflate as he chokes out sobs. I let Liam cry and I cry too, trying to recommit how he feels in my arms to memory. Can I carry this feeling with me into the next world?

The crackling of the fire breaks through our silent reunion. I hoist him up and lumber into Liam's bedroom. I head for the door, lowering a protesting Liam to the floor, but he won't let go of me.

"It'll be easier if I set you down, okay? Please, Liam," I beg. "I'll hold your hand. I won't let go."

"You promise?" He sniffles.

I hug him again. "Promise." When I set him down, he grabs my hand so hard I wince. Keeping hold of his hand, I lean toward the door. Grabbing the doorknob, I jump back in pain; it's as hot as an iron brand. My palm burns and I bite my lip to keep from crying out.

"What's wrong?" Liam asks anxiously, wiping his nose on his shirtsleeve while I shake out my hand.

"Nothing," I say, forcing a smile. I bend down and hold his shoulder firmly in my uninjured hand. I need him to know I'm serious. "Listen, Liam, okay? She's on fire. It's spreading really fast and I...I—"

"She's going to kill us, Rosie," Liam interrupts. "She won't let us leave." His little cherub face is tear-streaked and red with heat. "She'll never let us go."

"Oh, squiggle worm," I say with a resigned sigh. Until this moment, I'd convinced myself Liam and I would be the sacrificial lambs. We would die so others could live. We're basically orphans after Mother was taken anyway. No one will miss us, not now. It's the right thing to do. At least I *thought* it was. That was the course I'd determined to take from the moment I heard about Eileen's death. But now, I'm filled with the sudden will to live. A protectiveness rears up inside me, and I realize I have to save Liam's life. I'm his big sister and I can't let him die. I might have to die, but Liam doesn't.

"But we're not going to let her," I find myself saying, squeezing Liam's shoulder so hard my knuckles turn white. "We're going to get out of here. I'm going to open this door in a minute. There's going to be fire, but we're not going to burn."

"We're not?"

"No," I say firmly. "We're special."

"Like superheroes?"

"Exactly, like superheroes. And our super ability is that we won't burn, right?"

"Right," Liam nods. He takes a deep breath and wipes away his tears, trying to be my Big Man.

"So I'm going to open this door, and I'm going to grab your hand, and then we're going to run out this door, and down the stairs, and out the front door, okay? And we're going to run as fast as we can, and we're going to ignore all the fire because —"

"We won't burn."

"Right." As I look at Liam, staring into his innocent blue eyes, my own sting with tears. This is ludicrous. It can't work, but I can't think of anything else to do. To stay is to die. "I love you, squiggle worm."

"I love you too, Rosie."

"Ready?" Liam nods. I pull down my sleeve so it covers my burned hand and use it to turn the doorknob. I ignore the intense pain as I grab Liam's hand in the other.

Together, we run into the hall of flames. I'm immediately blinded by the bright fire and thick smoke. Without my vision, I'm disoriented and lose my sense of direction. I hear Liam choking behind me, and only the sensation of his hand in mine is confirmation he's close. Flames surround us now, licking at our clothes. As the fire touches my skin, I scream from the white-hot pain.

Ladybird, Ladybird, fly away home
Your house is on fire and your children will burn.

Chapter Fifty-Six
Demolition

Beckan shoots up off of the floor, looking wildly around his darkened bedroom. He'd fallen asleep with the television on somewhere in the middle of *Letterman*. I must've rolled off of the bed, he thinks. Wouldn't be the first time.

The television blares some gaudy infomercial for jewelry cleaner with an obnoxious over-excited man yelling about how well this cleaner works on all your most precious jewels. Beckan rifles around in his bedclothes for the remote and turns the television off, returning the room to the tattoo of rain, so constant now that he equates it with silence.

No. That isn't right, he thinks. Something woke me up. A sound. A scream. A banshee-like screech intruding into his dream. Before he has a chance to figure out what it was, he hears it again; a terrible cry throbbing with pain and desperation. The sound spurs him into action.

No! he thinks as he throws on his boots and runs for the door. No, no, no. *Please, no!* He nearly collides with Derry, already on the porch, staring up the hill with an anguished expression glistening in a sickening orange glow. Lady's at his side, growling and barking, chomping at the bit to run for the house, but Derry restrains her with a firm grip on the scruff of her neck.

Slowly, Beckan's eyes follow his father's to the source of the light and his heart nearly stops beating. The first two floors of Wolfhowl Manor are engulfed in flames. They lick up at the sky, some of the highest and hottest flames he's ever seen. Against the dark purple backdrop of storm clouds and through the mist of falling rain, it's an awesome sight.

Beckan starts forward, but one of Derry's strong arms blocks his path. "It's too late."

"No," Beckan says in disbelief. "I heard her screamin'! Rose is in there! She's burnin' alive, Pop!" he screams.

"And what are *you* goin' tah do 'bout it?" Derry asks sharply. "Get yourself killed too?"

"Call the fire department!" His voice cracks with desperation.

"Cahn't," Derry says simply. "Phone's dead. She knew what she was doin'. I told you befah, she's cunnin'. She didn't want no one stoppin' her tah-night. Just let her go. Let the girl go."

Another wild howl rips through the storm, quickly followed by a burst of lightning and thunder. Lady renews her anxious barking and makes another attempt to get away from Derry's vise grip.

"You might be afraid, but I'm not!" Beckan pushes his father's arm away and takes off. "I won't just let her die!"

The freezing rain shocks him. He expected it to be hot, to burn his skin like a fire would. Beckan scrambles up the hill, fighting against the muddy ground. He falls several times and is nearly dragged back to the bottom of the hill with the flowing current on the ground. Cresting the top, the pure power of the fire before him, roaring in his ears like a dragon, brings him to an awe-struck stop. It's devoured the first floor completely, and is nearly finished with the second. A sudden rush of failure and hopelessness washes over him. The house will collapse any minute.

The ground shakes beneath him. Another scream rips through the air and this time, he realizes, at least one of the screams wasn't Rose. It's the house. It's Her. The ground shakes again, stronger this time, and Beckan's knocked to the ground. The tremor subsides and he gets to his feet, catching movement on his left. Another dark figure is coming over the top of the hill, climbing the driveway on all fours and then running toward him.

"Beckan!" Adam yells. "Beckan! Rose is inside!"

There's another tremor as they reach each other and Beckan reaches out, grabbing two fistfuls of Adam's soaking shirt to hold him steady. "What's goin' on?"

"She drugged us," Adam says urgently. "She drugged all of us. I couldn't stop her! She's inside!"

A sudden explosion rocks the hill and both boys fall to the ground. The saturated earth peels itself apart, opening a crack between them and the house. Fire erupts from the second floor windows. The tinkling of shattering glass comes with the shock wave, peppering them with beads of melted glass.

Beckan sits up on his hands, staring at the demolition happening before his very eyes. The house is tearing Herself apart.

*   *   *

I fall back against the wall, my arm burning with pain as my skin boils. When I opened the door to the hall, a rush of air brought the flames straight to us and I held up my arm, as if that were any real protection. The heat's unbearable, unbreatheable. Liam crouches next to me, coughing and crying. My eyes search frantically for a way out. Tears spring to my eyes, evaporating almost immediately in the dry air.

But then – darkness. A hole in the fire appears. Relief floods through me – we still have a chance. I haul Liam to his feet and lead him toward the strange void in the flames. As my eyes focus on the darkness, it begins to change, to grow. I think the flickering flames are is playing tricks on me. But then the hole in the fire takes shape, a *human* shape. It grows arms, and then legs. The body tapers at the waist and long, thick hair sprouts from the head. The eyes are two black holes, sucking in everything around them. The fire, the thinning air, our breath. The apparition comes for us with its terrible glaring eyes. Its mouth opens and the foul stench of death permeates the air. Liam whimpers behind me as a low growl begins from the strange specter, becoming a high-pitched scream. It's then I realize I'm staring into Her soul, Her energy, the source of all the evil in this house. I see all of the women of Wolfhowl Manor in this shadow of evil. It's each of them and none of them; the most terrible version of the women who had lived and died here.

How could you? How could you do this to me?

The apparition advances toward us. Liam screams. I hide him behind me and back up as far as the fire will allow.

You don't get to leave me, Rose! No one *gets to leave me!*

The black mass rushes at us and, terrified, I close my eyes.

You die TONIGHT!

The rush of cold black overtakes us and we fall backward through an open door. I bounce back up like I'm on springs. The spirit is gone. Grabbing Liam's hand, I realize we're in the fire room – where all the death in this house has occurred.

No. It can't be. We can't die in here. Not here, *in this room.*

I close the door against the fire and try to think. The fire is already glowing through cracks in the door. It'll be in here any minute and make quick work of the already fire-eaten room. And then me. And then Liam. I choke on a sob, pulling Liam close.

Oh, God, what do I do? And then I scream, *"What do I do?"*
DIE!

Think, Rose, I urge myself. *Think.*

"Rosie!" Liam points to a corner. "The closet!"

Smoke is now rolling into the room like a freight train and we start coughing. I search the room for anything better than crawling into a closet and dying, but find nothing. We dive into the tiny turret closet. The door still lays crumbled on the floor and there's nothing to shield us. I push Liam into a corner behind me and watch as the fire fells the room's door. I watch the hungry flames crawl into the room, eating up floorboards, licking the wallpaper, and chewing the weakened ceiling beams. It won't be long now.

"Huddle close, squiggle worm," I say, pulling Liam close against me. "I love you."

"I love you too, Rosie."

I cover Liam with my body as we wait to die.

Welcome home, my children.

Chapter Fifty-Seven
The End

The explosion of fire into the room breaks the windows and shakes the foundation. Liam screams and I hug him tighter. The flames engulf the fire room and make their way toward the little hole in the turret with ease. The air is so hot it actually begins to feel cool, like a cool breeze on a hot summer day.

"Where's that cold coming from?" Liam asks, his voice muffled at my side.

"What?" The air around us *is* cooler. I lift my head and look around. Near the ceiling of the turret is a small gap – just small enough to squeeze a body through. What's up there? My brain works quickly. Alva's reading alcove in the library. Going up might not save us, but it'll give me time to think, and maybe work out a plan.

"Up here, Liam!" I shout over the roar of the fire. "Climb up through there!" I hoist him up, shoving him toward the crack. He grabs the edge and pulls himself up as I push him from below.

"I'm stuck!" He cries. All I can see are his legs dangling from his waist. He kicks both feet in furious panic.

"You're not stuck," I urge him. "Don't panic. Take a deep breath." His little legs swing slightly as he obeys. "Okay, now let out all the air in your lungs. Let it all out and suck in your stomach. Pretend your pants are too tight. You can do this, squiggle worm! I know you can!"

I grab Liam's feet and start pushing him up again, begging him to suck in his Little Debbie gut and climb. Finally, his weight disappears as he pulls himself through the crack.

"Good job!"

"Hurry, Rosie!" he shouts from above. "Hurry!"

I jump, hoisting myself up as fire pours into the closet. The flames lick at my ankles, blisters springing to my flesh. The rubber soles of my sneakers start melting. I get stuck at the hips just like Liam did. I take my own advice as Liam grabs onto my arms and pulls on them so hard I think he'll pull them off. I cry out as the wood scrapes my skin and my ankles roast above the flames before I finally work my way through the crack.

It's dark in the old library and I'd lost my torch downstairs. Flashes of lightning illuminate the room that had once captivated Enit with its treasure trove of books. The glow of the fire lights up the cracks in the floorboards and I'm seized by the urge to see it all burn, my suicidal plan returning. I finger the pack of matches in my pocket. I think about holding them to the books, about watching the old dried out pages curl and turn to ash.

"Rosie?" Liam's voice brings me back, and I think quickly, trying to remember the floor plan. *The balcony!* Maybe we can somehow climb down, or yell for help. It's our only chance.

"Stay here!" I tell Liam and run out of the library, heading for the balcony. I fling the door at the top of the stairs open, letting the wild rainstorm and a gust of drenching wind in. The balcony's there alright, but not for long. The flames haven't been beaten back by the downpour, and climb through the rotting wood. Even as I watch, the fire eats through the balcony. With a sickening creak, the structure pulls away from the side of the house, crumbling in midair. It falls into the darkness below, a hundred tiny torches hurtling to the ground. *"No!"*

Harsh laughter fills my ears, drowning out the crackling fire and howling wind. I scream in reply, a terrible, wolf-like howl. My rage starts taking over like a feral animal.

"You die tonight, you rotten old bitch!" I scream. *"You* die! Not me!" I run back into the library and grab Liam. I put him in the center of the open space outside the library. He cries and worries his hands in the fabric of his shirt. "I'm scared, Rosie! I'm scared!"

"It's okay," I say, though my tone is not the least bit comforting. I sound manic, crazy. "It's okay, I promise. I just have to do one quick thing, and then we're going to the attic. We're going out onto roof, okay? And when we get there, we're going to scream. We're going to scream as loud as we can, and someone is going to come. Someone will help us."

"Really?"

No. "Really. Just wait here."

I leave Liam and stalk down the hall of portraits. I grab first one, then another, and another. I take all of them, grabbing ours last. Setting it on top of the stack of paintings, I stare at my family. A new face peers out at me – my own. I'm pale. My eyes are dark empty pits. My body has wasted away, become skeletal. My long hair is dull and frayed. I look like Mother.

The house owns us all now.

This realization strengthens my rage. I leave the portrait hall, hefting the paintings to the library, ignoring Liam's terrified sobbing and the flickering light of flames as they creep to the top of the stairs. I throw the paintings on top of the pile of displaced classic literature and first additions. Then I pull out the pack of matches and smile – the old books and paintings won't need help from gasoline.

I strike a match and hold it up to the matchbook. The remaining matches blaze to life. I drop the burning pack onto the pile. It's slow to start, but when the tiny flames catch the single page of an open book, the pile goes up like so much kindling. The canvases bubble and boil, the melting faces of the dead winking back at me.

Noooooooo! The whole house shakes with her wrath. *My collection!*

I stumble out of the library and grab Liam's hand, dragging him away from the flames. Together, we run up the stairs to the attic and the widow's walk, out into the storm.

From here, the storm is awesomely terrifying and wild. I feel like I can reach out and touch the dark purple clouds, grab onto a spike of lightning and wield it like Zeus. Wind and rain lash at us from all sides and we're both forced to grab onto the rickety railing for support. All four sides of the house are covered in flames, which leap higher every second, laughing at the rain. I pull Liam close. Then we scream for help.

*   *   *

Back on the saturated ground, Beckan and Adam freeze.

"Did you hear that?" Adam asks.

"Shh!" Beckan closes his eyes and concentrates, waiting for the rumble of thunder to die out. And then he hears it again – the screams – *"Help!"*

Adam and Beckan back away from the house, shielding their eyes from the rain as they look up, up, up to the flaming turrets piercing the sky, to the roof and the widow's walk.

"There!" Adam shouts and points as a flash of lightning lights up the scene before them. "I see them! They're on the roof!"

Beckan sees them too. He's full of both relief and dread. He's glad he's not too late, but how on earth is he going to get up there?

"We need a ladder!" Adam shouts over the wail of the storm.

Beckan heads for the hillside, Adam right behind him, but they're met by Derry's bulldog face as he grudgingly drags a ladder up the hill. Lady rushes by them, barking rabidly at the inferno.

"Hurry!" Derry yells. Adam and Beckan each take part of the ladder and help Derry carry it the rest of the way, skirting the crack in the ground. They stretch out the ladder and lean it against the side of the house. With great disappointment, Beckan realizes the ladder only reaches the second floor balcony outside Rose's bedroom.

Adam races up the ladder without waiting for an invitation. He's already scrambling over the balcony's railing when Beckan follows.

"Adam!" he shouts. "Wait!"

Adam steadies himself on the railing and reaches up to the bottom of the next balcony.

"Here!" Beckan shouts, holding up his hands after he stumbles onto the balcony. Adam puts a foot in Beckan's linked hands and hoists himself up. Once over the railing, Adam reaches down and helps Beckan. Together, they climb up the last floor of the house, bracing themselves and finding footholds on the window frames and in the twisting ivy. What seems to take hours takes only minutes, and they're finally on the roof.

"Rose!" Beckan shouts.

*   *   *

I turn to see Beckan and Adam climbing over the side of the roof. I'm sure I'm hallucinating until Liam starts scrambling over the railing of the widow's walk. Adam reaches us first.

"Adam!" I cry, half relieved and half full of regret. "What are you doing here? How –"

"We can have our happy little reunion later!" he shouts and grabs Liam by the armpits, pulling him over the railing. "I'd like to save your ass and get down from here. Then we can hug it out."

Despite the seriousness of the situation, I laugh. As Adam hands Liam off to Beckan, the door of the widow's walk bursts open, a torrent of flames arching for us. The shingles have grown hot under my feet and I know we have only minutes, maybe seconds, to get off the roof before it caves in.

"Hurry!" Adam yells urgently.

I grab Adam's outstretched hand and climb over the railing. I watch as Liam holds tightly to Beckan's hand. Derry's head pops up over the edge of the roof. He holds out a hand for Liam and Beckan passes him off quickly, but gently. I'm filled with a powerful relief as they disappear over the side.

Adam leads me to the edge of the roof, and to Beckan. Adam holds one arm tightly as I reach out to Beckan with the other. He squeezes my hand reassuringly. "Crazy girl!" he shouts with a tense smile. "We'll have tah climb down tah the balcony," he cautions me. "It's slick and hot all at once. Be careful."

Beckan and I begin climbing down. Peering into the glowing night below, I see Derry and Liam climbing down the ladder. When my head is at the roofline, I shout to Adam, still dangerously close to the widow's walk.

"Hurry, Adam!"

"Don't stop! I'm coming!" he shouts back.

The house shakes as Beckan and I reach the third floor balcony. I fall back into Beckan, who steadies me.

"Keep goin'," he says with a growing sense of urgency. "Go!"

"Adam!" I yell when I don't see him scrambling over the side above me.

Beckan doesn't wait for Adam. He grabs me by the waist and practically throws me over the railing. "Go, Rose! I'll get Adam, but for the love of Gawd, go!"

As I start lowering myself to the second balcony and Beckan turns back to get Adam, a huge tremor shakes both house and mountain. My heart sinks to my stomach and I hear the familiar creak of wood as the balcony pulls away from the house. Beckan's eyes fill with horror as he realizes what's happening.

The balcony falls away from the house. For a few agonizing seconds we're weightless. Then we're on the ground in a tangle of wood and wrought iron. I land hard on my back, the air leaving my lungs. Liam cries out behind me. Lady barks frantically. Beckan screams, grabbing at one of his legs, which lies at a sickening angle. I look back to the house and watch Her last seconds of life flicker out in a grand explosion of fire and thunder.

It starts at the top. Her roof caves in. A burst of flames reaches into the clouds, connecting with a dazzling array of lightning. Thunder rolls as She screams and the ground shakes with Her rage. The attic collapses into Her third floor, Her second, Her first. Flames shoot out in all directions, soaking up all the oxygen around Her and for several terrifying seconds, I can't breathe. Then, finally, I scream.

"Adam!"

Epilogue

A_{pril}

Liam screams before falling into contagious giggles. I set the
last paper plate on the picnic table and turn around, shielding my
eyes from the sun with a hand. My eyes linger only a second on
the terrible burn scar running from the palm of my hand to my
shoulder. It becomes more and more a piece of me each day, a
reminder of how wonderful it is to be alive, to be happy, and to
really _live_.

Beckan holds Liam upside down by his ankles with one
hand and tickles him mercilessly with the other. Mother watches
from a blanket spread over the grass. She's a greyer, weaker, and
less vibrant version of who she once was, but even this is a
miracle. Doctor Fleur believes with time and therapy, she'll
recover most of her former self. But even if that doesn't happen,
I'm just glad she's finally home and smiling again. Moira Delaney
has not been beaten.

I spent several weeks in the hospital recovering from the
severe burns to my right arm and lower legs. Although the scars
are permanent, surgery and skin grafts have made them less ugly.
For the first time in my life, I don't care much about my
appearance. To simply still be breathing is my miracle. I should
have died on Christmas Eve, had _intended_ to. But in the end, it
was Adam who saved us, who saved us all. I think of him every
day, sometimes with thanks, sometimes with guilt and confusion.
Did Adam come to Wolfhowl to save us? Or did he come to die
for us? I'll never know the truth, but I owe Adam my life, and
I'm determined to make his death worth the sacrifice.

We moved into an apartment near the hospital, although we
can certainly afford more with the insurance settlement for the
"act of God" – officially an earthquake, mudslide, and a
convenient strike of lightning – that destroyed Wolfhowl Manor.
But for the moment, we're comfortable in a typical, small

apartment building without the space – or darkness – of a larger home. And this way all three of us are close to the hospital for our various appointments. I still have regular checkups to make sure my skin grafts are healing as expected, and rehab to work my damaged muscles. Liam, who suffered burns down his left side, has healed well physically, but still has appointments for his mental wellbeing, as does Mother. Hopefully by summer, she'll be ready to return to work.

Beckan suffered a serious leg break in the fall and now walks with a pronounced limp. The injury required surgery to insert pins, but his doctor is confident the limp will fade with physical therapy. He always stops by to see us after his appointments. He also visits when he doesn't have appointments, just to spend time with me, which makes me feel special. He's very supportive. He helped me find a local dance studio where I can continue to study dance and teach a class to children. He helped me study for my G.E.D., which I received, and he's helping me look for colleges to attend in a year or two; I can't leave Liam or Mother until I know they'll be okay without me, no matter how many times Beckan and Derry promise to take care of them.

Although we're living in Bar Harbor, we do visit Port Braseham. Since the total destruction of the house, the townspeople have suddenly realized they don't have to hate us. They held fundraisers to help us cover our medical bills. They also paid for Adam's funeral and began checking in on Enit and Laura, inviting them to church and other events around town. Liam's little friends from kindergarten missed him, and they have play dates from time to time. Mother and Laura O'Sullivan have become good friends since Adam's death, and comfort each other, which I think is good for both of them.

Port Braseham is enjoying a renaissance of sorts since Wolfhowl Manor was destroyed. The historical society hasn't decided what to do with the land yet, but it's agreed that building another house there is out of the question. For the time being, they've set the issue aside and are focused on more important things – like money. Tourism's up and the local businesses can afford to spruce up and advertise. Money's being spent to renovate and reopen the waterfront businesses. People are always out and about, bustling around town and spreading happy news of pregnancies and talk of the beautifully seasonable weather – there hasn't been a storm since Christmas – and spreading the news of the burgeoning fishing business. The attitude seems to be: Curse? What curse?

Things are looking up for everyone. Even Ol' Derry's figured out how to be happy. After Adam's death, he and Laura formed a bond over the son he'd never been able to claim. Though there's a fifteen-year age gap between them, they've found their own happiness and are starting to recover together. Now that he and Beckan are both out of their caretaking jobs, Derry has begun the process of opening his own furniture restoration business where father and son will work together, and Laura will help them manage accounts. When Derry made the announcement, that grumpy, bulldog face smiled for the first time since we met. It looked so strange on him that I asked if he was alright. His response was a hearty, cheerful laugh.

I survey the scene before me now. It's the first seasonably warm day in late April. A few geese glide along the glass surface of Beaver Dam Pond. Beckan finally releases Liam, setting him on the blanket next to Mother, completely exhausted. Letta's arrived with her parents and they're setting down a blanket for themselves, and for Shane and Patty, who are holding hands and whispering cheerfully behind them. Derry and Laura stroll together near the tree line. Enit trails behind, holding onto Lady's tail as a guide and pretending to enjoy the chirping birds while she eavesdrops.

Everything seems so perfect I'm afraid it's all a dream. Will I wake up any moment, still trapped in the burning house? Things had been so very dark for so very long, I'm almost afraid to admit how good I feel. I allow myself a small, secret smile, and warmth seeps into my heart.

Beckan smiles and waves as he walks over. He takes my hand in his and kisses it lightly. "How's it goin' ovah heeah?"

"Good." I smile and pop up on my tiptoes to kiss his cheek. At the last minute, he turns his head and puts his warm, soft lips on mine. I close my eyes and kiss him gently back before lowering myself back to earth. I lean into his chest, grinning from ear to ear.

"All set?" he asks.

"Yep."

He turns, shouting to our family and friends, "Let's eat!"

Everyone gathers around the picnic tables, eyeing the spread of delicious food. Letta and Patty smother me with hugs before moving into the loose circle we've formed. Each person takes the hands of those next to them and bows their heads. As Derry begins the prayer in his low, gravelly voice, I keep my head up, looking at each of the people around me. I'm moved by the sudden feeling of bliss that overcomes me and fight back the happy tears.

Then, I lower my head and thank the Good Lord, not for our food, but for our lives.

*   *   *

The grapefruit sunset has finally faded on Wolfhowl Mountain, pink fading to purple and then black. It's nearly silent save for the waves crashing beyond the cliff, yearning upward under the command of the full moon, high up on her perch in the night sky.

A heap of black debris and detritus lays in the darkness, a black mountain atop a black mountain to the townspeople below, who pay it no mind, not anymore.

Ash, scorched wood, melted metal. Just scraps really.

Against the black landscape, two shadows move in the moonlight. They may seem indistinct to the distracted eye, perhaps just some birds flying across a streak of light, but to anyone who looks, *really looks,* they might convince themselves these shadows are really silhouettes. Two silhouettes moving through the pile of scraps. One a woman, her body bowed by misery. The other a boy, slightly hunched at the shoulders, skinny to the point of malnutrition, hair hanging in front of his eyes. They don't speak, or even acknowledge each other as they work, but one would not be here without the other; this is clear. They could be mother and son, plodding through the ruins of the house, looking for anything that might've survived the great blaze.

Beneath the shadow of a hand, a rusty nail leaps up from the blackness, along with a small wood beam, seared, yet salvageable. Nail goes to wood, poised and ready. An invisible breath of wind sends ash from the wood into the air where it will drift out to sea and eventually become part of the ocean.

In the still air over the sleeping town, a faint sound echoes. *Chink. Chink. Chink.*

It almost sounds like the power of a hammer against a nail. But what follows next is a voice. Yes, definitely a voice, low and hissing, slithering through the darkness like a snake.

Rooosseee... I haven't forgotten about you, Rose...
Come home, Rose.

Come. Home. Rose.

Acknowledgements

I owe a great deal of gratitude to my wonderful butterfly of a friend Brooke Ackerman, who was the first to read *Wolfhowl Mountain* in its entirety. It was her interest in Rose and her family that helped me push through writer's block and make it to the end of their story.

I am in even greater debt to my good friend Daniel Cramer, who acted as my editor and helped me finalize this book and ready it for the eyes of the general public. Without his help, this last step might never have happened.

A big thank you also to Chris, for his support, troubleshooting, and endless patience. Publishing is often a pipe dream, but you helped make it a reality. Thank you and I love you.

My parents always told me that I could be whatever I wanted and do whatever I wanted. Thank you for meaning it, for helping me when I needed it, and for just moving the family computer into my room and allowing me to monopolize it for all my little stories; it's what ultimately turned me into a writer.

Don't worry, Kira, my amazing sister, your hard work has not gone unnoticed. You constantly balance my negativity with positivity, and you read my first draft without complaint. That, perhaps, means the most.

Lastly, to every teacher I ever had: Thank you, thank you, thank you! But a special thanks to Mrs. Casserly for loving my quirky little shorts. It had a deeper impact than you'll ever know.

About the Author

Dian Cronan Beatty lives in Virginia with her fiancée, Chris, and their children – I mean cats – Catsiopeia and Soma. You can find her works in progress and shorts on Wattpad (dcronan). She is on Twitter (@DCronaBeatty), sometimes updates her completely unsuccessful blog: My Name Isn't Diane, and fiddles with her website: diancronanbeatty.com.

69399137R00260

Made in the USA
Middletown, DE
19 September 2019